Devoured

Devoured

Anna Mackmin

propolis

First published in 2018

by Propolis Books
The Book Hive,
53 London Street,
Norwich, NR2 1HL

COVER: Studio Medlikova

A CIP record for this book
is available from the British Library

Printed and bound by TJ International, Padstow, Cornwall

For Scarlett
With love to Michael and the memory of Phoebe Clare

CHAPTER ONE

Here you come. Bike ride with your beloved. Ms Jessica Dog. Irish Setter, persuasive ears, shocking fleas, extraordinary pulling power. Look at her now, pulling away. She's got you attached to the other end of her lead. Your lead-end's slung over your handle bars. Jessie's doing all the work. This is travel. Will you ever walk again? Unlikely. Smell that, as you hurtle along? That near to cough inducing taste-smell is dust. Sun's baked the fields dry. Plus, there's not a hedge in sight. Nothing left to break up this field-Sahara. You're a flint-headed arrow through that dust.

Last year you and Star did a field protest. It was an outrage, what did the bloody farmers think they were up to, hacking down all the hedges? You got Daddy and Rod, as usual, to drive you around until you spotted a farmer. Daddy and Rod hid, because children are far more effective at guilt than adults. Then you and Star sprinted over to the farmers, forced them to stop their tractors, each climbed up a side and sort of hung into the cabs, and then you asked them some good questions. 'Did you know hedges can be at least seven hundred years old? How would you like it if my sister and I dug up your grannies? Actually how dare you dig them up just because somebody in the bloody EU is bribing? Don't you realise it's a false economy because without hedges the earth will completely die of starvation? Do you want your legacy to be Earth Murderer?' You. With Star doing nodding. Star isn't that keen on chat. One farmer just revved his tractor and went haring round his field with you and Star hanging from its sides, until you fell off. Into the mud. Daddy pissed himself laughing. He'd been spying from the White Saab. Rod didn't. He was in the middle of doing ruminations. Having to wait for you and Star to get back in was frustrating to his ideas. Rod's a spiritual explorer, he's one of Your People, he might be Daddy's best friend, he might be a poet.

Field protest had surprisingly little impact. Why? Hence current absence of mud and that taste. Whizzing home along the road to Norwich. 'It's the road to London, my darling. Never forget that.' Clarissa. Your un-godly godmother, to you on a terribly dull walk. Last year. Nineteen seventy three. When you were still only eleven and Star was just eight. She's nearly nine now. Why do people care about ages? It's the soul's age that counts. Grown-ups can't stop pretending away that they don't care about each other's and it's only the kids they need to pin down. But they bloody do care. May as well rummage around in each other's mouths. Totting up teeth. What it boils down to is this: kids need to get a move on and grow up lickety spit and adults need to screech to a halt. Slow things right down. Young is the thing. If you're old. And human. Old is only good for trees. And look. Six gargantuan oaks one mile apart from each other, lining the absurdly long flat road, are the only thing for miles attempting to hold back that dust. No chance. You're only four lonely oaks away from the village now. Flat road. Singing. Also flat.

"And did those dogs, in ancient times, pull all their owners on their bikes? And did those ho-ly dogs of god use just their leads to pull those bikes?" You. Loud. But really who cares? Song releases the heart vibrations.

That really is a crappy, frankly, old ladies' bike. Why is that bike not an orange chopper? 'Absolutely no. Take a moment to study the form. They can't possibly work. They can have no momentum. They're illogical. And corrupt. It's the last straw using design to flaunt materialism at fucking kids.' Mummy. Last birthday and about why no orange chopper. 'Plus they're thirty four quid.' Daddy. 'Extraordinary.' Mummy. 'And, despite the fact they fall apart immediately, you still can't pick one up second hand.' Daddy. Compounding.

It's a valiant heave-ho from Jessie. The wheels of your second hand, unnaturally tall, old ladies' bike, flying round with legs dangling. No need to pedal – even if you could reach the bloody things – your setter-sleigh dog will get you home. Jessie's foaming at the mouth. That dog is running hard. The singing's louder. You're closer now. Look. Brown hair in five-day-old plaits. Jeans. Truly filthy those jeans. Bare feet. Same. Light brown smock thing. 'Darling? You must promise never again to let her near beige.' Clarissa. To Mummy. About you, before you were twelve. And about the light brown smock thing. Actually, Clarissa isn't anything to you. Her title's a pretend. You did ask her to be it but it wasn't your place to ask. Grown-ups do the arranging of extra adults for kids.

"And did the dog-gy dog divine, pull forth its owner on her bike." You.

Jessie is breaking the speed limit. Your eyes are closed. Your dog is in charge. Feel that hot-air blanket being forced past your face. For god's sake open your eyes. Free-wheeling into the village. Isn't it small? More of a row. Past the church. Flint, round tower. Past Ma Burt's shop. One room at the front of a white-washed cottage, for stamps, marge and penny chews. One room at the back for Ma and Pa. Pa Burt's loopy. Ma Burt used to be a nurse. If there's an accident, get her. 'Although why on earth one would ask for medical assistance from someone who still pisses in a bucket in a shed, god only knows.' Mummy. After telling about Ma Burt as a nurse. 'Surely a more immediate concern would be why buy bacon from the shed pisser?' Daddy. Ma Burt's got two hairy face warts. Past the pub. Samc kind of deal as Ma Burt's. One room at the front for the bar. It's a long, low, flint house and thatched. You take a jug, they fill it with beer, you take the jug home. Kids can fetch the beer. Never buy their crisps, they're always soft. And processed. No processed food at Swallow's Farmhouse. Uncle Rob will be sitting at the bar. Uncle Rob will attempt a digging-in tickle, if you let him. So don't. Why the hell is everyone in your village pretending to be a relative? Especially the people with no friends. Or family.

"Bring me my dog of burning gold." Top vol.

If one of the lorries that thunder down the endless Norfolk roads came now you'd both be dead. Two months after today Jessie will be dead. One of those bloody lorries. You're through the village. Jet-speed past the last gargantuan oak. Oak bedecked in tatty ribbons and ancient bells. An avalanche of dream-catchers that have been there so long their tinkle's all tinked out. And. Home. Bike skidding down the packed-earth weed drive. Past the converted bread vans, one working van, two decomposing vans, and you're scraping your ankle on the back of the White Saab. Tight corner number one.

"Bring me my dog-gy of des-ire." Bit quieter. But no less intense. Tight corner number two. And.

Swallow's Farmhouse. On its defiant own in the middle of its acre of field. Clinging to the village by its flinty nails. A lush, abundant, tangle-weed field. Full quota of hedge. Your house is more of the same long lowness and it's flint too but no thatch. 'Thank fuck. Can you imagine? The amount we all smoke.' Mummy. When anyone's chatting about thatch. Although might thatch be easier to patch than tiles? There are holes in the roof of your home. Those mossy tiles are in a secret race with each other to see who can bop one of Your People on the head first. As they clatter to the ground.

"I will not cease from mental dogs." Strangled, crashing past the assembled transport to drop your bike out front.

Watch out for Mummy's White Saab. Once, somebody from the village, presumably, put a note through the door telling Mummy to get into her White Saab and pack the rest of the gypos she lives with in the boot and go back where she came from. London. As if you could get ten people and a dog, and a cat, and a goat, and various fowl, into one Saab. Let alone the bloody boot. This was before Your People started investing in bread vans. Obviously.

Mummy had wanted and wanted the White Saab and then, finally, one of her shares coughed up. 'Buy it. You deserve a moon white chariot. Your Phoebus Carr. And it's not real money.' Daddy. So she did. It's terribly sad that Mummy isn't up to that much travel anymore. 'It's a fucking symbol of flight.' Daddy. Trying to take Mummy for a spin last week. 'We only moved here for the famous fucking sky. I, for one, am sick of the tiny acre of sky lowering above this house. Please love? It might be beautiful out there.' Daddy. Begging. 'You go. I'll be fine. I just really don't feel like outside today. There are lots of lovely people here to keep me content.' Mummy. Smiling back and then smiling at Bryan. Daddy did go. Slamming the door. Didn't actually start the White Saab. Just sat in it and tooted the horn, until Bryan went out to him. Poets can be very angry. Daddy is a poet. 'Keats was decomposing by the time he was thirty-two.' Daddy. Same night and starting another list of dead young writers. With Bryan. Bryan's not a poet. He isn't anything. Yet.

Your cartwheel-sized back-bike wheel's still spinning. If you put your finger on spinning tyres they'll burn your skin off. Friction. So don't. There're more rotting bikes piled beyond the bread vans than there'll be people inside. 'It's a form of cartography. The map made by this collective's bicycle choices.' Mummy. On a day before the conversion. To bread vans. Rod first arrived on the racer he'd had since Durham. Dragging an exceptionally poorly constructed go-cart. Piled high with Shakespeares. 'Make way, make way. I bring you language.' Rod. Wobbling in to land, braking right at Mummy's crimson toe nails. 'Travelling along this coast, I here am come by chance, and lay my arms before the legs of this sweet lass of France.' Go-cart packing up and hurling its burden of Shakespeares to earth. Mummy, Daddy, you and Star (who was side-saddle on Daddy's hip) did some grinning. Rod's hopeful blue eyes, peeking out from his liquorice-black specs, looked a bit pink round the edges. Dust. 'Yes. Right-o. Well, Anthony says I'll be interested in your mind. Which usually means he will be. But, anyway, welcome and all that.' Mummy. Turning and doing her sashay walk back into the house. Has Rod's bike been biked since? Nope. 'Sweet lass indeed, hey Tony? Grunt. Puff.' Rod. 'Not Tony, please. I'm not an antique dealer.' Daddy. You and Star made excellent use of that go-cart. Wheels have been in service ever since.

Mummy was planting cornflowers, out front, when Bryan tipped up. She came hurtling into the Big Room. 'Anthony, where the fuck are you? Anthony? An absolutely miniscule Greek god is flying towards our house. Looks like he's got a pet Nymph clinging to his back. Come. Immediately.' Mummy. Shouting. You all poured into the front garden. There they were. Zooming past the pub. Bryan and Pretty Justin on a sparkling Raleigh ten speed, with touring panniers. Pretty Justin was perched on the rack with his feet stuffed in the panniers, arms stretched to the sky and his long, palest auburn hair streaked out behind. 'Weeeeeeeeeeeeeeeee.' Pretty Justin. Screaming and laughing and sliding off onto the grass. 'We're like yeah, like, so, like totally, here.' Pretty Justin. Everyone was laughing, gathering them up and welcome-welcoming. 'I found this pretty thing. He was at the airport. I claimed him for us.' Bryan. Chucking the Raleigh ten speed down, giving Pretty Justin a shove forward and tossing a great heap of black curly hair out of his smiley eyes. 'Bryan.' Bryan. Holding hand out for mass shaking. 'Looking forward to giving you guys a try.' It was all laughing and gathering up of more bags than should have been possible on a Raleigh ten speed. Especially cos the panniers were fully occupied with feet. 'I can honestly say I have never seen a more beautiful specimen.' Mummy. Later that night, tucked into a chair with Daddy and whispering about Bryan. 'Which one?' Daddy. 'Dark one. The red-head's just pretty.' Mummy. 'Yes. Yup. Are we sure it's this house he wants to join and not the girl's doll's house? He's small enough.' Daddy. That Raleigh ten speed got itself stolen. Only two days after arrival. Bryan nearly left from the shock. Stealing wasn't to be expected in such a remote and peace-loving community. He didn't leave. Couldn't face the walk.

Eric took a year to arrive. On a girl's bike. Sturmey-Archer three speed, tiny white tyres, massively high seat, massively low handle bars, basket up front. Eric is large. There was an autumn-howler blowing but that didn't stop Your People, all on the grass, waiting to cheer him in. Finally he could be spied. Hunched right up and over, pedalling like a nutter. The icy wind had blown his beard round his neck. Handy scarf. Your People did him a war dance. Probably mainly to warm themselves up. Then whisked him in. No one noticed he didn't have much to say for himself. Until later.

None of the bikes in the bike-decay-heap have ever belonged to Laura. One day Laura was just with you. Everyone was eating. Veggie stew with goat's cheese crumbled up top. And there she was. Standing extra tall at the end of the table carrying a bunch of daffs. Daddy leapt up like he'd sat on a wasp. 'Fuckinghellhello.'Daddy. Then he went quiet. Sat back down. 'Look at all of you. Not one bit what I'd imagined and hey, you have kids. Hello, you.' Laura. Beaming round then handing you, and a bit Star, the bunch of daffs. 'Oh how glorious another woman, hello and welcome, come, come, sit beside me, you must be starving. Girls, fetch her a bowl. Laura. It is Laura isn't it? Laura, you are an oasis for me. Sit, sit. Anthony? Tongue back in, darling.' Mummy.

Cartwheel slowing to safe levels. Stop it with one bare toe. Done. Didn't even hurt. Extra thick foot-skin.

You're hovering, quick breather, one hand on the cracked black door knob. Wriggle it, push the knob bit back up the twisty stick bit, turn it slowly or the whole thing will come off in your hand. A flake of cracked white door paint will always drift down as you do this. There you go, flaky-door white-paint dandruff, all over your grubby little paw.

"Till we have dogs and dogs galore all over England's green and dog-gy laaaaand." You. Whispering now. Finished. Crouching down, laying your whole chest up top of Jessie's back. Not heavily. She needs to breathe. Just for a sniff of her and a feel of her being yours. In you go.

Inside. There's the red pamment-tiled floor and one of the long, low walls covered in squares of dark green Biba wrapping paper.

That paper's peeling away on each of its corners. It was supposed to wrap presents not walls. 'What was I thinking? It's sodding paisley for a start and there's absolutely no repeating pattern.' Mummy. Three weeks into the home-made wallpaper glue. There's the wall that's all fireplace. That wall's actually just a hole. With a grate. And a mound of ash that reaches up the grate and beyond. Even in high summer. 'That fire is a thief. It steals all the warmth in this bloody house.' Mummy. The fire coughed at her, filling the room with smoke. 'As if the sodding ash wasn't enough of a trial.' Mummy. Daddy's found all the house furniture at junk sales. The furniture looks like queues of achey old people. Seized up, looking down, leaning into each other to stop themselves crumbling floor-wards. The furniture idea is renovate, sell on, make real money. There's the white Aga. White's the only colour for domestic objects. White and dark green. Although how much white's actually visible? That white Aga's so festerous the grease has formed a new, crisp, black surface all over the Aga top. There, in the middle of the red floor tiles, is the massive wooden table. Made from railway sleepers. And left overs. Left over crumbs have formed a table-cement that joins the gaps from one railway sleeper to another. If a person were bored enough they could take a trowel and excavate those cracks. The table's not a geriatric. It is home-made. Real money idea?

The table's covered in everybody's everything. Rod's filing system for his Tarot interpretation is scattered. The system is to make sure everyone's doubly amazed when Rod does his uncannily accurate readings. The filing system has each card's meaning on it. After the troubled person has asked for Tarot Support and chosen their cards, all Rod does is lay their deck and read out each card's pre-ordained meaning. Then sits back to do a serious face at said amazement. He's done one for the I-Ching too. Bloody good job, all those shiny foxes leaping over western rivers at sunset can do your sodding brains in. There's Laura's notepads. Covered in her slanty, clever person's handwriting and her stack of gum. 'Do not steal my gum. You will regret it. I will breathe on you.' Laura. When you and Star helped yourselves. Laura's an American. That's why she needs her gum. The breath's a joke. Laura's not a writer. 'This? Just dreams. Random doodles.' Laura. Laura's immersing herself in experiential learning. The table's also covered in poetry. Books, magazines, ideas for poems. And, of course, there are many plates with ends of suppers, unwashed up, that have evolved into ashtrays. Why do people who live communally like to stub out their ciggies in old eggs? Look under the table. How many years worth of newspapers are stacked there? Why does Eric buy so many *Eastern Daily Press*es? He never seems to read them. He never seems to read anything. Eric likes gardening. 'Where does he think it's leading?' Rod. Muttering to Daddy, watching Eric dig. And dig. And dig. It's good to have a constant supply of newspapers. Papier mâché, animal pees and poos, temporary funnels, precious object wrappers. And the like.

Loud door bang and here you are in the Big Room, looking for a gap amongst Your People, who are scrummed in, hunker-munker, round the table. Isn't it unusual to see them together like this?

"For Christ's sake, do you have to make an entrance every time? You're destroying the doorframe. And where the hell have you been? This meeting's been going on for an hour. An exceptionally long and tedious hour, I might add." Mummy. Welcoming.

Jessie's breathing in gulps of water, trailing slobber, slumping into her basket. Home-made basket. Real willow. Watch out for eyes when in vicinity.

"Pant gasp. Pant gasp." Jessie. Good dog. Might she be about to have a dog's heart attack? You've slept in that basket with her. And her fleas.

It's a House Meeting. Never say commune. Say House. 'We're experiencing some time. Some togetherness. In this House. This space.' Rod. Ages ago. 'Experiencing some free accommodation cosied up in my inheritance.' Mummy. To Daddy and leaving the room.

Why are you late for the House Meeting? You like House Meetings. All the grown-ups trying to get the meeting done, from the moment it begins. Resenting and resenting that they have to have a meeting and why can't they be the in-charge one? It is exceptionally hard work living in an egalitarian community. It stretches one's patience with humanity to breaking point. But it is the only way to truly face one's inner being. So, meetings are a necessary evil. Plus, at least one grown-up will do crying.

"Aye. Grunt. Puff. People? Can we re-focus on the issue? Puff. Work space? Living space? Shall we open ourselves to the possibility of a discussion about defining the space?" Rod. Rod's from Lancashire, before Durham. Rod does grunt puffs a lot. When he wants people to listen to him but he doesn't want to say – shut oop and listen to me. Does Rod know he grunt puffs?

"Define? How define? Define the literal space? We have The Work Room. Which it's fair to say is colonised by you. Beth has the pottery. What more space do you need defining?" Laura. Laura came from New York. New York is packed with radicals. Laura would never grunt puff. Laura would just say – shut up you all and listen to me. She'd also be using her extra strong, honey-coloured legs to stretch right back in a chair, taking up all the floor. Then she'd half smile and close up her tulip-leaf green eyes, just a weeny bit. Beth is Mummy's real name. Bethan is the long version which only her parents use; if anyone else ever does, by an accident, there's a danger of Mummy becoming horribly repressed.

"No need to be defensive. Let's resist the impulse to become emotional about this." Rod.

"I am not and will never be 'emotional' about space. Let's resist the impulse to resort to underhand misogyny." Laura. May as well have said shut up. You're edging into a corner of the House Meeting. Next to Star. Star's on the floor. Doing something with the Action Girl doll so you've got her seat. The three-legged stool with one leg four inches shorter than the rest. The Limping Stool. You're limping it back and forth with your bum.

"Stop that. It's irritating." Daddy. Hand on shoulder.

"I take offense at that. That is offensive. Grrunt." Rod. He isn't talking about your stool limping.

"Hey easy man. I'd hazard a guess that was her point." Bryan. Another New Yorker. House is infested with them. Although they're the best kind of American. Full cultural life. If Bryan pulls his hair, like now, into a pretend ponytail, then lets it spring back, the whole room stops. For a second. To watch. Bryan's lucky because he's a beautiful man. It's possible he might have a good mind too. 'Perfection. Just in mini miniature.' Mummy. Whispering with Clarissa, on Clarissa's last visit, after Bryan first joined in. 'Perfection? Too poodle for me, my darling.' Clarissa. Whispering with eyebrows.

"Thank you, Bryan. That was her point. Great to have an interpreter." Laura. Doesn't look too pleased to have one. 'I've worked it out. It's her bones, don't you know? Great big bones. Not fat, exactly. Like a farmyard wench.' Mummy. On Laura's second day.

Daddy laughed. He and Mummy slipped off for a chat. One of Laura's experiences was spending a year in Paris doing mime. Good idea. But, speaking in French is a bit of a worry. Speaking's one of your things. You speak English.

"Darling? I fail to see how the purpose of rooms has anything to do with misogyny." Mummy. Smiling, doing a sweet thing with her mouth, at Laura.

"Oh, beautiful Beth. Do you really not? It's about language. It's always about the fucking words." Laura. Smiling back. But no extra mouth stuff.

"You got that right, lady." Daddy. Looking friendly. At everyone.

"You betcha." Laura. Having a bit of a stare at Daddy.

"Grunt puff...

"'He, when the rising storm of party roared,
Brought his great forehead to the council board,
There, while hot heads perplexed with fears of state,
Calm as the morn the manly patriot sate;
Seemed, when last his clarion accents broke
As if the conscience of the country spoke.'

"Puffity puff. Emmerson. Puff." Rod. Has got a pretty big forehead. Come to think of it. Bertie Big Head.

"Emmerson? Ain't that a surprise." Laura.

"I'm sorry if I'm being thick but who is it here that can lay claim to the – clarion accent? Are you referencing your good self?" Mummy. Her and Laura are grinning now. Bit wildly.

"Just a bit of apposite musing on the power of language, hey Rod?" Daddy. Is Daddy attempting to table-excavate? He'll need more than his thumb nail to get that cement moving.

“Thank you Anthony. To re-cap, all I was attempting to say, and please forgive me, Laura, if I was offensive – I’m at a loss to see how I might have been but I have no desire to offend – all I was attempting to say is we all need our own space. Sometimes. Space within the group. Puff.” Rod. He’s sort of square. As in square-shaped, not a person with nothing of interest about them. With a fluff of hair up top his massive head.

“Jesus, Rod. What does that mean?” Mummy. When Mummy’s irritated she sits up very tall. Mummy is short but Mummy’s short is petite. Like one of those dolls in an oval plastic box in immaculate national dress from somewhere you never knew had national dress, like Poland. The dolls always have exceptional hair and that’s like Mummy too.

“Exactly. Please Rod. What does it mean? You can’t be talking about defining the ‘emotional’ space, can you?” Laura. Pouncing. Right forward in an old pub chair (now white) with her soft brown hands splayed, hard, on the table. Looks like she’s about to do a handstand on it. Which she could. If she fancied one. Laura’s bendy.

“I do not want my pottery brought into this argument. Do you understand? All of you. I have a very real need of that very real space. I feed us from that room.” Mummy. Growly loud. Where did that come from? But it’s shut ’em up. Does she? No. But she does need the real space. Because she doesn’t really go anywhere, apart from this house and its field. These days. Unless it’s, ‘A quick nip into Norwich because I am desperate for clothes. Tops. And skirts. And maybe just something summery.’ Mummy. There’s a long quiet bit in the Big Room. Bit of scuffing of toes on red tiles. Laura’s slumped back and has managed to dislodge a large lump of old floor-pastry.

"Let's not get too hot under the collar about all of this and let's not forget Eric's contribution to our diets." Daddy. Hand on Mummy's shaking one.

"Yeah. Thanks, Eric, man. Thanks for the kale, man." Bryan. Why's he laughing and tossing his curls about like an irritated pony?

"Eric, I value your work with the earth, on all our parts. Beth, I had hoped you were aware of my admiration for your own work with the earth. The earth in its more evolved form, shall we say? Puff. I have a sense that the space the pottery inhabits is both. Both spiritual or, if you will, 'emotional' but also practical, and here-in lies its sacred nature. And, indeed, the source of my admiration. Laura... Ahhh? Puff." Rod. Blinking heck.

"Forget it. Whatever it is you admire about me, great. Let's move on." Laura. Why is Daddy winking at Laura?

"I've got ma kale to weed, Bryan. So if yous are all done here I'm away back to ma field." Eric. Standing up. Eric is Aries. Hitler was Aries. They can be quite controlling. Although Hitler was from Germany and Eric's just from Scotland. Scotland is another country.

"Technically, it's my bloody field." Mummy.

Silent bit. Your People are having a look at each other but pretending not to. Rod's doing extra looking at Laura. Is he trying to make her look back at him? That won't happen. Bryan and Daddy just missed small-smiling to each other. Eric's leant on his chair back. Chair bending dangerous amounts due to largeness. You've resumed stool limping. Star's getting up, resting her chin on the table beside you. Action Girl's taking a stroll on the table. Watch out eggy ashtrays. It's Action Girl.

"Ok. Good point, Eric. What we scheduled for is the Rota crisis. Can we just sort this, please? Quickly." Laura. There's one of those breathing out, shifting around things happening. Eric's checking his watch. Eric is the only one of Your People to sport a watch. 'Time. One of the true, great, remaining mysteries.' Rod. On why no watch. 'If you glance up, you'll notice it's 10.45. Precisely.' Mummy. Pointing to the wall clock. 'But, that clock stopped at least two weeks ago. Mysterious.' Laura. Mummy and Laura smirked into their porridges.

"Great. Yes. Let's sort the Rota. Shouldn't be beyond us. Stop that. It's irritating" Daddy. Hand on shoulder.

"I have had to state this before and I must say that I resent being made to do so again. However, I am obviously not being heard so – I will not be forced to commit to a timetable. I must be free to sense a moment." Rod. Look closely. Rod's eyes have gone slate blue. Rod's never been observed washing his glasses. How does he see out? Swirls of grease polka-dotted with finger prints. Good job he isn't a burglar; the fuzz would nab him in an instant. If he'd been foolish enough to leave his specs at the scene. Which he might well have been if the people he'd been burglaring had serious literary taste and he'd got himself side-tracked.

"It's kinda obvious when the moment has come to clean the bathroom. All your senses will be picking up on it." Laura. When Laura's eyes go casual someone is about to weep.

"I wouldn't be too sure about that and there's our problem. Hands up who actually notices the shit?" Mummy. Dollop of choc eyes ziggity zagging over all Your People. You included. "Sit up. You look like a sack of potatoes when you slump like that." Mummy. No need to shove, thank you. But you are sitting up. Whilst maintaining full stool-limp.

"I vote the kids do their share of the cleaning. They do poopies in the bathroom too. Tee hee." Bryan. What? Is he trying to make you be the crying one? The loo's disgusting. You've been known to poo up the field. You dug a hole and buried it. Of course. You didn't leave your poo lying around. You aren't Jessie, for god's sake.

"I really do have to draw the fucking line somewhere. I will not scrape your crap off the bog walls. I am engaged in important work. I will not degrade myself with fucking toilets." Rod. Loud. Rod is the editor of Norfolk's first radical poetry magazine. Everyone's speaking faster now.

"Toilet. Singular. And that's groovy, man. But you know, whom will it be scraping off yours? Like I say, I vote we set the kids to work." Bryan. Pretend Britisher voice and more tee-heeing. That means he's joking. Bloody well hope so. Stay shut up. Just in case not. Action Girl's waving. Ignore.

"Right that's it. I am fucking—." Rod.

"Cool it, Rod. It's not worth it. Beth and I are serious about the kids committing to their share. Leave them out of it, Bryan." Daddy. Interrupting in his big-Daddy's voice. That voice always makes everyone cool it. Has done now. Rod's glancing at Daddy. Possibly trying to work out if he dare ignore the Daddy voice? Rod and Daddy share a lot of ideas. 'Except humour. In which department dear Rod is sadly lacking. Typical Northerner.' Mummy. Once, Rod did an orange juice fast. You and Star made bacon sandwiches and kept dancing them around in front of him. He cracked. After not even one whole day. Had ciggies and cake. It was all your fault. People were irritated by how childish you were. Apart from Mummy. 'Girls? Take this. Get bacon from Ma Burt's. We'll time how long Rod can resist the true whiff of tut North.' Mummy. Handing over money. 'Do not tell a soul I gave you this.' Mummy. To your retreating backs.

"I sense a need to lead the meeting in meditation. Just hold the thought of a Rota in our minds." Tammie. Squeak. Bloody hell, look at Squeaky Tammie. Had you forgotten about her? Easy to see why. Only her head's visible, peeking above the table. Why's she sitting on a floor cushion? Tammie always looks like she's smuggled her teeny body into a real grown-up's clothes. When you can see her body. 'Tams? I sense she'll find peace once she gets back to Middle America.' Laura. To Mummy about Tammie, when Tammie first joined in – red infant's bike, with pretend golden metal mud guards. Solid rubber tyres. 'Or a nunnery.' Mummy. Back to Laura. 'What on earth she's doing with us I have no idea. We are fecund with masculine energy. She seems oblivious. Maybe she's a lesbian. Christ, the nuns would lap her up.' Mummy. Wish Tammie would go to a nunnery then you could visit. It'd be useful to meet some nuns. Problem. Tammie's god, if she exists, could never be a male god. So 'fraid Mummy's wrong, those nuns would kick her out, quick sticks. Shame.

"Oh for crying out loud. No. No. No. I will not hold anything in my sodding mind apart from who is going to pick up the fucking Ajax, apart from me." Mummy. Pink cheek dots.

"Or me." Laura. No dots.

"How about we try, once again, with the sensible option? Everyone, including the kids, cleans up after themselves?" Daddy. Ignoring Tammie. Like everyone does. And, bloody hell, that means you and Star will be the first ones on the loo Rota. Again. Keep eyes on floor.

"But that doesn't work, Anthony. Hands up who's cleaned the bathroom after themselves this week?" Laura.

"Loo. Say it over. LooLooLooLooLooLooLooLooLoo. Crazy word." Bryan. Gurgling with delight. Showing off his – 'Perfect fucking teeth. My god what isn't perfect on this man?' Mummy. Same, tucked in a chair with Daddy, chat. 'I believe it's an American trait. Ice-cube trays full of square teeth.' Daddy.

"How fucking old are you? It's two in the afternoon. This meeting's been in the House Diary for a week. Have you been fucking well smoking?" Rod. Goody. When Rod starts shouting it means crying really can't be far off. Rod has a short fuse where Bryan's concerned. Doesn't understand why Daddy sometimes shares his ideas with Bryan as well. 'Consider him Rod. He might be our Holy Fool.' Daddy. At the beginning of Bryan. Rod snorted, stomped off. 'Holy spoilt little prick'

"Rod? Yeah? Bryan's like there's way too much tension for him, yeah? So you know? He's smoking to like, centre, yeah?" Pretty Justin. Pretty Justin never talks at meetings. Must be serious. Maybe start listening to what they're actually saying. He's perched on the painted, chipped, white cupboard, with dropped down curtains instead of doors. Another American. Southern, 'It was like so inevitable I would, yeah, join, yeah, an oppressed minority.' Pretty Justin. Ages ago and about being An Homosexual. Pretty Justin loves Bryan. Men can love men just like they can love women. 'Maybe like more so, yeah? Secrets, they're like the heart of love, yeah?' Pretty Justin. Sometimes you wake Pretty Justin up, get into his bed and tickle his greasy back with your finger nails. His back's mountainously spotty.

"If you can't stick to the point will you please just stay silent, Justin? There is always tension. Does it really matter whose or what fucking tension we're having to negotiate? Does it? The point is simply, the bog. Clean or filthy?" Mummy.

"Grunt. Puff." Rod.

"Yeah? Sure? I'm just, Bryan is hurting." Pretty Justin. Is he going to be the crier? Pretty Justin's eyes are the colour of the water that's left when someone's tried to mop up spilt syrup. Empty of tears. He's being very brave. Bryan looks perky as anything.

"The rumour is that Bryan is a fully functioning adult and can speak for himself. Is this what everyone wants to talk about? Shall we? In the group forum? Eric? Bryan? Any-fucking-one?" Mummy. Dry eyes.

Does Bryan want Pretty Justin to be doing Bryan's talking? Feel the room's knicker-elastic tightness stretching? Stay still. You are invisible. Everyone knows the rule is No Personal Shit At Meetings. Although there always is. 'Secret, like, don't tell, like, Eric is in love with someone yeah? But Bryan needed to sleep with that person, yeah? So, Bryan, like, did.' Pretty Justin. Early one morning. 'Are you sad?' You. Same morning. 'No. Love is about loving, you know? Adult love yeah? Is like fluid.' Pretty Justin.

"Eric, man, yeah? This tension? Yeah? Bryan's needs? Yeah?" Pretty Justin. Un-stoppable. May as well have an arm up Bryan's shirt and be waggling his head around as he talks.

"I canee stop her. I woodnee stop her if I could. Free world." Eric. Low speaking. Stroking bosom length ginger beard. Doing silent slow turn of head. Making eye contact with whole group. Apart from you and Star. Action Girl's waving at him, now. He's ignoring. Questions are, stop what and who?

"Yeah, sure, man. Just, Bryan, must have whatever Bryan's needs are." Pretty Justin. What needs? Pretty Justin's nearly still a child. Just nineteen. He decided to stay, for a year, to get a break from existing in America. He's being Mummy's assistant, cleaning the pottery, doing the stuff she had to do for her Clay Master when she started. He's looking forward to making something, soon.

"Bryan's the big man here, Justin. Bryan can fight all his own battles. Drop it. Drop it right fuckin' now." Eric. Chesty voice. Then bit more silence. Looks like it's dropped. Pretty Justin's picking red polish off his toenail.

How did Eric find Your People? Doesn't appear to be a thinking man or even a spiritual explorer. Might not be a serious person at all. But his head does nearly touch the roof and it's pretty certain he could smuggle babies under that beard. And he is useful. Planted half an acre of kale last autumn. People aren't mindful of Eric. You are mindful. Impossible to ignore his relentless lack of interest in you, and Star.

Look, Daddy's stretching across the table, picking up Pretty Justin's tobacco box, smiling his sarcastic smile into Bryan's face. Bryan's snickering, Daddy's stretching back, smiling into Eric's face, smiling into Bryan's, rolling his ciggie. Looking down. Not smiling at all now. Daddy is the big man. Quiet. Whoops. Jessie farted. No one is laughing. Don't you laugh. You're sneaking a peek at Star. She's trying to make Action Girl hold her nose. Arms not bendy enough. Why can't you stop stool-limping?

"Stop that. It's irritating. Anyone noticed my wife's beautiful black mane has three silver strands in it? How did they get there?" Daddy. To you, then stretching again, picking up Mummy's hand, kissing her finger where her ring sits. Mummy's hair is exceptional. 'I will never succumb to The Fringe.' Mummy. She hasn't. She's the only one of Your People to have resisted its lure. Everyone else at Swallow's Farmhouse believes in The Fringe. Right down over the eyes. If achievable.

The elastic tightness is stretched to pinging point. As if a huge laugh were waiting to snap everything apart. It'd be a dreadful laugh, kind you can't help, have to run away from. A fart laugh. Jessie? All eyes watching Pretty Justin. He started this. Is he going to tell who slept where?

Goldilocks, get out of baby bear's bed. Big Room waiting. Get on with it. Tell.

Hear that breath? The room's swivelling away from Pretty Justin. Look. Laura's trying to hide that she might be doing the crying. Big surprise. 'One of the things about Laura is her remarkably masculine energy. Have you noticed?' Mummy. To Daddy. When Laura wasn't joining in being sad about a batch of kittens that needed drowning in a bucket. Why's she moping? The fart laugh would have been better than this. Made a change. Daddy's letting go of Mummy, turning to Laura.

"I warned you. The lioness runs the pride. She gets her pick. Add to that, lions are fucking lazy beasts who can't be arsed searching around for new and interesting mates and who'll simply fuck whoever's standing nearest their particular tree, if she'll let them, and you don't stand a chance. Did you drink and see the spider?" Daddy. That nature chat has sorted out Laura's maybe tears.

"S p i d e r." Laura. Staring at the ceiling. Everyone's talking SO s l o w l y, n o w.

Bryan and Eric are staring at Daddy. Daddy is the big man. Although actually he is nowhere near as tall as Eric. Daddy is normal. Skinny as a post, with skinny brown hair and eyes a mix-up of you and Star. Hazel. Daddy gazes out from under his cup-shaped top-eyelids and glitters at people. Most days.

Bloody hell. Why's everyone (apart from Eric) looking at you and Star? Do not glance towards the Ajax tub. Stare back. Stare back. Well done. Shame though because you were about to learn something. Ajax tub may as well be doing a little dance over on the windowsill. Ignore. Star's doing some friendly Action Girl waving at them but if they're looking at the kids they feel guilty. Or not sure what's next. Apart from wonky smiles. Action Girl has lost her nerve. Star's abandoned her to the old eggs.

"This is my house. Mine." Mummy. It is because her daddy bought it for her ten years earlier for two thousand pounds. Norfolk's a long way from London.

"Grunt puff. Why does it always come down to this? There's a world out there that needs our ideas but it always descends to this." Rod. Bit too loud. Again.

"Ahh, Rod. Lonely?" Mummy. Tinkle-laugh. Hear that silence? That is the sound of lots of breath being held. And Daddy smoking.

Mummy's doing secret smiling and peeping at everyone, shaking long hair out of its knot-bun. Laura's looking at Mummy. Very level gaze. Star's doing her hair twisting. Why the hell's she started doing that? Action Girl needs rescuing. Star's head is bleeding, again, where she's tugging the hairs out. Time for someone to do a proper bit of crying. Squeeze out a couple of tears, why don't you? Very good little girl crying routine. Try some trembling too for good measure.

"Please stop. We need the house to feel right. I'll cook. A House Meal. Star and me. We'll cook. P l e a s e." You. Plop goes your first squeezed tear. Slow talking's working, too.

"Sure. Good idea. Peace-making meal. We'll stop but only if you stop crashing that fucking stool backwards and forwards." Daddy. Stool stopped. But not the crying. Need to get a few more fretful, sympathetic glances first. Laura, one, Pretty Justin, two, Tammie, nearly three.

"Tut". Mummy. Bit mean. Ignore.

"Plop." Second squeezed tear.

"Oh, Honey, there there, one of your amazing feasts would be far-out. Really magical. There there, Sweetie." Laura. And, oh yes, those leafy eyes are brimming.

Your People are stretching, standing. Ajax tub is still. Hey, why's no one noticing your crying anymore?

"You've such sweet eyes, Laura. Let's see them smiling. I'm happy to lend but why would I hand over a man who knows more about clothes than I do? He's a demon in Saxon's. Let's go for a walk. Just a teeny stroll. Down the lane. Then home. I'll henna your toes later. Ok?" Mummy. Must really, really need Laura cheered up. Mummy is going for a walk, down the lane. How far will she get? Should you go with her, to help Laura?

Saxon's is a shoe shop in Norwich. You chose a pair of blue wedges with your birthday money from there. Weren't allowed to wear them. 'Shoes as an instrument of torture. They will wreck your posture.' Mummy. On wedges. Blue or otherwise. 'Does nobody understand the foot anymore? My girls will always go barefoot. Whenever the weather allows. It's the least I can do for them.' Mummy. The weather allows for a surprising amount of the year. The wedges went back, bought all the *Malory Towers* books by Enid Blyton. Who's a fascist but her books, 'Are like opium to little girls.' Daddy. About your whole box of books.

Mummy's got Laura's hand tight. Is Mummy really going to leave? Wouldn't it be better if she stayed? Rest of Your People, apart from Tammie, watching.

"Sweet eyes, don't you think?" Mummy. To her watchers.

Laura's doing a throaty laugh. Where did that come from? Mummy's got Laura pulled in, kissing her sweet eyes. Disgusting. Bit annoying how quickly everyone stopped counting your tears although not sure you could have squeezed another and you've got the adults cowed. Apart from Eric.

"Grunt. Puuuf." Rod. His other variety of grunt puffs. The one that's a groan. Like a goat pulling at its chain. Stop staring and close your mouth Rod, it's possible to count your fillings. Lots. When Rod was at Durham he sent his washing home, every two weeks, and his mother returned it with chocolate nestling between his sheets.

"Rota, umbaala. Rota, umbaala." Tammie. Chanting. Squeakily. Umbaala is Tammie's mantra. It was given to her when she was studying in Guatemala. Goats. And god.

"For fuck's sake take that outside, Tammie." Daddy. Not shouty just a bit bored. And going out to the Work Room, with Rod, and Bryan. Why's Bryan trailing Daddy?

"Slam." Back door. That'll be Eric off to his veg. Tammie's ignoring Daddy. Lugged her floor cushion, to the middle of the Big Room. Mummy's heading door-wards.

"Rota, umbaala. Rota, umbaala." When Tammie sits cross-legged, her clothes puff out and ride up so far she looks like a Chinese pin-cushion. Mound with head. Black, bobble-topped, pins for eyes.

Pretty Justin's wrapping his apron on, and gliding towards the pottery. Mummy's dragging her feet but her and Laura are on their way to the back door. Meeting done.

"Rota, umbaala. Rota, umbaala." People stepping over her. Letting her get on with it.

Looks like Mummy's going. You'd better get cooking.

"Mummy? Mummy? Can we make anything?" You. Need to know the cooking rules before embarking. Mummy's stopped. Holding onto the back doorframe. Two hands.

"Rota, umbaala. Rota, umbaala."

"It's ok, Sweetie. Think you can let us go? Good girl. We're only going for a little wander. You cook what you want. Yes, Beth? See what we have in. You let us get on." Laura. Leading you back into the kitchen bit of the Big Room. Leaving Mummy gripping the frame.

"But Mummy might need." You. Half turning between them.

"Rota, umbaala. Rota, umbaala."

"I know, Sugar, but Mummy might like her little walk. Let us go." Laura. Tricky. Should you let Mummy go? Do need to sort the food ground-rules. It'd be sensible to get her back. "Ok. So. Let's just sort this menu." Laura.

"Rota, umbaala. Rota, umbaala."

"No. Dairy. Do. You. Hear. Me?" Mummy. Yell whispering.

"Ok? There we go then. A meal for ten with no terrifying dairy. Easy peasy." Laura. What's it going to be? "Sooo, hows about we go loco and buy some meat?" Grinning. Meat? Yum. Star's been glued to the wall watching Mummy but that mention of meat's got her attention.

"Rota, umbaala. Rota, umbaala."

"Laura, sometimes you are rather marvellous. Yes. Let's have something indulgent. A little hurrah for the House." Mummy. Letting go and holding her arms out to Laura, with a final turn to you. "But absolutely nothing fatty. And please, for christ's sake, can you sit on your sugar impulse? Just this once. Star? You're in charge of puds. Right. Walk." Off they go. Did you catch that big wink from Laura?

"Rota, umbaala. Rota, umbaala."

A House Meal Menu.

Vienna bread with mackerel pâté.
Boeuf en daube.
Haricot beans with sorrel.
French beans with garlic.
Lemon solid.

Back on bike, into Aylsham to shop. Two miles. Each way. Home. Pick produce. Star's onto the pud. And she needs to be cos it takes flaming hours to set. Even in the back of the fridge near the elements with a chair jamming the door properly closed. The used-to-be white foldy seal's getting to be a bit dodge.

LEMON SOLID – Your great grandmother's recipe. Antique recipe. Ingredients for six people. Doubling recipes is experiential learning. This recipe is unique. Your People marvelled when you first magicked up this trembling mound.

1 pint milk. If it's a party you can swap half milk for cream. Today is not a party. It really is impossible to make a serious pudding without some dairy.
2 juicy lemons
3oz sugar. Less will do but never use less. Star doesn't.
1 packet agar. Gelatine's made from horse's hooves. No one should eat it. Mummy ate horse in France when she was starving and eighteen. She was in bed for a year. Woke up scared. Gelatine works much better than agar.

Milk into saucepan. Peel strips off lemons. Drop in milk. Shake on sugar and agar. Don't stir. Leave to stand for an hour. Extract peel. Stir until sugar dissolved. Heat until near boiling. Mustn't boil. Off heat. Lemon juice in. Do not stir. It'll curdle and that's right. Pour into waiting mould. Your jelly mould's Georgian, lion on a mound. The lion's for Mummy who's Leo. Leo's the most complex of the star signs. The Great Lion. You're Cancer. The word cancer makes people uncomfortable, they don't understand that cancer is for crab. Crabs are homely. They go at things sideways. Into fridge to set. Star's got this done, and jammed in, as you're arriving back with meat.

"Where did Tammie go?" You. To Star, plonking down meat. Star's flicking eyes at ceiling. Tammie's gone to her bedroom. "Still at it?" You. Unwrapping meat. Nod, nod – from Star. Bloody hell – head shakes. From you both.

THE DAUBE – Mummy's absolute favourite and will pave the way for slight dairy infringements in other areas of menu. This comes from Elizabeth David. She's a genius. Peasants have been eating like this for hundreds of years. Elizabeth David's idea was to write it down. 'Oh my goodness me. This is, um, yes, chew-chew, this is food as it is meant to be eaten. So blissfully simple and yet somehow, chew-chew, fully complex. How have we travelled so far from this elemental relationship to creating food?' Mummy. First time she made this. She can only manage a tiny mouthful at a time because of the richness and she doesn't like it when people talk about anything unpleasant when she's eating because then she has to stop eating and control her sickie tum. Then she sounds like a cat being sick. It's quite hard to keep eating when she's doing this. Mewl, swallow, mewl. But you always do.

3lbs beef. Not sure which cut. 'The rounded one Mummy gets.' You. To John the Butcher. Once, John The Butcher locked Mummy in his freezer room to talk about how short her skirts are. Mummy whacked his balls.
½ lb of bacon. Cut up.
Lots of garlic. Chopped.
Few carrots

Lots of black olives. Olives are almost impossible to buy in Norfolk but Clarissa brings them from France every year. Clarissa's a real princess in Nigeria where her parents live. 'Christ, absolutely not, m'dear. Bless your sweet heart. French Sun. London. London. French Sun. It's the only way and your mother knows it. In her heart.' Clarissa. When you asked her to join in at Swallow's Farmhouse.

Tomatoes. The greenhouse is small. It's rammed with tomatoes and a passion fruit vine. It's a gloom inside that glass house. The smell in there is one of the great smells.

Herbs. Whatever you fancy.

"Slam." Back door. They're back. You and Star are pausing. Listening.

"Clack, clack, clack." Two sets of Indian sandals. Slapping from the back door, swerving into Mummy's pottery. Listen a bit more. Muffled chat. Smell of ciggies curling under pottery door. Back to work.

A marinade – ¼ pint red wine, tea-cup olive oil. Clarissa has to drive her Peugeot to France and back. 'Think of me like a Victorian grocer boy. Basket up front. Bringing you all the good things you need to survive in your ghetto.' Clarissa. About olive oil as well as the other stuff. Celery, some shallots, onion, garlic, pepper, more herbs.

Heat oil. Chopped marinated veg, in. Cook a bit then add everything else. Cook bit more. Let it cool. Pour over meat. You're supposed to leave it for a day or so but you never have. Soak for as long as poss. Then put all, apart from olives and toms, into big pot. Mummy's made a chocolate brown earthenware pot with a proper fitting lid for this. Why oh why won't Mummy make these to sell? Real money. No doubt about that. But Mummy's work is focused on her My Pots, pots. Let daube cook in its practical pot for two hours. Add olives and toms. Cook more. This tastes all salt, sweet tomatoes and the soft mud flavour of beef.

HARICOT BEANS AND SORREL

Haricot beans
Sorrel. Big handful.
Oil. If no oil can use butter or, in extreme emergency, marge. Ma Burt sells marge. Top of her marge has usually gone a bit yellow. Warm fridge. Plus, it's processed food.

Boil, for sodding hours, beans. Drain. Cool a bit. Add chopped Sorrel. Add oil.

"Go easy with the bloody oil. That's got to last us at least six months. Clarissa isn't as generous with it as she used to be. She's withholding. In a pathetic attempt to punish me for not liking aeroplanes." Mummy. Nipping out of the pottery for a progress check on beans. 'I wish I'd never introduced you to my precious Elizabeth David. You're becoming dependant on the spoils of the Med.' Clarissa. Plonking down four big wine bottles full of oil. Before the withholding set in. These beans are very good eating with the beef. Their wet softness soaking the juices of meat and it's got this ting, ting, tang from the lemon sorrel too. Lemon sorrel has nothing at all to do with the Med. It comes from hedges.

FRENCH BEANS

Boil. Add hot to bowl with more olive oil. Big scrunch sea salt. Loads black pepper.

VIENNA LOAF

It's a spiritual experience making bread to break with the community. You've been knocking this one out since you were an infant. Mainly because it's the only time you're allowed white flour. 'I don't care if my children never brush their hair or say thank you to anyone but I will not tolerate them consuming processed flour.' Mummy. Once a week. Whenever someone, not you, is consuming white bread.

1lb strong white flour
½ a pint milk, water mixed
1 egg
1oz yeast. Get yeast from baker's. In a lump, like cheese. Squeaks when you squash it. Like Tammie. Put on back of Aga with spoon of honey. Fizzes up.
Salt
1oz butter or oil

Put flour and salt into bowl on back of Aga. Melt butter in warming milk. Beat eggs. Mix all. Knead. Not as if you're wedging clay. With clay knock air out. With bread push it in. Rise. Back of Aga. Plait it. Rise again. Bake. About twenty mins hot oven. It's pretty. At the solstice you made eight loaves, each one a letter. You wrote 'Solstice' in bread.

"Thought I said – No. Dairy." Mummy. Poking her head out from the pottery door. How the bloody hell did she know you were pouring milk? You're paused, milk bottle suspended in mid air. The milk bottle's leaking its last few naughty drops into the pan.

"Um." You. Oh, come on. You can do better than that. Mummy looks very angry.

"Ha, ha. Only joking. It all smells delicious. Carry on." Mummy. Pottery door closing. Massive tittering from inside.

MACKEREL PÂTÉ

Some smoked mackerels, skins peeled off and fed to available cats.
Small bowl yoghurt. Yoghurt does not count as dairy. Because it is crawling with live culture. Daddy makes yog with Prune's milk. Prune is Star's goat. Prune is absolutely mad.
1/4lb melted butter
½–1 lemon

Smash fish. Mix everything. Fridge to set. If fridge can muster up the energy having given its all to the lemon solid.

If only Your People would have a think about the idea of a course system. They like all the food up top of the table at the same time. So that's where it's going. It is exceptionally tedious attempting to get the whole House sat down together. Why do you bother?

"People? People? Daddy? Mummy? People? FOOOOOOOD." You. Silence. Light a few candles.

First to arrive, Tammie. Always is. Although she'll only pretend to eat. Ten minutes later, Eric, but he has to spend hours scrubbing earth from his spade-shaped hands. Then five more mins and it's Daddy, Rod and Bryan. As a mass. Bryan and Daddy have already been in and out for tastes and wine.

"How did we breed such a throw-back? Such a prissy little middle-class number? A fucking hors d'oeuvres." Daddy. Ripping a big chunk off the loaf, wiping it into the pâté biting and sitting, all at the same time. When people talk with smooshy food in their mouths you can see great stretches of food stalagmite connecting their teeth.

"Believe me it has absolutely nothing at all to do with me. She's a changeling. Left here by some fairies. Fat ones." Mummy. Floating out of the pottery surrounded by Pretty Justin, who has his soft pale hair twisted up in a bun secured with paintbrushes, and Laura. Looking a bit smug.

"Wouldn't that make them trolls. Or gnomes?" Daddy. Big glass of red, big heap of meat.

"You have a pathological need to re-write me. Have you noticed?" Mummy. Plonking herself down with her saucer of daube. Next door to Eric. He's looking worried at his empty plate. Reach across, dollop him some daube. Aren't you helpful? Not even a simple thank you. Rude. Frankly.

"Darling? You are pretty as a fairy and you really do need to remember about heating the plates. It's what the bottom oven is for. Especially when you've gone to all this bother. It's wrecking this daube having to eat off ice. It's congealing." Mummy.

Laughing adults. But kind ones. Candles dripping down dark green wine bottle holders and all Your People, apart from Tammie, who is doing some hand-waving over the table, eating. Bloody finally.

"Christ this is sickeningly rich. Veggie week next week, people." Daddy. Stalagmite, stalactite.

"Mewl, swallow, mewl." Mummy. About sickening richness.

Smell it. Garlic, hot wax, ciggies, distant dead mouse, damp earth. That is the smell of Swallow's Farmhouse.

"Hey, Miss Twinkle? You gonna eat something other than dessert?" Laura. To Star.

"Star's fine, she's self-regulating. When she's hungry she'll toddle into the garden and graze. Inspiring." Mummy. But not true. Star's pockets are stuffed with the crumbs of filched biscuits. Inspiring.

"Make sure you leave some for the rest of us." Mummy. Over your shoulder. You've a little bit of everything. The cook must taste what they provide. Otherwise how will they know? Is bread and butter the best food ever? Big butter teeth marks. Press that buttery bread into the beef juice. Juices bleeding in. Extra salty from olives. Salty butter. Sweet milky bread.

"Go easy and this is way too salty. You must learn to check your seasonings." Mummy. She's right. Horribly salty olives. But still, quite nice.

God all bloody mighty. What's that smell? Look. Bryan's already rolled a joint. What has he eaten? Just pâté. Now he's spooning up tastes of Pretty Justin's daube and smoking at the same time. Get yourself a proper helping. Great, he's using his same spoon to try the lemon solid.

"Tasty. Cool Jell-O stuff, Kiddos. Who's paying for all this nosh? Is it coming out of the House kitty or what?" Bryan. Waving licked spoon at you. Smoke, smoke, smoke. Now Pretty Justin's smoking too. Why can't Your People follow the order of the menu? And what, in the name of buggery, is wrong with serving spoons?

"I gave them the money for it. Thank you, girls." Laura. Any minute someone's going to get high. High is fine in the day but at night it's edgy. All that work and now it's bedtime.

"You're welcome. It was nothing. So sorry it's so salty. And the meat's a bit dry. Don't know why. If that mackerel needs more lemon there is some. Sorry. I think the lemon solid is set enough but maybe eat it soon, looks like it's melting. Anyway. Star? Night, night." You.

"That's no changeling. That is pure Beth. Never apologise for cooking, sweetheart. Night, night." Laura.

“Yeah? Like, yeah.” Pretty Justin. Blowing kisses. But mostly smiling at Bryan.

Will going upstairs always be scary? When you have children, if you move them to a new house, you’ll ask them if they think there are ghosts before you move. The staircase is circular. It’s called a Stairwell. There you go, twisting up the well. The stairs are wood. Painted black. The walls are papered in silver cooking foil. It’s hard not to pick at the foil as you pass. Once, Star scraped your name on the wall, you both got hit for that. ‘Don’t you see how hard I’ve slaved to make space for you both?’ Mummy. On discovery of the first scrape, post the hitting.

You’re chasing Star like a monster, quite a freaky intense monster, to the bathroom. She’s nearly enjoying it but not really. Loo looks normal, it always has those streaks of brown all down the bowl. Those are old-loo hard-water stains. Did someone clean it? Quickly, quickly it’s cold. Even tonight. Washing. Teeth face fanny, teeth face fanny. A race along the landing of doors. Get to bed before the loolooloo flush changes its tune. Or else.

Now it’s just you in your blue bed. Star’s sleeping on the other side of the room. Her bed’s red. Daddy painted birds on them. Mummy did lilies. Alone in bed awake. Hair still in plaits. Both you and Star have nightdresses, scrappy and pink. A present from Grandma. She has hopes of you becoming a nurse. Ha. Nobody will see the nighties. You’re allowed to keep them. Unlike the fruit jellies and tan tights she also always sends. Mummy usually keeps the random boxes of tissues. ‘She’s just worried that we never wipe their noses.’ Daddy. To Mummy when she was laughing at the tissues. ‘She’s right. I refuse. They’re plenty old enough to take responsibility for their own snot bubbles.’ Mummy.

Curtains open, watching the moon and the clouds chasing it. Moon bathing helps you grow into more of a woman. Women are spiritual beings.

You're sleeping. Listen to your puffy breath. Look. There are mice. Quite a lot of mice. Great Uncle Elizabeth's here. He's jumping onto Star's bed. Great Uncle Elizabeth was taken away from his mother before he learnt to wash his bum. He's a smelly cat but Star doesn't care. The mice do. Great Uncle Elizabeth, Star and you, all sleeping. No mice now. Music from downstairs. The answer my friend is blowing in the wind. Everybody enjoys Bryan's singing but, don't tell, he actually sounds like the bees that have made their hive in the end wall. One big, dull hum. Thick cloud is swallowing the moon. Night, night.

CHAPTER TWO

Good morning. Golly you've woken straight up. Listen. Only birds. The house is yours. Star will have been up for hours. 'Star has too much going on to sleep.' Daddy. You've plenty going on too, of course, but not when you're sleeping. Usually. No doubt she's ensconced in her ditch. With her cat and her goat. She's made a den in the ditch at the top of the field, woven a roof from branches and blankets – what will happen when it finally rains? A floor from doors. She has fires in there. Hazardous? Invites Prune for tea. Prune's a surprisingly good guest. They lounge around assessing the top twenty which Star records, plays back and mimes to. She doesn't sing anymore she jigs around in silence. Star doesn't know you know this. Why would she need to?

Out of bed. Hair still in plaits. Fuzz round your head. Don't wake the adults. Creeping along the landing dodging creaky boards. Pretty much every other board's a creaky board. 'This house is ancient. You can sense the generations crowding around you, when you sleep.' Laura. After her first night in your house. That put paid to any sleep (without anything going on) for you, for a good few weeks. Generations? Crowding? Spit it out, say what you mean. Ghosts.

Star's not in her ditch. She's on her beam in the back garden. You're behind the landing window, spying. She's made a gymnastics beam from a railway sleeper, binder twine and table legs. You can cartwheel, under normal circs, but that beam is exceptionally unstable. It's impossible for an average person to cartwheel on. 'That bloody thing will collapse and crush her one of these days. I will be left wiping her bum and pushing her wheelchair for eternity.' Mummy. Look. Cartwheels. Slow ones. Wobble. Into the crab position. Wobble. Hoopla, twiggy-leggy-legs spinning above her head. Wobble. Imagine how good she'd be if she didn't have to stop it wobbling as well as holding herself on? Pretty good. Once, the time you went to Grandma's, for two days, even though the dark furniture was suffocating Mummy's sense of self, and – 'I have a profound desire to commit a Greek execution. Ancient Greek.' Daddy – you were allowed to watch TV. And there was Olga Korbut on her wobble free beam. Star evolved detailed plans for a meeting with Olga. Although Olga's from an oppressive regime so the plans had better be canny.

Jesus Christ. Look out. Star's crashing to earth. Crump of head on wood. That bloody thing. Wheelchair. No blood, no sound. What're you thinking just standing there like a gormless idiot? Race to her aid. Oh. She's poking her spider's legs straight in the air. Breathe. That's Chanticleer crowing. Those sodding hens need feeding. She's probably ok.

Winding downstairs, trailing your little finger nail in the silver foil. Making just a weeny rip. Everybody's at it these days so it doesn't matter, that much. Who made that lovely CND sign? Taa dah! You'd think they'd have been pleased but they're not sure it was you, which is interesting. Not as interesting as it would've been if you'd thought of doing stuff that shifts the blame, instead of Star getting in first. But still.

Into the Big Room. Crash of last night. 'This house is a total pigsty.' Mummy. Every time she thinks about organising a Saturday Morning

Clear-Up. The idea is everyone has to do a bit before the weekend can begin. 'Since Saturday's exactly the same as every other endless day.' Daddy. Saturday Morning Clear-Ups never get much further than you and Star polishing the tiles in the Big Room wearing Daddy's winter socks and doing some ice skating. Watch out for cat poo corner. The poo's been there so long it's a fossil. Might not even have been Great Uncle Elizabeth. Might've been a cat before.

Now there's this table full too. Will the Hoover Constellation (white) ever be taken from the box it came in? Twelve and a half years ago. 'Your mother knew life would be complete if I spent the last of my university grant on it. Might have been an idea to find somewhere to live first, but hey.' Daddy. Teaching about the arrival of the Hoover Constellation, on their honeymoon. Laura's right, it's better when there's adhering to a Rota going on. But you did the cooking and House Rule – No Cleaning For The Cook. Smell that. Dead ciggies, wine turning acid, sweet rot of crusting meat, adult sweat and dog. Jessie's up and at you nipping at your hair, pushing you over. Whispered morning barks. She knows not to wake the adults.

"We lived. Another day. Let's run." Jessie.

"Good doggy dog. Pee time. Find Star." You. Shoving her through a teeny opening of the back door. Closing the back door before you have to see Star. Now you can both pretend you're the first up. Alone.

That back door is a big, scarred door. The whole house is covered in those marks where the Sellotape being removed has ripped off paint. They're left over from the home-made signs that used to label everything. Until Star was four and you could both read. 'Kids will learn what they want when they need it. Formal education is torture of creativity.' Rod. Not that he was anywhere near your House when you and Star taught yourselves to read.

Breakfast.

FRENCH PORRIDGE

Small child's handful pinhead oatmeal, per adult. 'Less, less, less. Consider your poor tummy. The stomach is only the size of your fist.' Mummy. About most quants.
Small child's handful oats, per adult.
Double amount water to oatmeal and oats. Supposed to be milk but – 'All dairy is rotten cheese in waiting and too much milk creates mucus which is a frankly grim start to any day.' Mummy.

All in pot with fitting lid and room to spare. Swells as cooks. Bottom oven Aga over night. Making house breakfast is one of yours and Star's jobs.

French Porridge is a real shame. Almost anything would be a better breakfast. It's grey. Why? Oatmeal's a summer colour, originally. Take your portion bury it in the bin. You've had plenty of practice in the ritual of burials. When Star and you were young you spent hours trawling for stuff killed by lorries to give the smashed-up corpses a decent burial. Dirges, speeches, flowers placed in grave, dancing around grave – covered in ashes. No shortage in supply of ashes. Then light refreshments, biscuits and water. So reviving to spirits of tragic mourners.

Chuck in an ashtray's contents, make sure that grey blob's well buried under ashes. Someone's stubbed out a joint in the lemon solid. Bloody Adults. Eat the good end. Bit watery but still slippy and good. Gone. Cold beans are worth it. Better not eat too many. People will need them for lunch. Don't breathe on anyone. They'll smell the garlic and there will be... accusations. This beef tastes foul.

Too strong. Too much one taste. Too salty. Harsh. Lamb's delicious the next day. This beef is not. Just a couple more beans. There's bread left on plates. Real leftovers. Rod has ripped his into tiny bits. He'll have been sharing ideas. Why take bread in the first place? He can only cook Spaghetti Bolognese and he doesn't even know that if you use tom puree or tinned toms you have to add a pinch of brown sug to prevent an acid tang. Rod has no concept of the sacred nature of bread. Get Tammie's untouched hunk. 'Tammie has an over-developed sense of the sacred.' Daddy. Tammie pretends to eat but doesn't ever, in public. She eats a lot of peanut brittle, from Ma Burt's, in secret. She thinks. Big smear of butter. Butter's a bit day later but not too offal. Licking the knife, need more butter. Need jam. Bread in one hand hitching up your nightie. Greasy stains on it now. See? clambering up to the cupboard. Balancing. Balancing. Get that jam.

RHUBARB AND ELDERFLOWER JAM

This is The Great Jam. Apart from strawberry which everyone knows. And raspberry. Which is so sweet it makes your ears feel pink. The French should try jam.

1lb rhubarb
1lb sugar
4 or 5 heads elderflower

Saucer into fridge. Chop up fruit. Large saucepan, sugar, chopped rhub to boil. Can add juice of orange. Boil ten-ish mins. Until looks jammy. Drop blob jam-ish goo on icy saucer. Give it a push. If it wrinkles it's perfect. 'Unlike me.' Mummy. If no wrinkles keep cooking, try again. At last min shred elderflower heads into jam. Fills with tiny flowers. For a second. Cool, a bit, before you put into jars or jar will explode. All jam makes this stuff called scum. White jam froth. People put butter in to get rid of. Why? It's delicious. Simply scoop and eat. Put lid on. Jam is another job. 'Teach them a healthy respect for heat. If they once scalded themselves with boiling sugar they'll make bloody sure never to do it again.' Mummy. When the heap of strawbs she'd harvested two days before, but not had a second to turn into jam, were crying out for help and the kids making jam job came into being.

Got the jam. Got the bread. Leg dangling down.

"What're you snuffling up, little piggy?" Bryan. When the hell did he creep in?

Stay statue still. Head feels huge and tight and hurts. He's not looking at you. Get down. Careful now. He's hovering, picking at the pâté. Big wobbly blob on his finger. Look at that, his finger is hairy. Into wet mouth. Suck. Another big blob. In. Suck. Should have had a proper helping last night, shouldn't you, Bryan?

"Um." You.

Does he even really know you're here? Look, he's only wearing shorts. Wow. He. Is. Hairy. All. Over. He's got hairs on his teeny body just like his head. So much hair. Curly and black. Hairy Dolly Man. You're sliding to the window. Hopping onto the ledge. Get away from that bread. It's abandoned to the sink. Bye, bye sacred bread. You're perching, watching that Hairy Dolly. Does it hurt when the hairs first push their way through those skin holes? Legs swinging. See those skinny bruised legs? Yours. You've got hairs too but yours are perfectly reasonable. That nightie's a bit small. Very pink. No one wears pink here. Your arms are like a trout. Pink and brown freckles down the top, underneath a white that's nearly silver. Hairy Dolly's found its cigarette box. The box's got The Hanged Man painted on it. Pretty Justin did it. If only the Hairy Dolly wanted to sleep with Pretty Justin. Although Pretty Justin has a single bed. Comfy for you and Pretty Justin to cuddle in but no real room for another adult.

What has that Hairy Dolly seen?

"Can I roll your ciggie? Daddy lets me. I'm good at it." You.

It's handing over the box, smirking. Stop smirking Hairy Dolly. Pretend it just walked into the room and it's all about ciggies and nothing at all about private breakfasts. Hairy Dolly's seeing you. So, get comfy. Push back into that wrinkled old window pane. Roll the ciggie. Lick its paper. Liquorice paper sticking to your lip like it does to Daddy's. You look perfect. Ciggie paper's sweet, a taste that melts in a second. Look. That is sun shining clear through your nightie. You are nude. See those? Those are breasts. Acorn nubs. Can you see your ribs? Tummy button? The start of hair. Hello, when did that start? And that didn't hurt come to think of it. Great lengths of body all hanging off you. Has that Hairy Dolly noticed your nudeness? No. Has it noticed the bread? No. It's just breaking its hairy-fast, that's all. Have a good old stare at that Hairy Dolly. Interest it. That's the way to handle this. Take its mind off your blinkin' garlic feast. Adults are always interested in you. 'She's the creative one. Star has a mathematical brain. Where did that come from in this family?' Mummy. Star has tried with the maths brain thing. She snapped when she got given a radio set for her birthday. 'But darling, I thought you'd adore to make it and take it apart again.' Mummy. Star had asked, repeatedly, for a doll that you can feed water to. The water trickles through, then the doll does a real pee. She couldn't have been clearer but Mummy was determined.

"Can I light it?" You.

"Does Daddy let you do that, too?" Hairy Dolly.

"Come on. I want the hit." No you don't. It's completely disgusting. But that's what they say. So.

It's searching for a match. Keeping on looking your way. Noticing? Striking the match.

"Mmm. I like that." You. 'Sulphur. Smell of the devil's farts.' Daddy. When you said you liked it. 'Have you smelt them?' Laura.

"Yeah. It's nice." Hairy Dolly.

It's coming up close. Holding its match. Hey, Hairy Dolly, get back. It's sort of leaning in more than it needs to, to light its cig. That is its arm sliding up your chest. Cheese grater. Does it mean to make its arm do that? Cigarette spark. Swallowing smoke. For Christ's sake you aren't an actual smoker. That smoke needs to get out of your lungs. Puff it out and at it. That'll make it budge back. Bit of a cough-splutter but not too much. Why don't you pick a pretend scrap of baccie off your bottom lip? Look in its eyes whilst you do this picking bit. This would be a good moment to do a smoke ring. If you could. Like Mummy. You and Star have done a fair bit of practice with smoking. You go to Star's den, you get hollow-dried cow parsley stalks, you stuff them with newspaper and they make excellent ciggies. Almost as chokingly vile as the real ones. You've achieved smoke rings but not reliably enough to risk one now. Hairy Dolly's sucking in puffed-out smoke. Your head's rolling back against the pane. Lovely, lovely air. Isn't your neck long? And dirty. Wormy curls of black filth. Hairy Dolly's taking the ciggie.

"How long have you been doing that?" Hairy Dolly. What does it mean? Rolling ciggie? Inhaling ciggie? Practising ciggie? Ciggies in general? Take a guess. Come on. Just guess.

"Oh. Years." Deciding against the full guess this early on. The Hairy Dolly's nodding. Sagely. Good. No guess necessary. Work out what you've committed to later. It didn't mean the leftovers.

The Hairy Dolly's leaning right in. Resting its hard little scrubby body against yours. Doesn't feel like any of yours or Star's dollies. Not that you play with dolls anymore. You've just become twelve for heaven's sake. Unless it's Action Girl for story telling, which you do still do. Very occasionally. Taking Action Girl on a day-long adventure, talking the story out loud as it happens. It's nearly out of the question now that Your People have filled up your house. How long is it going to do this pushing bit for? And ok. You can look up. The Hairy Dolly's moving off.

"How old are you?" Hairy Dolly

"Nearly Thirteen." You.

"You should go now." Hairy Dolly.

Should you? Why? You were here first. The sun's warm. Why have you started to do that little rocking thing with your bum? The Hairy Dolly seems to be insisting on hanging around to do its smoking. It's walking to the pâté. It's dipping in its finger. Again. It's sucking it all off. There won't be a scrap of that pâté left for anyone else, if it doesn't watch it. It's having a bit more ciggie. It's looking at you again, so that rocking thing is interesting. No need to goggle Hairy Dolly. It can keep those marble-round, too dark eyes in its head. Its eyes look like you could pop them out with your thumb. Mummy used to know someone who actually could pop out their eyeballs. Give them a lick. Then pop them back in. Very much like to meet that person. How useful to be able to do that. You did try but it hurt like buggery, and your eyes were fairly serious about staying put. Maybe the Hairy Dolly has New Yorker's eyes? Is it possible it might be trying to ask you something with its bulby doll's eyes? Like Star does. Mind you, you're fluent in Star. This Hairy Dolly is un-translatable. So, stay shut up. Shutting up might be the best thing all round.

Here it comes again.

Don't breathe, keep on with that tilting, goggle back at it, let it do the bloody translating, keep on shutting up, and you've got a plan. It's stopped, in front of you, it's putting just its face up to yours. Really don't breathe now. It isn't blinking. So don't you bloody blink. Hold your breath. Come on hold it. Argghhh. Running out of air. Eyes being massively disloyal and fucking watering. Don't blink first. Have to breathe. Done. That's a pathetic gulping baby's breath. No way that Hairy Dolly won't have noticed that. Yup. It's off. Nipping towards the door. Blink, blink, blinkety, blink. Stop watering you fucking eyes. This rocking and clinging to the window ledge is really hurting the old bum bone. Simply must shift. Lovely big wriggle. Oh. Hairy Dolly has ceased all movement. It's standing with its back to you. It's turning. Could it smell the wriggling? How did it know you wriggled?

"Wanna hit?" Hairy Dolly. Can't say no can you? Do, for heaven's sake, stick with shutting up. Just nod. Yes.

It's moving back in. That's some jolly casual strolling towards you it's doing. When did you open your legs? It's facing you. It'll entirely be able to sniff your garlic. So what. Let it. It's so close, it must smell it. The Hairy Dolly's laying the ciggie on your bottom lip. Close your mouth. Do the tiniest suck you can. Blow it out around the ciggie still in your mouth. This is quite a French way of smoking. Very glad indeed you've had a go at this way of blowing out before today. And you're staying shut up. Good girl. Hairy Dolly is stepping in between your legs. Sort of prancing in. Taking back its ciggie. Phew.

Feel that? That is its willy. How the hell do women get that inside them when they make a baby? And, come to think of it, is this what all willies feel like? Know what they look like. Seen Daddy's loads. When he flops along the landing for a pee. And there's a pony at the far end of the village called Fella. Fella's just a bit bigger than a huge dog. Which is tiny for a pony. You and Star have spent quite a few hours hanging on Fella's gate, poking his willy with long bamboo garden poles. 'Fella's willy is exceptional even by horse standards.' Mummy. Fella's willy is like the trunk of a silver birch tree. Peeling. You and Star try and peel it for him. With the poles. The trick is to hold the poles like extra long chopsticks. He doesn't seem to mind. You've seen Rod's willy too. In passing. Walnut whip. So, Fella's willy is long. Daddy's is normal. Rod's is stumpy. Are willies like breasts? Changeable? 'Christ look at my breasts? They used to be something. You two have dragged all the goodness out of me. Dragged it. Look at what's bloody well left, just two nipples like fucking...dates.' Mummy. About her breasts. Which are just big brown nipples, now. You've seen Tammie's Jammie Dodgers and Laura's, 'Look like they might amount to something serious. Puuuufff.' Rod. So. Breasts and willies can look very different but is this rock-like-ness to be expected? You're breathing in jags, right up in your throat.

"Are you just like your mummy? Baby girl." Hairy Dolly. Whispering.

Baby? Bugger. Baby? Which kind? It's pushing at you, nudging. It's got you. It's getting hold of your legs. Ow. It's pulling you up against itself. It's pulled your fanny next to its willy. Its Big Silly Willy. Does its willy have hairs on it? Are you going to fall off the window ledge? That ledge is really difficult to balance on. You're clinging on with your fingertips but it's got your legs. You're not going to fall. Its thumbs are near your fanny. It's moving them, circling them on your near-fanny skin. And rocking like you did. Only more.

"You wanna kiss? Little piggy." Hairy Dolly.

It's still rocking. You are not.

"Um. Maybe later." You.

That Hairy Dolly's breath stinks of fish and ciggies and drains. It's stopped. It's smoking. Holding you with one hand. Its thumb's still moving, a little.

"Why don't you fuck off then, Nearly Thirteen?" Hairy Dolly. No need to shove. That'll make a bruise.

"That's a fucking silly game and you're a stupid little cunt." Hairy Dolly. Wheezy laugh.

Gone. Tittering's following. Absolutely do not look back. Through the door, upstairs, down the landing, don't wake the adults, into your room, slamming the door and pushing back against it. 'Why would we want locks? Locks say no. We say yes.' Rod. On your bed, on the edge. What to do?

Cunt?

There's no one else awake. Get outside and away.

Edging off the bed, sneaking your ear to the floor. Can you hear it? Can't be hearing it smoke. Hear that? That's the front door opening. Why are you crawling to the window? It can't see inside your bedroom. Peeking out. It's in the front garden, finishing its ciggie. It's glancing up. It knows where you sleep. It did see you. Crawling away from window. Lie down flat on floor. Nightie, off. Pants, on. Pale brown smock thing and jeans, on. Done. Go. Crawling from room. You know this house better than any of them. It's your house. Stand up. Fast to the landing window – at the back of the house. That Dolly's out the front. No way you can go downstairs so, grab hold of the landing window ledge. Jump to the ledge. Missed. Jumping again, clinging and climbing. Up. Scraping through the window, onto the roof. Sliding down the tiles. It's a vast distance to the ground but not impossible. The tiles are loose and want to come with you. Of course they do. Bloody tiles cannot wait to exit Swallow's Farmhouse roof. Having to hold them in place and get down. You've done it once before but never since. You're stopped, teetering on the edge. Go on, jump. Maybe you'll fly? The first time you attempted this exit you were trying out flying, just in case it was like your dream. In your dream you're running. Lots of effort goes into the running. You have to push against the air, means you can only run slowly. When you've got a head of steam up you tip forwards, your feet float up until you're flat, about a yard from the floor, then you're doing front crawl through the air. Excellent means of travel. Second favourite dream. First favourite dream's a dancing and jumping one. You're dancing and very quickly it turns into jumping, then you're jumping higher and higher until you're jumping higher than buildings. But all in nearly slow motion. Thick air again. You've a chance to chat as you float-bounce up and down. And, of course, many, many lucky people get to observe this phenomenon. Even in Dream Land you're miraculous. You told Rod, because he is the House Dream Analyst when you need a Jungian interpretation. He was a bit shifty looking. 'It's not a dream you're ready for.' Rod.

Perching on the tiles pulling the window closed behind you. This is not a dream. Jump. It might be coming round the side of the house. Although it's scared of the bees' nest in the end wall so possibly not. Jump. Barrelling earthwards. Ouch. That crack feels as if your heel bones have entered the earth. Massive jolt up your legs to your shoulders. Job done. In the garden and not where that Hairy Dolly expects you to be. Star's wobbling on her beam goggling at you – that's not flying – across her mud coloured eyes.

"Come on, nippety-pip. Top of the field. Come on, Star." You.

She's doing what you tell her to. Top of the field is Child Land. Unless it's full of Eric and his hoes. Or Mummy, in the sun-bathing nest she's made for herself in the wilderness at the very top. There's a Mummy-shaped flat bit in the grasses up there. That Hairy Dolly won't bother with fields. Take a break, have a breather, you've earned one. It's going to be another scorcher.

"Come on, for heaven's sake, we need to let the bloody chickens out of their coop." You. Another job.

Star's having a think about whether she can be bothered with that. Look out. Jessie's arriving, at you. She's been waiting. Your dog really does have exceptionally bad breath. Has she been smoking?

"She's been scoffing pig poo again." You. Breathe in that Jessie Dog's breath.

Oh well. To the hens. Star's relenting and following. The hens are rightly pissed off with being left so long and clearly they're expecting corn. Crowding round a bit too close. Nag, nag, nag with their pointy little beaks. Shove them over. No chance of corn, it lives under the sink in the kitchen. The kitchen's part of the Big Room. The Big Room leads to the front door. Clambering into the coop. See how dark it is in there? Few streaks of light between slats and dust motes stuffing into those streaks. Reaching into the strawy boxes, feeling round. Gentle, gentle don't knock them. It's dark and hot and thick with hen poo in here. Look at your feet. Bare. Ignore the poo. It's mostly dry anyway. Although one of the things about hen poo is how dry even the wet stuff looks. And then it's too late. Get the eggs. Eight eggs. Three of them warm. All of them poo stained. 'Oh for Christ's sake, a bit of chicken shit won't kill you.' Mummy. About smeary eggs. Pig for dogs, hen for you. Star's outside keeping the child murderer Chanticleer at big stick's length. Once, Star shone a torch into his eyes, at night, he went crazy-beans. It was an accident for heaven's sake. The torch shining. Not Chanticleer's endless revenge attacks. They're clearly planned. Vicious cock. Flies at your neck with his claws like talons. Vital to arm with big sticks to collect eggs. Star won't go in the coop. She doesn't want to get trapped. Neither do you but someone has to get the shitty eggs.

Many good things to do with eggs. Shitty or otherwise. Best of all, which might be the best of all things to eat – apart from a tomato sandwich on home-made bread made with 81% white flour with very salty butter and a little bit of pepper – the best of all things to do with eggs is meringues.

'Meringues are the reason to have a bloody Aga.' Clarissa.

MERINGUES

Are childishly simple. 1 egg white to 1 oz sugar. Soft brown sugar mixed with caster is sweetest, stickiest. Sniff of toffee flavour.

Whip egg whites for an age. Done when bowl's upside down over Star's head and nothing moves. Apart from Star. Cut sugar into eggs. Dollops on greaseproof tray. Bottom oven Aga. For hours. Can leave over night. Once, Daddy made them and threw in a handful of wild strawberries. Mummy was inconsolable. Why?

The only way to serve them is a sandwich with a whipped cream middle. After meringues you'll have yolks left; sensible thing to do with them is curd.

SEVILLE ORANGE CURD. First thing Mummy taught you to shoplift was oranges. On the fruit and veg stall in Aylsham when she used to go shopping, for fruit and veg. 'Say, I'm just helping myself to four of these lovely oranges. Then point to something on the other side of the stall and ask its price. He'll look at that thing. You swipe two more oranges. He's a hideous racist. Told me not to worry, no darkies had touched his South African fruit. He deserves to get it swiped.' Mummy. Teaching.

2 egg yolks

1 egg

4 oz white sugar

1 Seville orange. The point with these is they're almost a lemon. But not quite.

1 lemon

2 ½ oz butter

Pan water to heat. Bowl to sit in pan not touching water. Scrunch up tin foil to line top of pan, make a steam-proof nest for bowl. Stops touching.

Grate rind off. Sugar, juice in with rind. Whip egg yolks, add to sugar mix. Balance bowl, on nest, over simmering water. Drop butter, small chunks, in. Stir often. Thickens to creamy curd. Takes about 15 mins. Let cool. Thickens more.

Once, years ago when you were tiny, before you had Jessie, Daddy and Mummy had been shouting for days. 'Right. I am done. I have to get away.' Daddy. Mummy had Star because Star was still needing breast milk. 'Although what was I thinking with all the endless breast milk on demand crap.' Mummy. About letting you breast-feed on demand until you were at least four. Clarissa came to look after Mummy, you and Daddy went to sleep at the beach. You took blankets, matches, a bottle of water and Daddy had some whisky.

"Please don't talk to me. Can't you just entertain yourself?" Daddy. Of course you could.

You collected wood. It was windy but warmish too. Not warm enough to swim but warm enough to sleep outside. You collected all the wood you could find.

"We don't need that. We aren't planning on burning down buildings. Or maybe we should. We could." Daddy.

Stopped him thinking that by starting to get big stones to make a fireplace. He stopped talking, joined in, you made a circle with high stones and put the smallest, driest twigs in first, some sea grass too, then Daddy let you light that and then, using your bodies to break the wind, you kept the flame alight and added more wood and when there were glowing embers you left it with a little dried tree trunk across it. You and Daddy went fishing.

"Look, always look, where the sea birds are. Follow the birds for fish." Daddy.

You went right to the crumbled end of the jetty, where the water was properly deep.

"Dangerous but fuck it. As good this way as any other." Daddy.

You sat and let down your lines – no rods just thread with a hook and some teeny worms you'd scrabbled from sand – Instantly you had mackerel. Two. Daddy smoked, put his arm heavy on your shoulders, you ached to stay scooping up fish but Daddy finished his ciggie then you left the jetty. Daddy taught you to use his penknife to slit the bellies and wash the guts into the sea. The gulls came shrieking to guzzle those guts. You took the fish, pierced them onto long sticks, sat and toasted them over the fire. From his big coat pocket Daddy found a jam jar with Bearnaise Sauce. You both laughed. I mean really, Bearnaise Sauce. He said he'd taken it from the fridge. It was leftovers from the Poetry Pleasure and Pain Happening.

"Fuck it, I made it, why not? It was too good to leave." Daddy.

And here it was, to dip the blackened smoky skin and still pink drippy fishy flesh into. Oh the goodness of that sweet fish, butter, salt and tarragon. The wind was getting up and the smoke from the fire was in your eyes, sparks were cracking past.

"Who cares? Wrap up warm. Tuck up." Daddy.

You did. You made a line with your bodies, heads touching, stretched alongside your fire. Wriggling down into the broken shelly sand, made a dip, scrunched your head into the sand, filled your hair with it, closed your eyes, opened them and stared. The sky was rammed with stars.

BEARNAISE SAUCE

Slosh vinegar
Chopped shallot. Shallots are so small you can chop them before they make you cry.
Few black peppercorns
Teaspoon dried tarragon
2 egg yolks
Blob mustard
6 oz butter
Lemon juice. For tasting.
Handful fresh tarragon leaves, chopped. 'You are a beautiful, ridiculous snob. What the hell will you use it for?' Daddy. To Mummy when she first planted tarragon. Now he knows.

Vinegar, shallot, pepper, dried tarragon, few spoons of water, reduce two mins.

Tin foil nest over boiling water. Strain liquid from reduction. Chuck bits. Liquid into bowl with mustard, egg yolks. Whip. Drop little chunks butter, bit-by-bit into bowl. Don't stop whisking. Butter melts, thickens, becomes mayonnaise-like sauce. When thick, it's done. Add chopped tarragon, squirt lemon juice.

Only ever ate this once with mackerel but it is the only way. Sea and earth. Nose food. Smells as it tastes. Complete.

You have the eggs. You have Jessie. You have Star. Star needs to know what will happen with the day.

"We're these two kids. We're orphans. We've been at sea for weeks. Um." You. Cooking up a plan. Flaps of soft, dog-ear-muscle running through your fingers. Setting off together further up the field. There's really no need to go back to the house for hours. Why isn't Star following?

"Ok fine. Not sea. We're in Russia. We're world-famous dancers. But shockingly poor ones. It's snow as far as the eye can see. Endless winter. The sledge has lost a slidey bit. Again. We have no choice. We must walk. You have a broken toe. It's chronic pain. For you. We can't limp on. Your broken toe's turning yellow. It stinks. Most likely gangrene. Oi, come back! What do you want to play then?" Where is Star buggering off to? Bloody Jessie's suddenly all perky-talking-eyebrows too. What the hell do they want?

"No. Jessie. Heel. Jessie. Bloody. Heel!" You. You have to pretend to be a man for a dog to take you seriously. Jessie does take you seriously, on a psychic level, but she is fucking disobedient in real life.

"Phup, phup, phup." Sound.

That's what stopped Star. And Jessie, as it happens. Why didn't you notice it before?

"Phup, phup, phup." Music – infection loud – from inside the house.

Star's running, she has the back door swinging open, the sound is thunking out, the door's closing behind her, sound's reverting to phup, phup, phup. You have to follow. You are. But slowly. Holding Jessie close by her collar. Hovering for a second. It'll be fine. In you go. Crash.

"You know that I would be a liar, if I was to say to you, girl we couldn't get much higher." Music.

The Big Room's choked with them. Just out of bed. Tie-dyed shorts – Eric. Indian cheese-cloth sarong – Laura. Arm full of tiny silver bangles, wrist to elbow – Tammie. 'Clothes decorate the soul. Not the body.' Tammie. Ages ago. 'As long as your soul can carry off a bias cut.' Mummy. Ages ago too and about Tammie's excessively drapey dress.

"Come on baby, light my fire. Come on baby, light my fire." Music.

They're cleaning the mess and almost everyone's dancing. Where's the Hairy Dolly? Green velvet hipsters – Daddy. Nothing else. Where's the Hairy Dolly? Jumble sale vest, long like a dress – Mummy. Towel – Tammie. Tammie can't have meant to join in. She would never dance around in just a towel, normally. Look over there. The Hairy Dolly's still in its shorts and its hairiness, lurking by the Aga. Not noticing you. Pants – Pretty Justin. 'Those relentlessly hideous Y-fronts.' Mummy. About Pretty Justin's pants that he sleeps in. They're baby blue and grey that was once white. 'Saggy in all the wrong places.' Mummy. Again. Pretty Justin doesn't care, he looks. Um. Yes. He looks delighted. With it all. With the dancing, the loudness, how far it is from America. 'Ohhh this country is yeah? Is yeah? So far, far, far, far out. So far out, yeah? From Amerikee.' Pretty Justin. About why he likes your country most. He's seeing you, grabbing you, singing for you. Jessie, desperate to be taken seriously on the dance floor, is jumping. You look stern. Stop looking at the Aga.

"Come on baby. Come on baby. Come on baby." Pretty Justin.

A bit less stern. I'm not a baby like that. I'm a baby like this. I'm a come on baby, baby. You. Signalling in the general direction of the Hairy Dolly. Clearing up a few facts.

It's not interested. Why? It's lurked over to Tammie. Tammie? Has it ever even spoken to her? Swinging her round. Tammie's very pink. Let the laugh at Pretty Justin squeeze out. That Hairy Dolly, and its silly pokey willy, is going to be nothing. Have a dance.

"I'm here. I'm here. I'm here." Jessie. Barking. Well of course she's barking, Jessie can't actually talk. Yet.

Star's on the table doing tapping over Great Uncle Elizabeth, who's snoozing. She's passing plates to Daddy. He's doing his hip-thrust walk. Wish he wouldn't insist on that kind of dancing. 'It's good enough for Jagger.' Daddy. Knees bent, thrust, step. Knees bent, thrust, step. Catching plates, flipping them to Laura. He's stopping for a second behind her – stood at the sink – thrust, thrust, thrust on her bum. Bit childish. Laura's taking plates, plopping them in the soapy sink. Laura moves differently. Look out, here she comes. Arms straight up in the air softly waving. Soap bubbles dripping down her arms. Closed eyes and she's off, glide-waving round the room. 'Fascinating how graceful Laura can be. Considering her bulk. I suppose she had some training, or something.' Mummy. To Daddy. When Laura first danced and people were captivated.

"The time to hesitate is through, no time to wallow in the mire." Music.

Laura's feet are covered in brown scratchy henna paintings. Mummy's lily paintings. With roots growing round her ankles. Must have done it last night. Laura's skimming past Rod who's jigging about in the corner. Rod is uptight. The Hairy Dolly is not uptight. 'Oh and he flows when he dances, too. Liquid beauty.' Mummy. To Daddy about that Hairy Dolly at the first House celebration after it arrived.

"If Rod could just let go, he might seriously surprise everyone." Mummy. Passing Daddy.

Planning to be around when that happens. There goes Laura, wave-glide past Mummy, stopping with Mummy, who's stepping into her but no, Laura's off again, back round Rod's end of the table. She's like the bus that's recently started up, from Aylsham to Norwich. The 178. Only goes once a week but when it does go it stops at all the stops. Rod's ready at the bus stop, he's jerky jigging, clicking his fingers all over the shop. That's not dancing. Nor is it the way to stop a bus. That's shouting with his body. Oh, look, he's made a snatch at her. You're whipping a look to Pretty Justin. Did he see? Oh yes he did. He's winking at you, waltzing you over. There goes Mummy. Mummy dances slowly too. No matter what the music. Swings her hair around a lot. She's swinging it between Eric, who can move. Big Surprise. 'Eric, you can dance. I assumed you were jointed like Action Girl.' Mummy. To Eric when he first danced. And between Daddy. 'Your Papa has snake hips, girls.' Mummy. About Daddy's good moves.

Pretty Justin's dipping you. Wink your eyes so it can't see you peeping and check its whereabouts. Still twirling a Tammie. Pretty Justin's been teaching you ballroom dancing. This is the wrong music. But he's forcing it into the right music. Step, step, dip and you're in the queue at Rod's bus stop, floppy in Pretty Justin's arms. 'Let me, me like lead. Stop, yeah? Trying. Give me the, you know, the, like, control.' Pretty Justin. To you. Doing the teaching. You've got the hang of floppy now.

You and Pretty Justin are doing good pretending that you're flop-dipping, but you're only interested in Rod who you're both following with your sideways eyes. Is he about to let go? He looks shocked. He needs to touch Laura, doesn't he? Bus coming round the corner. Queue shuffling forwards. Here he goes. Spectacular snatch. No contact. Rod nearly ended up on his bum. Has she noticed? The 178 has arrived. It's opening its doors. The driver is ready to issue the tickets, big dip and up from Pretty Justin as Laura's squiggling down to the ground. Arms in the air. Her head's in front of Rod's tummy.

"Grunt puuuuffff." Rod. Goat variety. Glancing up at Daddy. Daddy's playing pretend drums on the table, Star's hopping between his hands. Oh look. Rod's sensing the moment and getting on the bus. Rod's copying Daddy's thrust walk. He's grabbed Laura's head, holding it to his tummy. Pretty Justin's screaming with delight and nearly dropping you. Rod is a rubbish dancer. The 178 has stalled. Engine off. Laura has stopped dancing. She's yanking herself away, standing up, Rod's static, up go her hands and she's miming. Brilliant. You really are very interested in learning mime. She's miming a wall. Walking away. Like she never even danced. Walking back to the washing-up, passing Daddy, he's trailing an arm out for her, wriggling his hips, she's ignoring him, he's sniffing at her neck, twirling her on her way. Engine back on, the 178 will complete its journey, she's back in the rhythm, back to the sink. Brum, brum, brummm. Daddy's glancing at Rod. Rod didn't even get a ticket for the 178. How did Daddy see what was happening with Rod and Laura?

"Come on baby light my fire. Come on baby li-i-gh-t my fire." Music.

Pretty Justin's laughing too much, he's swung you off to do your own thing, so you're breaking a house rule by gathering some forks and spoons, shaking them together and now Daddy and Pretty Justin are in each other's arms. Rolling and Rocking.

"And our love become a funeral pyre." Music.

Rod's straight back to jerky-jiggy-finger-clicky, alone. You're delivering spoons to Laura.

"Thank you, sweet thing. You and Justin are the belles of the ball." Laura. Yes, you are.

Now. Sneak another speedy look at that Hairy Dolly. Peek. It's leaning against the fireplace rolling a joint. Watching Mummy with its bulby eyes. Mummy's doing slow motion head banging. Hairy Dolly is not interested in you, anymore. That didn't take long. Check the rest of the room. Star's trying to do a handstand. Wheelchair. Eric looks like he's gone insane. He's got Jessie by her front paws making her dance on her hind legs. She's still barking.

"You know that I would be a liar, if I was to say to you, girl we couldn't get much higher." Music.

Tammie's running in circles flapping her hands. Who told her that was dancing? Tammie and Rod should apply to you to teach them a few moves. Eric's dropping Jessie, catching Mummy's hand, she's banging to him, Hairy Dolly's sneak watching under its hairy lashes.

"Try to set the night on fire. Try to set the night on fire." Music.

Silence. Record's over. No more barking either. Great Uncle Elizabeth hasn't stirred. 'Epic powers of control, that cat.' Daddy. About Great Uncle Elizabeth stalking the Mouse Cupboard, for days at a time.

"My Love?" Daddy. Calling to Mummy who's stepping from Eric, "Play that at my funeral. When the curtains are closing and my coffin's sliding away."

Star's gone rigid in the centre of the table. Looking to you, starting to twist a handful of hair. You're gathering Jessie into you. Feel her slump? Breathe in her stink, like coagulated earwax. With a hint of pig. Peeping at Mummy. She's pulling her hair back to tie it into its own knot, smiling her open moon-daisy face at the room. Did she even hear him? Great Uncle Elizabeth's standing, stretching and leaping from the table.

There's laughter. He's serious, you know? People are resuming the tidy-up. Apart from Rod who's laughing and leaving the room.

"Gotta jot that down. Aye, nail that thought." Rod. On his way out.

Hairy Dolly's sneering as Rod passes. You're pushing Star off the table. She's jolted but she's stopped her hair twist. The Hairy Dolly's passing behind you. Smacking your bottom as it goes. Hey. No thank you. Listen. Jessie's lip's curled and she's growled. Very quietly. Don't think the Hairy Dolly heard her. Everyone's working together. Apart from Rod. And Jessie. And Great Uncle Elizabeth. And Prune who, how come? Is standing in the doorway, observing.

"Christ, I am starving. My children used up a week's worth of food last night. We have nothing in the house. Bloody hell." Mummy.

But you do have, look at Mummy remembering, going to the freezer and getting it out.

FROZEN CHOCOLATE CAKE

This is, quite simply, the pinnacle of cakes. If a person's ever lucky enough to get offered this for breakfast, they must never ever say no.

3oz butter
3oz sugar
6oz wholemeal, of course, self raising flour

2 eggs
And, strangely, a big spoon of yoghurt mixed up with a slosh of milk. Tammie whispered this trick to you. Mummy pulled a bit of a face but yum. It's good. Extra bounce and keeps for ever. If you let it.
Couple of spoons cocoa powder

Cream butter, sugar. Whisk eggs. Mix eggs, butter, sugar. If it curdles, which it probably will, cake can be so grumpy, add spoon of the flour. Mix then add rest flour, cocoa. Dollop into two small greased tins. Bake top oven, twenty mins. Cool. Make butter icing. Butter, icing sugar, cocoa, splash milk. Sandwich cakes up with this. Freeze.

To eat this cake take it out of freezer sit it up top of Aga for ten mins, turning it over. This almost defrosts the sponge but leaves the middle rock hard. Soft, sproingy sponge and ice-hard chocolate butter. Unparalleled eating. Listen. No one's speaking whilst they eat this. No one can believe their luck. Everyone, apart from you, has forgotten about French bloody Porridge. Oh my goodness, see Mummy walking to the cupboard under the stairs? The Mouse Cupboard. Watch her open the door. Get a whiff of the smell of dead and living mouse that wafts up from the open cupboard door. She's bringing out an old Corona bottle.

HOME-MADE GINGER BEER

For this you need to have a friend. They have to give you a bit of their ginger beer plant. Luckily some bloke called Bob who Daddy knows at the Erpingham Commune really wanted to try and make friends, for his sons, with the kids at Daddy's commune. You. 'Bob's boys, the lonely heroes.' Daddy. Daddy did try telling him you aren't a commune and you don't need any friends but it was vital to expose Ginger Beer Bob's boys to a female influence. Endless and unutterably dull afternoon. Apparently playing together. Outcome, ginger beer plant. Worth it.

Blob of ginger beer yeasty plant
8oz sugar
1 lemon, juiced
Half teaspoon cream of tartar
As many spoons of ginger as you want. Start with two big ones.
3 ½ pints water

Put everything apart from plant and ginger into big jug, stir until sugar dissolved. Plant and ginger into muslin, tie up, hang into liquid. Lid on, leave for 5 days. Into bottles with screw tops. Leave for week. Longer you leave it the more it fizzes. And the more pissed you get. Last spring everyone, and some cousins you'd just met, and their parents, an aunt and uncle, must have been. Anyway, that day, everyone was in the garden when suddenly you all jumped and screamed because it sounded like the house was exploding. Bombs. Everyone rushed into the Big Room. The uncle was crying because he could easily remember The War. The walls were running with brown liquid and the floor was covered with glass. Six bottles of ginger beer had all exploded at the same time. 'How are we to describe this synchronised exploding phenomenon? Psychic Pop? Fatalistic Fizz?' Rod. Staring at a wall. 'Another fucking mess for me to clean?' Mummy. Picking up glass. She was interrupted. A sound. Unmistakable, unless you were the uncle who hurled himself under the big table and sort of wrapped himself around, like a hedgehog. It was a crop sprayer. Teeny tiny plane. Mummy went screaming back into the garden. 'Stay in here. All of you stay inside and cover your mouths, those fucking rural imbeciles, I will fucking kill them.' Mummy. Hauling her top off and racing along the field with The Dates on full show, screaming at the sky. The plane flew low, pretty much brushed the tips of the pear tree, you could see the trail of pesticide snowing down. All over the field. 'Fucking morons, fucking rural morons, fucking rural inbreds.' Mummy. End of field. 'Father? Father? You can come out now. It wasn't a bomber. Why has your mother removed her clothes?' Oldest Cousin. Standing beside you and watching Mummy through the window. 'Bethan is under the impression that the local farmers care about our communal, and indeed agricultural, lifestyle choices. She believes we're under attack. That when they've finished killing caterpillars they fly home over our den of iniquity and empty the last of their tanks on us.' Daddy. Picking up glass. 'Why the breasts?' The Uncle. Uncurling. 'Thinks they'll be distracted by lust and crash.' Daddy.

"I'm just going to check this isn't poisoned." Mummy. Having a gingery swig. She always says this. Once, you went on a picnic and at the end of it you and Star were so thirsty your throats sort of buzzed. There was a mistake. Only one small bottle of drink. Mummy said the poison thing for the first time. You believed her. She drank the whole bottle. You both tried crying but it was too strange. 'I didn't mean to do that.' Mummy. Handing the empty to Daddy. 'No, of course you didn't, you were thirsty, I assume.' Daddy. Turning the empty round in his hand. 'I always put them first. Always. I was thirsty.' Mummy. 'Yes, you were thirsty.' Daddy.

Mummy's handing round the long, thin, bobbly bottle. Everyone's taking deep glugging swigs. Enormous burps. Mummy's triumphant. Although you cooked that cake. And that ginger beer.

CHAPTER THREE

Four days later. Still proper summer. That Hairy Dolly seems to be treating itself to lots of long, sunny walks. It toddled to Norwich yesterday. Twelve miles, each way. Swallow's farmhouse front lawn is pretty much gone. White dead grass, bleached cracked earth. Path lined with dead poppy heads. What's left after the Hairy Dolly tried bleeding them in July. No high. The cow parsley hedge is thick with seed-heads. Never bring cow parsley inside. 'Ooow. You little beggars. You asking for a death in the family?' Ma Burt. You never do bring it in, you never will, but there will be a death in the family. Soon.

'Only boring people get bored. Make yourselves useful. Make something for Eric's birthday. Don't say I said, he's so dull about fusses being made. See if you two can charm him.' Mummy. Never been known to duck a challenge, so sweets it is. Star's made a box for them. 'Clever thing.' Mummy. To Star. Wandering past. Old shoe box covered in silver foil with grass glued on the top. Field effect.

HOME-MADE GLUE

Handful flour. White's best. Which supports Mummy's point.
White flour creates glue.

Water
Mix together. Glue.

SELECTION BOX

Chocolate-dipped pineapple chunks

Treacle toffee. Grown-ups like this back-of-the-throat taste better than normal toffee.

Sugar mice. Only not mice. Other shapes you will think of. Grown-ups don't much bother with this. So you and Star can.

CHOCOLATE-DIPPED PINEAPPLE CHUNKS

Tin of chunks
Bar of chocolate. Grown-ups like Bourneville best so does Star. They're wrong, milk's best. Dark choc removes some of the point of choc. Sweetness.

Melt choc – bowl, tin foil nest. Don't stir. Drain chunks, dry slightly. Soon as choc melted dip in chunks. Work with speed. Choc dries fast. On greaseproof to set. Sweet juicy surprise burst when you bite through crack of choc. You and Star invented this recipe when you needed some sweets but no one had even two pence to spare. 'Do not badger me for dough. You're horribly spoiled as it is. Ten pence every Saturday to stuff your faces with crap.' Mummy. Lie. You get it some Saturdays and you're saving your ten pence in Post Office Stamps to buy a pony. One without a peelie willy, please. So you have to convince Star to share her ten pence. On the weeks that she isn't hording hers, for the sojourn with Olga. Tricky work. This makes five pence worth of sweets, not even every week. However, Mummy always has a stash of chocolate in the pottery, (blood sugar levels), which you borrowed the first time you made these chunks. Doing the same again today, she says you can. This time.

TREACLE TOFFEE

Could not be easier.

10 oz soft brown sugar
6 tablespoons black treacle
12 oz butter. Salty. Again.
5 fl. oz water

All into big pan. Boil ten mins. Do dropping into cold water test. Done when squidges. Pour into greased tin. When set, smash into chunks with hammer. 'It isn't an enemy.' Mummy. Wandering past. Return trip.

SUGAR MICE

8oz icing sugar
1 egg white
colouring

Whisk egg white until fluffy. Add sugar, colour. Make into mice. Stuff in string for tails, silver balls for eyes. Why mice? Mice have an absence of bladder. They leak pee constantly. Make some cows, Eric adores farm things. Apparently. A tractor. Failure. Tractor colours mixed up to plasticine sludge green. Transformed into cow poo. 'Why do you have to wreck everything?' Mummy. Wandering past. Again. Those cow poos are life-like. Eric is going to be made to be happy. And then he is going to do some happy sweet-induced chatting. Betcha.

Star's ripping up green tissue paper, nestling each sweet. Tucking them up for bed in their meadow box. Sandwiching each layer with a cardboard roof. Four layers of tooth-rot delight. Star's putting the finishing touches to her box. Trying to glue a couple of plastic cows to its field. Ee–i-ee-i-oh. Looks good. Real money in sugar, for certain, but how would one stack a heap of these boxes for wholesale?

If you need help getting to sleep you plan how you will share your real wealth. There's satisfaction to be had from sharing wealth with the collective. Unless it's the profit from Mummy's shares. This comes once a year and Mummy used to stop off at Biba, when her and Daddy were in London seeing her Jungian Analyst. Mummy got what she needed then you and Star got a little something too. Last time it was trousers made from T-shirting. Stars are dark purple and red. Thick stripes of colour that wrap around the legs. Yours are yellow and orange. 'Hey People, look out, ain't that a heavy plant crossing sign that just strolled into the room?' Hairy Dolly. On trews first outing. Everyone laughed like drains. After sharing with the collective, the profit skim will be spent on a pony. Thorough-bred. And riding lessons. If it turns out you need some. Unlikely, as you have excellent balance (despite quarrels with Star's beam) and the idea of horse whispering, as a means of control, is interesting.

An early real money scheme was Swallow's Tea Shop. Star made a big sign and you stuck it up by the road. Tea Shop Open. You'd baked piles of flapjack, scones for cream and jam, obviously. Coffee cake with walnuts. Ginger biscuits and thin bread and butter, in case people were still hungry. Or unconscionably greedy. You did a minor ritual before you opened – expressive dance based, willing car loads of Greedies to tip up. Think of the profit. You made four tables, out of the old door pile, covered them in the table cloths that Mummy got when her granny died. Then you waited. It took about an hour for your first customers to arrive. They looked quite straight and a tad surprised. A man and a woman. Skinny as sticks. You stuck with the plan. Home-made notebooks for the order which, unsurprisingly, was a simple cake and tea.

"Please choose a table. Be careful not to lean on it. It's a bit wobbly." You.

"Ok." The Customers.

Problem was the bloody Aga decided it had had enough, after all that baking. The water for the tea would not boil. You and Star stood by the door waiting, smiling at The Customers

"Just waiting for the kettle." You.

"Ok." The Customers.

But this really did take far too long.

"Where are your parents?" The Customers.

"Up the field. Harvesting the kale." You.

The Customers got the giggles. They were quite nice, tried to hide it but the kettle Would. Not. Boil. There was nothing for it, they had to leave. They did pay for the cake and said it was good cake. Although the cheeky buggers left half of it. You were quite tired by then and a bit bored of trying so hard. Star took down the sign, everyone came back in and ate up all The Stock.

"Good try girls." Daddy. Flapjack.

"Real money should flow, effortlessly, towards one. Especially now there are so many was to avoid paying taxes." Mummy. Second slice of walnut cake.

"Cash from your daddy?" The Hairy Dolly. Walnut cake, ginger biscuits, scone and cream.

"Although not your daddy, girls. Don't even think about it and don't call me Daddy. I am a person. I have a name. Even if I'm too broke to be liable for taxation." Daddy. Same flapjack.

"Of course we're liable. We are also clever. This fucking government aren't getting a penny from my shares. That is family money. It's my legacy. That money has been handed down through generations. I'm fucked if it's going to be frittered away on surrounding us with nuclear missiles." Mummy. Thin bread and butter.

"Yes, fuck 'em. Biba never aimed a missile at anyone." Daddy. Scone with just butter.

Sweets? Real money? Star's finished wrapping. It is vital to clean up after sweets cooking, regardless of the Rota crisis, or the house will be simply covered in flies. There are too many pig farms round about to risk another fly invasion. A while ago some idiot, Rod, hid a stash of sausage (raw) in his room for a month. The stink. The flies were like a writhing skin, constant movement and sound. Star had a nightmare after she saw it. Her scalp was hairless, covered in crumpet holes and worms were peeking from the holes, she had to pick then tug them out. Thank you, Rod. Why didn't he notice the smell building up? Or see the maggots before the mass hatching? Rod doesn't notice much. Unless it's a new way of laying out the Tarot or someone else's book of poetry getting published by a serious publisher. Not just him and Daddy with the ink blocks in the Work Room. This sticky mess will have to go before you can do the enchanting birthday surprise. Always use ice-cold water to remove burnt sugar from pans. Hot will just seal it on.

You and Star are scouring the bits of the kitchen that sugar dust has landed on. Not doing the whole kitchen. You haven't got all week. Star's in her blue tank top and towelling shorts, shaking free the dust clouds of powdery Ajax. That whispy hair's getting to be a concern. The knot at the back is fine, only needs time and energy to sort but the hair is getting patchy. 'Ignore her, it's just strong feelings, she'll grow out of it.' Mummy. 'What if her baldness makes more strong feelings?' You. 'Aren't you a sweet Mummy-Sister?' Mummy. Giving you a cuddle. Mummy-Sister's what Star called you for years, until she packed up talking.

The kitchen's looking a bit flooded. Least it's cold water. Might it be time to change those filthy jeans? Feel that. That is your hand clinging to the stick on your thighs. Damp too. Same light brown smock thing. 'If you girls want to be endlessly changing your outfits, you need to learn to wash them. I've more important things to do than keep white socks white.' Mummy. When you asked for a real school uniform, grey with white socks preferably, for Christmas one year. Easiest to stay in the same things for a few weeks at a go. You're children, you don't smell. 'Oh no you don't, Laura. Stop waving that Daz around, immediately. You reek of accusations. Washing their own gear is experiential learning.' Mummy. Not that anybody needs any more of that.

Right. The moment has arrived. Time to unveil Eric's – melt in his mouth, melt his heart – birthday-box. Low-level tussling over box, Star's jolly determined to win the glory of the handover. Sod it, let her carry it. Shrugging and conceding. Right. Where is he? Shouldn't be too tricky to find a giant in a haystack. Hang on. It's very quiet all of a sudden. Jessie's in her basket chasing pheasants in her sleep. Great Uncle Elizabeth's soaking sun on the window ledge. Other than that, where the hell is everyone? Daddy's at work. Some days Daddy drives into Aylsham and works for Gerald Frank in his antique shop restoring crappy old pine junk. For money. Not real money. He only does it on days when Mummy is cool and has lots of My Pots ideas. 'She won't have a panic. I'm here. I'll answer the phone if anyone from the shops with orders calls. I'll tell them process etc.' You. Just to Daddy.

So Daddy's at Gerald Franks. Pretty certain the Hairy Dolly's roaming, again. Star's clutching that box, one finger holding the not dry cows in place. Check the pottery, Mummy will know where the rest of Your People are. 'Only sensible to keep a track of all the comings and goings.' Mummy. Please let Mummy be finishing an order. Been five months and although you told Daddy you could handle the phone it's getting a bit tiresome doing – 'There's a creative process to hand-built work.' You. On the phone. At least once a week.

Pottery door. No matter what the urgency, always stop to sniff the dusty wet clay smell. Mummy's hair smells like that too. That and Tweed perfume. Star has a cotton wool ball soaked in Tweed she takes to bed. Pretty Justin's mixing a bucket of glaze.

"Is it the Copper Chung for the orders?" You.

"No. Yeah? Something hedgerow we like just found. She was yeah?" Pretty Justin.

Where the stink is Mummy? You promised Daddy you'd be in charge.

"It's fine. Fine. Don't squeeze the bloody box so tight. The sodding cows will topple." You. Calming. Good job Star's hands are occupied, mind.

Work Room. Pongs of ink. Boxes of old printing blocks. Boxes of paper. The obsolete printing press. Obsolete because it's a hand turning one. Printing has moved on. Books and newspapers fly off electric presses in factories these days but Daddy and Rod need to be connected to the language, so they hand turn away. Tubs of ink, stacks of *The Major Arcana*. Unsold. *The Major Arcana* is Rod's, and sort of Daddy's, magazine. They sold seventy-two copies of the last print run which is exceptional in such a cultural black hole as Norfolk. Rush matting squares on some of the floor, the rest's crumbled concrete. There are also boxes of empties stacked along the window wall waiting to be returned for money. Not real money. The empties are the reason you don't play with the other kids in the village. Those kids came over one day and saw those empties then everyone for miles around said Your People were alcoholics. The back room's empty of Your People. The trotting is now a gentle canter.

"Stop joggling the bloody box. You've lost a cow." You.

Star isn't slowing. Back garden. Short-cut tour of the field. No Eric in the field and worse no Mummy. No Eric near the hens. No Mummy. No Tammie. No Laura. No Hairy Dolly. No Rod. Not worried about Rod, he nearly always goes to work with Daddy. Sits with him, rolls Daddy's ciggies. Talks. Keeps Daddy's mind fertile, whilst Daddy strips the paint off pine junk with Nitromores and wire wool.

"I bet Eric went into Norwich on the bus." You.

Star's staring hard at you. Spit it out, for heaven's sake. Knowing what she's saying without hearing makes her words crash about in your head. Gallop-a-trot back to Pretty Justin.

"Bryan, yeah? Bryan's like swimming, yeah? At the lock gates. Maybe Laura? Tammie? Or yeah? Tammie. Umm." Pretty Justin. Intent on glaze. Really does work very hard in Mummy's pottery.

Tammie will be meditating in her room. So, fine. Where is Mummy? Upstairs. Straight down the landing flicking open all the doors. Bathroom? No. Eric's room? No. Tammie's? Found Tammie, standing on one leg. Laura's? No. Hairy Dolly's? Paused outside, ear to door. Star, why? Tiny head shake. Has Star caught the extra whiff of worry? Silence. Absolutely do not open its door ever. Rod's door is open. No.

Up ladder to attic. Star up ahead. What is that distant and insistent sound? Pushing Star to one side, carefully, overtaking her on the ladder. What the blinking heck is that sound? Listen. Of course. It's the same sound that comes in the middle of the night at Harvest Time, when the normally empty roads are busy all night with lorries full of grain. That sound is the sound of one of those lorries reversing. Eurngh eurngh eurngh eurngh eurngh. Reversing into the farm yard next door to unload its grain into the enormous grain silo. But it's the middle of the day.

"Mummy? Mummy?" You. Almost on top rung.

"Eurngh. Eurnghhello! Darling! One sec." Mummy. Oh big phew. And that lorry's finished backing up.

Your little face is peeking into the light and airy attic room. 'They are the biggest investment we made when we were rescuing this place. Velux windows. Divine. They actually work, plus you automatically moon-bathe all night long. Probably should have spent the money on a damp proof course but look at this space.' Mummy. About her attic, to everyone she shows it to.

Star's shoving you over, there's her face too. Both, justifiably, pink with anticipation and look. Eric. Great. Eric's by the window staring at the sky. Mummy's been having a nap, she's stretching and sorting out her, 'Miraculous lake of hair.' Daddy.

Singing.

"Er, er, er, er, err, errrr. Er, er, er, er, err, errrr." Star. To the tune of Happy Birthday. If a twig could sing it would sound like this.

"Birthday dear Eric. Happy birthday to yoooooou." You. Joining in with the actual words. Mummy's sitting, wrapping herself up in her lilac shirt.

"Hello, girls. What's this? Who made this crazy field? You know

Eric doesn't believe in birthdays, don't you? Eric? What do you think? Might you allow my little ones the pleasure of spoiling you?" Mummy.

One with brown eyes. One with sludge. One with green. All varieties of eye on Eric. Eric has a damp, excessive, chest. Splodged with freckles all over his blue-white skin. Apart from the skin that's burnt red on the arms. Star's bounce-sitting on the bed holding out the box. Why's Eric's beard so wet? He looks shifty. He's flicking his glance round the room searching and pouncing on his T-shirt. Just the sunburnt arms poking out now. Stuffing on sandals.

"Eric, please. Yes?" Mummy.

Eric's starting towards the ladder. No. Change of plan. Stopping again. One foot still in the room. Crikey it's only sweets.

"They didn't mean to upset you. They adore birthdays. They just want to spoil you a little." Mummy. "And any excuse to top themselves up with sugar."

Star's turning to you. What the hell does she expect you to say? Right. If it's business as usual on the silence front, someone needs to take full charge. Get that box. Tussle. Stretching up to Eric, he's bending. Has to, he's too tall for normal reaching. You're pushing the box at him, stretching up for Kissing On The Cheek. This is a new idea. Clarissa started it. You have to do it for birthdays. You can do it to say hello to good friends but it can get to be a bit much. Grandma nearly fainted when you tried it on her. Your People do it for birthdays only. So, reach, reach, reach up to just beside Eric's mouth. Do you feel dizzy so far from the ground? Pooh. What's that stink? Wet Tweed perfume and something like, yes, like pansies. Eric's hand's up, wiping your kiss away. Beyond rude. Kiss gone. Box delivered. Star's fidgeting with pride. Eric's opening the box inspecting the top layer of sugar cows. Tipping the box for Mummy to check.

"Moo. Moo. Goo. Goo." Mummy.

"Aye. Very thoughtful." Eric. Oh, come on, a smile wouldn't kill him.

"Well. Happy birthday. There are Pineapple Choc things which you need to eat today before the pineapple rots, there's excessively good toffee – that's Mummy's favourite kind – and actually, Mummy? I think Bryan and Laura might have gone to the lock gates, Pretty Justin's nearly finished, it's so hot, and we're sticky, so we should all go for a swim. Come on Star get some towels and Mummy? Daddy and Rod have the Saab but Eric? You drive the van and take us all and we'll leave a note for Daddy because he will be home, really soon, for lunch, then he can come and meet us and he'll only be about half an hour, if that, and Tammie's in her room but she might come. I know she doesn't like getting her head wet but me and Star quite need a swim. So, come on, that's what we need to do." You. Star is bouncing, she's bounced up, caught the attic beam above the bed and is swinging from it.

"You know I hate being hijacked like this. Now is not a good moment. Really not. The sweets were a kind thought, if you actually meant them for Eric and this wasn't some clever ploy to manipulate your sugar rations into the red. But either way, thank you and no swim." Mummy.

"I'll take 'em." Eric. Wow. It worked. The sweets worked. Eric is claimed.

"Christ, Eric, there's really no need. She's capitalising on her imagined generosity with the present. Really don't rise to it." Mummy. Out of bed into her skirt and everything.

"I'd like to. Come swimming, Beth. It'll be grand." Eric. Eric's not waiting to hear if Mummy is a yes or a no, he's escaping towards the ladder. Star's right behind, she knows a serious offer when she hears one. Mummy's sucking the end of some of her hair.

"You've got a fucking nerve." Mummy. Doing a long grown-up stare at you.

But, looks like it's decided. Mummy is going to leave the house. Down the ladder everyone's climbing. Eric's lifting Star, dangling her through the trapdoor. Because he's so long he can just plop her down the hole to the floor below. Star looks far too pleased with the miracle of Eric's bigness. Eric's busy being captivated by how like a fairy Star can look. Nipping after her along the landing, collecting towels from the airing cupboard.

"I love your father." Mummy.

Father? The only *father* you're aware of is Father Christmas and he hasn't shown his crazy white beard in these parts for years.

"This is between me and him and it's nothing anyway so please keep your mouth shut. For once." Mummy.

"Between you and Eric?" You.

"No. Your father." Mummy.

"And me?" You.

"No. It isn't all about you." Mummy. Laughing. Waiting. And? What? That's your lot. She's giving you a tiny push, hard and friendly.

"Get a move on, we don't want to miss the sodding van." Mummy. Brave.

Downstairs. Wow. The house is suddenly full. Although it's just Star, Eric, Mummy, you, Pretty Justin, Tammie and Jessie. Jessie's wagging her tail neurotically, terrified she might be left behind. Mummy's writing plenty of notes, to make sure Daddy sees them, terrified she's got to go. Everyone's leaving in a stumble of bodies, you're last to the door. Stop. Look. On the dough-bin by the sofa, it's a proper grown-up's swimming mask and a snorkel. There's a scrap of paper, scribbled note. Quick check, no one else has seen them, they're all pouring out, one stride to beside the pile and picking up the note.

Nearly 13, these are for you. Laura and I are at the lock gates. B

How come none of Your People have noticed this pile? How come you didn't see it when you were hunting an Eric?

Grasping the absolutely tremendous present tight to your chest. Smell that rubber? How thick are those black rubber straps? This is a completely professional adult's set. Nearly 13? Nearly 13? What to do? Where to go? Look. The van's ready. Jessie is up front in the driver's seat, preparing to fire the ignition and get the show on the road. Mummy's gesturing with flappy hands.

"Come on. Stop dawdling for Christ's sake. I thought it was you that wanted this. Come on." Mummy. Shouting. It's gone quiet. Mummy's looking stretchy mouthed.

"Lovely cold water, darling." Mummy.

"Time alone can be healing." Tammie. Squeak, squeak right in your ear. How the hell did she get herself behind you? Levitation?

"Will you tell them?" You. To Tammie.

Tammie's nodding, going to the van, leaning in the window. Mummy's thinking. Eric and Tammie are watching her, she's nodding and brushing their looks away. The van's starting. Honking a couple of merry toots and jerking away. Brave, brave Mummy. You have let your mummy drive off without you. And Star with her. Tammie's coming back. She's not looking at you, she's gliding to the fridge. She's reaching in. She's gliding back plus the tray with all the leftover sweets. She's sitting on the floor. Cross legged. With the leftover sweets. You're sitting too. Also crossing your legs and placing that swimming bundle close by. Why didn't you go? The Hairy Dolly is with Laura. It hasn't even looked at you, for days. The Hairy Dolly is friendly. This is the friendliest present you've ever been given, since Laura got you the sledge. And it hasn't snowed since the sledge arrived so that doesn't count. Why didn't you go? Tammie's offering the tray, you're taking a reject cow. A big one. Tammie is not taking one.

"I guess I sense what just happened to you and I wanted to say that I believe the body is sacred. I believe that childhood is sacred." Long silent bit. Not unusual with Tammie. Take another cow. Two is fine.

"It's entirely cool. Mummy and I spoke about it. He's so dull about fusses being made. He really is allergic. Don't tell Daddy." You. A toffee this time. Cough splutter as it jags down your throat. Is Tammie guessing about Eric being ungrateful? Why do you need healing?

"A little sweetness for your soul." Tammie. Squeak up Tammie, it's almost impossible to hear you. Oh. This is intolerable. Everyone knows Tammie is absurd. Mummy needs you. Look at your gear. How can you not try it? You can't. You must.

"I'm going swimming now. Bye." You.

Off down the long, straight road. The lock gates are only two miles away. You're so quick on the heels of the van you can smell its petrol trail. The sun has melted the road's tarmac so you have to bounce-run. Make sure you don't break through the surface of the hot, soft tarmac. That toffee-tarmac will burn your bare feet, if you let it burst through its upper layer. Run fast. Run light. Maybe you can grow up to be an Olympic runner? Star can be a gymnast, you can be a runner. You can both be pals with Olga.

Two miles for a tar hopping Olympian? Pah. It takes minutes.

Straight down beside the mill. Ah, that breeze from the mill's river is good. Hot face. Need more air. Jump down that little ledge into the meadow, straight through the centre of the meadow and there it is, slap bang in its middle. A round, dark green – almost black – pool with all the meadow tumbling up and over its sides. Reeds crowding at the edges. Be very careful of reeds; they will grab your legs, tangling you down to your death. Children have died in this pool. In the olden days but they did. There are the lock gates. High, solid, wooden gates that the water foams under before rushing down and over the concrete slope, that drops to the pool below. In the spring and winter the gates are wound up high so a proper water fall gushes beneath them and floods over the concrete. It's less now but it's still pouring through. Olden dayers made these gates to stop flooding. The water made its own pool. Laura's poised on the top rung of the gate. Laura's body is complete. Tall. Strong. She's wearing a proper navy swimsuit with little shorts over the top. The Hairy Dolly and Eric are in the water both shouting how they will catch her. Jump, jump.

"I don't need catching, you shit for brains. I can dive." Laura.

Bloody hell, she can. She has leapt high enough to somersault and get herself straight again as she hits the water. No splash. No crashing to death on the concrete. The Hairy Dolly's not giving you a glance.

"Girls, you are never to try that. Do you understand? Hello, darling." Mummy. To you both, then to you alone. No one's surprised to see you. No one's asking how you got there. Shame. Notice how Mummy is pushing that big breath out between her clenched teeth? Eking it out.

There is much noise. Everyone's in the water. Apart from Mummy, who is lying on a towel in her small Biba bikini. Just covers The Dates. Purple sprinkled with cream stars. She's shiny with suntan lotion.

MUMMY'S SUN LOTION

Half jam jar olive oil
Few splashes wine vinegar
Put all in jam jar, shake. Smells delicious and really works.
Mummy's very, very brown.

Ripping off your clothes. Stopped with light brown smock thing raised. Pull it down, swivel your back to the pool, glance over your shoulder but look, the Hairy Dolly is racing and splashing Laura, so that's all fine. Top off. Trousers off. Swim in your pants, you always do. Quick check of general chest area. Normal. In. Surfacing. Hairy Dolly is right beside you. All its woolly curls above water, have slicked down. All its woolly curls underneath, are floating. Pond weed. You can tread water. You are doing. Treading and flicking water from your eyes. No one, not even Star, who's being swum along on Eric's back for a Dolphin ride, is looking at you. Slicked Hairy Dolly's still there. Treading water too.

"Thank you." You.

"Give me the snorkel, Nearly 13." Hairy Dolly.

"Wet the inside of the mask then put it on. Sorry if it's a bit big. Here, I'll tighten it." It is. With the snorkel under one arm. You're both treading water, hard. You're an excellent swimmer. Excellent all round sports woman, as it goes.

"Open your mouth." Hairy Dolly. It's slipping its little finger along the inside of your bottom lip and smiling. Friendly. See? Keep your mouth open. It's very gently putting the snorkel in. That snorkel is huge and so rubbery.

"Bite down." Hairy Dolly. You are.

"The ping pong ball at the top will automatically suck closed if you go down too deep. It'll take a bit of getting used to but. Well. Try it, Kiddo." Hairy Dolly.

Tentatively putting your whole face in. If you could see under water you would see that your eyes are open wide. Listen to the suck of your own loud breath in the snorkel tube as you're searching around under the water. The colour is sludge green but somehow see-through whilst also being dense. There isn't any wildlife to see, apart from hundreds of tiny wisps of weed and mud floating close by. Mud motes. Graceful. The water's so thick it's impossible to see for any distance. See this unforgettable colour, with bits, like thick light. You're enclosed. Letting your legs softly float up to the surface and stretching out your arms. The water's warm and firm in this glowing upper layer. The water's private and big. The Hairy Dolly's face has arrived in front of the mask and you're both floating. Its eyes are open too. Its wool is billowing around. Grinning at each other. It's holding its arms out and coming towards you. Still grinning. Its hands are feeling up and down your ribs searching for your waist. Feels slippy and nice. It's found your waist and is holding it tightly. Hear your breath sucking in and out of the tube? It's nodding at you and here we go. It's whooshing you up in the air. It's strong. Surprising for such a little dolly. You're simply flying through the air then crashing back into the water. Teeth gripping hard on the rubber. Warm then ice as you plunge down to the pond's murky depths. Yes. This is good. You're kicking to the top spitting out the mouthful of muddy water you accidentally sucked in, ducking down again. Swimming along. Searching everywhere. If only a fish would come visiting. See over there? The Hairy Dolly's swimming off, it's flipping round under the water, waving. Hurrah for The Hairy Dolly. Your legs are being magnetically dragged back to the upper layer so you're floating, laid out on the pond's dense surface. Staring into the green. What if those drowned, dead children's underwater ghosts were to float by? Spin around. In case one is behind you with an armful of weed. Ghosts always want living people to die their same way. There are no ghosts. There are no ghosts. You're spinning off alone, count the shadowy legs all kicking about. Your People. One two three four five. Once, I caught a fish alive.

Last summer Rod developed a positive mania for fishing. He came to the lock gates every day. He was determined to catch the monster pike that famously haunts the lock. The year before there had been a sighting and then the pike might have eaten a puppy that went missing. Pike can eat children. If the reeds haven't got to them first. They'll certainly give you a nasty nip. So, luckily, Rod caught it. It was gigantic. Had to be cooked in three fish kettles. Who knew there was such a thing? But there is. Mummy borrowed one from the fishmonger although he was really pissed off that she didn't want to buy a salmon to cook in it. But Mummy had cleverly got the kettle off him before revealing that she wasn't going to purchase. The pike got chopped into three kettle-sized chunks. It was nearly midsummer when Rod got the pike so there was a massive feast. It took three hours for all the pike to be cooked. It was served cold. Which wasn't the plan but you can't really warm up a mile of fish.

HOW TO COOK PIKE

1 pike
Herbs
Garlic
Onion
Carrot or two

Fish stock cube if no real stock handy
Other stock-ish stuff

Boil up stock bits, half-hour or so.

Clean pike. Careful of the teeth. They've stuff on that will make you carry on bleeding for extra long if you get a cut from them.

Slice pike into kettle lengths.

Pour stock over.

The kettle might be big. The pike might be small. If so you will need to keep swapping it so each end gets a go on hot plate of Aga. Time consuming.

Pike's not worth the bother, it has hundreds of tiny bones and tastes like water-mud smell. But the grown-ups made a big fuss. Rod was swelled with happiness. You'd have thought he'd have got the bug for fishing after all that pike worship but he went back to poetry. As his thing. His creative impulse was throbbing. You ate the pike with new potatoes. Boiled then half smashed up, soaked in butter with huge amounts of chopped thyme, mint and wild garlic leaves. Potatoes were jolly good. And now it's safe to go back into the water at the lock gates. Your People made a sacrifice to Belisama the Celtic water goddess. She's the goddess for loads of useful things so she gets plenty of sacrifices. This time it was to appease her vengeful temper for taking the pike. Belisama and Chanticleer would get on like a bloody house on fire. The pike's jaw bones have been buried in the meadow.

Listen to that whooping yell. Daddy, Rod and Tammie have arrived. Daddy and Rod are splash-crashing into the water in their clothes. Jessie has leapt in too and Star is being whooshed over to Daddy by Eric. Has Star had to make a single stroke unaided? Isn't it interesting how dogs have to go so slow in water? Work so hard to keep their heads above water? Even fast dogs. No wonder the pike nab 'em so easily. Jessie is not an Olympian. In water. Mummy's standing at the top of the gates and Your People are turning in the water, Tammie's settling on the rug and turning too, all turning towards Mummy. Mummy's making a gigantic sound. Might that be ululating? Everyone's replying. Mummy's leaping in. She not attempting a dive. It will be quite hard for anyone to dive again, having seen Laura's brilliance.

"It is fucking freezing, you are all demented." Mummy. Surfacing.

There's a scramble to the banks, Daddy's lifting you and Star out. Pretty Justin's out, holding his towel for shares. Star's inside Daddy's towel, Daddy's reaching over to kiss Mummy.

"Hello, my lovely love. Good diving." Daddy. To Mummy. With his spare hand Daddy's handing round the perfect feast he's brought to sustain everyone. And taking off his wet shirt.

PERFECT FEAST FOR AFTER SWIMMING

Mrs Pritchard. Sliced, thickly buttered.

All Your People, apart from Tammie, are ravenous. Simply must have a second Mrs P slice.

"Finish your first slice. There's plenty." Mummy. Tapping your big toe with her scarlet one.

MRS PRITCHARD

1 heaped tea cup All Bran – This is an American recipe, from Tammie, so it's done in cups. 'What is wrong with the English? Why aren't all recipes this transparent? Why all the endless

disguise?' Mummy. 'By disguise do you mean numbers?' Daddy. Mummy ignored him. It is well known that Mummy is not keen on numbers. Unless it's a quick shifty at the *Financial Times* for shares. Mummy failed maths O level three times. 'One of the many things you girls have to bless me for. I will never subject you to the horror of an exam.' Mummy.

1 heaped teacup sugar
1 heaped teacup mixed dried fruit
1 teacup milk
1 teacup self-raising flour

Mix all, apart from flour. Leave to soak and swell for hour. Add flour. Pour into greased bread tin, bake medium heat for 50 mins to hour. This is a tea loaf. Excellent eating.

"Yes. Very clever, Bryan." Mummy. The Hairy Dolly has a slice of Mrs Pritchard in each hand and one balanced on each knee. It's biting them in Rota. It's just about to take its first bite from its left knee slice.

"Point made." Mummy. The Hairy Dolly's opened its mouth to disgust her with its half-chewed food and now it's plopping the left knee slice back on the heap. Urgh. That slice will be hairy.

"Mewl swallow mewl." Mummy. Handing her slice, with a baby bite out, for Daddy to finish.

"Yous all fancy some of this here toffee?" Eric. He's reached into the bottom of his old school satchel, with the handle held together by just Sellotape (how?), and is producing...The Sweets.

"Great box. Happy birthday. Is it a happy birthday? It is today isn't it?" Laura. Stretching across and extra carefully taking off the lid. Those cows look a little sad to have travelled so far in the depths of a satchel.

Most of them are lying down. A sign of rain? No chance. That sky is aching with blueness.

"Aye. Maybes." Eric. He's pushing the sweets over. She's taken a toffee.

Laura's passing the box Star-wards. Star's crawling over to beside you with the box. Star's got her first cow pat in her mouth and another in her left hand. You're glancing in. The choc has departed from its pineapples like blankets from a bed. Once, you were lucky enough to sleep under a silken quilt. At Grandma's. Silken quilts are the best coverings for bed departures known to man. Or woman. You lay, like a princess, with a sheet and a blanket and the silken quilt. You smoothed your fingers to sleep on the silken pockets of the quilt. You awoke. Seconds later. It wasn't a pea that'd done it. It was the absence of bedding. Everything had whispered its way, oh so gently, to the floor. Eric's choc has done the same. His pineapple chunks are now exposed and drying out, sitting glumly in the pool of their formerly glorious covers. Sun. No other adults are bothering with sweets. Don't you bother either. It is actually too hot for sweets.

Your People are sinking into the earth. Staring up. Meadow pippins are doing their on-the-spot back-stroke flying, above your heads. Filling the top of the sky with their expectant peeping. That meadow is rammed with wildlife. Turn your head to one side, scrunch up your eyes and see. Bluey pink swathes of cornflowers slashed about with yellow corn marigolds. More pinkness from weasel's snout. Not as pretty as snap dragon but like it and just as good a name. The best is pheasant's eye. Especially when there's as much of it as there is here. Blood-red splatters all through the sea of harebells. The smell is wild mint. The meadow is colour. Even though it's August. In April, you and Star always do a bike ride to this meadow and then take Mummy coffee and freshly squeezed orange juice, in bed, and cover her tray with bunches of fritillary. From here.

"We are the cobalt blue drawings on a nineteenth-century plate. Rural scene." Mummy. Her voice floating through the hot dry grasses.

"Except they are Chinese." Daddy.

"I am not talking about Chinoiserie, or Majolica or Delft for that matter. I am talking about plain old English willow pattern. Spode. Staffordshire." Mummy.

"I am in love with my wife." Daddy. Leaning up on his elbows and looking around at the hand-painted peasants scattered hither and thither. "I would like that to be clear."

"Gruuuuunt. Puff. Indeed." Rod.

"Fuck. Just look at all this. Us. We are brinked in time." Daddy. Rod has jolted upright. Chewing his mouth. Bet he's resisting the urge to ask if brinking's a real thing.

"Puff?" Rod. Whispy one. "Puff?" Even whispier. 'It's the poet's duty to shift the language for his times. Use your own words.' Daddy. To you, when it became apparent that spelling might elude you.

"Puffffffy puff?" Shoulders now twitching with effort.

"Let it be, my friend. If it is the fucking brink we might regret not simply staring at the sky." Daddy. Lying back down.

"Or the butterflies." Mummy. She has one arm in the air. Looks like she's dipped a finger in the choc blankets and two swallowtails are seriously considering landing on it. Wiggle, waggle goes her hand. Shall we, shan't we, go the miniature flakes of light. Shan't. They've gone. No more butterflies. What do butterflies do when it rains? Daddy has Mummy's finger in his mouth and is sucking, softly.

Only Rod can resist the drag of hot earth. He's still upright. Cross legged and flicking his greasy speced gaze about. What's he looking for? Who? When Your People first discovered the lock gates they met the owner, Will Gibson. As they approached the mill, its massive wheel was turning. Water was crashing everywhere. Storm levels of sound. It made everyone most uncharacteristically shy. They all stood, with Star at the front of the queue and you just behind, trying to make enough courage to cross the slim wooden walkway that straddles the front of the wheel. They waited too long. An exceptionally tall man, covered head to toe, and all of his head too, in the whitest flour, was suddenly there at the opposite end of the walkway. Everyone looked at him. He looked at all of you. This was Will Gibson. He came towards you. Slow but extra long strides. He stopped at your end of the walkway. Tiny, iridescent brown eyes unblinking in the sun shone through his extreme whiteness. A screech owl. Your People waiting, waiting. Swim bundles clasped. Would Will Gibson blink? No. Would he swivel his head entirely around, like a real owl? No. Course not. Eventually, 'We demand the rights of wayfaring folk. This mill lies upon one of England's strongest lay-lines. Our House also. We have been compelled here by forces more ancient than time.' Rod. Will Gibson stepped aside. Your People flowed into his meadow. 'Bless you. For this is truly Eden.' Rod. Attempting to shake Will Gibson's hand. On the return trip. 'I do not know much about gods but I think that the river is a strong brown god – sullen, untamed and intractable.' Will Gibson. It was like someone had poured electricity into Daddy. 'Elliot? Yes? Or fuck, is it not? Pound? Which of those buggers? Elliot, yes. Must be.' Daddy. Grinning. 'Oh, Aye. Mind yourselves with that there pike. He's a handsome bugger. He'll have your legs off.' Will Gibson. Turning on his feathered heels, returning to his lifetime of grinding.

Your People are stirring, standing, packing, leaving.

"Great gear." Daddy. Handing you the snorkel and mask.

"Yes." You. Does he wonder where it came from?

Everyone's careful not to trample the grave of the jaw bone. Rod's dropping a red campion spray on it as he passes. Look at him, straining to see if Laura noticed, lolloping after her. He looks like Jessie when she's spotted prey. Ears pricked. Star's on Daddy's shoulders. Daddy's still in his sodden jeans and has Mummy pulled close to him, in just her bikini. On her free side, Mummy and Laura are holding hands swinging their arms. Eric's alone, almost at the Mill.

"Nearly 13?" Hairy Dolly.

No stopping. Pretend you haven't heard. Got your happy Jessie by the collar and Pretty Justin's taking your other hand. Both noticing Rod's puppy-prance. Pretty Justin's stroking you. Doing the top side of your arm. A bit as if he doesn't notice he's doing it. That not noticing stroke is going inside your skin. No Will Gibson today. He packed up his milling last year. 'No call for it. They make that plastic bag bread with something different to flour. I reckon.' Will Gibson. Home you all go.

CHAPTER FOUR

It's that beginning bit of autumn that's June some days and October others. Plums covered in wasps, day. Two hot water bottles not enough, night. Poetry Reading for The House. No kids allowed. But the door's open to Local Poets. There are massed heaps of Local Poets. Rod and Daddy apply rigour to the vetting procedure. So the door isn't that far open. Poems must be submitted in advance. Poets must be willing to have their ideas discussed by the collective. Rod and Daddy do most of the discussing because they are real writers. 'We should charge. Charge for telling them how to write a poem. Charge to publish that poem. We'd never need an original idea again. Charge for an enforced purchase of the magazine. Charge a fucking entrance fee to readings.' Daddy. On a charging roll. 'Hee, hee, hee.' Rod. Doing the little pretend laugh he does to keep the conversation going his way. 'Aye, aye we might but teaching will always be a noble pursuit. The art teacher who first credited me with more than average creative powers will live inside me for all days.' Rod. Conversation going his way. 'Mrs Braithwaite. Yup. Nice tits?' Daddy. It's draining putting your creative energy into other people's ideas. It can create a drought in the imagination. Rod will make reasonable money from Creative Writing Classes. In years to come. When they have been invented.

Tammie, you and Star are in the Work Room, setting out the cushions for today's reading. The cushions are big enough for two big bottoms each. 'Laura, love, just squat on this and give it a size test would you.' Mummy. Measuring. Mummy made them. Patchwork. 'Invented just after fucking embroidery, to fill all those extra hours women have left over after they're done floating around looking sexy.' Mummy. Determined to finish the second patchwork cushion. 'What's wrong with just two big patches? One for each gargantuan butt.' Laura. Joining in and finishing six cushions, with the two-big-patches idea, in the time it took Mummy to finish her proper one. 'Main thing is you managed to look sexy at the same time as doing the fucking patchwork. So no time wasted.' Daddy. Admiring the two proper cushions. And Mummy. The patchwork is from antique velvet curtains that Daddy got from junk auctions when he was buying stock for Gerald Franks. The cushions still stink of auction. Musty cloth rot. You're having your customary sniff of the mostly saffron one. Star's loitering. Trying to look extra spiritual. 'It's possible that Star may have a definite spiritual bent.' Mummy. After she caught Star making up hymns. For Prune. Your idea, if anyone had been bothered to ask. Tammie's got the salt jar and a massive bunch of dried sage leaves. Look out. It's going to get smoky in here.

"Girls? Get something to cover your heads." Tammie. Looking truly spiritual.

Excellent. Means Tammie needs you to assist with the space cleansing. Luckily you have planned ahead. In case. Headscarves out of pockets. On. Eyes down.

"Umbaala, Umbaala, Umbaala." Tammie. Umbaala from Guatemala. 'They are a unique people. They embraced me fully. They immersed me in their culture. Into the centre of their community and families.' Tammie. Squeaking so hard it was tricky to follow clearly but that was the gist. They also gave her a 'whole goat bag'. Tammie. Again and to Mummy when Mummy was testing out the softness of Tammie's huge leather bag. 'Fuck. This? It's a fucking goat?' Mummy. Quickly stopping the testing. 'It's a whole goat. The goat's a talisman creature for the Guatemalans. When their breeding cycles cease they're ritually slaughtered, drained, emptied, dried and then look...' Tammie. Showing Mummy how the strap is actually two empty legs sort of stuck together at the hooves. It even has its tiny tail hanging down at the very bottom. 'Jesus. I've been dreading the menopause but now I will welcome it. I will wallow in it. Safe in the knowledge that I am not a Guatemalan goat. Poor dears.' Mummy.

"Girls? Please join me when you sense it growing." Tammie. Squeak. Sense what growing?

"If it doesn't grow within you, that's cool. Just hold the silence." Phew. Silence holding it is.

"Mutter, mutter, mutter." What is she saying? Vital not to miss a good bit but this is hard listening.

"Mutter, mutter, umbaala, mutter, mutter." Bloody hell this is going to get boring. But no, look, Tammie's doing a private kind of spiritual person's nodding at Star. Oh typical, Star's got the message and is nipping over, pulling the thick, dark green, velvet curtains along their bamboo pole stick. Closed. Definite spiritual bent in operation. It is now dark in the Work Room. Star's back beside you. Head down. Tammie's lighting the ten-hour candles. Watch out. Tammie's handing you a candle each. Do not drop your candle. Do not shout when hot wax starts trickling onto your hand. After you've banged into something because of the darkness.

TEN-HOUR CANDLES

Actually any candles but the ones for readings need to be long burning. Got to burn through the space cleanse. Burn alone waiting for the poetry reading. Burn through the reading. Really could be twice the length of these Fella's-willy whoppers.
Candle stumps. You ask at the church. The warden is quite enlightened, saves them for you. Means the candles are beeswax. Beeswax purifies the air as it burns. The Warden also lets you graze Prune in the grave yard, when the grass at The House gets thin. He ignores the village moaning about goats being the devil's children. You try to ignore the fact that the grass turns into milk and you eat that milk. So, the grass that made the milk has been grown from the juice of dead bodies.
Essential Oils. Bergamot for creative energy. Lemon for focus. Jasmine for self-awareness.
String
Mould

Make mould. Cardboard inner tube of tin foil roll. Balance tube inside tall pot to keep straight. Stuff around with tin foil to steady. Dangle string down middle. The wick. How did people make anything before tin foil?

Candle stumps into saucepan that's only for wax. It wrecks pan. Onto hot plate of Aga. Pick old wicks out. Hot. Watch wax like hawk. Once, it caught fire. Just, pouf, a serious ball of flame. What to do? You watched. Then remembered to put a wooden board up top, it went out, it stank. The board has a massive burnt circle on one side. No one mentioned it so you didn't bring it up. No need for anyone to stop you making candles again. You're a bloody quick learner. When wax melted, add oils. Pour into tube. Let it set. Peel off tube. Trim wick.

Right. Candles. They're so heavy. Those nuns and people must have massive arm muscles. Tammie's doing more secret nodding. Star's off. Slow-drag-walking to the centre of the cushion circle. She's doing quite well with not dropping hers. Must be the Olympic training regime. Candle down on leather mat. That mat was hand-tooled by Eric. Raised design. Celtic knot of wheat. Your turn. That bloody wheaty knot's making it extra wobblesome. Tammie's beside you. Taking over. Three candles done. Just.

"Umbaala. Umbaala. Umbaala." Tammie. Squeak. Squeak. Squeak.

"Umbaala. Umbaala. Umbaala." Star. Straight in. And frankly pretty squeaky too. Vocal chords certainly not Olympic strength. Sense it growing yet? No. Might it be possible that Star's going a bit far? She's glued on Tammie. Round the candles they go. They're at the salt pot. Tammie's handing it to Star. Star's off round the room. Stopping in each corner to pour a little heap onto the floor. She's stopped at the first corner. Turning to Tammie. A question.

"The salt from the last cleanse hasn't been swept up. It's covered in bits of fluff." You. For Star.

"Umbaala. Umbaala. Umbaala. Just pour." Tammie. To Star.

There she goes. A heap in each corner. East. West. South. North. The salt will gather any excess anger that might leak from the poets. Oh for heaven's sake. They really should get rid of the old stuff. Those piles will be overflowing with leftover issues.

Ok. Here comes the best bit. You're darting forward. Hands out. But no, the bunch of sage is being given to Star too. That's shut her up with the bloody Umbaalas. She's surprised she gets to do this bit too. You're not. Back by the door, watching. Again. But hurrah, Tammie's giving you the oyster shell. Yes.

"Umbaala, umbaala, UMBAALA." Tammie. No need to shout.

Tammie has the matches, Tammie's lighting the sage, it's catching, it's flaring, Star's stubbing out the flame onto your shell. Smoke. Star's off, you're following, shell out-stretched to catch the ashes. Star knows to wave the smoke in each of the corners again.

"Sense the smoke absorbing. Sense it obscuring the negativity. Sense it remove that negativity. Sense it cleansing all the air. Cleansing all our air. Umbaala, umbaala, umbaala." Sense the smoke being very, very thick. Tammie's clapping now. Clapping her hands all over the room. That clapping's to shatter the old vibrations. Then more clapping to make new ones.

"UMBAAAAAALAAAA." Tammie and Star. Clappety clap.

You're trying hard not to cough and whizzing about after the clappers to catch ash. You are coughing, but it's a strangled cough. Those clapping umbaala-ers are hard at it. The corners are done. Tammie's spinning and clapping and secret nodding at you both to stand over the candles. Ow. Too close. Three big final claps above you.

Silence. Phew. What now?

"Cough." You. Can't help it. Had to.

Tammie's taking the sage. She's wafting the smoke over Star. Star's cupping her hands gathering the smoke. Oh please no. Not, Smoke Showers. Star's pushing the smoke over her face, like washing in water. How is she not choking? Your turn. Hold your breath. Hold your breath. Hold your breath. Tammie's turn. Done.

"Umbaala." Tammie and Star. Only Star's Umbaala is just her mouth going.

"The space is cleansed." Tammie.

Look. Your eyes are shockingly pink and pouring with tears. You are all choking with coughs, all three of you wracked by them. How on earth did Star and Tammie hold on so long? You and Star are in a race to get out of the Work Room. The three of you blowing your noses, wiping your eyes.

"Admirable ritual." You. To Tammie. 'Tammie needs no praise. Her faith in her own faith is unshakeable.' Laura. Once, a while a go. Tammie isn't responding.

Sage burning is a shamanic ritual from the Native Americans. The Native Americans are a lot like Elizabeth David. They thought of stuff before other people did. Once, you had a dream. Pretty normal monster dream. You were being chased. As you were about to be caught you had a rush of anger. Bigger than anything you've ever had awake. You turned to the monster, who was invisible now, you shouted, shaman in its invisible face, then woke up. It was actually the first time anyone had discussed Shamanism in The House. The word had never even been mentioned before so how did a nine-year-old know the word? The adults marvelled. You marvel that it's Star who has the Spiritual Bent and not you. Maybe it's because of the looking like a fairy thing? You're, 'Altogether more earth bound.' Mummy.

Mummy has to cook for the poetry reading. 'Bless you for the sustenance.' Rod. Poetry readings can go on for quite a few hours.

SUSTENANCE FOR POETS. 'And it really is remarkable how much those greedy bearded fuckers can tuck away.' Mummy.

Pastry Tart
Clarissa's Chicken Liver Pâté
Grandma's Chocolate Date Thing

PASTRY TART

Cheese Pastry
Onions
Thyme
Tins toms
Garlic
Goat's cheese. If you can be bothered making it. If not, Philadelphia.

Make pastry usual way but swap half butter for grated cheese. So 2oz butter, 2oz cheese, 8oz flour. Make pastry. Roll flat. Onto baking tray. Stab all over with fork. Mummy's made three Aga trays full. Doubling.

Fry onions with lots garlic. Scatter over pastry. Chop up toms. Scatter. Not too many toms. Absolutely no juice. Soggy Pastry is truly horrid. Little dollops of cheese scattered. Loads thyme. Scatter. Loads black pepper. Aga. Until no sog. Cool. Chop into little squares. Little squares will shame Local Poets into eating less as each time they reach for another square they will – 'Expose their innate greed.' Mummy.

CLARISSA'S CHICKEN LIVER PÂTÉ

First thing Local Veggie Poets always eat. 'My organs need regenerating.' A poet. Veggies can't absorb enough iron. Their veggie bodies are starving for this. So is yours. Iron can support women's organs too. Although poets are usually male. 'The female imagination is formed differently. Its genius is instinct not ideas. Men gravitate towards nations and kings. Women towards the hearth.' Rod.

1lb chick livers
3oz butter
1 shallot
Parsley
Thyme
Pepper
Salt
Slosh sherry

Fry chopped shallot. Add everything. Fry. Until livers stop leaking blood. 'For gawd's sake do not cook them like the English do.' Clarissa. Meaning too much. Whizz in Moulinex. Fridge to set. Done. Might it be possible to eat a whole pot full? Yes. If you ignore the manure heap in summer smell.

GRANDMA'S CHOC DATE THING

Why, why, why is Mummy giving this to poets? Total waste.

'Her one true creative act. This recipe. That and your father, of course.' Mummy. About Grandma and her Choc Date Thing. And Daddy.

3oz butter
1/2lb chopped dates
1lb chocolate
3oz gran sugar
3oz rice crispies

Melt half choc spread on greaseproof in Swiss roll tin. Melt butter, sugar, dates. Stir in rice crispies. Cool bit. Press onto choc. Melt rest choc. Pour over top. Fridge to set. Cut into tiny (tonight) chunks.

Dates are a whole food. Means Grandma's choc date thing isn't as evil as Mars bars. 'Which only an idiot with no regard for their intestines would eat.' Mummy. Mummy does, however, have a reasonable stash of miniature Mars and Crunchie, in the pottery. 'Because they are practically invisible and I am an adult. My colon is formed.' Mummy. Grandma's choc date thing is the food Daddy wants served at his funeral. 'What about my Summer Fruit Tart?' Mummy. 'But it isn't yours is it, my love? It belongs to Mrs David.' Daddy. And it might be a winter do.

Local Poets are flooding the Work Room. Three of them have fallen out of a green and white, with one red panel, 2CV. That's some precarious parking. Might need Jessie to re-park that. Another six are screeching up in an old bread van. Copy cats. These ones are all from the Erpingham Commune. Open doors for writers in Erpingham. The strays have been gathered from around north Norfolk by someone Rod used to run a magazine with but who's too intellectually constipated to include in the *Major Arcana* running gang. The constipated poet's poems are always very short. 'Three lovely big cheers for the haiku.' Mummy. Your People are tucked up in the Work Room. Guarding the choc date thing. Hopefully. You and Star are perched on the garden wall ticking off arrivals. And digging dry moss from between the flints. Only one Local Poet even notices you.

"Remember him? He's Ginger Beer Bob. Remember his Heroes?" You. Nudging Star.

Looks like that's it. Many, many Poets have arrived. You and Star are dropping down from the wall, nipping to the window of the Work Room, leaning your foreheads on the filthy glass. To observe. To teach them how wrong it is to exclude kids. To teach them how much you care about poetry. To teach them it would be a good idea to change their minds about no kids. Mummy's avoiding your pleading eyes. Daddy's giving you a callous wave. Nothing much is happening. Poets all sitting, sometimes even three bony bums per cushion, in a circle on the floor around the candles. It's actually quite rude to exclude you. Considering how much psychic energy you shed getting that room ready for them. Not to mention the sore throat from all that bloody coughing. The Local Poets are men. The only woman to read, ever, is Laura. 'Laura has an impressive grasp of the masculine form.' Daddy. Heads down. Silence. This is how all House Meetings start. Group silence. Quaker ritual. Quakers talk an awful lot of sense; it's just a pity they believe in a Christian god. Anyone can break the Quaker silence, when they feel the power of speech rise up inside them. Another pity about the Quakers – it's always the same people who feel the power of speech. Rod's talking. You can feel the window rattle every time his voice drops to a breathy whisper. Which it does whenever he utters the word creativity. Which he's doing. A lot. 'The problem with Rod's fixation on the creative impulse is that he's only really interested in his own. But boy can he preach about everyone else's.' Laura. 'Let's see. He may surprise us. He has a good mind.' Daddy. He will surprise Daddy. That's for sure. But not this evening.

Rattle, rattle, rattle. Here they go. Looks like Rod's up first. 'I'll open with something in a looser form. Possibly a work in progress. Something fluid. Good to keep the tone experimental. To open.' Rod. To Daddy. At breakfast when they were planning. 'You can smash them into submission at the end. Why don't you give those sexy flower pieces an airing?' Daddy. Encouraging. And planning too. Rod can't start because Mummy's having a bit of a stretch. Getting comfy. The Local Poets are more interested in the getting comfy than Rod's loose form. Rod's right leg is tapping up and down. Mummy's snuggling, resting her head in Laura's lap. Laura's stroking her hair. Daddy's stretching out his long legs and he's stroking Laura's back. Lots of stroking and now smiling at all the left out of the stroking Local Poets. Rattle, rattle. Rod's getting on with it. Local Poets are doing some listening now. Quite a few with their eyes closed.

Local Poet after Local Poet after Local Poet after Local Poet, reading. Plenty of window rattling. You're maintaining your plaintive vigil but not one single Poet has even smiled at you. Surely it's important they realise how deeply you can be affected by their words? Even if you can't actually hear them. Do not move from your position of protest.

Alright, you can twist round a bit. Have a look at that Hairy Dolly. This window is so dirty it's possible it might not have realised you're there. Maybe none of the Local Poets know? Have a jolly good peer at it. Still the hairiest thing to be found in these parts. Without paws. Its head hair's got even longer. The curls are un-twisting a bit. Flop curls. Those curls are creeping over its shoulders dropping down its back. Like a well-established clematis. It has a long, with a hump at the top, nose. 'I tolerate him purely because of his classical beauty. Look at that exquisite snout.' Mummy. Ages and ages ago. Is it? Will the Hairy Dolly read? It did once. Daddy asked and asked it to do it again. 'That piece you shared. Where did that come from? I was interested in that.' Daddy. He even asked to see it written down. But that Hairy Dolly was having none of it. 'Oh, Anthony man, I just thought I'd see if I could, you know? It's not my bag. Too relentless. All that fucking thinking.' Hairy Dolly. To Daddy. Saying no to more sharing. Star's still beside you but she's given up on the vigil. She's leaning against the wall, reaching Great Uncle Elizabeth onto her lap, twisting her hair with one hand, his with the other. Gentle twisting not worrying twisting.

Rattle, rattle. Bang. No. The Hairy Dolly's completely in front of you. Its face is pressed right up on its side of the glass. How did it get so close to the window so quickly? You're leaping back as if you've been stung. It's staring at you. Bulb eyes. Its mouth is open and it's flicking its tongue back and forth over its very white teeth. It's dropped back to where it came from. All you can see is the back of its head. That was a shock. Look at Star. Still half asleep. Look at the Work Room. Rumbling on. Daddy? Mummy? Who saw that happen?

"Star? Wake up. Come on. We're gate crashing. Write a poem. Write anything. I'm getting mine." You. Up and to the box under your bed. Box is for keeping your thoughts books in. Thoughts books are beautiful things. Real school exercise books. You have eight all filled up with thoughts and recipes. Daddy made the under-bed boxes. You've crammed the boxes with distractingly interesting stuff, to cover up your books. In case the adults become compelled to spy. The stuff covers all the standard interests of a captivatingly clever child. Mice skeletons with added attraction of skulls wrapped in tin foil and dresses from hen feathers, lucky stones (all with hole right through the centre), bit of rusty tractor metal that looks like a dancing person sculpture, rat's teeth. Usual rubbish.

Back outside Work Room door. Thoughts book in hand. Star's scrunching up a bit of paper. Both got your ears pressed on door. Why do people in books do this? This and the glass against a wall thing. Neither works. It isn't working now. Can't even feel the rattle. Scratchy little shy tap. Nothing. Try again. You are. Even shyer. Scratching away for a very long time.

"What? What is it? Can't you entertain yourselves for a single hour without badgering us for something? This is an important meeting." Mummy. Grump-y. But, in open doorway, however.

"We wondered if you would like us to serve your food to you?" You. Doing some good begging-dog eyes. Star is not doing a dog face but she is looking fairy which will no doubt swing it.

"Very clever. Anyone hungry?" Mummy. To you then swaying round to Local Poets. Of course they're hungry. She knows this as well as you do. Look at them. Beards all perked up at their tips and look at that little one, with the pink nose, in the corner. That one is actually rubbing its tummy.

"Fine. Get the food. But do not make a fuss when you bring it in." Mummy. Going back to Laura and Daddy. Leaving the door so wide open she may as well have taken it off its hinges.

You're back. Chicken liver pâté, pastry squares – Star. Choc date thing – You. Eric's leaping up and helping Star. Quick head pat when he's done. Star's smiling at him and sitting next to him. Mummy's sighing. Quite loudly. Poets are elbowing each other out of the way to get the biggest portion. That Pink Nose wasn't joking, he's piled six squares of pastry and he's got a choc date thing in his mouth. This has started a freefall of Poets eating pudding first. Pudding panic has erupted. Choc date thing has gone and you haven't even sat down. You're risking a look at Mummy. Mummy can't resist. She's pulling a very good gobbling pig face at you. Mummy is funny. Quick. Whilst she's smiling get yourself sat down.

"Hey, hi, will you like, yeah? An onion thing, yeah? Please." Pretty Justin. Helpful. You're grabbing a couple of slices and turning to him but look, Pretty Justin's bum is pressed up against that Hairy Dolly's on their cushion. Don't slow down. You aren't. Handing over the slices.

"Hel-lo Nearly Thirteen, fancy seeing you here. Wanna squeeze in? Be the jam in our sandy-witch?" Hairy Dolly. Budging up. So you are. Squeezing in. Good job you changed into your Laura Ashley puffy out skirt. See that little blue vest like Mummy's? That looks good. And right. Shame about the big grey circle of window dirt smudge obscuring your forehead.

"What's this?" Hairy Dolly. Tapping your Thoughts Book. You're looking round the room. It's noisy. The food has made a break in the reading. No one's seen you getting yourself sat down. Not even Mummy. Who's moving to beside Eric, getting Star off him and on her lap.

"Poetry. General thoughts. Ideas. Mainly poetry." You.

"You gonna share?" Hairy Dolly.

"She, like, should, you, like, should." Pretty Justin.

"I just want to listen." You. This is, of course, an errant lie. You actually want to stun and amaze. Listening is merely an aspect of the stunning and amazing plan.

"Ok. People. Shall we? Resume. Resume." Rod. Standing on the pedal of the printing press. To be taller. More of an oblong than a square. Temporarily.

People are resuming. Bums back on cushions. Quite a few Poets have got stacks of food on the floor in front of them. One Poet has got three slices of choc date thing. Did Star get a slice? Why does cold choc do that beads of moisture rolling on its roof thing that glasses of wine also do? When the wine has come from a fridge. Other cold stuff doesn't do it. Why choc? Why wine? Look at that. There really only is one pastry slice left. Why do adults leave just one thing? Even these hungry ones? You're getting up, gliding over to the lonesome slice. Good floaty skirt puff. You're picking up the lonesome slice. Listen to that. The Work Room is holding the silence. Are Poets about to leap on you (snarling), wrestle you to the ground, and shed blood over that final slice? See Mummy and Daddy? They're looking worried at each other. You have the slice. You're twisting in the middle of the room. You've found Jessie and you're feeding her the lonesome slice. No greedy poet is getting his little yellow teeth on your slice. Look at Mummy and Daddy. Relieved. Relieved the slice went to Jessie.

"Right girls. Out." Daddy.

"Aye. There's work to be done here." Rod.

"Yes. Yes. Yes. Much to share." Ginger Beer Bob. Who does he think he is? Joining in with the banishing. Damn. Big mistake getting up again. Now you're stuck in the middle of the room. Looking belligerent. And smudgy. Not the plan.

"Star and I felt we might value the experience if it were possible just to listen?" You. Head down. Bit of fiddling with the corners of your thoughts book.

"Snort." Mummy.

"Star? You got plans to become a Lady Poetess? You need this experience?" Daddy. Tricky. Maybe you should have left Star out of it? It's usually more effective if you bring her into it. Possibly not this evening. Star's gazing at the candles. Probably giving spiritual bent a whirl.

"She might. I don't know. I have something." You.

Everyone's looking at Star but she's giving nothing away. Apart from general fairy-nun charm.

"Ok. It will be an experience for us all." Daddy. Good. Fairy-nun charm working in most corners of the Work Room.

"Grunt. Puff." Rod.

"Ttch. Ttch. Ttch." Ginger Beer Bob. He's very annoying. You're smiling at him doing your best glide-walking back to your sandwich. It really is most tantalising how this skirt fuffs up when you sit down then takes just long enough to let it's air out as you get ready to read. You're riffling through your book. Oh just pick one. Any one will do. You're opening the book at random.

"So?" Daddy. Leaning back. Uncrossing his legs, laying them straight across the floor. Long, green velvet legs. Button fly. Red buttons that Mummy sewed on. 'For fun and attention where it's due.' Mummy.

Read s l o w.

"This is called HIM THERE

Him there. Him in the corner of that room. Him there.

There are dark days ahead. Days of silence and tears. Days of solitude and rain. And him there. Always him. The clouds will wash the moon and you will think you see him. You will stand on endless burial mounds and howl at that moon. You will rake your heart with ashes from his fire and you will cry and you will wait. Him there. You will taste the salt in the secret places of your skin and you will wish him. You will stare at the sky and will him on. Will him home. You will sing his ship onwards. Rock it gentle on the sea. Lullaby him to the harbour. Bringing him home.

Him there. Him there.

And he will arrive. Yesterday tomorrow all the days together he will arrive. And he will be beside you. And the flames will soften to ash and those ashes will be blown around the room but he will be there. You will share the hearth. And he will lick the salt from your arm. And he will breathe you home.

He is an adult." You. Done. Quite a long silent bit.

"Yes. Yes. Yes. How old is she?" Ginger Beer Bob. To Daddy. That old Chestnut.

"Nearly Thirteen. Aren't you? Hey people, I'm going for a pee." Hairy Dolly. It's gone from the Work Room.

Oh, how funny. That Hairy Dolly thinks your poem is about Hairy Dollies. No. You just wrote it. You've listened to hundreds of poems, you know how it's done. You need to do repeating and aching. It's also useful to make it sound like it's come from by-gone days. People like birds in poems too. Birds, weather, boats, all sea-related stuff, hearths – obviously – random mentions of bits of bodies. What they taste or smell like. It's easy. You just get it all down then read in a clear s l o w voice. It's interesting what you find yourself writing. Your box is crammed with stuff like this. You're just not allowed into readings. Usually. But now. Taa dah.

"Well, obviously, it is an immature voice but the repeated images of home, the moon and sea are archetypal female ones. We can see that, even in children, there is a reaching towards expression of Jung's Anima and Animus. Gruuuuunt. I am struck by the motif. Him there." Rod. He's so struck by it that he'll use it himself in his next Nature Poem. About a bull in a field. "These powerful female images are used hysterically here. Childishly almost." Rod. That Hairy Dolly did not need a pee.

"Jesus H Christ, Rod. Childish? She's only just twelve. Twelve. Where do you guys get off? What do you want to do about this?" Laura. To Mummy. Going on. Waving towards you. She means your poem not Rod's thoughts.

"Darling Laura, this isn't really anything to do with you and now is absolutely not the time." Mummy. Fierce and kind.

"It is everything to do with the whole house. We have agreed collective responsibility." Laura. Ignoring the timing.

"These are my kids." Mummy. Also ignoring. Now.

"They come through you, they are not of you." Laura. Is that from a song?

"They are mine." Mummy.

"They are not property. We are all invested in their future." Daddy. They're all doing shouting in whispers now.

"The future is contained in the present." Sqqqueak. Tammie. That's caused a teeny quiet bit. Maybe the Poets are all trying to fathom what she actually said.

"Tammie, honey, not now. I think these children, this child is telling us that something is..." Laura. Doing embarrassed smiling in your general direction then searching round the room.

"This is the reason we don't invite kids to an adult event. This poem is an immature attempt to mimic tone. It's simply feelings. Can we please work to stay focused on what's important here. We have twelve serious pieces still to share." Rod. Straight into Laura's pause. Not whispering at all just shouting. Seven of those pieces are Rod's smashing into submission ones.

Laura thinks your poem's real. Don't look at her. Is your poem real? Tammie does too. Don't look at her. Mummy? Daddy? Local Poets? Bit of general munching on leftovers going on but also a fair old bit of staring, at you. Stunned and amazed. You're staring at the floor. The modest Lady Poetess cannot quite lift her (dirty) neck, she is suffering most cruelly from the vapours.

Feel that? That's Star. She's crouching beside you, pushing her scrunch of paper into your hand. Bloody Hell. Two Lady Poetesses? One was quite enough. You did tell her to write something. Fine. You're standing. Bold. The circle's egalitarian. No one stands.

The occasion seems to demand it.

"Star's poem. It's called..." You. Un-scrunching. Scanning. "It's called, Baked Beans. Ingredients. Beans. Tomatoes. Water. Sugar. Modified Corn flour. Spirit Vinegar. Salt. Spice Extracts. Herb Extracts. Emulsifier. Baked beans." What a cheat. It's the label from a can.

"Twinkle, twinkle little Star. Brilliant girl. It's a masterpiece. Rod? You must publish it. Promise you will?" Mummy. Local Poets looking towards Daddy. Apart from Ginger Beer Bob. He's checking to see if his own Serious Pieces are as good as yours and Stars. Shaking gingery head at floor so probably not. Daddy's grinning. Getting up. Picking up Star. Doing a big hot potato on her tummy. Laughing. Local Poets laughing. Bit too hard. Wasn't that funny. Enough of this nonsense. You're gone.

Back garden. Prune's on her extra long chain. 'Give that goat her space, man.' Hairy Dolly. To Eric when the shorter chain kept failing. Extra long chain worked. She hasn't used her horns to lever up the stake-anchor for ages. Prune's eating thin dry grass. Giving you the Evil Yellow-Eyed Wink. Once, Eric tried blunting Prune's horns. He stuck those blue rubber tubes you can attach to tap ends, to swoosh your water in all directions, onto the horns. Lasted two minutes. Prune levered them off. Ate them.

Ciggie smoke. Grey trail winding up from the dip down to the field. Are you going to visit it? The sky's as blue as Laura's linen granddad shirt. Herbaceous border's still full of tangley scarlet roses, over-blown artichoke thistle heads, dead lavender. And weeds. Go on. You are. That grass sounds crunchy. The Hairy Dolly's on its back down the dip. It's turning its head to you. Bulbing at you. Offering its ciggie. Bloody Hell. Not ciggies again. Wafting the offer away. That linen sky is just too absorbing to bother with ciggies.

"I've given up." You.

"You're very wise, Kiddo. For such an infant." Is it joking? Don't risk it. Just nod. After all it is true.

"Sooooo. Nearly Thirteen. Poetry. Hey?" Good-O. This is perfect. You're plopping down beside it.

"I've been working on a few pieces."

"Don't bullshit a bull shitter. Don't waste your pretty fat mouth on it." Fat? But also pretty. Your mouth is now enormous. It's hard to make it do normal things. It's twitching. Is your mouth so fat it will wobble as you twitch? Stop mouth twitching. The Hairy Dolly's putting its hand, with the ciggie in it, up to you. It's touching your twitchy bottom lip. Ow. Its smoke is going in your eyes. Hand back down. That hand smelt a bit of cheese. "Tell me a secret, Thirteen." Big drag on ciggie. Great. Easy. You're lying down too. Mouth back to normal.

"Star wants to be an Olympic gymnast. Daddy might suffer from something that is an actual illness called depression, occasionally. Tammie eats three quarter-pound bags of peanut brittle a week. In her bedroom. Remember those sweets you liked that we made as a surprise for Eric? Mummy asked us to but said don't tell Daddy. Mummy has agoraphobia. Always put lots of small dollops of butter in with the fruit and sugar to make a perfect crumble." Is that too many secrets?

"Jeeez am I glad I asked. Agoraphobia eh? Fear of the market place. That ain't it. I'd say your Mama is the High Priestess of them there markets. She's the shopping goddess."

"It's more that the market's in the middle of town. You have to get there. Then, when you do, it's rammed with shoppers. Other people." Is that right?

"Those friggin' bastards, people, getting their strangers' hands all over the gear before she can. Ya know? That peanut brittle ain't a secret. You wanna know a secret?" Yes. Please.

"Ok. If you want."

"I do. I have shared some of that peanut brittle with Miss Tambourine. She was most ladylike. Most generous."

"That's not a secret. I told you real things. Don't tell mine. Promise you won't? Please." What if it does tell?

"Seriously, Kiddo? I thought you were observant. I never tell anybody anything. Anything that counts. You wanna know another secret?" You thought it was observant.

"Only if it's one that counts." This is fun.

"Hah. That's more like it." It's sitting right up then half back down then balancing towards you on one elbow, stubbing out its ciggie. Make sure that's actually out. Don't want to start a forest fire. The Hairy Dolly's shuffling up to beside you. You're kindly rolling over to face it. Right. It's taken hold of your chin. "You are smart, Kiddo. That's not the secret. The secret is, I liked your poem."

"That's not a secret either."

"Oh, is it not? Ok. Promise you won't tell a soul and I promise to tell you a real secret." Talking of breathing. Its breathing is a bit too close. Its breath is early morning smoker's breath. Acidy burp breath. It's evening time now.

"Promise." Can you feel that knocking feeling? Like you've got a door buried inside you and an insistent visitor is trying to get in.

"You've gotten a dirty mark, in the shape of Africa, on your forehead. It's been there for as long as I can remember." You're jolting to sit up. It's still got your chin. It's pushing. Firmly. You're staying put. "I'm gonna work some magic. I'm gonna make it invisible." Hairy

Dolly. Spitting on its finger. That's got hairs too. Rubbing all over your forehead. Spitting more. More rubbing. Big smudge, gone. Forehead smelling of cheese spit. Why isn't it letting go? Looking at each other. Door banging. Hairy Dolly's hand is up again. Grazing your eyebrows. Grazing your fat mouth. So close that one loose hair curl's flopping onto your face. Your skin is flickering like a horse when flies land on it. Do not speak. You aren't. It's letting go, lying back down. You aren't lying down. Both watching the stubble field beyond Star's den. You're shaking like that time you touched the electric fence, just to check it was electric. Hairy Dolly's skinning up. Sighing. You're getting up, stroking skirt fuff down. It's watching that. You're doing it again. You're trying stretching, up and back. It's watching that. That visitor has left your inside door. You're leaning right over it. Your face is in its face. This is daring. Your fat lips are a little crack open.

"Your breath smells like cherry drops." Hairy Dolly. Nearly shouting at your leaving back. Never had cherry drops. Sound tasty. Must get hold of some and give 'em a whirl.

Back inside the Big Room. Not a single Local Poet in sight. Check the corners, just in case one has crept back and is lurking. Waiting for crumbs to drop. Your People are flopped about the place. Daddy's smoking, doesn't even glance up from the book he's reading.

"Bed." Daddy. How does he know it's you that's come in? Where's Star?

Don't move. You're just inside the door by the high-backed flaky-paint, white-wicker chair Daddy's in. His velvet legs slung over one chair arm, hand with the ciggie dangled to beside ash tray on the floor. His book is flat, open on his lap, a Georgian rummer brimming with red wine's beside the ash tray. 'He doesn't pay me enough to merit loyalty.' Daddy. About borrowing the glasses from Gerald Franks.

Chance it. You're inching in. Bending down until you're leaning on his legs.

"Bed." He isn't looking up, he's trying to flick you off his legs. You're actively leaning on them.

"Don't be a bore. Get off me. Bed." Flicking harder. You're climbing onto his lap. Why? That looks a bit silly. Like a display sculpture-person, from a shop window, draped on a real person.

"Get off me. Leave me alone. I'm busy. I don't need you now." He's continuing to read, whipping the book out from under you, holding it over your head and also reaching for his glass. He's drunk half the glass in one glug. He is very busy. Must be a good book. Wonder what it's about? You're leaning even further down. Hanging your head sideways to get a look. "Don't be a tit. Get off me."

"What's it about?" You. Jolly.

"Why? Fancy an educational debate dissecting its literary merits? This evening's experiential learning not enough for you?" Daddy. Finishing other half of wine in second glug. Turning page. Drag on ciggie. No looking up. You're re-arranging head. Snuggling it against his chest, he smells of beeswax wood polish and ciggies.

"Off. Off. Get off."

You really must insist on staying. Check out the rest of the Big Room, from the safety of your perch. Pretty Justin's curled up small on the floor by Mummy's chair, rolling his ciggie, grinning at you. Rod's staring at you. Doesn't he know you can see him looking? The others are not looking.

"Bed." Too loud. He's resorted to using his tummy to push you off him. Un-comfy. You're relenting, climbing down and moving away.

Stopping before the upstairs door, turning back. Look at your daddy. He's still not looking at you. All Your other People have stopped doing their own thing and are now watching. Right. Do not slink. You're doing a sweeping the room look.

This is to remind them what a Serious Poet you might grow into. With their continued guidance.

Eric's breaking first, sliding past, trotting upstairs. Very light footfall. For a giant. Tammie's moving to the sink, pouring water. Laura's smiling. Looks a bit shy and silly. Look out. Mummy's made a move. Towards you. Mummy has her hands against your chest, she's giving you little pushes. Joking pushes.

"Bed. Bed. Bed." Mummy. With each little push.

Don't budge. You're giving her Prune's Evil Yellow Eye. She's giving it right back. You're side stepping. Mummy's made a sudden grab. You've swerved. Escape. You're walking back into the room. Mummy's glancing at Daddy. For assistance. Nothing. Don't you look tall? You're pausing at the table. Take your time. Have a sift through the book pile. *Narcissus and Goldmund* by Hermann Hesse. You're opening it, reading a couple of lines. Quite good, actually. And now you're going to the upstairs door. Mummy's doing a little curtsey as you pass. You're giving a gracious head tilt, pausing just a second. Have you gone too far? Maybe Mummy didn't see. She's sitting back down, picking up her sketch book. Daddy hasn't looked up. Pretty Justin's got up from where he was sitting with Mummy. You are in-step, he's holding the door to upstairs open for you.

"Yeah? Like? I thought, like, your writing, was like far out?' Pretty Justin. Pretty Justin is your friend. He's kissing you.

"Night." Pretty Justin.

"Yeah. Bed." You. Waving your book at them. You were going to go anyway.

CHAPTER FIVE

Morning. Stop, look at yourself before you wake up. No splodges, no veins, no sad torn cracks and sags, no dark and anxious smudges. Perfect apricot skin complete with the baby fuzz of ripe fruit. It wouldn't matter what order the features are arranged in, the newness of you is all that counts. Who could resist?

Still sleeping in that pink nightie? Has it ever been washed? Pop. You're awake. Up and out of bed leaving the antique sheets tumbled. Star's long gone, of course, entertaining visitors in her ditch, no doubt. Still hasn't rained so it still has a roof. You're dragging that scratchy nightie off when there it is. So you're twisting your legs together to check but, yes, you're right. Your fanny feels damp, in a thick and frankly sludgy way. It's faintly chilly where the damp meets air. Not an unpleasant feeling more like something that has been nothing, is now present. Twisting your legs again. Big brown smear on the top of your thighs. Reaching down, touching the outside of your fanny so now your fingers are also smeared with it. What is that? Oh. It's blood, brown, stringy, sludge blood. Not very much actually. That cannot be right. Staring. Test it. Get your fingers right in. Yup, more brown strands but not much more. You're sniffing it and with the very tip of your tongue tasting. Iron mud. That is why chicken liver is important. It's a replacement. You're rubbing brown fingers together, rolling the viscous blood until it rolls into little worms which you're brushing to the floor. Look at your hand. The finger nails stained with it but your hand nearly clean. Moving quickly now. Wad of loo roll, wiping away as much brown goo as poss. Wrapping stained paper inside more clean paper. Jeans and tight pants, on. Tuck the goo parcel into your pocket. Deal with that later. Another wad of loo roll, to soak blood that might gush, inside tight pants. Little T-shirt is the first thing on the clothes pile. It's light blue, has an ice-cream-cone transfer on it, you've had it for years and it still fits, just. Off to find Mummy.

Outside the pottery door. She's definitely in there, that's her making Pretty Justin laugh and that whistling-crunch is the wheel turning. Finally. She's working. Bum-holes, this is bad timing. No one, no matter what, should interrupt the creative process. 'Unless it's shopping for shoes.' Daddy. But that's not true because Mummy can't get to Norwich any more. Go on, go in. Tell. 'My daughters are more like sisters.' Mummy. To everyone. But will she want to see her sister-daughter at this particular moment and with this news? Do you have to tell? 'We have no secrets. I tell them everything.' Mummy. Do you want to tell? Just get on with it. Smell the dusty clay-whiff. Mummy's sat at the wheel. Headscarf, work smock, clay-smeared jeans and sandals that Eric made everyone from car tyres. This is how you will try to picture your Mummy, for ever.

"What? Go away. Can't you see I'm working?" Mummy. This is how you will actually picture your Mummy.

"Yes. Sorry. Can you come here?" You. Shifty looking.

"What? What have you broken? Whatever it is I really don't care. I'm working." Foot back on treadle.

"Nothing. Sorry. Can you come here?" Not moving. Long bit where Mummy just throws and you are invisible, apparently.

"Now look what you've made me do." Very tall vase shape wonking completely out of control and cork-screwing at the top. She's eyeing it, kicking the treadle slowly round, wonk, wonk, wonk, round it goes. "That's rather brilliant. Thank you darling, now fuck off will you." Regrettably there is no fucking off to be done. Wonk-vessel isn't that interesting, surely it's about to go back into the slip-bucket? It's rubbish.

"Bloody hell. Alright. You win." Getting off the wheel, rubbing clay hands on her smock. Eyes fixed on wonk-vessel.

"So? What's so important?" Mummy. More obstinate eyeing.

"Can you come here. Please?" You.

"You can say whatever it is in front of Justin. Surely?" Is she in love with the wonk-vessel?

"Please. Mummy." Two pleases does it. She's flicking a look of bloody hell to Pretty Justin but she is coming. She's hovering in the doorway, holding the door half closed behind herself. That'll do.

"What's the great and urgent mystery?" Doing pretend whispering but looking back over her shoulder making big eyes at your rival, Mr Wonk.

"I am a woman."

"What?" Ha. Not so tall and shiny now are you, Mr Wonky Wonk?

"I'm a woman. I've started my periods. I think." Quieter this time.

"How do you know?" Dragging her eyes away from him.

"Blood." Reaching into jeans, retrieving the wads. Pocket one and inside one, unwrapping and showing. There's very little to show. Mummy's grabbing them, swinging the pottery door open.

"Look-look. My first born is a woman. My god darling we are in sync, I have mine too." Waving the papers at Pretty Justin. Mr

Wonky-Wonk is no more than a lump of clay entirely abandoned. Pretty Justin looks unsure. So do you. You're snatching the loo roll wads back. Mummy's off. Really, truly, actually skipping.

"We must tell your father, he'll be so proud. Oh." Mummy. Screeching to a halt mid-skip and poised one knee in the air. "We must have a Happing. Darling, we're going to have a Red Party. We're going to submerge our community in womb-worship. We are claiming this glorious moment for all the women in this house. Even Tammie, who let's face it probably hasn't started menstruating herself yet, she is so un-formed, but you, my darling, oh, I am so proud of you." She may as well do one of those little sideways jumps where the dancer taps their heels together in mid air, both feet to the one side.

"It's not really red. It's more brown." You. Calling but quiet calling not shouting.

"Yes but it will be red and who wants a bloody brown party?" Shouting over shoulder having given up on the dance moves and now just running to find Daddy. "Every single freak in this house must be dressed head to toe in red. Including the dog." Did you hear that right? She's practically in the attic she's travelling so fast. Dressing up? Um. Ok.

FOOD TO HERALD THE ARRIVAL OF WOMANHOOD

Roast tomato and basil soup.
Garlic bread with red garlic butter.
Beetroot crisps.
Blackberry and rose geranium water ice.
A bowl of figs.

First things first, you and Star have to bike to Aylsham to buy French bread. French bread is unadulterated white flour. 'This is an impromptu happening, there isn't a minute to slave over bread.' Mummy. Clearly nonsense but why argue when there's white French bread on offer? 'We need to ritualise the needs of a woman at this point in her cycle. She needs cosseting. White bread's a marvellous cosset-er. If you're anything like me you will crave it.' Mummy. This is not nonsense, this is good news making the brown sludge aspect of periods less... absorbing. Cravings sound interesting too.

ROAST TOM SOUP

Nearly as good as Heinz tomato soup which is a desert island food, if you're lucky enough to have a few tins on board when you're ship-wrecked. You might have because tinned food's so practical it can last through nuclear attack. 'Proves my point about it being fucking dangerous stuff.' Mummy. About why no tins. Apart from tinned tomatoes. And beans. In an emergency. Which a nuclear attack would surely be? But still no soup.
Heaps of toms. Good time of year for this soup, there's an endless glut of toms choking the greenhouse.
Stock. Chicken if you have it but why would you? Don't use beef or lamb or it's just beef or lamb soup. Make veg stock, standard method or stock cube. Not too much cube or it tastes cubey, which is an insistent taste you can't shake.
Whole garlic heads
Thyme
Basil. Never use dried, it's simply not the same.

Chop top off garlic heads, slosh oil or chunk butter up top. Put them, and toms, into biggest Aga trays. Sprinkle fresh thyme around. Roast until garlic squidges out of jackets when pressed. Chuck tom and thyme stalks and garlic cases. Smoosh all up in Mouli, add to stock. If you want to be fancy, sieve it. Too dreary. Sometimes you add cream. Sometimes you don't. Today it must be red as poss. So no cream. Only add basil as you serve or it goes grey and seaweed-like. Tangy, tangy soup that keeps the smell of the green bit of tomatoes intact. Brilliant. Now that would be an excellent perfume idea. That green-bit smell. Someone should talk to those Tweed people. Potential real money idea? You and Star did a road-side stall last summer selling your home-made rose petal perfume. Rose petals brewed in water. Remove petals, cool, add fresh and bottle. 20p per bottle. Sold no bottles. Went worryingly brown in the sun. But smelt ok. For a couple of weeks. Then the rot set in.

Mummy's already in a bright red headscarf she's made from one of the dishcloths she dyed in a job lot. 'New house rule. All white linen must be gathered and dipped. I am sick of grey tea towels, grey towels, sheets, fucking stinky grey fanny-flannels.' Mummy. Last winter, issuing the coloured linen edict. 'Not sure changing the colour will improve the smell. I'll say one word to you, Beth. Rota.' Laura. Joining in with the mass dipping. Half red, half green. Mummy is now singing and slicing.

"Star? Star? Put that bloody cat down and help. Get the red duvet cover from my bed and put it over the sofa and have a rummage and see if you can find something to cover the Big Room light. Something red." Mummy. What other colour could Star have possibly thought she meant? Has Star ever moved more grudgingly? Is it possible to walk sarcastically? Apparently it is.

GARLIC BREAD. RED

White Bread French Loafs. French loaves taste so good because the French have invented ovens that work with steam. 'Don't be a fool darling. They don't have a steam oven at the Spar in Aylsham.' Clarissa. To Mummy when Mummy was being thrilled about French steam. 'It's hardly my fault I can't tootle round fucking France, all summer long, stuffing myself with steamed bread.' Mummy. Hurt and crying back at her. Daddy would love to drive to France all summer but that can't happen. 'I'm perfectly happy with the Spar's version. Thank you.' Mummy. To Daddy when he tried to tempt her. Great. So are you.
Butter
Garlic. In spring there's wild garlic in hedges so use those leaves instead. Chop small, add instead of crushed bulb. Very burpy mind.
Salt
Cochineal. This is red food dye. It's made from insects. Don't tell the veggies.

Smash up butter and salt with loads of crushed garlic and that's it, usually, but today Mummy goes crazy-beans with the cochineal. 'This must be vivid, let's force the men to face the reality of our lives.' Mummy. Shake, shake, shake with the red dye. Cut loaves into slices but don't cut through. Smear both sides of slices with mix. Really big smears. Wrap in tin foil, heat until bread's crisp and butter's melted and the whole house stinks of garlic. Daddy should think about serving this at his funeral. You will at yours. But not red.

Star's back. Getting into the swing of things, lugging two football-shaped bunches of scarlet geraniums and she's got her boyfriend,

Eric, in tow. Look at that, will there be any red climbing roses left in the herbaceous border? Wow, Eric is a walking bush.

"Oh, Eric, oh, thank you. Those are just...well...they are perfect. Really so lovely. Gosh. Thank you. Star, be an absolute darling and get a stool and see if you two can't do something exquisite with them draped over the windows. See if you can get them to, to, cascade. Heavenly. Thank you." Mummy. That is the world record for Mummy saying thank you.

"Neigh bother." Eric. World record for saying pretty much nothing. Most of the time. Wish he'd stop all the gormless petting of Star. Maybe he's got a thing for bald fairies.

BEETROOT CRISPS

Beetroots. Use the French mandolin. 'Darling, I beg you not to let the kids near this, it will take their hands off.' Clarissa. Unwrapping and flicking her thumb over blades to show. 'Bless you, darling, it's exactly what I wanted. The kids will be fine. I trust them. And I do so want them to experience a proper slicing method.' Mummy. She's right. You are fine and blinking heck sliced stuff flies off it.

Wash beets, slice with mandolin. They fly off it just like real packet crisps. 'What is it about kids and Salt and Vinegar?' Mummy. The only time you and Star were allowed them. She wasn't asking you so you didn't tell her. If she had it would have been your pleasure to inform her it's the way they burn layers off your tongue. Heat oil. Deep fry for moments. Out and shake off spare oil. Massive scrunch sea salt. Done. Sweet beet and salt crunch.

They're back. Eric seems to be dragging a tree this time.

"Eric, I am in love with you." Mummy. She's dropping the figs. Hey, watch out, figs bruise. She's got Eric's face and she's kissing him on the mouth. "I would never have thought of it. Copper beech. Was it a nightmare to steal? God it's beautiful. Just ram it into any corner you can. The room is transforming. I am so grateful. Darling? Aren't you thrilled? All of this, for you." Are you thrilled?

"Neigh bother." Eric. Once, you and Star went for a riding lesson. Once. The riding lady said to all the ponies 'Trot on.' Constantly. You and Star couldn't stop laughing. Or telling each other to trot on, at the least provocation.

"Trot on." You. To Star. She's pretending she hasn't heard. But she clearly has. The back end of the tree's quivering.

BOWL OF FIGS

Figs. Many as can be eaten. 'On your return trip from Aylsham stop at Bad Dog Farm, see if you can scrump whatever figs they have left. Don't get bitten. Try and get them home intact.' Mummy. Hard when the backpack is full of bread and you're on bikes and you have Jessie who never wants to stop for anything and will alert the Bad Dog but scrumping is an important egalitarian lesson. Despite Star and Jessie's understandable horror at the Bad Dog. Once, that dog was off its chain, you and Star were on your bikes, and it chased you for at least a mile. Star tried to kick it away but the Bad Dog was very bad. It sprang up and bit Star on the tummy. Hung off her for a good few yards. There was an emergency tetanus visit to the doctors. Which was very boring but better than the emergency visit to the chemist when you had thrush. Laura took you. The chemist is a sadist. His customers always whisper whatever it is they need. Of course they do, they are shy but he responds by shouting their ailments at them. 'Is the thrush in your vagina?!' Sadistic Chemist. Yelling so hard he went a bit red. 'No. It's in the vagina of an eleven-year-old girl!' Laura. Topping his vol. Taking the roof off the chemist's. Your People were delighted with Laura's balls. Shame the whole of Aylsham now knows you once had a thrushy fanny.

Mummy breaks open the scrumped figs, dollops lumps of Prune's cheese up top then pours runny honey over.

It's candles now. Star's got a roll of red (surprise) crepe paper and she's wrapping candles in it. Eric's jamming them into wine bottles. Fire hazard? Eric needs to pay more attention to his hazardous candles but he's too busy watching Mummy and the split figs and smiling.

"Shush, you naughty, it's not that funny." Mummy. To Eric. He isn't actually laughing. It's just the northernmost reaches of his mouth slightly tipped up.

BLACKBERRY AND ROSE GERANIUM WATER ICE

You don't have to make this today, the freezer's packed with it. Kid's job. You get paid five pence per pound of this you make. Why do people like Beatrix Potter always do field mice and blackberry kind of drawings to show autumn? Blackberries are always springing up, juicy and ripe, from end of June onwards. Then everyone goes on about what a good summer it's being. Usually in the pouring rain.

1lb blackberries

3 oz sugar. Elizabeth David recipe, she says ¼ lb 'This is too much even for a child's lunatic palate.' Mummy.

¼ lb water

6 Rose geranium leaves. Says three but more's good. Not too much more or you're burping Grandma's rose soap for hours.

Boil water, sugar, half the leaves until got syrup. About 5 mins. Cool. Sieve blackberries into syrup. Chuck away bits. Mix, add fresh leaves. Freeze. Americans are enchanted by this flavour. So English. Probably the hint of old ladies' soap. Don't be put off. Eat in January when it's vital to remember picnics.

Bang. Front door. Feel that breeze? Look at Mummy, Eric, Star and you all noticing that teeny shift. Is the weather about to change? The Hairy Dolly's coming in. He's been to the pub and has gallons of wine. Red no doubt. He's stopping in the Big Room door.

"It's a friggin' whore house." The Hairy Dolly. Taking in your party.

"Yes. A whore house in fairyland. Right, my friends, my family, clothes time. Eric, you're first, follow me, and Bryan you come too and get your nails done. Everyone's getting red nails. You can choose if it's toes or fingers. Both if you want to express true solidarity. Come, come, you delicious men, girls – you too. Gather anyone else and bring them to me and make sure they bring whatever they're planning on wearing for me to inspect its hue. Tout suite." Mummy.

Mummy and Daddy's attic. The wardrobe that's only got two legs – the other two are piles of books – has its single door wide open. It's always open on the other side, it only has a door on one half of it. All garments that have even the faintest connection to red are heaped on the bed. The Hairy Dolly has Mummy's octopus-pink silk French knickers tucked into its purple shirt pocket, as a hankie. It's painting its own toes. Badly.

"Bryan? Is that shirt ensemble really the best you can do? What about these harem pants? Admittedly they might drown you but they are truly scarlet and so festive." Mummy. Holding them up for consideration.

"Not even for you, Beth. This not a potent enough symbol of my empathetic commitment for you?" Hairy Dolly. Sliding its pants hankie from its pocket and giving it a sniff before tucking it back and trying again with the left big toe. All hairy elbows. It's knocked over Mummy's stack of Elizabeth David's that she puts her Wee Willy Winky candle up top of.

"Humph. Eric, my sweet? Please take that off and try this." Mummy. Offering Daddy's Liberty-print burnt orange shirt. What will Daddy wear? Eric has his shirt off. Laura's arriving, head coming through the trap door and stopping to stare. Hairy Dolly's pausing mid-paint. All taking in the chest of the resident ogre. Fe fi fo fum. Daddy's shirt won't do up over Eric's huge whiteness.

"Just sling a handful of these around your neck and I think that'll do. Laura? What d'you reckon?" Mummy. Handing over heaps of love beads to Eric. He's draping.

"Sure, Beth, whatever, guess you don't have to alter the beard, what with it already being so red." Laura. Clambering in. Eric's passing her and leaving.

"Mind your toe nails on the way down, they aren't dry yet." Mummy. To the top of Eric's head.

"Look who I've found." Laura. Presenting Star in her red mohair jumper with the silver wire stars that Mummy knitted. 'I'm reclaiming all the ancient crafts.' Mummy. She'd moved onto macrame by the time it was your turn for a mohair jumper. Star looks warm.

"Great. See if you can make these fit." Mummy. Passing Star her red silk PJ trousers. Star will make those fit, no question. She's had her beady eye on those since Daddy first gave them to Mummy.

You've already caught Star trying them on four times. Star's in them and wrapping them around herself with red wool holding them up at the waist. "Bryan, do Star's nails will you?" Mummy. Star's plonking her hot and silky self down beside the Hairy Dolly. Watching it trying to do its own nails, claiming the brush and taking over.

"So hey, all you Lay-Dees, what colour would you say this is? This particoolar rouge? Crimson?" The Hairy Dolly. Lying back to get comfy as Star sets to work. Watch out for that toe hair, Star.

"Blood-red. That's the point. It's a sanitised reminder – we bleed, we breed – that's why men are such boys about red nails." Mummy. Tossing her puce clothes heap hither and thither.

"Not cherry-red then?" The Hairy Dolly. Impossible not to glance at it. You are. Was that a wink?

"Here it is, come here my Womanly Woman and try this." Mummy. To you. It's her red silk bomber jacket with the paisley sleeves. On. This beats even the PJ trews. "Red enough and such a good fit. You look very sexy, darling." Mummy. Undoing the zip right down to between your breasts. If you had any. How does it feel to have your Mummy looking so hard at you?

"Beth, for Christ's sake, you can't say that. She's a child." Laura. Picking up Mummy's wrap around dress and doing your zip back up. A notch.

"Ah but she's not and I just did say it because she does and the sooner she learns to take control of the effect she makes, the better. It's basic economics. Fundamental currency. Not sure that'll reach darling but do try." Mummy. About the wrap-dress and re-un-zipping. Mummy's in her pants putting on her denim mini. The one she dyed with the tea towels. "Do you think this'll work for me? Really can't face the thought of suffocating myself in cloth in this endless heat-wave we're enduring." Showing the attic the skirt.

"You look beautiful, Mummy." You.

"Thank you, my darling, I need to make sure you don't get all the attention now you're such a rampantly sexy miss. This is the only top I've got left that's even remotely red, since you swiped the jacket." Mummy. Adding her tight burgundy vest up top.

"Right. Dressed. I'm gonna skip the nails, thank you, I hate the feeling. And the look, actually." You. "Come with me. I have something for you." Laura. In Mummy's wrap-around dress. To you. But stopping to lift Mummy's face and kiss her. Lucky Mummy. Laura's lips feel like the underneath of crumpets. Un-cooked.

Bathroom.

"Ok. Do you know what these are?" Laura.

"Mummy's cotton wool." You. Taking the packet.

"Lil-lets. They're sanitary protection. Stops the blood going everywhere. You can use pads but it's like walking around with a nappy on. Persist with these; it's the only way. Ok. Wet the tip with spit, push it in, if it's hard to get in, bear down, kinda like you do when you're pooping. Push them up but make sure you're guiding them back a bit too. If it's real tricky, get a mirror. Have a good look down there, if you haven't already." Laura. Smiling. Why haven't you thought to have a good look down there? "Make her your best friend. And, Sweetie? Never use Tampax. They come in a cardboard tube that's sharp and jagged, it can cut you inside. Women who are freaked by touching their own cunts need help, they need pity. Don't be one of those gals. Put a chair under the door handle, it works. Here you go, have a practice." Entirely sticking with Lil-lets. And door-chairs.

Mummy and Daddy's attic.

The Hairy Dolly and Star have gone. It's just Mummy doing her Kohl. Extra thick black lines inside and outside her eyes. She's smoking and she's doing her beauty by candle light. The candle goes back for a hundred years reflected in the densely speckled mirror. Ghostly.

"Hello. You need some?" Mummy. Waving the Kohl wand. Most certainly you do. You're on her little stool quicker than she could say eyeliner.

"What did Laura want? Don't blink. Keep your eyes open. I know it feels weird but you have to get used to it and actually whilst I'm here I'm going to sort these bushes out."

"Owowow. Stop it, what is that? Ow, you're scalding me." Jumping away from her.

"Don't be silly darling, it's just tweezers. You have horribly overgrown eyebrows, they need doing. It gets easier as the skin thickens. Sit still." It's like being bitten by hundreds of famished ants. The ants or the massive Lil-let jabbing away like a badly parked submarine inside your fanny, which is worse?

"Finally. You've been gone hours, I was just starting to picture the Saab wrapped around a tree, but you know what? We've been alright. Haven't we had a wonderful time darling?" Mummy. Putting her face up to be kissed by Daddy, who has arrived. Where has he been? Why didn't you know he'd gone? Mummy hasn't even once said anything.

"As predicted. Who've you been captivating to keep you company? Whoever it was is a lucky fucker, you look exquisitely gamine." Daddy. Putting a tiny box down in front of Mummy. Gamine is the only really beautiful way to look. Means you're a woman but you don't look like one. You look like a boy. William Shakespeare thought of it first. 'All those legitimately fuckable boys. He must have gone to private school.' Daddy. To Rod at the – Shakespeare, A Relationship With Women? – workshop. 'Not really.' Laura. At the end of the workshop, when it was open for discussion.

"Oh. Anthony, for me? La Luna. Do it up will you?" Mummy. She's taken a beaten-silver crescent-moon necklace from the box and is holding it round her neck. "I adore the symbolism almost as much as the lovely thing itself." Mummy. Daddy's got his eyes closed with his face in her neck hair, having done it up.

"It isn't every day your daughter turns woman." Daddy. Doesn't seem that interested in the real-live daughter-woman. Interested in Mummy's neck. Mummy's fondling her lady-moon. How come you didn't get one? It is you that's just become a woman. Oh. Look.

"These are for you." Daddy. Holding out a Jean Junction bag. Jean Junction's a tiny shop on the corner of St Stephen's which is the best street for shopping in Norwich. Jean Junction only sells jeans. You're reaching in. Hear that scrunchy crunching? Feel the tissue slipping off new jeans? Look at them leaving their bag. And yes, they are red. Loose, already soft, perfect red jeans that did not come from a jumble sale. Will you ever own a better pair of trousers? Unlikely. You've got your filthy old sticky jeans off and these glorious trews on. Daddy has swung away from you.

"Adorable. Such a Gent. She does look different doesn't she? Sleeker." Mummy. To Daddy. Noticing his spikishness but liking it.

"Thank you very much, Daddy."

"I have a name. It was your Mother's idea." Daddy. You're sticking your arms out to hug him thank you. Why are you waiting? Just hug him. You are. Daddy isn't hugging back. He's got his arms to his sides. You're stepping away and now his arms are going up but you've moved. Must have been odd timing.

"Yes. Sorry, Anthony. Thanks then, both of you." To Daddy and Mummy who are peering at you in the candlelight. Do they like what they see?

The whore house in fairy land.

"And I was dying there of thirst

So I came in here

And your long-time curse hurts

But what's worse

Is this pain in here" Dylan. Loud.

"Ain't it always the way? The man's pain is worse than her long time curse." Laura. Opening the red – as predicted – wine and waving the bottle at Mummy. "Beth? You gonna make a toast to our warrior-gal? Something about our vow to create a world where her woman's body ain't gotta price?" Pouring. "Hey there, panda eyes. Ok?" To you. Is she asking about the submarine? She can't expect you to tell for heaven's sake.

"Darling Romantic Laura, have you been at the Erica Jong-bong, again?" Mummy. Taking the wine and doing a silent cheers your way. Then glugging.

Tammie's removing the candle wraps, scrunching up the crepe, making nests for the bottles instead. Good job as the candle flames are all leaning hard, away from the breeze. The windows on the front wall are open. You were right, that air's smudging the faintest whiff of autumn into the room. All Your People are in the Big Room. All Your People are looking at you. Some of them a bit sideways, admittedly, but none the less you're being closely observed. Do they expect you to start doing tricks? Yodelling? An 'I have my period' Jig?

"Please don't let on that you knew me when
I was hungry and it was your world
Ah, you fake just like a woman, yes you do
You make love just like a woman, yes you do
Then you ache just like a woman
But you break just like a little girl." Dylan. Finishing up. Your people still most fascinated by your new-found status. Good. Possibly captivated by how appropriate the music was for you?

"Menstruation munchies, people?" The Hairy Dolly. To the whole room and doing an unlikely herding of everyone towards the Big Red Table.

"You're particularly childish and irritating tonight." Mummy. Stroking its hair.

"I'm mortified for your daughter. Is all." Taking Mummy's stroking hand, opening it, kissing the palm, looking at you. Mummy's taking her hand away wiping off the kiss. All very friendly. That Hairy Dolly knows you have a bloody fanny.

Daddy's borrowing the Hairy Dolly's hankie to mop his brow on the way to putting on his new favourite music. And then pocketing it. Nina Simone. Forbidden Fruit. He always starts with this track then goes back to the beginning and plays all the tracks. Daddy and Star are doing their tap dance to the clickety-clack bit. Daddy's lifting the figs, offering them round, Star tippety-tapping behind.

"Go on and eat.
It's mighty sweet
Go on and taste it
You don't want to waste it." Nina and Daddy. Pushing the figs at Rod.

"Vul-Vic." Rod.

“I rather think that is the point, old boy.” Daddy. In a funny posh voice.

People have stopped looking at you. Completely. Is this better? Hard to know what to do with one’s body positions now one is a woman. Try just sitting with Laura and Pretty Justin?

“I am genuinely surprised that Rod picked up on that visual clue.” Laura. To Pretty Justin as you’re attempting your joining-in with them. Maybe don’t sit down? Don’t want them to stop talking. You’re doing some good back-of-chair lean-stretching. Quite womanly. Daddy and Rod are gobbling down figs.

“Go ahead and bite it

I bet you’ll be delighted.” Nina.

“Has Rod ever gone down on anyone? A question for the group.” Laura. But it’s not for the group, just Pretty Justin. And certainly not intended for the delicate ears of that newly hatched woman stretching away over there.

‘I’ve a suspicion Rod’s dick’s kinda like a Christmas tangerine, still wrapped in its tissue-paper jacket. Untouched, hopeful.” Laura. Whisper, whisper. Pretty Justin’s squeezing himself with giggles. Stop the stretching, you look silly. Do some cushion lounging. See if you can get to the figs before Rod scoffs them all.

“I hate to tell you what followed the Lord was most upset

Saw them making love and hollered what have you two ate?” Nina.

“Lawrence will never be bettered. Grunt Puff” Rod.

“Hey Oup. Our Rod is aboot to take tut floor.” Mummy. Secret-talking to Daddy. Your People are all world experts at secret-talking in a full room.

“The fig is a very secretive fruit.

As you see it growing, you feel

at once it is symbolic: And it seems male.

But when you come to know it better, you agree with the Romans,

It is female." Rod. Did he hear Mummy?

"Rod? You become even more deliciously northern when you quote. Did you know?" Mummy. This is one of the main techniques to perfect when attempting secret-talking in full rooms. Say the funny secret thing to the person who needs to hear it then, in next breath, say a kind version of the funny thing to the victim.

"Lawrence may never be bettered on figs but, oh boy, did he have a distance to travel on women." Laura. Calling across the room.

"Did he need the 'very'? Wouldn't 'secretive' alone have swung it?" Daddy. Doing some half-dancing with Star and smiling all round. What to do, what to do, what to do, with all your lady limbs? Has The Hairy Dolly noticed you're wearing make-up? Do not look at it. Damn. Why did you look at it? Think it might have noticed. It was looking at you.

Rod's galvanized, hunching up and forwards, arms on knees, ready for the real party to start. The Talking About Poems Party. Is Eric even listening? He's reading, drinking wine and ignoring the figs. Tammie's cross-legged and of course not drinking and not smoking and certainly not eating. She's staring out the window.

"Go ahead and bite it

I bet you'll be delighted.

You all went and did it now your gonna get it.

Forbidden fruit." Nina. Done.

"Just put your mouth to the crack." Hairy Dolly. That English voice it does when it's quoting poetry. With its mouth full. Giggling. "Eric, man? Mouth to the crack?" Thank you Hairy Dolly for making such an effort to get everyone talking.

"How stoned are you, Bryan?" Rod. He can get angry with The Dolly so quickly.

"Weeell, Rodney... I am half as stoned as I will be in one hour. Ok?" Hairy Dolly.

Daddy's changing the music. Not back to the beginning of Nina Simone, but to 'I Love To Love'. Great. Dancing time. Did Eric hear The Dolly?

"This fucking song will never get out of my head now. Can't we have something serious?" Hairy Dolly to Daddy. The Dolly has serious musical taste, it's even interested in Folk, in a mild way.

"No, Bryan. We cannot. We can all have a jolly dance to this, then we can eat some of the Sani-pad bread and then, possibly, we can get an early night. Ok?" Daddy. Why's he sounding so mean? Hang on a second. What the hell's going on here? Star's stopped dancing and is hair-pulling. Pretty Justin's got his head in his hands. Laura's got her hand on Mummy's arm. Tammie's staring out of the window. Good to know there are some constants in this crazy world.

"I'm taking Star to bed. Thank you, no really thank you, all, for ruining my daughter's remarkable day. If you want to stay up with these people a little longer, you may but do not push your luck." Mummy. What? Who said what? And should think so too about the womanly bedtime hour.

"Eric?" Mummy.

Big door-slam and off upstairs they go. Eric's on his feet.

"Oh no you don't, Tiger." Daddy. Is this all about the fig poem? Poets can be very angry but really? And the Hairy Dolly isn't a poet. And, is the remarkable day ruined? That bread looks tasty.

"My wife's menstruating too, didn't she warn you all?" Daddy. Bit to Eric but mainly to everyone. Really do wish people would stop going on about it. It isn't your fault you are a woman and Daddy had to spend £12.99 on new jeans.

"But my baby just loves to dance."

But no one is. Fine. Food time. Healthy portion of soup, cold now, chips and bread. Sani Pad? Come on everyone, don't they see that your sitting and eating is an invitation to join in? The marbled crust is sticking in your throat. Plough on.

"She loves to dance, she loves to dance just loves to dance."

Pretty Justin's coming to you, putting a titchy bit of soup in his bowl. Wish you had too.

"Mmmm. Yeah?" Pretty Justin. Drinking from the bowl.

Hairy Dolly's sitting on your other side. No looking at each other but this is good. This is a Dinner Party. Tammie's floating over, sitting at the far end of the table. Whole table paused. Will she eat? No she won't. Whole table resuming mild munching. Eric's still where he stood. Doing some big thinking, although it won't be deep.

"Rodney, would you be so kind as to pass me my stash, please? It's on yonder chair." Hairy Dolly. Leaning back in its chair, gesturing to the empty chair next to Rod's.

"My name is Rod." Rod. Passing the stash. Ha. Hairy Dolly is the winner.

"What? Your mother in her quaint Britisher way gave you half a name? Had she no thought to the solemnity of your future?" Hairy Dolly. Burning the end of its dope.

That stinks, worse than burnt sage. Might dying feel like nostrils full of hash smoke? Hope not, there's enough to fret about with the period that everyone's obsessed with without adding death to one's expanding list. The crisps are delicious.

"Provocative. Nasty music, man." Hairy Dolly. To Daddy, who has swapped the track to 'Dancing Queen', but not aimed at him so Daddy can ignore it if he wants to.

He does. Daddy's doing some lovely moves over to Laura. Invitation to dance? Laura's standing up very slowly. Laura has a candle lighting her up from behind, she looks like that picture of earth taken from the moon.

"Grrrruuuuunnt puuuuuf." Rod. Goat on chain variety of grunt. Laura's re-tying Mummy's dress she borrowed. Daddy's swaying in front of her, doing a bit of a silly smile. Frankly. Arms out, fingers tickling her air to get her moving. She is but she isn't dancing with Daddy. She's making him have to follow her around. Which he is. A bit. Everyone else is watching Planet Laura. Hairy Dolly's pushing back on its chair so far it might topple backwards, sucking in clouds of hash smoke, passing the joint to Pretty Justin. Pretty Justin's not seeing Laura because he's gazing and gazing at the Hairy Dolly. The Dolly's reaching over taking Pretty Justin's hand, like he did to Mummy's, opening it and kissing the palm. Pretty Justin's holding smoke in his lungs, his eyes are filled with tears. That crying is not hash-based.

"It's like, just, like, oh man." Pretty Justin. Sad whispering and floor staring

"Pretty Justin is in love with me. Should I sleep with him?" Hairy Dolly. Normal whispering, in your ear. Did no one hear that? Not even Pretty Justin? No, still crying at the floor.

That feeling is all your blood pushing up to the top of your skin and making you blush all over. Has even your fanny blood, what there is of it, been diverted for this new blood purpose? You're aching with blushing. You match your own party.

How could you have been so childish? Sleep with him means sex. You understand about sex, you have known about sex all your life. We have no secrets. Of course you know it's for making babies and love and everything and you do also know it's something that sometimes happens because adults are complex and have complex needs and you will understand fully when you're an adult but why did you not hear them when they said 'sleep with' over and over? They have tricked you. How violently do you wish this party was not happening, that you'd stopped it, said no? You are a woman. You are. But this fucking party's just a pretend of it. How dare they not have realised what you actually are? How dare they have tricked you?

'Nearly 13? What'd ya recon? Him There?" Hairy Dolly. That Hairy Dolly thinks this party's wrong too, doesn't it?

Tammie, Eric, Rod, even Pretty Justin now, are watching Laura and Daddy dancing in their own bits of the party. That Hairy Dolly isn't moving from your ear. You're stretching out for the crisps, it's pulling them to nestle between you. You are sharing. It's stoned and hungry, you're hungry. Handful and in. Handful and in. Handful and in. Dolly's waiting for its answer. Munch, munch, munch you both go. Stare, stare, staring at the Big Room. Eric's moving. Looks like he's done with the party too, heading upstairs.

"Just this once and then you're done. Get it?" Daddy. Eric is silent. And big. He's nodding a kind of yes. Eric is sleeping with Mummy.

That wet smell. Pansies.

And, of course, Mummy has slept with the Hairy Dolly before him. Hasn't she?

"Eric?" Tammie. Not squeaking. Calling. "Eric? Could we talk?" Is this the first time she's ever spoken to him?

Eric looks dazed. Look at Your People. They all look dazed.

"Good girl, Tams." Laura. She means the squeaking up.

Are you having a panic attack? Your heart is fluttering. Not like one of Mummy's panic attacks, which are all pinching your arm, spitting in hankies, breathing in terrifying spikey jags and begging you to find Daddy. Your heart is jumping around but you're moving smoothly, taking hold, with your small cochineal-stained fingers, of the Hairy Dolly's chin and turning its face to you. Your eyes look exactly like Liza Minnelli in Cabaret. Cabaret is the only film you and Star have seen and having seen it there is no need to ever see another. It is perfect.

"No. I think you should sleep with me." You. Big eyed Liza stare at it and back to your feast. Let it wonder if that ever happened. You're getting good at this.

Nothing's changing in the Big Room. Nothing in that room will change for weeks. Those rose branches will still be hanging there in December. Crinkled and twisted with most of the leaves and all of the petals gone. But still there. Music's done. Another handful of crisps, in. The Hairy Dolly's up, racing Daddy to the record stack, Laura's laughing at them. Daddy and the Hairy Dolly are playing at a fight. Another bowl of cold soup, in. Daddy's pretending to be some kind of snarly cat, Hairy Dolly's beating its chest like a Gorilla. They're having fun. Tammie's standing, brushing down her faded pink denim pinafore dress, gliding over to the upstairs door, Eric's following. An ox and a kitten. He has to duck his head to get out of the door. Don't get your horns stuck, Oxy. Bread. Still warm. Pretty Justin's lighting the joint he and Laura rolled, going to her and sharing it, they're swinging their held hands. Rod's on his feet. He isn't going to dance is he? Phew. Just trying to join in with the hand swinging.

"So sorry, Rod, but we don't want you on our team. Try the other lot." Laura. Would that be Public Talking? Saying the whispered thing entirely to its victim.

Pretty Justin's flicking you a look that might be saying – but we want you, if you want us? Doesn't actually say it though. Rod's over by the music animals looking very seriously through the LPs. It's possible to eat two slices of this bread as if they were one. That was not a panic attack. Your mouth's vivid with cochineal stains. Looks like you slaughtered something with only your teeth. Crisps gone. Just those last few salt-dust crumbs to get up. Lick a puce finger then press down. The bowl is shining. You're nipping out to the pottery. Smells extra strong tonight. Does menstruation heighten all one's senses? You're opening the chest freezer. It's long enough to keep a dog carcass in when no one can bear to bury it for days. But there's no dog today. Well there is but today she's just asleep in her basket. You've the roof of the freezer balanced open against your head and you're reaching the water ice out. You have the tub and you're letting the roof smack down as you walk back, prizing off the lid, stopping for a handful of spoons. Back at the table, waving spoons. No one's seen. Good. Tuck in. Jessie's sloped up to rest her drippy muzzle on your thigh.

"Achoooo." Jessie. Shame you can't train her to use a hankie.

Scoop in the crystallized ice. Hold it in your mouth. Let it float down your throat. Again. Again. Daddy and the Hairy Dolly have agreed on 'Space Oddity' by David Bowie.

"A one off from a true original." Hairy Dolly.

"Like your good self?" Daddy.

Daddy and the Hairy Dolly are floating around their pretend spaceship and the Hairy Dolly's opened the upstairs door.

"And the papers want to know." Hairy Dolly and Daddy. Singing very loud up the stair-well.

"Whose shirts you wear?" Hairy Dolly and Daddy. Are they both stoned? They're finding that ever so funny.

Another chunk of water ice. They're floating in their tin can again. Oh, right, now everyone's floating in tin cans. Apart from you.

"Achoooo." Jessie. Will dog snot mark and wreck the red jeans? That would be a shame.

"It's time to leave the capsule if you dare." Daddy and Hairy Dolly. To each other.

"Tell my wife I love her very much." Daddy. To the ceiling.

"She knows." Hairy Dolly. To itself.

Daddy's stopped dancing. He's standing in the middle watching the others. But not you. His tight, slightly curved-in, chest is rising and falling. He's brushing his long, thin, brown hair away from his face. Daddy is horribly sad. Will Daddy die from love? Spoon going in. Bugger. Spoon's hit the plastic box. That's that then. Bed time. Of course your Daddy isn't turning to watch you or wish you sleep tight. You're not turning back. Up you go. No ghosts tonight. Jessie's pushing past and coming with you. It's too smoky for dogs in the Big Room. Time to get this gigantic achey lump of cotton wool, out.

Bedroom.

Asleep. In your blue bed. Jessie's draped like an old coat over your chest and one baby's hand is on her ear. Star's in her red bed with the sheet kicked off and her nightie twisted up around her tummy. Softest whistle of children's breath. Look. The door's opening and the Hairy Dolly's in the room.

"What? What? What's happened? Where's my Daddy? Is Daddy

alright? What's happened?" This is panic. There's toothpaste in the corners of your mouth.

"Sorry. Nothing. It's cool. Sorry. Wrong room. Sorry. He's downstairs. It's all cool." Hairy Dolly. Fleeing your room. Closing the door softly. The music downstairs has changed again, it's Elgar now. Your absolute favourite. Elgar's cello concerto in D Minor played by Paul Tortellier. 'So much grief in waiting.' Daddy. To Mummy when he first played it. Daddy and Rod must be discussing Englishness. Daddy's still alive.

Clambering over, tugging Star's nightie back down for her. The Hairy Dolly saw her like that. And she looks un-comfy.

"Leave me alone." Star. Hitting your hands away in her sleep. Hasn't forgotten how to do it then.

Would it be safer for her if you got in with her? Sleep with her? Door chair? Wouldn't it be so nice if Mummy or Daddy came in now and fed you a bowl of Flum Flum? Like they do when you're starting to get better from being really ill. Or really, like they used to do, because think about it – no one has eaten Flum Flum in this house for at least two years.

FLUM FLUM

1 large tablespoon cornflour per person. Beauty of Flum Flum's that it's only made for one person at a time. Because there's usually only one person ill enough at a time.
Milk
Cochineal. Important. Flum Flum must be pink.

Heat milk, when warm take spoonful to mix with cornflour, then all milk in and stir until no lumps. Back into saucepan, drop cochineal, stir on Aga until custardy thick. As it begins to boil the bubbles go Flum Flum Flum.

If you've been really ill, Mummy pours a whispy curl of golden syrup up top, to serve. Wonderful forbidden syrup. Processed food.

'Flum Flum has miraculous healing powers.' Mummy.

CHAPTER SIX

Morning. Late. That's people talking downstairs. Good, up you get. Oh yuck. You've been sleeping in warm tight pants stuffed with paper. Submarine was too painful but had to have some security hence the stuffed pants. Checking for leaks but there's absolutely nothing there, apart from a whole copy of the Eastern Daily Press. Totally clean. Good. Farewell hideous nappy. Going to have to give protection some serious consideration. How much dough's needed to procure protection? Where's it procured from? Will it involve period chat? Will ten pence, on random Saturdays, cover it? You need a fucking job lady. Is the EDP laughing at you?

Down to breakfast in the ice-cream T-shirt and, yes, the new red jeans. Just put them on. If you don't wear them today you never will again and they're too good to waste. Brave it out. And, if there's a flash-flood it might be hidden by the jeans? How much blood is normal? Now you know how the poor mice feel. Leak, leak, leakity leak.

The Big Room. Mummy's washing-up, Laura's writing in her big scrap book. This is very good. It's so nice when the sink's empty.

"Where is everyone?" You. Meaning, where is that Hairy Dolly?

"Fuck knows." Mummy. Still in her bad mood. "Oh, Darling?"

Remembering and cheering right up. "How are you feeling? Is your tummy aching terribly? God, mine's a nightmare."

"Fine."

"It's ok to tell. It's all women here." Why didn't she go the all women route yesterday?

"I'm fine."

"But so menstrual. There's no need to be sulky. It's hard for us all. The sooner you learn to control your moods the better, for the whole house."

"I am fine. I have no more blood. I told you there wasn't very much. It might not even have been a period."

"I saw it. Of course it was."

"We scared it off." Laura. Laughing.

"Where is everyone?" You.

"Star's in the garden preparing for her life as a paraplegic. Daddy's at work. Bryan's fucked off somewhere. Justin's finally getting that pot-ash glaze mixed. Eric's watering the vegetables and Tammie's in her room staring at her navel. I assume. Ok? Everyone where you need them?" Mummy. Daddy at work explains the snappishness. Does Mummy know Laura's looking after her? Mummy's turned her back on you and is flying through the last of the washing-up. Good. No Hairy Dolly.

"Fucked off where?" You.

"Somewhere. How should I know?" Mummy.

"Kindergarten. Hopefully." Laura. Mummy's snickering.

Laura has a handful of blackberries, she's half squashing them then adding them to some oats, raisins, grated apple, soft brown sugar and condensed milk. She's pulling out a chair at the table, sweeping a gap in the rubbish, gathering greasy red crepe paper squashing it into a huge ball, lobbing the ball in the general direction of the fireplace wall, nodding at you to sit and putting a spoon into your hand.

"There you go, Little Lady." Laura. You need no second invitations. My goodness this is a magnificent breakfast. Let this goodness fill you right up. Star's coming in followed by Great Uncle Elizabeth, Jessie and a random hen. Laura's making the same mash for her.

"There you go, Littler Lady." Laura. You're both simply gobbling this new loveliness down.

"There's far too much sugar in that, Laura. You can tell by the silence." Mummy.

"Yes. But they are eating some breakfast. Want some?" Laura.

Isn't it interesting to be watched and fed in this way? Both of them leaning against the Aga, dipping their teaspoons into the concoction, considering you. Your eyes look like a joke of a coal man, still rimmed with black make-up smudges.

Today's a day you and Star always have a plan for, which is another reason it's useful the Hairy Dolly has evaporated. Breakfast finished.

"Hel-lo. Wash those up please." Laura. Resuming her scribbling as you're about to leave the room. You and Star are busy being enchanted by this new bossy version of Laura. You will happily wash up your bowls for it, so you are. Mummy's raising one eyebrow at you. This is a trick you and Star have worked and worked to master. Raising one eyebrow can be so useful. You can laugh at someone, without them knowing, by doing it. You can use it for questioning and you can use it to show you're in a secret club. The time Mummy used it best was the bad birthday. Daddy and her had been arguing and arguing for two whole days. Just argue then silence, argue then silence, on and on.

Then it was your birthday and they had forgotten. You waited until lunchtime to remind them which took impressive levels of self control for a person who was nine only that morning but it would have been unacceptable for the whole day to go without drawing their attention to it. You hadn't done birthday chatting for days because obviously there was going to be a surprise but by lunchtime there hadn't been a single unsubtle clue dropped and you knew it had been forgotten. They'd have felt terrible if you hadn't helped them remember, so you did. Mummy screeched to a halt mid-arguing and raised one eyebrow. This told you to follow her to the White Saab. 'Come on my darling girls we're having a secret party.' Mummy. Checking and checking her seat belt. Obviously she'd forgotten but she was doing first-class pretending so you joined in. She eventually got the White Saab started and drove you to the party. You all had a glass, a real glass, of Babycham (two little bottles between you) with a maraschino cherry each. You then shared a whole packet of Squashed Fly biscuits. None of you could resist so you finished the jar of cherries with sips of their juice then, and from nowhere, Mummy wound down the car window. 'Listen. Shhh. Do you hear? Shhh. Listen.' She leant her head against the steering wheel and cried. Then stopped. 'But do you hear it?' Neither you nor Star knew what 'it' was. Although you were both trying, very hard, to hear something. 'Never mind.' She wound the window back up and started the White Saab. The last of the cherry juice slopped onto Star who then spent the journey back sucking it out of her top. Star might have been drunk. Soon as you got back to Swallow's Farmhouse Mummy swerved down the drive, left the engine running and you and Star to get yourselves out and follow her. Which you did. Mummy ran straight up to Daddy and chucked herself into his cuddle. 'Brave girl. Brave girl. Brave girl. How far did you go? Brave girl.' Daddy. 'Just to the lay-by.' You. No one heard. 'Oh, Anthony. There was a curlew.' Mummy. They both started crying and Daddy was kissing her eyes. Then Daddy held one arm out and you and Star joined in. The White Saab was still humming away on the drive. This was just before Your People shared the house. No present that day, had to wait a week before anyone could face a trip to Norwich and then it was books which are fine but are not ideal for birthdays. You did, however, manage to strike a bargain. Four pony books and you only had to read *The Hobbit* in exchange. What is it about grown-ups and fucking Hobbits? Terribly dreary creatures. Bad birthday.

Bowls washed. Out back you go. In no time it'll be bonfire night. Bonfire night's the best night of the year. Better than Christmas and birthdays. Bad birthday anyone? Bonfire night's always better than a Solstice Happening. It's better because there are fireworks and a bonfire as big as you and Star want to make it. Very big indeed.

'It's remarkable she's a water sign. You'd think, with her addiction to pyrotechnics, she'd be a fire sign. She must have Leo in the ascendant.' Mummy. Last year, about you and fire. 'If the kids insist on this crazy festival they have to earn the money for the fireworks.' Daddy. The year before that. This year you've had a masterstroke idea. 'Mistress-stroke surely?' Hairy Dolly. Weeks ago, when you shared the plan. 'We all want one of those.' Rod. The laughing at Hairy Dolly's joke had stopped by the time Rod thought of his but people still laughed. Here's the plan. You'll dress Star up as a Guy, put her on the go-cart and drag her around the village doing Penny For The Guy.

Back garden beside Prune's shed. You've got an ancient man's suit saved from the village school jumble. Stinker. Must've been a pig farmer. Must also have been as small as one of his piggies as the suit's nearly a fit. Brave to have gone to the jumble because whenever the village kids see you they race after you yelping on about how you're 'Gypos' and 'Scum Bags', droning on about fleas and 'too poor for shoes?' You've tried to explain about shoes and posture but why waste your breath? Anyway, you did the jumble, got the suit and some black shoes that have definitely been prized off a corpse. The toes are curled right up and cracked. That's what happens when rigor mortis sets in. Dead man's shoes for sure. All this gear came to 60p so that'll have to be skimmed off profits and given back to Daddy. Star's struggling into the suit. You've given her your ice-cream T-shirt inside out to go under and look like a vest. She's got the turned-up toes shoes on. Impossible to walk in them so she's shuffling to the go-cart and flumping on.

"Watch it." You. That go-cart isn't one of your best. Pram wheels and three layers of cardboard-box base which you got Star to sew on with binder twine. It'll probably hold. If Star sticks with the keeping-still plan.

"It'll be easier to stuff you if you stay put." You. Getting going on stuffing straw round her neck, poking it out of the sleeves and the bottom of the trews. A Scarecrow Guy.

Needs to look like her stuffing's exploding. Look at that, that is some skilful stuffing. Right, make-up. You've a lot of white eye shadow and a lot of black mascara which you're mixing up. What would you call this colour? Ashen grey? Get that smeared all over her face. She looks very ill indeed. Excellent. Now get scribbling. Needs lines. Done. Crag-gy. You've got a massive floppy felt hat from Mummy. Once, Mummy and Daddy had a friend who was a photographer and he took pictures of Mummy in hats and they went in Vogue. She was paid in hats. This is one of them. 'You may as well have it. It's far too larky for my life now.' Mummy. Kissing the hat bye, bye. Real kiss.

Great. Looks perfect on Star, covers most of her face so the make-up that's visible looks real. Now you've got the scissors and are snipping a few choice holes in the suit and hat, to stuff selected strands of leaky straw out of. Look at that. Star looks exactly like the shrivelled dwarf who begs on Norwich market. Apart from the Scarecrow straw. The dwarf doesn't have that. He doesn't need it. Star does and it's the finishing touch.

"Right. Do not move a muscle when we get up to the front doors. Don't even blink." You. Real money time.

You've harnessed yourself to the go-cart and are off to start at the far end of the village where the new people from Sweden have moved in. People think they might be going to dig a swimming pool. This means you'll be able to inspire them about Penny For The Guy and how much money English people usually give. Vast acres, obviously. Bloody hell their drive is long and pebbly. Star's attempting a clamber-off to make it easier.

"No. Stay. They've millions of windows, they might see us. I can do it." You. Can you? It's not you that's been in training for the Olympics.

Star's wobbling back on, one curly shoe falling off. Stop and shove it back and get all the straw into its right place. Off you go. Shoe about to go again but look, the big blue front door's opening and a very tall lady's coming to meet you. Uh oh. Is she going to shoo you off?

"Hello. I saw you coming. What is this?" Her hair's so blond it's actually white and her eyes are like a blind cat's. The weakest blue. Is she blind? Can't be, she saw you coming.

"Penny for the Guy, please?" You.

"Oh yes. Of course. Very good. Very good Guy. Wait here. I'll get some money. I was sunbathing." The blind lady. Sunbathing would explain the glittering extra-long shawl she has wrapped around her. Like a towel. And the redness of her skin.

"She knows about Penny For The Guy." You. Sharing profound disappointment. Whilst you're waiting. It took at least twenty minutes to get even halfway up her silly drive and she's clearly completely up to date with currency and everything Guyish. Damn. She's back. In a dress now. Pink. A Prawn.

"So how much is usual?" The Prawn. All may not be lost. Nice smile and look at how her pussy-cat eyes stay with yours. She isn't shy, she might be trying to teach you something. Or laughing at you. But don't think so. Most likely she just thinks this is the best Guy she's ever seen. Which it will be.

"As much as you think it's worth. We're going to have a massive fireworks party. You can come if you like." You. Look at Star, she's so surprised she's stopped holding still and has turned to look at you. Bugger. That blows the cash. Again.

"I think this is easily worth... um... one pound." The Prawn. This is remarkable. No one has ever given you one whole pound for anything. Ever. Look at Star, she's grinning like the village idiot. Like the real village idiot. He's called Nigel, he's forty-six but he looks about fifteen and he bikes around the village all day on his Chopper (why him?) which he's attached at least ten wing mirrors to. Grinning. Who does he think is following him?

"One pound, each." The Prawn. Might you faint?

"It's best when you don't smile. I think. More scary and threatening. People will give more if they're a little bit worried by you. Don't you think?" This Prawn is clever. Star's no fool either. Not smiling now. Or moving.

"Thank you very much indeed. Do you want to come to our party?

We live at Swallow's Farmhouse." You know she'll know what that means and she does.

"Yes, I thought so. Thank you. I've friends staying that night but maybe we'll drop by." That seems to be that so you're turning the go-cart. No mean feat on her gravel marsh land and off you go. Look at her. She's not going back to her house, she's just watching and now calling.

"Good luck. I hope you make your fortunes. You deserve to." Clever and wise Prawnie. You don't turn but you are waving back and Star too can't resist one big wave.

"Like the snow queen from Narnia. That hair. Did you see the dress? I like that kind of pink. Prawnie Pink. I think she'll definitely turn up." You. See how thoughtful you both are?

Galvanized by her approval you're positively flying through the village and the generosity's caught on. The woman at the top farm whose husband hits her and whose husband might actually also be her brother gives you 50p. Uncle Rob gives you 20p each. But he does also try to lure you in.

"A biscuit?" Uncle Rob. This is what prompts Star's cursing.

"May all your biscuits be eaten by mice." Star. Mumbling under her breath as you whizz the go-cart away. Tarmac is the preferred surface for speedy getaways. Uncle Rob doesn't seem to have heard.

This is the summit of the whole morning. More glorious even than the one pound each. Every time someone doesn't cough up, or just slams the door, Star curses them. The curses get better and better.

"May all your warts be hairy." To Ma Burt. She's the meanest person you've ever met. You only ask her so Star can curse her. She'd never give money away.

'I'm not giving anything to you lot. You owe me. I see how many sweeties you tuck inside your sleeves.' Ma Burt. Last year. 'She doesn't see or she'd stop you.' Mummy.

"All her warts are already hairy." You. Scampering off. It's downhill from Ma Burt's.

"May all your beer run dry." The pub.

"May all your dogs be cats." Bad dog farm.

"May all your kids have enormous ears." At the house where they do. She's abandoned the go-cart, only worth getting into position for likely houses.

"May all your ciggies be damp." To Apricot Lil and her chain-smoking daughter Fag Ash Lil.

"May all your budgies poo on your head." To Old Mac the farmer who lives on his own in Burgh and has a garage full of budgies. You're both hysterical. It's not at all surprising to hear Star speak. Home you go. Star with the curly shoes off and pulling you now. See?

Home. Look at that. The bloody cheek of Eric. He's done it again. That is yours and Star's roadside stall. Purloined. Piled high with sweet corn. Only it isn't sweet corn. It's fucking un-tasty, rock hard, dry corn. Eric only looked at the picture on the seed packet. Didn't bother to read maize. When will Eric learn no one wants to buy veg riddled with insects and covered in mud?

"Watch out for the bloody road holes. Sixteen pounds and twelve pence." You. The go-cart has ceased all movement. You're both still. Listening to birdsong high in the air. Might that be a curlew? It has happened. You are rich. This is going to buy so many fireworks. Even after you've paid Daddy back. The millionaires are entering the house. Shame there's only Tammie to welcome you back. She's eating an apple. Not for long. Soon as she sees you it's in the compost bucket.

"How are you feeling?" Tammie. Has your new-found wealth changed nothing? She must mean the period. Why the surprised face? Had you forgotten? You're wriggling to double check. Feels normal. No leakage.

"Fine." You.

"Eric's in the field." Tammie. Eric can be on the moon feasting on clotted cream teas with all the characters from *Apple Bough* (which was your favourite Noel Streatfield book for three years) for all you and Star care. You've your earnings to double check and then you have to get someone to drive you to the firework shop in Norwich. This'll be the toughest challenge of the whole event.

"What's wrong with the sodding bus? It's only twelve miles." Mummy. To you both when you ask if her and Daddy will take you. The bus is 20p each. Each way. No chance. And it doesn't always come all the way back to the village.

Eventually Rod, of all people, agrees. He wants to collect something from Head In The Clouds. The new, surprise, head-shop. He gives you twenty minutes, says he'll pick you up at the clock tower and don't be late or he'll just leave without you. Fine. You could hitch. You have before. But the fireworks are big. You make speedy choices. Easy. Then it's home. With the best-ever collection.

What feels like a year later, it has finally arrived. Remember, remember the fifth of November? Still no Hairy Dolly and you've settled into this now. Daddy says it'd talked about doing that retreat at Findhorn in Scotland that's supposed to be miraculous. Eric was jealous. He wanted to do that retreat. They grow veggies by the cycle of the moon and their cabbages are notorious. As big and round as a beach ball. By all accounts. Why bother? Isn't there enough cabbage, no one knows what to do with, in the world? Your People are very interested in macrobiotics. Especially because it's ok to smoke when you do macrobiotics. Someone who thought of it says 'Smoking can cause or cure cancer.' So that's good news. 'Please not macrobiotics. It's all so dreary.' Mummy. Although Daddy did try the ten-day brown rice and water fast. It didn't make him as grumpy as Rod got on his one-day orange juice fast but it did make him very thin. And sleepy. So that's that for macrobiotics at Swallow's Farmhouse. For now.

It's getting dark. You've been sitting by the window in the Big Room waiting and waiting and here it comes.

"Please can we light it now?" You. To Daddy.

"Of course. You can light it whenever you want." Daddy. This is annoying. You'd been told to wait by Mummy. She wanted a grown-up near. Unusual. Daddy's finding the matches and taking his lighter fluid, just in case. One thing's for sure, he won't be needing that.

YOURS AND STAR'S PERFECT BONFIRE

Six newspapers
Dried cow parsley stalks. Pile as big as Star. Or dried bracken.
Cow parsley's best as stalks are hollow, suck flame up selves.
Dried twigs. Really dried. Pile at least as big as you.
Dried small branches. No quants, many as you can fetch.
Dried normal branches. Same.
Old rotten fence posts. Dried. Whole field's worth. Ideally.
Old doors. Dried. At least ten.
Buckets water, in case. 'One of my very few rules.' Mummy.
Others are: limit all sugar and fat and no motor bikes.

Pile all up in order. Start small and build in teepee triangle shape as far away from house as achievable. Right at the top of the field.

On the other side to Star's den. Save the doors a little way off (so they don't catch light) to be chucked on when fire's raging. And that's it. Takes about two days to build as you've to do plenty of trips to the wood to load the go-cart with vital branches and extra bracken.

Up the field you go. You, Daddy, Star and Jessie. Look at it. A magnificent pile, heaped to the sky. It's at least as tall as a bungalow.

"Don't bring the dog for Christ's sake. Take her back and put her inside. Make sure she can't get out." Daddy. To you.

"You can't start without me. Don't start without me." You. Taking Jessie by her shiny, soft old collar and tugging her home. She's resisting. She's so self-centred, can't bear the idea something interesting will happen without her. This drag and shove's taking longer than you need.

"Come on, Jessie. For Christ's sake. Bonfire's are not for dogs." You. Jessie's laughing at you. Prune's giving Jessie a wink as you pass. You're getting her into the main room. Good, there's Eric and Tammie. She's roll pressing out the pastry for her Spicy American Apple Pie. Eric's smoking and slicing apple.

TAMMIE'S SPICED AMERICAN APPLE PIE

2 cups (hurrah) SR flour. Usual.
1 Tablespoon allspice
1 Dessert spoon cinnamon
1 Packed cup dark brown sugar. Dark brown sugar hasn't been messed about with to the same extent as white so is almost a health food.
4 oz butter
1 egg

Splosh of milk
Apples, more butter, more sugar for filling.

If you were doing an Aga tray, double up a few times.

Mix dry ingredients then rub together with butter. Normal pastry. Egg whipped up with bit of milk to bind. This is an exceptionally sticky pastry, if you try to roll you'll still have to patch into tin. Simply squash in with no holes and fill with sliced apples. Do not peel. The goodness of fruit and veg's just under skin. 'You're massacring nutrients.' Mummy. When you did try and peel. Dollop apples with butter and fair bit more sugar. Top with rest of pastry. Bake until puffed-up and crusty. Cut into chunks to eat, like cake. The Americans understand a thing or two about apple pie.

"Jessie must stay inside. You need to keep her in. And Great Uncle Elizabeth. If you see him." You.

"Please." Tammie. Where's her squeak gone? What's happening to the women in your house since you joined their ranks? They seem to be on a mission to talk to you like a child.

"Yes, of course." You. Don't give her the satisfaction. Did Eric just do a tiny little tut-tut head shake at her? Might it be time to start charging Eric rent, for the use of your stall idea?

"Whine, whine." Jessie. Begging not to be abandoned with these rude people. You're giving Jessie a final chest squeeze and big sniff of her oily fur before hurling yourself back up the field.

Daddy's waiting. He's standing with the matches held out for you. He's looking right at you.

"Apparently you're a woman these days. I guess you're old enough to light your own bonfire." Daddy. He's doing a small checked smile into his scraggy beard. He's stopped looking at you again. Right fire.

You've left a tunnel into the heart of the heap to worm your way into its centre. You're on your tummy. Star's reaching for Daddy's hand and Daddy's reaching for Star's. Do they know they're holding hands? This bonfire has been built tight, you're crouching so far inside your feet have disappeared. Long quiet bit. Go. You're striking the match. You're dipping the match down so the flaming end is pointing to the earth, the flame's growing, working its way up the match, you're guiding the match to the newspaper. It's caught. It's vital to work quickly now. Do as many touches to as much paper as you can before the match burns your finger and you flick it out of your hand. Another match and another. All the places you've touched the match to are catching. Tiny licks of flame are instantly flame-poles. It's getting smoky in the tunnel. Your eyes are scrunched tight. Your breath's held, doing the next match almost blind. Flames keep touching your arm as you push to get it catching evenly on all sides. The whole centre must burn together.

"Get out of there. Come on. You're going to set light to your hair. You maniac." Daddy. That's real, true panic in his voice. Good. Stay for another match.

One match too many. It's dropped and you're squirming hard to get out. Daddy's grabbing hold of both your feet and he's dragging you out of the tunnel. Yanking you out like a carcass. He's let go. No one's speaking. Look at you. Eyes watering. Front smeared with earth. One long cut on your cheek, from a passing trunk. Your hair has been pulled through a hedge backwards. Still no one's speaking. The three of you are just watching. This is a truly memorable bonfire. It hardly needed any matches and it didn't need the lighter fuel. Not one bit. Its bonfire night crackle's in full voice. Will it be all burnt up before it's dark enough for fireworks?

"Very dry summer." Daddy. Finally.

"Oh bugger. The potatoes." You. Remembering the most important food of the night.

"It's fine. We'll just poke them in. They'd be done too early if they went in now." Daddy. Comforting chat. All of you are just staring. Star's tugging her hair. She's also leant against Daddy and his hand's up top of her head, stroking. Seems ok. She hasn't spoken since the curses.

BONFIRE NIGHT SPUDS

Potatoes
Bonfire
Butter

When you're building your bonfire shove as many potatoes, that you've pricked with a fork to stop exploding and sending lethal splats of hot potato flying, around the bottom, and close-ish to middle, of fire as poss. You'll need at least three per person. These are the best potatoes a person will ever eat and even Tammie could eat two. So really must think about numbers. After the fireworks are finished use a long stick to drag the spuds out of the embers. They'll be crusted in an amazingly thick and hard charcoaled skin. There won't be much potato inside as the burning up seems to shrink them but what there is needs only a dollop of butter and you eat them by holding the halves in your jumper-wrapped hand and munching. No forks or spoons. Just hands and teeth scraping out the goodness. Careful you don't burn that little strip of skin between your front teeth that's so easy to burn. You get a fair bit of gritty charcoal in your mouth too, this is part of it. 'When I was pregnant with you my craving was to lick coal.' Mummy. Explaining why the charcoal crunch is acceptable as well as delicious.

You're standing and staring at that fire for a long, long time.

Half an hour later. Here come Your People.

"Whoop, whoop, whoop, whoop." Pretty Justin. Skipping up the field in a headscarf and one of Mummy's pottery wrap-around pinnies. Pretty Justin loves fireworks too.

Mummy and Laura carrying the wine. Rod, he's got the box with the fireworks. That's thoughtful. Here's Eric with a box full of empties. You'll need these to stand the rockets in. He's also balanced an Aga tray of Tammie's Spiced American Apple Pie up top. Very thoughtful. Tammie's coming last. What is her costume? Nobody mentioned dressing-up. It's some kind of endless white robe and she's carrying a wooden crucifix. She's a nun. Finally. Oh please let that be so.

"Can we form a circle around the fire, people?" Tammie. That squeak really has gone. She's stern. This is even more interesting than Druidie-Tammie. You and Star are skipping up close to this Nunnie-Tammie. Your People are doing what she asks, although look at Mummy. Did you catch that eyebrow to Daddy?

"Raise your arms. Stretch to your neighbour on either side. Send your loving energy, finger tip to finger tip, around the circle. Ignite your care of the group." Tammie. All fairly standard but now she's raising the crucifix to the starry sky. Muttering.

"Hey. Hey. Tammie. No thank you. Absolutely not. None of that on my land." Daddy. Sounds like a farmer returning Jessie when she's got out and frightened their livestock.

"And certainly none on mine." Mummy.

"What the fuck are you playing at? I'll happily go along with any of the rest of this nonsense but I draw the line at a symbol of torture being waved around at my kids' party." Daddy. Wow. This is good.

"Hear, hear." Mummy. Clearly not wanting to be left out because it is good.

Tammie's lowering the crucifix. She's looking around, trying to catch the eyes of all Your People. Failing. She looks a bit smaller again.

"I wish you all very happy with your fireworks. Especially you guys." Tammie. You guys meaning Star and You. Looks like Tammie's going back inside. That's a shame. It's weird enough without The Hairy Dolly. Why does Tammie need to go? Especially Nunnie-Tammie. Everyone should be here. Tammie's stopping by the food, holding up the crucifix, ever so quickly, over it and muttering again.

"Tammie. Please fuck off with that. It's. A. Pie." Daddy.

"Yes. I hope it nourishes you." Tammie.

"Thank you." Daddy. Will this do the trick? Will Tammie stay? No. She's off. Dragging the train of her robe behind her. The back of that robe comes up so high it looks like she's got no neck.

'Umbaala." Laura. Sideways mouth to Pretty Justin.

"Right. Fireworks." Daddy. The men (apart from Pretty Justin) are leaping into action. Pretty Justin's just leaping. They're dotting bottles round the field. Each bottle has it's own rocket and they're organizing a Rota for lighting. Mummy's spooning out the smoking hot cauldron of mulled wine that Laura's balanced on a couple of bricks nearish the edge of the fire. Laura's slicing the Eggplant Parmigiana. Sipping mull.

BONFIRE NIGHT MULL

Red wine. Cheap and lots. Cheap wine's what French peasants keep for themselves to drink. They trick the English into thinking

the expensive wine's better. French peasants worth consulting for real money ideas? When you've learnt to speak French.
Oranges, lemons and apple too, if you like.
Brandy. Whole small bottle.
Cinnamon
Cloves
Sugar 'Yet more. What is happening to this house?' Mummy. Watching Laura spoon it in. She did use dark brown, though.
Bit of water.

Pour wine and brandy into massive saucepan. Laura uses the one for making marmalade and tie-dying clothes in.
Stud orange with cloves. In. If you want apple, chop and add.
Spoon Cinnamon. In.
Squeeze couple oranges, small lemon – to cut sugar – in.
Plenty of sugar. To taste and water for same.
Boil if don't want to get pissed. Heat gently if do.

EGGPLANT PARMIGIANA

This is Laura's mummy's recipe, you'll never be able to taste it properly because the Brits just don't do cheese in the right way. So what? This is still good eating.
Aubergines. This is what the American's call Eggplant. They say it looks like an egg. Which is nonsense. Aubergines are purple.
Cheese sauce
Tomato sauce

Slice aubergines. Laura says you should salt them but she never does so neither do you. Layer over bottom of big baking bowl which you've rubbed with oil. Layer tomato sauce. The sauce is so easy. Tins of toms (so recipe will serve in event of emergency), well smashed, with heaps of garlic, sugar, left-over red wine (check no one's dropped a ciggie end in, thyme or rosemary, or both, which you chop small. If you've got some, glugs of olive oil. Laura says olive oil's another thing the Brits don't get. Her and Clarissa agree about this. Boil all up. Sauce.

Thin layer cheese sauce. Then more aubergines. Keep layering ending with cheese sauce. Bake. The thing Laura says is very wrong is the sauce. It should be some cheese made from Buffalo's milk. How do you milk a buffalo? It's hard enough getting Prune to stand still. Not sure you fancy that cheese but you'd give it a go. Of course. The cheese sauce's just a béchamel with lots of strong cheddar. The whole thing mustn't be runny and needs to bake until eggplants are soggy. Balance. Best just warm then it sets and you can cut into holding lumps. Eggplants are an excellent meat substitute. Although they're shocking sponges for fat of any kind. 'Like Laura.' Mummy.

Whizzzz BANG. Here we go. Fireworks. Fireworks pouring in a relentless cascade. So loud. So very bright. Grown-ups are snatching turns at letting them off. Everyone's standing back between each one to admire and compare. They're lasting and lasting. The endless black sky's now green, BANG, red, BANG, silver, BANG, gold, BANG, purple. Over and over. Everlasting colour. Everywhere is hazy with firework smoke. Catherine wheels.

"Dangerously badly attached." Mummy. Attached by you because it's terrifying when they un-attach, taking flight to the back of the sky.

"Watch out, watch out, stand back! Fucking move back!" Mummy. To everyone. No one does. The assembled company are mesmerized. Awestruck.

"It is fucking amazing to be forced to stare at the stars in this way. Man, my heart is pumping. I am alive. Bloody good work girls." Daddy. Very loud.

See how bashful you and Star look?

Who ever had the idea of sparklers was a brain box. The end of fireworks is a dangerous low but then there they are. Sparklers. Tonight there's a sparkler for everybody with two left over because no Hairy Dolly and no Tammie so you and Star get an extra one. You're twirling them, scrawling your names, stabbing constellations. Hold tight. They're fizzling, drooping, down they bend and done. Out. Finished.

"Drop that bit! Drop it! It's scalding metal! Let go!" Mummy. You both do.

The fire's higher than trees, it's screaming with flames. Fire can be so loud.

"Anthony? Anthony? This is out of control! The grass is a tinder box! We're far too close to the church! I really think we might be about to burn something expensive down! Anthony?!" Mummy. Daddy's staring at the sky with his arms stuck up like an electrocuted scarecrow. Yikes. Mummy's gone early with the water. Chucking the buckets-full round the base. The ground's instantly dry. Mummy's starting her anxious phase. She always does, every year, but this fire is wild. You and Star are wild. Racing round and round the fire. Get the doors.

"I am eating your oxygen. I am eating the world." Fire.

"More, more, more. Gunpowder, treason and plot." You. Door spinning through the air, slamming into fire, wall of sparks smashing out. Bloody hell. Top of the fire's sliding sideways into the field. Wow. A second fire. That door's been consumed by flame.

Pretty Justin's twirling and whoop whooping.

"Will somebody please control the kids, this is very dangerous! I'm calling the fire brigade. Now. I'm going to call them. Stop the girls. Oh fuck, Anthony?! This is out of control. Justin, for fuck's sake!" Mummy. Not calling the fire brigade. The fire brigade are in Aylsham. Probably at their own bonfires. The whole village would be ash by the time they were roused.

"I think it's going to be fine. Look. I know it's mad but it's less than it was five minutes ago. There's no wind. The sparks are dying in mid-air. It's contained. Let's just wait it out. Have a toffee apple. It'll keep you busy." Laura. Handing her one. "Star. Put that door down. Enough both of you." Laura. Better abandon the doors. Pretty Justin's twirling. Daddy's worshiping the universe, cooking up the twentieth century's great poem?

TREACLE TOFFEE APPLES

Exactly same as regular toffee just mostly treacle and boil for ever. Done when instantly hard on contact with ice water. Use twigs for handles. Dip apples into toffee holding twig. Twirl round, whip out and stick them in icy water to set. Greaseproof tray to dry. The toffee usually slides off a bit but who cares? You can't really have a bonfire without these. Even just a burn-up-all-the-rubbish-bonfire and not a real one.

This is a very real one. Are the grown-ups drunk? Are you drunk? Everyone might be. That's your second mull. Get a slab of pie to soak and munch. Right, spuds time. Need a long stick. Got one. Star's joining. Easiest if you crouch down low, less body exposed for roasting. Dig and delve. Get those spuds.

"How many times?! Get them away from the edge." Mummy. Yelling. Chucking the apple into the blaze. Instantly eaten by fire. Oh bugger, your poking stick's a goner too.

"Shhh. Shhh. It's alright. Calm down it's all fine." Daddy.

"Do not tell me how to behave or how to feel. I am not fine. None of this is fucking fine!" Mummy.

Long silence. Apart from the massive shout of the fire itself. Hey, where the hell's Eric? When did he go? He lit some rockets, didn't he? Has he spontaneously combusted? You're interested in the idea of spontaneous combustion. Not for yourself but to witness, please. It's just Mummy and Daddy, Pretty Justin, Laura and Rod in the field. Will Mummy and Daddy have a row?

"Anthony? Anthony, man? Anthony? Can you come here? On your own. Anthony?" Voice. From house.

"Bryan? Bryan? That you?" Daddy. Shouting.

Daddy's taking Mummy's hand, for a second, passing her and going towards the Hairy Dolly's voice.

"Anthony? Anthony, man? On your own, yeah?" Hairy Dolly.

Everyone seems to have forgotten about the fire. Which is alright because the fire's fine, occupying itself. Why are you all just waiting? Straining towards the house as if you might hear something. Waiting. Finally, here comes Daddy. Here comes the Hairy Dolly. With very short hair. On its head. Tammie, and that's Eric too. They're all walking slowly and they aren't seeing the marvellous fire because they're looking at the ground. Although it's tricky to see them because the fire's blinded you to everything else and the night is beyond darkness, out there, near the house. Here they are. They've all stopped beside the fire. They're still all looking down. Long quiet bit.

"Oh no. What is it now?" Mummy.

"Can you please control your hysterical response to every fucking thing?" Daddy. Whoops.

Mummy's marching straight to the house. Daddy's crouching down holding his arms out to you and Star. You're taking a step towards him. No one's watching Mummy.

"My little loves I am so very sorry but Jessie is dead. It seems an articulated lorry caught her head on. She got out somehow. She was having a lovely time chasing pheasants. She won't have felt a thing. I'm very, very sorry." Daddy. Star's crumpling into Daddy. Crying. Really crying. Like a tiny baby cries. Bleating. You're looking back to the fire and sipping your wine.

Mummy's stopped her march, turning back. Weeping. Daddy's hugging her and Star. Mummy and your daddy have a spare arm out for you. Will you join? You're sipping again. Considering the fire.

"How did she get out?" You.

"We'll never know." Daddy. Why not?

"My poor doggy." You. To your fire. Rod's actually sobbing.

"Yes. She was a great dog." Daddy.

"Where is she?" You. To the fire.

"Bryan was given her body by the driver. She's in the deep freeze." Daddy.

"Right." You. You and Star both know why. You've eaten roadkill enough times. Usually pheasant come to think of it and it's usually delicious. You sort of roast it with big chunks of apple, garlic, whole shallots and supposedly calvados but the house never has that so Mummy uses Harvey's Bristol Cream, which is always in the mouse cupboard, and when it's all roasted you add lots of double cream to the collapsed apple mix. You're not going to eat Jessie but it'll stop the decay until someone's ready to bury her.

The fire's snapping away.

Tammie's moving to beside Mummy, Daddy and Star.

"Eric and I have some news we want to share with The Group. Might be that it'll cheer us." Tammie. Clear voice. Still in the robe and still with the crucifix.

Your People are watching her. You're still watching the fire. The crying's quieter. Apart from Star who is making a strangled gulping. This isn't stopping Tammie.

"Tammie Love, I think we all just need a bit of quiet right now." Laura. But Tammie's un-stop-able.

"I'm pregnant. We're going home. To the U.S. Eric and myself. Eric has asked me to be his, bride. Star? We'd love for you to be our bridesmaid." That's shut Star up. She's goggling at Tammie. You too now. Tammie's remembering herself. "Oh and also you, of course. If you want to be a bridesmaid."

"How would we get to America?" You.

"You and Star will always have a home with us. You can come for as long as you like. You can come and live with us, if you like." Tammie.

"And this wedding. Will it be Christian? And will you send my children the money for their fares before you adopt them?" Daddy. Standing now. "Eric, what the hell is this?"

The whole gang's swerving their focus onto Eric. His beard has never been redder. It's wagging. He's about to speak.

"Tammie's carrying my wean. She's... blessed me. She's given me hope. So, aye, it will be a Christian ceremony. I am a Christian, by the way. So is Tammie, now. We're plannin' on four wean, in time. The girls will just be...welcome." Eric. Tammie's settling into his thigh.

Rod's clapping. He's still crying about Jessie but he's applauding them and raising his glass.

"Fertility. Fertility. Fertility. Let's drink to all new life." Rod.

"When did you fuck Tammie?" Mummy. Nearly spitting her name.

Eric looks caught. What have you got to do with it? Why's he staring at you?

"After. I'm neigh that kind. Never with. Tammie is my. She's only just." Eric. Beard chewing mumble. "I apologise." To Daddy.

"Can I remind everyone that I am no one's property." Mummy. She sounds exhausted.

"God no. No way." Rod. How come he's getting so involved?

"Shall we all have some food? I think it might be sensible. Soak up some of the wine?" Laura. Notice how close to her Pretty Justin has moved?

Amazingly no one has anything more to say. Your People are clustering round the food which is gathered on a door. They're all being jolly kind and careful. Giving plates, pouring wine. Rod's kissing Star on the head as he passes, Mummy hasn't taken her arm from Star, Laura's slicing and handing and you're still fire-watching. Sipping your wine. Your front's burning hot but your back's cool. The season has changed. At last. Don't think you'll fancy any potatoes tonight.

You're sitting on the ground. You're looking at the Hairy Dolly who's turning to you and coming over. It's carrying a sloppy mug of wine. It's sitting down.

"It's the saddest day I've known." Hairy Dolly. About Jessie. Not Tammie and Eric.

One hot tear is oiling down your face.

"I'll be fine." You won't though.

"I know she was yours but we all loved her." Hairy Dolly. Oh no they didn't. That's absurd. They had no idea of her beauty or her meaning.

Look at it thinking it's feeling a big thing. Oh, what is the point?

The rest of Your People are settling down in front of the fire. Eric's got the Hairy Dolly's guitar, he's singing to Tammie. Yuck. We've all got to listen to that, Eric. He's going for 'Rocket Man'.

"Mars is not a place to raise your kids. In fact it's cold as hell out there." Eric. Mumble stumble. What's he stopped for? Oh more yuck, he's popping teaspoonfuls of the apple bit of pie into Nunnie-Tammie's open mouth. Open beak.

This is Star's complete favourite song. She's being driven nuts by Eric messing about with it. Mummy will have to take her to bed soon. When Star spoke she used to sing 'Rocket Man' exactly like Elton John, she's devised a dance that works with the words. Laura taught her some mime for the 'I'm a rocket man' stuff. 'Laura has a serious talent for rockets.' Daddy. Watching them.

"I've been in Norwich." Hairy Dolly.

"Is that all? I thought you'd gone to Findhorn." You.

"Why would I go there?" Hairy Dolly. "Hello You. Nice frock." To Pretty Justin who's coming to sit on its other side. Blowing you a kiss.

"I know it's gonna be a long, long time" Eric. Hitting his stride. Although not the correct words.

"You'll, like, miss her, like, for ever. I guess you'll kind of judge all your, like, loves by this one. Yeah?" Pretty Justin. Yeah.

"I know it's gonna be a long, long time." Eric.

"Snort." Star. Disapproval of Eric's key choice. Not sure it's an actual choice mind.

"We could cremate her." You.

"You'll need a grave." Hairy Dolly. "Even when you're all grown-up and gone, you'll need to know where to find her."

Pretty Justin's leaning over Hairy Dolly to reach you. He's tapping his heart. Yes.

"Gonna be a long, long time." Eric. Quieter now. Thank fuck sticks. All Your People are sat in the field. The sky is black and massed with stars. Like someone threw huge sacks of glinting rice that just stuck. Bonfire. Almost contained now. No one has anything to say. For a very long time indeed. Mummy's stretching, a normal sleepy stretch. She's standing, holding her hand out for Star. Look at Star's face. Puffed up and shiny. Looks like snail-silver where her tears and snot trailed over her tight face.

Star's being led off. Star's stopping, breaking away, running back to you, you're standing, Star's sort of knocking into you, you're tottering back but keeping hold of her. You're standing together, holding on. There's just you and Star now. No one could count Prune or even Great Uncle Elizabeth.

Everyone's so young standing beside that fire, staring at the real young people. They look scared don't they? You and Star are not scared. And you won't be going to America. Well not for now. When Star's sixteen she'll hitch and beg her way there. She'll find Pretty Justin in New York and sleep on the floor in his one-room apartment. She'll find Laura, strap Laura's baby to her chest and carry Laura's baby to work with her whilst she washes up in a diner. She'll go to contemporary dance classes, form her own one-woman dance troupe, performing in derelict buildings for three years. She'll come back to England with a shaved head and talking. Then she'll have her first break-down.

"Night, night." You.

"Night, night." Star.

What's that racket? Oh, just Rod. Sobbing again. Surprised Mummy isn't joining in. 'Your Mother's a deep feeler. All those tears from such a tight little bundle. One might say lachrymose.' Daddy. Years ago. 'One might but that would be bitchy. Tears are natural, for fuck's sake.' Mummy. 'Careful you don't use them all up.' Daddy. Mummy and Daddy are taking a hand each of Star's and leading her back into the darkness towards bed.

"The tears aren't a surprise but they are a cliché." Laura. To Rod. She's getting up and gathering a handful of mugs to take with her.

"I am very sorry for your loss." Laura. To you. She's moving off, stopping and turning. Listen. The big back door's clunking closed behind Mummy, Daddy and Star.

"Will one of you make sure the fire's safe before you come in, please?" Laura.

She doesn't mean you but you'd already thought you would spade some earth and put it up top to contain the end of the fire. When you decided to go to bed.

"Sure." Hairy Dolly. Not making eye contact.

"Seriously, Bryan. I need a promise." Laura. Pushing at its back with her toe.

"Sure. Like I said." Hairy Dolly. Ignoring the toe.

"Jesus." Laura. Leaving. Stopping to touch your shoulder with the edge of the bunch of mugs.

"You ok?" Laura.

"No. Yes." You.

"Ok then." Laura. Moving off. "The fire, Bryan. Ok?" Shouting back.

"Fucking nag." Hairy Dolly. Under its breath.

"I know what you think." Laura. From nearly at the house "And I care not a jittery jot. Got it? Fire." then "Night, Sweet Thing." To you, as she goes inside. Hear the big door clunk closed?

"She really is an impressive woman." Rod. Rustling up to go after her.

"You don't stand a fucking chance, Rodney. She's queer, man." Hairy Dolly.

Look at you and Pretty Justin. This is news. Pretty Justin looks thrilled.

"Really? Like, are you sure?" Pretty Justin.

"She wouldn't fuck me." Hairy Dolly.

"Ahh. Case closed then." Rod. He's scampering off. Tangerine-tissue crackling.

"Did you fuck Tammie too?" You.

The Hairy Dolly's snapping round to you. It is trying to work out if your 'too' means you know about Mummy, isn't it? Its twinkling at you. Looks glad you know.

"Very, very nearly. Tammie's hot to be fucked. She'll have been a push-over for Eric. I decided against at the last moment. Too damaged." Hairy Dolly.

"No." You.

"No, possibly not. That was the act. But I didn't wanna give her the satisfaction. Way too needy." Hairy Dolly.

"I'm not needy." You.

"I am." Pretty Justin. The Hairy Dolly's really laughing. Stretching out and up to the deep sky.

"Well I sure am glad I came on home." Hairy Dolly. Snuffle laughing.

"Do you think about sleeping with me?" You.

Uh oh. Pretty Justin has gone rigid. White round his eyes. Never seen that before. On anyone.

"That's a beautiful mouth and what occupies too much of my current thinking is putting myself inside it." Hairy Dolly. Wish it'd stop touching your mouth with its stinky fingers. This would all be so much more fun if it left you alone.

"Bryan, like, Bryan? I love you, yeah? Like, love you. And you can, like, fuck and fuck me if you, like, need someone but, like, please don't say that. Yeah? To her. Yeah? Please?" Pretty Justin. Whispering. His mouth doesn't look too beautiful, it's gone oddly stretched.

The Hairy Dolly's still. Stiller than still. So are you.

"Consider it un-said. Come on, you pretty thing. Let's have that fuck." Hairy Dolly. To Pretty Justin.

They're both up and The Dolly's chucking the dregs of its mull onto the fire. It's fizzing and burning.

"Oh. Yeah. Yeah. Yes." Pretty Justin. Hovering beside it, waiting for the off. Pretty Justin's dreams are coming true. Maybe Jessie's in heaven doing her begging-dog eyes for favours. Maybe tomorrow Star will receive an invite from Olga? Maybe you'll be able to speak French, have a pony and have Jessie back. Alive.

"I'm sorry. I, like, I have to. You'll understand when, like, when you're older. Yeah?" Pretty Justin. To you. That again.

The Hairy Dolly's leaning down to kiss you good night. You're dodging away.

"Hey. You asked me, remember?" Hairy Dolly. Just to you.

They're leaving. Wish you hadn't dodged? You didn't mean it. You're twelve for heaven's sake. And Laura is a lesbian? Watch them skipping into the house. Hear the big door clunk closed? You are completely alone in the field. Your dog is dead. Is her ghost watching? Sit still. Do not run away into the house. Look at your hands. Your palms are nearly bleeding where your finger nails are digging in.

"Jessie?" You. Why are you whispering to your dead dog's ghost? Because the fucking church yard's next door to the field and very, very full of dead bodies. That is why. No reply. From anyone.

"Jessie? Jessie?" You. Still no reply.

"Jessie?" You. Argh. What was that? You've leapt ten feet in the air. Calm down. Grow up. The wind's touched you, ever so slightly, that's all. That crashing is your heart going mad with fear. Do not run into the house. You're licking your palms. Sweat, charcoal, flick of blood.

You're up and going slowly to the greenhouse to find a spade. It's ridiculously hard to see, all you can see is fire burnt onto the back of your eyeballs. Slowly, slowly. You've stretched your arms in front to prevent collisions. Even if it's Jessie's ghost arriving. Why would you want to touch anything you can't see? Big stumble on a grass hillock. Righting yourself. Pausing. Heart smashing. Straining to listen. Hear that? End of fire. Still loud. And night? Night is full of terrifying sound. It's almost silly. You've got the spade. Hard to get the job done whilst checking, checking, checking for Jessie's ghost. For any ghosts. You have to use the earth from the veg patch to damp down the fire. It's the only earth soft enough. Dig then check, dig then check. On and on. It takes an hour to make it all safe. Jessie is dead. The Prawn didn't show. Did she? You're standing back and checking your burial mound of earth. There's some smoke snaking through but no fire will start from this. Your eyes have adjusted to the exceptional dark. You can see everything and there's nobody else with you. No ghosts came. The field now feels like the safest place to be but you do have to go home. Spade back into the greenhouse. Hovering outside for one more moment.

"Bye, bye. My Darling." You. Out into the nothing.

Clunk, the big door's closing behind you. There's always such a struggle with the bottom bolt. Suck that tiny nip the hard metal bolt has made between your thumb and first finger. See how hard you're sucking your blood as you're hovered with your back pressed into the heavy big green back door and now. Go, go, go. Racing past the pottery door. Get past the room with your dead dog in it. Done. Up the stairwell, galloping down the landing, into your room, back against that door, breathe, breathe, breathe. No Star. Must be with Mummy and Daddy. Door chair. Jammed. Scanning all the corners, taking a flying leap onto the bed, so nothing can reach out and drag you under. Bedtime.

CHAPTER SEVEN

It's not the next day but it's very soon after. Breakfast. Eric's sitting on the long bench with Tammie nestled up beside him. He's feeding her cornflakes. You are not allowed cornflakes. Eric snuck this packet in.

"Jesus Christ Almighty, Eric. You know the house policy on processed cereals. What the fuck are you doing? My kids might get hold of some of that shit." Mummy. When she caught him doing the sneaking.

"I did neigh realize we had policies. That's pressed corn. Your girls will survive a wee stray flake. Mine might not. Unless she's fed." Eric. Big and firm.

Eric is right. You did survive. A whole bowlful. You and Star shared a bowl when the adults were in the garden. You had them with ice cold top of the milk and soft brown sugar. You ate them fast, with your eyes locked on each others. Bolted. You drank down the sugar milk and had a good long silent think about whether to risk a second bowl. But a second bowl would have been it. Discovery. Great shame. Bowl washed and dried, box shaken down and returned to shelf. Although look, Eric has since written, in navy felt tip, *Eric and Tammie* on the box.

Tammie's making a miniature sigh of satisfaction each time Eric posts in a spoonful. This is making Eric chew his beard with happiness.

"Shine and rise with Kellogg's." Hairy Dolly. Passing Eric and giving him a hearty whack on the back. Eric doesn't seem to notice. Next spoonful balanced and in. Not a drop wasted. Look at him shaving the corners of her mouth with the spoon.

"Practising." Laura. To you. She's caught you watching. "Try not to be put off." Look at you. Gripped. Look at Star. She has her fingers in her ears. To block out the sighs. You're both eating French Porridge. And wishing you were Tammie. It would be worth it for the flakes. And oh my goodness the Hairy Dolly has taken an empty bowl and is helping itself to a mountainous portion of flakes. Everything's stopping in the room. It's grinning round. It's taking the milk. It's pouring it on. It's pouring all the milk in the bottle on.

"Bottoms up." Hairy Dolly. To the room. Grinning and spooning them in. Making lots and lots of eye contact. Apart from with you. And Pretty Justin.

"Yum-baala." Hairy Dolly. Followed by an imitation of the sighs.

Daddy's really laughing at it. So is Pretty Justin.

"Please don't encourage him." Mummy. Daddy's stopping laughing, he's slamming the coffee pot off the Aga and pouring himself a very large mug of coffee.

"You'll have to have that black. Since Bryan has taken all the milk in the house." Mummy.

"I always have it black. As you know." Daddy. Jolly again, now.

"Black coffee anyone?" Daddy. Waving the pot.

"Yeah? Like, please, me too, yeah? Black. Yeah?" Pretty Justin. He doesn't even drink coffee. He's not looking at Daddy. He's only looking at the Hairy Dolly. He looks like he might cry. As well as laugh.

"Sure." Laura. Daddy's pouring. They're both watching Tammie and Eric. Eric hasn't really broken stride.

"It'll be boiled egg and soldiers for lunch." Daddy. To Laura. But still looking at the feeding. Tammie's looking up at Daddy at the mention of the egg. Daddy and Laura are nodding to each other. "Egg it is." Daddy.

The Hairy Dolly's abandoning its bowl and going to the table drawer, it's rummaging for a felt tip and walking to the egg tray.

"One egg or two, Tammie?" Hairy Dolly. He's scribbling *Eric & Tams* on two eggs. "Not enough room for your whole name. Sorry." Retuning to the table, reclaiming its flakes from Daddy who has swiped them and had three big milky spoonfuls. Not fair.

Look at Jessie's basket. Still under the window. Still full of her blankets. And her hairs. How long do fleas live after their dog is gone? Look at you glancing at it. For the hundredth time. You did try sitting in it just to see. It didn't work. Still couldn't cry.

"Ahhh, Rodders old man. How the devil are we this fine autumnal morn?" Hairy Dolly. In its Britisher voice. To Rod who's coming into the room. Rod never eats breakfast. But he does always drink coffee. With milk. The whole room, even Tammie and Eric, are watching Rod on his way to the pot. Pour, pour, pour. He's going to the fridge. Opening it. No milk. Looking round. Spying the bottle on the table. Not noticing it's empty, not noticing he's being stared at by the whole flock, picking it up and pouring. Shake, shake, shaking.

"New Policy. No dairy for breakfast." Daddy.

"Policy?" Rod.

"New idea. Policies. We're trying them out on food." Daddy.

"Did I miss a meeting?" Rod. Should one feel sorry for Rod?

"Very fucking funny." Mummy. But she is sitting down on Daddy's lap so don't think there's anything you're missing.

Listen. The post box is opening and a letter's being poked through and down. Nobody's moving. Everybody's feeling how quiet it is as the letter lands. No Jessie doing half-arsed barking. Just a letter. Although post is always interesting so no more moping. Get the letter. It's brown. Oh dear. Brown's usually quite bad news. Bills. You're handing it to Daddy. Eric has nearly finished the feeding, he's keeping going but the rest of Your People are watching Daddy open it up. And reading.

"Fuck Sticks." Daddy.

"What?" Mummy. "What, for Christ's sake. What?" Why isn't he responding? Bit more not responding.

"So. This is interesting. We are going to be inspected." Daddy. At last.

"What?" Enough whats, Mummy.

"By whom and for what?" Hairy Dolly. Seems to have forgotten about the flakes, in an instant. Total waste. It looks worried. It's over by Daddy share-reading the letter.

"Oh. Mellow. That's cool. Just the kids. Social Services or something. School services. Some kind of deal." Hairy Dolly.

"Karma." Tammie. A look from Eric. "Oh. Sorry. Divine retribution?" To Eric, not sure she's got the right form of revenge. Interesting to see Tammie all unsure. Being certain was part of her Tammieness. She just needs to get the hang of being a Christian. Which she will. Tammie will eventually be ordained, when her 'little guys' are all grown-up and there isn't so much need for her around the homestead. She'll have six little guys. All massive. All fathered by Eric. All Christians. Two of them will be ordained themselves. The other four will join their Daddy down on the farm. Pressing corn.

"What do they want?" Mummy and Laura. Sounds electronic them both speaking together like that.

"We have an obligation to fulfil section 12 of the 1973 Education Act to...um... to essentially educate our kids." Daddy.

"Is that all? That's nothing. The girls can sit any tests they want. Apart from spelling." Mummy.

"Or grammar." Daddy.

"Or math." Hairy Dolly. It's really laughing at the absurdity of this. It did once try to explain pi to you. But.

"Have yous ever had a history lesson?" Eric. To you and Star.

"In fairness they might do well on literature. They have a wide grasp." Rod.

"Tolkien, whoever penned that modern classic Jill's fucking Gymkhana and some of the modern and lesser poets doesn't constitute a knowledge of the syllabus." Daddy. Don't fancy getting tested on Tolkien. What are the fundamental differences between Elves and Hobbits? Answer – both simply ghastly bores.

"Science? Biology?" Tammie.

The grown-ups are on a roll. It seems that you and Star cannot do a test. Although everyone's still confident you could pass the test of life. This is a bit mean. It's not your fault you're living in a crucible for experiential learning. Or that you're a School Refuser.

"When do we have to do the test?" You.

"Friday." Daddy.

"What the fuck? Which Friday?" Laura.

"Four days Friday." Daddy. Eric's going back to scraping up the final droplets to feed the Tammie Bird. Hairy Dolly's rolling a cig, feet up on the table. It hasn't looked at you or spoken to you since bonfire night. Or Pretty Justin. As far as you can tell.

"Does it say a test?" Mummy.

"No. It says a meeting to evaluate." Daddy. "Here's what we're going to do. I'm calling Ginger Beer Bob at Erpingham." He's doing it now. Everyone's watching him dial. "Hi? Can I speak to Bob please? Anthony. Yeah, Swallow's Anthony. Cheers." Waiting while someone in Erpingham hunts down Bob. "Hello? Hi. Bob? Yeah. Yeah. Listen. You guys ever been inspected by the education team from Norwich? Oh. Oh. Oh. Yeah." Laughing and nodding. "Great. Excellent. No, great, come here. Yeah. Cool. See you then." Just about to hang up. "Yup. Um. Yup. No. Very powerful. Yes of course. Important work. No thank you." Now he's hanging up. And turning to Rod.

"Sorry. I had to promise him publication. Bribe." Daddy.

"No. Not the pelican poem. It's very poor. I'm not sure Bob's a serious person." Rod.

"He's pretty serious about education. He's bringing his kids over later. They're about the same age. Apparently you need numbers to be a school. We need to be a school to confound them. Then Bob can torture the inspectors with facts about education acts and get them off our backs. They've got the same letter." Daddy.

"Oh Darling, well done." Mummy. As if it's all accomplished. You and Star have still got to be made into a bloody school with the weird Erpingham kids and then do a bloody test. This really is ridiculous. You're practically a woman for god's sake. You don't say this but look how pissed off you look. Star too actually. And see Star? Twisting her hair? Why's Mummy being so jolly? 'If anyone understands about the hell of school it's me. I was abandoned at my boarding school. Can you imagine the fear?' Mummy. Often. You can imagine it. You're imagining it now as you digest this wretched news.

"Which kids? Who are they?" You.

"Bob's I assume. The Heroes." Daddy. Well that's just bloody marvellous, you can look forward to being bored to death as you chant your two times bloody table.

Later. You and Star have been waiting for an hour on the wall outside. Here comes the Erpingham bread van. Someone has painted a field of sunflowers over one of its panels since last time it was here. Looks like it was done by one of the Heroes. Very wonky work. Ginger Beer Bob's getting out. Let's get a proper look at him. Tall, skinny, bald, no purple hat today, and very long thin beard. Little round specs too.

"Bald Gandalf." You. Whispered.

Ginger Beer Bob's reaching back into the van, collecting today's hat. Great. It's pointy and felt. Too much joy. He is also swathed in a linen-ish cloak. Perhaps you could take the Tolkien test. Could certainly sort out who wears which hat 'n' cloak.

"Gandalf." Making sure Star gets the resemblance.

Ginger Beer Gandalf's noticing you. Tiny falter as he catches your eye. He's opening the sliding side door and here come The Heroes. They've grown since the last time you were forced into each other's company. A lot. The tall one's nearly as tall as his daddy. And they do both have hair. Lots. Longer than yours. They also have flarey jeans which they've grown out of. Flarey bit flapping above their ankles. How excellent it is to be attired in these comfy new red jeans. But they are both wearing sneakers. You and Star want sneakers. Mainly so you can say sneakers when people ask about your shoes. Sneakers is the American word for plimsoles. Sounds so much better.

Everyone's standing around. You're getting off the wall. Star's sliding off.

"Whatcha." You.

"Mumble." Big Hero. Looking at well-clad feet.

"Mumble." Littler Hero. Ditto.

"Hi, Kids. So. This should be fun." Ginger Beer Gandalf. Real money idea? Borrow the printing press and put together a pamphlet to assist adults with words. *Page one; 'Using the word fun at a first meeting marks you out as a hapless fool. You may never regain your assumed status as a result. Advice? No fun'.*

"Is Anthony around? Your Dad?" Ginger Beer Gandalf.

"Yes he is." You. Meaning yes he is my dad and not yes he is around. You'd like him to understand that you have a Good Mind. But no point risking detectable rudeness. Yet. Long, quiet looking at the ground bit. The Heroes scuff the dirt with their toes. Messing up their lovely sneakers. Gandalf looks shifty.

"I... um... I was impressed by your poem." Ginger Beer Gandalf. This is more like it. You're lighting right up. Big smiles.

"Yes. Good. Thanks. Anthony says you've done some important work too." You.

"Does he? Oh. Yes. Yes. Yes. Well. I hope so." Ginger Beer Gandalf. Yes, yes far more like it. Although Ginger Beer Gandalf doesn't sound so sure about his own poem.

"The Pelican Bleeds For Its Young." You. Remembering the title. Usefully.

"I was thinking just, The Pelican. Possibly?" Very unsure.

"Anthony says short titles are always the most effective." More helpful than he deserves. Look at those Heroes. The big one's having a hard look at you. Very good job you've got those jeans. The little one has just sat himself back down on the van doorframe and is reading a comic. A comic? Star's edging towards The Comic.

"Oh right. Yes. Yes. Yes. Good. He might be right. Yes. Yes. Yes."

Star's sat herself down next to the littler one and is reading over its shoulder. Another quiet looking at the ground bit. Apart from Star and the littler one who are both laughing and he's pointing to something in the comic and she's nodding. The big one's just doing his toe in the dirt thing. Is it really your job to get this bloody school started?

"Right. Yes. Yes. Yes. I'll find Anthony." Off he pops.

You're sitting down on what's left of the lawn. The big one's sitting down beside the van. Leaning on its side. Star and the other one are going somewhere. Did you miss something? They're still reading and pointing and just walking off somewhere. Who said what when?

"They're the same age. I think. How old is he?" You.

"Nine. Just." Big Hero.

"She's eight and three quarters."

"How old are you?"

"Nearly thirteen."

"When?"

"I'm Cancer."

"We don't believe in Astrology. It's Gumph. It's an opiate for the masses. We're interested in Astronomy. Cancer would mean you are only just twelve." Big Hero. Not very heroically.

"How old are you then?" You.

"I am thirteen. And a bit."

"How much bit?"

"One month and seven days."

Doesn't seem to be much more to say. The Big Hero's going back to scuffing. You're trying to sweat it out. The sky's grey. Is it going to rain? That might be nice.

"My dog's dead." You.

"When?" Big Hero. He's very caught up with dates.

"Bonfire night."

"Was it a firework?" Big Hero. He's jolly lively all of a sudden. Seriously tempting to say yes.

"Just a lorry. The driver was rushing home to let off his fireworks."

"How do you know?" He also seems to be quite needy regarding details.

"I don't. It's an estimate." You.

"My Dad says you're precocious." Big Hero.

"Mine calls you The Heroes."

"I'm going to get my name changed by deed poll."

"What to?" You.

The rain's starting, you're glancing up. Looks like you're both deciding not to go indoors. Yet.

"Ryan."

"Why Ryan?"

"Sounds similar but it's neutral. I'm a bit bored of the hero joke. Although I was a very big baby. That's why they called me it. I split my mother's vagina quite badly."

"Yuck."

"There's no need to be coy about body parts. That's its name and that's what happens if your child has an exceptionally large head."

"I didn't know he was big; I thought he was just a hunter."

"He was a giant and a hunter."

"Oh."

More rain, more scuffing.

"Have you considered a deed poll change?" Big Hero.

"No. I like my name." You. What's wrong with your name, for heaven's sake?

"You should. I think my dad regrets both our names."

"What's wrong with Wolfie?"

"Well that's obviously not his actual name. It's his nickname." Bit grand.

"What's his actual name then?" Two can play at that game.

"Beowulf."

"Oh." You're having a fairly straight look at each other.

"Why don't you call me Ryan?"

"Sure. Whatever you want."

"I don't want to be in a school with you."

"Why not?"

"You're too young and you've had absolutely no attention paid to sculpting your intellects. It's quite likely it's too late for you to develop a capacity for learning. You're allowed to float around doing whatever takes your fancy all day. We've had a system in place for quite some time. I think you might well hold me up. I plan on attending university. Do you have ambitions?" Big Hero.

This is fascinating. University? This is the first time you've even considered the word, apart from as a place where Daddy and Mummy met. They were both studying English Literature but Mummy was drowning in facts and the horse she'd eaten in France was having such serious repercussions. She'd started not being able to go to lectures and then Daddy missed sitting behind her lake of hair at lectures so he went to find her. Which he did in her digs. She was in bed crying and said she'd been crying for days and she hadn't eaten anything. Daddy got her up and washed her hair in the sink then dried it with a tea towel. This took an hour then he brushed it and de-tangled it. This is very impressive because long hair is so sticky. Then he held her hand and ever so gently led her down all the stairs in her digs and out into the street. They walked and as they walked he described all the things they could see along the way then he found a greasy spoon café and they went in and he ordered 'Double egg and chips, please.' Mummy ate it all up. They were in love. Mummy decided she'd had enough of university so she found her pottery master and waited in Newcastle whilst Daddy finished his degree and she waited whilst he did his PhD. Then they got married. They ate egg and chips on their wedding day. You've been to a greasy spoon café. It might be one of your favourite places in the world. It's called El Grotto. It's in Newmarket. Which is on the way back from London. Daddy and Mummy always used to stop the White Saab there on the way home from Mummy's Jungian Analysis in London. 'All those hundreds of pounds to learn that dumping kids at boarding school teaches them only that they're un-lovely and, worse, un-loveable. Fat lot of good learning those sad facts made.' Daddy. About not being able to travel to the analysis anymore. Or El Grotto. For that matter.

Anyway, it was getting dark by the time you got there, no matter what the season. Inside El Grotto one whole wall's been made to look like a cave. It has a real waterfall trickling down it. There are little lights that glimmer under the waterfall. You always, always, always have exactly the same thing to eat. A bowl of Heinz Oxtail Soup and a white bread roll which the lady thickly butters with marge. For some reason the marge melting and floating up top of the soup as you dip the soft roll in is one of the best bits. 'Please, darling, please, please will you try something else? They have egg and chips?' Mummy. Every time you order. 'But you said, whatever you like because we have been so good and quiet in the car and in the waiting room.' You. 'You've been a fucking pain in the arse in the car and you always are and for someone who suffers quite as boringly as you do with car sickness

I'm amazed you've the stomach for this crap but we did tell them they can choose and does it really matter?' Daddy. To Mummy. Sticking up for you. 'You do know that Oxtail is exactly what it sounds like, don't you?' Daddy. Again. Trying to put you off. So Mummy doesn't feel ganged up on. 'Of course. I don't care. I'm not a vegetarian.' You. Star has the egg and chips. Although there are serious concerns about Star and eggs cooked like this. They give her massive burps. Star can actually be quite windy. Pretty Justin nicknames her Fart Hog. She's a bit bored of this now.

"Of course I'm going to university. I think I'd like to go to Oxford. It's the prettiest. We always support them in the boat race." You. That's that sorted.

"I'm planning on Cambridge. I'll do Physics and then a PhD in Astronomy. Do you watch The Sky At Night?" Big Hero.

"We don't believe in telly" Finally. Something you can be superior about.

"That's silly. You have to be immersed in society, and, especially, its culture, to pose a serious alternative. Or else it's just bumming around."

"I've seen the Clangers." Big Hero looks horrified by this. He's going into the house.

"I'm going to get my dad." Over his shoulder.

"Orion? It might be time to ask for some new jeans. Yours and Wolfie's are far too short, you know?" Catching him just before he shuts the door. That's stopped him.

"What do you mean?" Orion. Just his giant's head poking back through the door at you.

"Your ankles are sticking out. The flares are good but they're too high up your leg so they're flappy. In the wrong place. You look...

unbalanced." He's checking to see if you're right. Which you are. So no worries there.

"How come you've got sneakers?" You. Been bursting to ask and now seems like a good moment.

"Plimsoles. Dad got them for himself so it was only egalitarian to get some for Wolfie and myself. They are exceptionally practical."

"Where did he get the sneakers from?" On his case.

"Saxons."

"Really. Wow. Recently?" Eager now.

"Last week. Why? Are they wrong too?"

"They're fine. It's the jeans you need to sort." Giving your correct jeans a stroke. This is all going much more smoothly. School will be fine. Long as it's only until this inspection's done. Orion's coming back into the garden.

"Do you know what the idea for this inspection is?" Orion. Looks anxious.

"I think we'll have to sit quite a few rigid tests." Ha. That's got him. Somebody in this garden understands a thing or two about fear.

"Who told you that? I'm not so good in a formal setting. That's one of my worries about Oxbridge. The entrance exam. I'll be fine with the papers. You can probably tell in an informal setting I'm art... art... art... art...... art...... art... ahhhhh.... art." He's stopped and is swallowing.

"Articulate?" Helpful.

"Please don't prompt me. It makes it worse. This is very annoying. I haven't stammered for sixty-two hours point." Pausing as he checks his watch. "Sixty-two hours point forty-eight minutes."

"Why do you say point?" Interesting.

"It helps me. As I was saying. You can probably tell I'm art... art...

art... ahhhhhhh..... art." You're doing what he asked but this is hard work.

"Articulate." Orion. Finally. Do not say 'not really.' That'd be childish.

"Yes. I suppose so. In a way." Look at you looking pensive and doing a bit of neck work. He's watching that. Why not un-plait your hair? You are. Slowly. Rake your fingers through it, get it all shaken out. This is a bit of a bore because it's been in those plaits over a week so there's a stubborn layer of knot to negotiate. Right, that's it. From now on this hair gets brushed at least once a day. And washed, for goodness sake, it's filthy. Hey, look at Orion, he's completely still, watching you with his mouth dropped open.

"That feels better." You. Tossing those filthy locks about. You're doing a bit too much tossing actually but Orion doesn't seem to know what's too much and it does feel better having it released. Do some eyes to the floor looking up at him slowly. That seems effective, he isn't going anywhere. It's raining fairly persistently now.

"Biscuit?" You. It didn't work for Uncle Rob but you're taking a calculated guess it'll be a definite cert for a thirteen-year-old boy.

"Which manufacturer?" Orion.

"What do you mean?" What does he mean? This isn't as straightforward as you'd assumed. Any of it really.

"Digestive by McVitie's. Custard Cream and Pink Wafer, Crawfords. Garibaldi, Peek Freans." He's so like Jessie. Suddenly. That's sad. What can you do about that? Jessie adored every single biscuit you ever fed her. You're shrugging and strutting on towards the house.

"Ryan? I don't believe in manufactured biscuits. These are home-made." He's panting after you.

"You can't believe or not believe in a variety of biscuit. That is nonsensical."

"Isn't the point of belief that it's personal? That one can believe in what one wants?" Clambering up as elegantly as possible to capture the biscuit tin and hoping, very much, that an adult doesn't come in and catch you handing around forbidden snacks.

Perfect biscuits to enchant a dodgy visitor.

CHOCOLATE IDIOT BISCUITS

Called this because even an idiot could make them. And no doubt has.

6 oz butter
3 oz caster sugar
6 oz plain flour
2 tablespoons cocoa powder
Slug of vanilla essence.

Cream fat, sugar and essence together. Stir in flour and cocoa. And that is it. Idiot proof.

Roll into balls, put on greaseproof-papered tray. Push down slightly with back of fork. This'll make them look manufactured. Bake middle of Aga for not a second longer then ten mins. If nobody has used Aga that day, and it's still got all its unreliable heat, do six mins. If it's somebody's birthday or if it's Easter and someone has an Easter egg they don't want and you've chocolate left over – as if – then it's truly delicious to stuff a small chunk of choc into middle of ball, attempt to seal, then fork down. Either way these are perfect biscuits. Melt when you eat them.

"And why nonsensical? What's wrong with just nonsense?" You.

Offering the tin. The tin may as well be singing to Orion. He's clearly serious about biscuits. You like him for this. And you like yourself for guessing so well.

"How many can I have?" Orion. Seems to have dropped the debate. "Please." Remembering his manners.

You're into very worrying territory here. Look at yourself wavering. Be good to be free with them but Mummy will know exactly how many biscuits are in the tin and you don't want her deciding to have some kind of tea party with Ginger Beer Gandalf and you to be caught. Do a quick tally.

"Oh. Three. If you're that hungry." You. Very much hoping he'll be shamed into two. He isn't. Lid back on, tin back on shelf. Quick. And down from the shelf.

"I don't think that is the point of belief. No." Orion. Bloody hell. Is there no stopping him?

"Did you like the biscuits? I made them." You.

"They were very good indeed. Thank you." Might you like to be friends with Orion? Even though he's fantastically annoying. And has shocking jeans. And you still haven't heard him laugh. Listen. You can hear Star and Wolfie laughing. You and Orion are noticing this together. You're leading the way to the back door. Past the pottery.

"My dead dog's in that freezer." Passing the open door.

"Really? That's disgusting." Looking shaky.

"Why? And why is that disgusting but a ripped fanny isn't? And actually you don't have any right to talk about what is or isn't disgusting about fannies because you don't have one. That's sexism." Got him.

"I don't think it is sexism if it's the vagina you came out of and calling it a fanny is disrespectful and that is sexism." Unstoppable.

"It is sexism and names is not."

"It is."

"Isn't."

"Kids? Kids? Where are you?" Daddy. Good.

You and Orion are taking in Star and Wolfie. They're both on Star's beam, they're holding hands, she's trying to walk up his legs with him holding her, wobbling like crazy and trying to stay on. It's a bar routine. Star's been hassling you to attempt a bar routine for two years. It's possible Star may have an aptitude for bar routines that you lack so you've resisted the lure of glory. See them? Wishing you'd had a go? Too late now. They're very serious. Cripes, Wolfie's singing their sound track. Another of Star's top twenty hits. 'There Is A Mountain' by Donovan. He lifts her up for 'First there is a mountain.' One of her legs is standing on one of his, supported by his knee, and the other's trying to point out to the side. One hand's being gripped, the other hand reaches up and is pointing to the pretend mountain. This is Norfolk. 'Then there is no mountain.' They're both looking surprised at each other, that the mountain has just disappeared, and she's almost clambering down. 'Then there is.' He's doing a massive push and she's back up and they're both being amazed, by its miraculous re-appearance, then he's trying to turn them both in a circle. The rain's pouring down on them. The circling's not working so well. The wobbling is serious. But it's a pretty good start. You're sneaking a look at Orion. What does he think?

"Its influence is Buddhism." Orion.

"Kids? Where the fuck are you?" Daddy. From somewhere inside.

"What?" You. To Orion.

"The mountain that is but is not there. Buddhism." Orion.

"Kids. We need you in the Work Room, now. Come on!" Daddy.

The gymnasts are clearly not hearing or pretending not to hear Daddy. They've fallen off but are getting straight back on. Just like you're supposed to. Wolfie has a massive scratch down one leg. He's not interested in it. He is interested in Olympic gold.

"Come on. Work Room. School time." You. To everyone. "Zen Buddhism." To Orion. May as well get his facts straight. You're turning and leading the way. They're all trotting in after you. Trailing you through to the Work Room. Heads hung low. True school children. Smell that. Daddy and Rod must've been printing whilst you and Star waited on the wall. Yes, there're slightly damp pages of the Major Arcana draped around and drying. Have a quick gander at them. Has that Pelican poem already been done before Ginger Beer Gandalf's had a chance to edit his rubbish title for your better one? Hard to tell.

All Your People are in the room plus Ginger Beer Gandalf. The Hairy Dolly's not looking up when everyone else does.

"Yes, yes, yes, inspections." Ginger Beer Gandalf. They've stopped looking at you four, they're teaching Ginger Beer Gandalf how seriously they take him by giving him focus. The Hairy Dolly thinks the coast is clear, it's sneaking a peek. Grin back at it. Ha. It looked. Knew it would. Eventually. Hairy Dolly's sticking its tongue out at you and stopping looking. The cushions are out and in their circle. This is a meeting. Or it was. There's hardly time for you four to sit down.

"The inspection's at nine a.m. this Friday. We need to demonstrate we're a school. Yes, yes, yes. We'll meet here in this room at 8.45 a.m. It's called The School Room. We'll demonstrate a school assembly. We'll gather, a pupil might sing or read a piece of work or speak about something that has caught their interest that week, then the pupils will disperse. There'll be two lessons running simultaneously. One for the older kids, one for the younger. We need to choose the subjects you think you'll excel in. Now. We also need to name the school. Ok? Got it? The inspector can then ask questions. Then it will be.... um.... playtime. The adults will do the rest. Ok?" Ginger Beer Gandalf. Play time? Sounds grim. That's going straight in the pamphlet.

"This is what we normally do. Why can't we do it at home?" Orion.

"Yes, yes, yes. I've already explained the reasoning behind this. It's just for this one morning. We have to have numbers. And a suitable space. It'll be fine. You can do all the talking. It'll be fine." Ginger Beer Gandalf. To Orion. Excuse me? Think you'll find another of this so-called school's pupils can talk. And, has a good mind, to boot.

"I can bloody well talk. Let's do a poetry lesson." You. If it needed proving.

"Oh please, not poetry. Who'll be impressed by that? Let's do Astronomy. I'm already completing work at A level standard in Astronomy. And Physics. And Maths, at university entrance level, obviously. You can't study the sciences seriously without Maths. I have Maths A level. I got an A. When I was t... t.... t.... t.... t.... t... t...." Orion. The room is waiting Mr Articulacy. Star's looking up for the first time.

"Tortured?" Hairy Dolly. Nearly too quietly to be heard. It's getting up. "If there's anything you guys need me for, just shout. I'm going for a walk." Leaving the Work Room. Pretty Justin's on his feet and following.

"I like, so, would have like, so loved my school, yeah? To have been like, this, Yeah? Cool School." Pretty Justin. A blur and gone.

"Ok. You two do the Astronomy and you..." Daddy. Pointing at you. Why? "Can illustrate one of Orion's many brilliant observations by quoting from some apposite poem, that just happens to spring to mind, then the lesson can take the literary angle or the science one. Depending. Bob? You wanna handle these two?" Ginger Beer Gandalf's nodding. Could anyone be trusted with Orion's good mind, apart from his wizardy self? Even for one blinkin' lesson.

"I'll take these two. We'll improvise. School name?" Daddy. Improvise? Not fair.

"Rainbow School." You.

"Black Hole Comprehensive." Orion. At the same time. Tittering. At him, not you.

"It's not a joke. A black hole is a mathematically defined region of space time exhibiting such a strong gravitational pull that no particle or electromagnetic radiation can escape from it. Isn't that the effect we wish to have on the examiner?" Orion.

"Rainbow school's a little less heavy, darling, it has a sweet logic. Like your daddy says, it's just for a couple of hours. I'm absolutely certain that no inspector, on this miraculous planet of ours, could fail to be captivated by your intelligence. Let's stick with Rainbow and you can do most of the talking. Ok? And you don't need to worry, darling, I really don't think he'll be an examiner. Bob? Your son's enchanting." Mummy.

Look at Orion. He's blushing. Look at Ginger Beer Gandalf. He is too. Look at you. You clearly have no interest in providing 'sweet logic' you'd be far happier with the 'gravitational pull'. But too late now.

"I'll gladly give some form to the assembly. None divisional. A discussion around spiritual needs." Tammie. Very long silence. Orion's blank faced. With horror possibly but possibly not as this is the first time he's met Tammie. Eric looks solemn, his beard is nodding sagely. Everyone else is looking at someone else. For help.

"Nice idea, Tams. Thank you. I think that'll be just great. I'll put some thought into it too, in case we need any left-field inspiration on the day." Laura. Standing and being suddenly large in the room. Just with her body she can make the meeting end.

"Bob, it's been a pleasure meeting you in this capacity and I look forward to Friday. It'll be an experience. And you guys are?" Laura. To The Heroes.

"This is Orion." Ginger Beer Gandalf. Gesturing towards him.

"Ryan" Orion. Muttering again.

"And this is Wolfie." Ginger Beer Gandalf. Wolfie's silent, he's gone back to sharing the comic with Star.

"Great. So, Friday. Thank you all." Laura.

Imperative to make sure The Heroes understand Experiential Learning has serious benefits, so you'll be laying on the following:

SCHOOL DINNER

Lemon and pea soup
Cheese and leek pastries
Lemon and prune jelly. The fruit not the beast. Bit of a worry about balance in the menu, with lemon twice, but jelly's such a winner and this jelly's the winner's winner.

LEMON AND PEA SOUP

You make everything on Thursday night. So it can all just be there when the Heroes are hungry and the inspector has said everything is an inspiration to him and he'll be advising all schools to take a look at yours so they too can turn out such exceptional human beings.
Frozen peas. Problem. Jessie's still blocking up the freezer and

there's no way you're going to fish the peas out from under her. You got Daddy to do it. 'I picked the fluff off.' Daddy. When he saw you wait before taking the packets from him. 'Sorry. Fucking silly thing to say. We'll bury her tomorrow afternoon.' Right.

Lemon
Stock
Slosh milk
Dollops of Prune's yog.

Boil peas in stock. Bring to boil then off Aga. Don't massacre peaishness from the peas. Usual stock rules apply. Whizz in Mouli. Sieve it. Important to make smart soup. Add milk. Milk's instead of cream. You'd never be allowed cream for a school dinner, cream's for celebrational eating only. Squeeze lemon in. Do lemon bit by bit. Don't want to curdle milk. Lots black pepper, even for children. Taste. Dollop yog to serve. Tangyyyy.

CHEESE AND LEEK PASTRIES

'Pastry and pies. The direct route to a man's crotch.' Mummy. Not that you're remotely interested in the Heroes' penises but you do need them to be impressed. And the biscuits were a kind of pastry so it's just possible she's on to something.

Pastry. Usual method.
Leeks
Strong and tasty cheddar
Potatoes

Fry leeks. Boil spuds. When cooked, chop spuds small, mix with leeks and grated cheese. Let it cool a bit. Roll out pastry, cut into triangles.

Dollop of mix in middle of each pastry. Wet edges of triangle with milk, wrap them up. Squeeze tight so no mix oozes. Brush with egg to impress. Leave plain just for taste. Egg wash it is. Bake until pastry's hard and brown.

LEMON AND PRUNE JELLY

A lemon
3oz sugar
Agar
A handful prunes.

Peel lemon, drop peel into saucepan with prunes, sugar, pint and half water. Cook prunes. Cool a bit. Prunes out, stones out and chuck. Prunes into mould. Chuck lemon peel. Lay agar over cooking liquid, when dissolved add juice of lemon. Pour into mould. Set. Very boring you can't just use packet lemon jelly with extra juice for zing. 'To justify one's carnivorous instinct you have to do the slaughter test.' Mummy. 'Which is?' Daddy. 'Before you cook a living thing decide if you'd be willing to be its executioner. If you are then you've a moral right to eat it. I couldn't slaughter a horse.' Mummy. 'Surely gelatine comes from any old hoof they've lying around? Cow and pig would be the most common and you'd eat those.' Daddy. The argument swung on but the essence was no hooves so no gelatine. This jelly's extra tasty with a lick of cream to serve. No licking today. Today it's school dinner. Exciting. You've eaten real school dinner a few times. You and Star went to the village school for six weeks. It's not in your village it's in Burgh where the lock gates are. There were about twenty children split into two classes. Children seemed to do a lot of peeing on the floor and the head teacher had a snake shaped ring she put on and scraped down people's legs when she hit them. If they peed on the floor. 'The definition of a vicious circle.' Mummy. The dinners, however, were excellent. Star still makes the snot pie you used to get on Fridays for pudding. It's a pastry case then you put a tin of condensed milk unopened into a saucepan of boiling water and boil for half an hour. Open tin and pour into the pastry case. Looks exactly like the snot from a horrid cold. At school they grated chocolate whirls up top to serve. And you could have custard too. You don't get to do those bits but the snot pie's enough on its own. The other terribly good thing about school dinner was a vat of beetroot in vinegar. You could have as much as you liked, it went with fish and chips. Also on a Friday. Friday was the only serious day for real school.

The Heroes arrive early for the first day of Rainbow School, with a bag of turnips and swedes.

"We start the day by making our own soup. Then it's ready for lunch. It's really easy. You just chop up some vegetables, add water and put it on the stove to cook." Orion.

You're clutching the bag of whiffy veg. Staring. He clearly thinks you're amazed by the recipe's simplicity and in a way you are.

"Then at lunch we make chapatis. They're an Indian snack." Orion.

"I know how to make chapatis. Wholemeal flour and water. Roll it up, flatten out and put directly onto the hot plate of the Aga for a minute each side. Lightly fried glue." You. Still clutching the horrid veg.

"Really quite nice. With soup." Orion. Is he keen to impress you?

"Come with me." You. He's following. You're leading him to the fridge, opening the fridge, inside are the pies and jelly. The soup's beside the fridge. You're lifting its lid, sticking your finger in and holding it out to him. "Taste." He is. Feels very tickly and wet that sucking of your finger. He's sucking a bit too long. Like a baby lamb when you're trying to teach it how to drink from a bottle.

"Gosh. That's delicious. Is that home-made too?" Orion. Staring at the pies. You're closing the fridge. Slowly. He's snuffling up that fuff of fridgey-pie whiff.

"That is what we'll have for lunch. We can offer the inspector some. If you fail your tests." You. But look at him, he is worried. "Don't worry. You won't fail. There probably won't be a test, will there? Sorry we can't have your soup but we could try it another day. Possibly." You. Relenting. "Yes. It is." Just so he doesn't forget you can cook properly.

Everyone's filing into the Work Room-now-School Room. Eric's carrying a big file. Is that his garden planner? Whatever, he looks very teacherish. Has he combed his beard? Did Tammie comb it, as a love gift? Mummy's almost the last of the grown-ups to go into the room. Star and Wolfie have been in there since the Heroes arrived. Mummy's dressed up in a long skirt, a buttoned-up-to-the-neck shirt and has her hair in a huge French pleat. This is the most beautiful way to do long hair. Why the hell didn't you do one? Although you did wash yours. Then slept in plaits so now it's down, shiny and kinky. Like the inside of corrugated cardboard. It's grown this summer. It's nearly down to below your shoulder blades. It'll never be as long as Mummy's (or the Heroes) and it'll always be brown and not black but doesn't it feel lively moving about against your back? Like a little coat hanging off your head. You and Orion are the last to go towards the door. Oh. Had you forgotten the Hairy Dolly? Here it comes, seems to be coming to school too. You three are nearly at the door but it's moving itself in between you and Orion. Orion's leaping to one side to let it through. You're all three stopping for a second. The Hairy Dolly's sliding its hand up your back under your hair, pushing its fingers through and tugging it down.

"Watch out for him." Hairy Dolly. Nodding towards Orion. "I think he might wanna be your boyfriend. Shall we tell him you already have a boyfriend?" Tugging a little bit more on your hair. Stick with the less said to the Hairy Dolly the better ploy. Has Orion heard? He's not looking at it. He's looking at his sneakers.

"We're going to bury Jessie later. Daddy says." You. To the Hairy Dolly. Failing to keep quiet but not answering the stupid stuff about boyfriends. Why have you gone pink? Quite glad it said that boyfriend thing, strangely.

"Did Daddy?" Hairy Dolly. Damn. Now you feel little and very silly.

"Happy first day at school, Kiddos." It's swerved at the last minute and is going out of the front door. Right, need to sort this all out. Or try to. Oh bloody hell, look who's coming down the drive. The inspector. The Hairy Dolly's doing a salute to him. The inspector looks a little surprised but he's doing a jaunty one back and now is standing and checking some papers. Can you hear how quiet it's gone in the Work Room? The grown-ups must have spotted him too. Well done you, opening the front door going straight up to him and holding out your hand.

"Welcome to Swallow's Farmhouse." You. Loud. He's looking positively shocked and checking his paper again. Oh bugger.

"Welcome to Swallow's Farmhouse home of The Rainbow School." You. Can you hear the breathing out inside the house? It is happening. The inspector looks quite friendly. He has brown hair too. Floppy and wispy and curling up where it meets his shoulders. He has a pale purple shirt under his grey suit and look, he has real blue suede shoes. His clothes look a bit big for him and he doesn't look remotely scary. You're nearly holding his hand. For heaven's sake don't forget it's a test.

"Please follow me. We're about to start assembly." You. You've read enough school books to know how the Head Girl should behave when welcoming a visitor to school premises. In you go. The Work Room's been dressed up too. They must have done it when you were in bed. It has all yours and Star's recent paintings pinned in one corner, it has a sort of patchwork of maps, it has half a wall covered in black crepe paper and someone has painted hundreds of white stars all over it. Are they stars? They look like stars. There's a huge heap of nettles and a roll of chicken wire (that'll be to do hand-made paper-making with. Easy), all the Shakespeares, the printing press has Rainbow School on its blocks and there are sheets of paper with Rainbow School printed on, drying, draped all over. There's a long list of war dates scribbled on a roll of lining paper that's going over the ceiling and down to the floor. And it has the cushions. In their circle. Look at Orion. He looks strained to bursting. He doesn't seem to be able to look at the inspector.

"This is The Inspector." You. To Your People who are all sat with the Erpingham Heroes and of course Ginger Beer Gandalf. Another combed beard.

"Oh no. Please. No. I'm just here to evaluate. Um. Yes." Inspector. Checking his papers. "Evaluate. That's the word. Um. Hello. Shall I?" Inspector. Hovering over the plumpest cushion. Laura's up and gesturing him to sit.

"Hi. Welcome. Please. What do we call you?" Laura. Being big in the room again.

“Um. Um. Giles?” Inspector.

“Oh Cool. Giles. Hello Giles. So?” Laura. She’s looking round to Daddy, Mummy and Gandalf. No one’s doing anything. “Right. Well. Ok then. I’m Laura and these are the kids and... actually... is there any point in going through names? You just want to see us in action. Right?” Laura. Looking at the parents again. Still no one’s doing anything. Why?

“Yes please.” Inspector Giles.

Long bit of people looking to each other and trying to make each other do something with their eyes or nodding at each other, ‘You start, no you start, no you.’ Parental eyes. Orion’s got hot-red splashes high on his cheekbones. Star and Wolfie are looking up at Laura like eager seal pups. Why isn’t Daddy talking? Or Mummy? Or Ginger Beer Gandalf? He’s supposed to be the big expert. They’re looking at Tammie. She’s clearly praying for guidance. Thought she was going to be in charge at the beginning. But then Tammie often thinks she’s in charge when she’s being silent.

“How long have you been a school?” Inspector Giles. Helping out. Clearly all that silence and nodding was getting to him too. The School Room’s flying into action. This is not a question that anyone has a plan for. “Are these the only pupils?” Giles. Two impossible questions? Calm down, Giles. Daddy’s on his feet, colliding with Gandalf, they’re both trying to get their separate class going, you four kids are getting up silently, milling and bumping.

“Hey. Hey guys? Guys? Assembly? Let’s just take it back down a notch. Hey?” Laura. Laura is the Head Mistress of Rainbow School. Sheepish sitting down.

“Gruuuuuuunt puuuuuuuf.” Rod. Means he thinks Laura’s plan’s a good one.

"So. Ok. Beowulf and Star." Laura. Why's Inspector Giles jotting the names down? Ginger Beer Gandalf's thinking about deed polls.

"So, Giles, we've been doing some work on time, what it means to us, we've been thinking about the ways a notion of something that is at once so concrete and abstract might be expressed. These guys have put together something to share. We are slavish about creative expression here at Rainbow." Laura. Wow. Very much want to go to Rainbow.

Star's crouched like a nut in the middle of the circle and Wolfie has reached behind him for a guitar. A tiny, child-sized one. He's tuning it. Star's peeping at him, he's nodding. The opening chord of 'The Circle Game''s floating out. Wolfie has a sweet, sweet girl's voice and he can play the guitar. Laura's humming a harmony so quietly it's nearly not there. The whole thing's quiet. Star, the nut, is growing into a tree. Floating her arms up to the sky for 'fearful when the sky is full of thunder' and walking, undancishly, over to Orion and sliding her hands down his face for, 'tearful at the falling of a star'. It's the chorus. The best bit. 'And the seasons they go round and round and the painted ponies go up and down. We're captive on a carousel of time.' Star's spinning for the 'circle' stuff and doing a fairly convincing mime of trotting up and down and round and round, complete with reins, for the carousel ponies. It just gets better and better. Although never louder. Skating miming, Clocks ticking for 'words like – when you're older – must appease him', then a big jump thing that really does show everyone about 'promises of – someday – make his dreams.' Each time the chorus comes Star's back to the slow circling with arms out. Now the song's building and look, Pretty Justin's standing, joining the singing. He sings very high too. Rod's joining, his eyes are closed, swaying his head and drumming, a slow single thump on the

Shakespeares. Mummy's up, singing and clapping. Tammie's prayer's done, she and Eric are singing. To each other. Daddy's watching Star, intently. Flash of a wish that you'd known this was happening and not spent the whole of last night in the bloody kitchen is crossing your face but the final verse is irresistible to everyone. Apart from Orion. And Giles. Everyone else is singing and Wolfie has upped the volume and he's standing and tapping his foot as he plays and Star's in the middle spinning slower than ever.

"So the years spin by and now the boy is twenty
Though his dreams have lost some grandeur coming true
There'll be new dreams may be better dreams and plenty
Before the last revolving year is through.
And the seasons they go round and round
And the painted ponies go up and down
We're captive on a carousel of time
We can't return we can only look behind from where we came
And go round and round and round in the circle game."

Who knew Your People could sing so loud? Laura's stopping singing and is stepping back, everyone else is copying her, all watching Star and Wolfie.

"And go round and round and round in the circle game." Which they both sing together. Quietly again. No guitar. Just them. Looking serious. And small. Both in bobble hats. Remember the hats? Star and Wolfie will love each other and be inseparable from this day until the day Wolfie is killed on his first motorbike aged seventeen. By a lorry. On the long straight Norfolk roads. That's when Star leaves for America.

"I'm twenty." Inspector Giles.

"So how old were you when you went to university?" Orion. Quick as a flash.

"I didn't. I did a bit of teaching abroad. English in France. And a one-year teacher training course at City College. I've been taking some time to find out who I really am. You don't need a degree to work for the council. My job is... well... it's being created as I go along. I am helping to... well... to create it." Inspector Giles.

The room is horrified. Giles is realizing. See Giles being horrified himself?

"I didn't think it was appropriate to join in the singing. Sorry. Was I meant to? I could have. We could do it again. I might be able to harmonize. Please can we?" Giles. He looks hopeful.

"What are you talking about?" Daddy.

"What is your evaluation of all of this?" Ginger Beer Gandalf. Speaking at the same time as Daddy and sweeping his arm round.

"Dad? Please can we go home now?" Orion. Might he faint? Do you need to get him a water? Hope not. This is gripping.

"Hang on. What happens next... Giles?" Ginger Beer Gandalf. Before Giles can reveal his plan for you.

"Jesus fucking christ almighty, this is a classic fucking classic fucking fuck off to the alternative way. How dare you wander in here? Mr One-Year's Teacher Fucking Training at Shitty College. We're a Community. We are nurturing these young people's minds with love and creativity and you wander in here exploding all kinds of shit-waves in your wake. Do you realize this kid's closer to his Oxbridge degree than you could shake a shitty stick at. He has an A at A level for fuck's sake!" Rod. Full shit-throttle then suddenly shutting up. Got a point, as it happens.

Long very quiet bit. Daddy's reaching for a baccie tin, Rod's pushing one over with his toe. Daddy's starting to roll. Giles looks very sorry. The test is probably failed. Isn't it?

"Dad?" Orion.

"I have to say, Rod, that I'm gladdened by your appreciation of my writing, and thank you for being so keen to publish me, but my son's A level has nothing to do with any of you. If we ever stood any chance of this evaluation succeeding you've just blown it out of the water. Do you have any children?" Ginger Beer Gandalf. Clearing his throat. Means it's going to get heavy. "I apologise, Giles. This 'school' is a fabrication. I educate my children alone and in my own home. Any credit you might afford to Orion's success is solely mine. Or rather his and mine. It has nothing to do with these people. I thought you might need to see a larger group. You don't care, do you?"

"No." Inspector Giles. He doesn't care?

"Dad?" Orion.

"In a minute, Orion." Ginger Beer Gandalf. That's very snappy and mean.

"Ryan. Ryan. Ryan... Please, Dad. Please call me Ryan." Orion. Star and Wolfie are getting up, taking the guitar and Great Uncle Elizabeth, who's been asleep on the press, and heading towards the door.

"We're going for playtime now." Wolfie.

"Your poem's a truly terrible piece of work and you can consider it un-published. You asked us to gang up in this pathetic union. You were the one so craven with anxiety that someone would take the privilege of educating your wee hero away from you, so sure that no one else has a good enough mind to entrust him to. This scampering need to disassociate yourself, at the first possible moment, is inelegant. Like your writing." Daddy. Quite a low big daddy voice like he always uses when he's getting going. That's exactly what you said.

"You called me. You begged me to give you my poem. Six other magazines are giving it serious consideration, I'll have you know. Yes, yes, yes. You begged me to bring my sons into this house. This house where twelve-year-old girls are encouraged to write about sex like they're middle-aged prostitutes, then encouraged to undermine the craft of good writing by reading out said puerile drivel thus wasting serious writers' precious time. You begged me to shield you from the authorities so you could carry on ignoring the fundamental rights of your children to an education. You should be ashamed. Ashamed by your lack of respect for craft. Ashamed of the paucity of general knowledge your verbally precocious children exhibit." Ginger Beer Gandalf. The whole of his big bald head has by-passed red and gone a deep and worrying purple. Orion might be crying. Hard to see.

"Right. Fuck you. Fuck you. Fuck you. Only one of our children is verbally precocious, the other is a FUCKING MUTE." Rod. He's actually jumping up and down as he screams this. Has Rod ever taught you anything? Apart from don't risk a fast.

"Sigh." You.

"I thought, yeah, you know? That singing, yeah?" Pretty Justin. Leaving.

"That is not a constellation. That is just a splat of white paint." Giles. Pointing at the black star painting. He may as well join in.

Orion's stopping nearly crying and clocking Giles. He's the only one who's heard, everyone else's fully geared up. Apart from Laura who, look, is sitting cross-legged, head down, picking her thumb.

"They're my children. Mine. And Rod, my darling, thank you. Thank you for your noble anger on their behalf." Mummy. Daddy's whipping a look towards Rod. Nobility check? Rod looks like nothing so much as a cockerel that's just sat on three hens in a row. Puffed-up.

"Yes, yes, yes. That's my point they are yours and the boys are mine and the difference between them could not be more clearly defined and I am not talking about fucking gender." Ginger Beer Gandalf. Oooooow. Swearing.

"How dare you speak like that about gender in front of my daughter. You hideous hairless sexist. This is a gender non-specific community." Mummy.

"What does that mean? What does it mean?" Ginger Beer Gandalf.

"It means you're bald and nasty." Mummy.

"And not a poet." Rod. Is Rod the dragon Smaug?

"I'm really sorry but I will have to go now. I've to file my evaluation. Thank you for having me." Inspector Giles. Going.

Orion's leaping up, jetting out of the door after him. Look out of the window, see them in some fast conversation running up the drive. Inspector Giles is trotting to his little red Mini but Orion isn't letting him close the door. Inspector Giles's nodding and nodding and trying to get the car door from Orion. He's got it. Slam. He's driving off. Orion's run into the road waving him goodbye. Now Orion's coming back. But not back inside just to his bread van. You're getting up and leaving too. Risking a very big slam of the Work Room door. The shouting's getting going again behind the door.

You're going to the kitchen bit of the Big Room. Opening the fridge. Taking out five, no six, of the biggest pies, rummaging for a bag and dropping them in. You're going outside, up to the van and Orion.

"Pies." You. He's taking them. "They'll be best slightly heated but fine just as they are only please wait until the fridgey chill has gone before you try one."

"Is my dad's poem bad?"

"Yes."

"Is your dad a serious writer?"

"Um." Look at you thinking. You don't know, do you? "I don't know. I think so."

"If he was you'd know. My dad's reached the limit of his capacity as my teacher. I'm outstretching him." It's hard to like Orion but he's the only child you know, apart from Star, so may as well keep trying. For a bit.

"Will the chill be gone by now?" Orion. Sniffing the bag.

"No. Jesus, have some self-control." You. Bit mean. That is why you gave them to him.

"What on earth were the nettles for?" Orion.

"To sting the inspector to death." You. Orion isn't laughing. It's possible you'll never hear him laugh.

"The kids were good. Weren't they?" You.

"I'm tone deaf." Orion.

The shouting from inside the Work Room's getting shrieky. You and Orion are having a look at the window then looking back at the ground in front of the van.

"Maybe my dad will sting your dad to death with them." You.

Orion's scuffing up his sneakers.

"Do your house meetings end up like this, usually?" You.

"Yes." Orion.

"I did some reading on stars and stuff." Look at Orion, his pale brown eyes are shiny.

"What? What reading? What did you read about stars?"

"I didn't have much time. I had to cook these and the jelly that's in the fridge and I had to finish... *The Golden Bough*... but I read up everything I could find in the encyclopedia." You haven't read *The Golden Bough*. It's in a very dusty pile beside the loo but it's the first grown-up title you can think of and Orion needs to knows that you do read. And you could easily have read it. You will read it. As soon as your dog's buried.

"I can lend you some reasonably simplistic books to get you going. I'll send you a list and then you can apply to the travelling library. I can educate you." Is that happiness? "What kind of jelly? Is it home-made?" He's obsessed with home-made.

"Was Giles keen on stars and stuff too?" Want to know what the fast chat was about.

"Yes. Lay man. But yes. Can we eat the jelly now?"

Ginger Beer Gandalf's running out of the house, he has Wolfie with him.

"Get in the van this minute, Orion." Ginger Beer Gandalf. Orion's hesitating. Clearly contemplating a dash for a mouthful of jelly. "Orion. This instant. In." Orion's climbing in. Dragging his sneakered heels.

"Bye, Ryan." Great big hair toss as the van doors are sliding closed. Just in case. And vroom. They're gone.

Right. How do you bury a frozen dog? You're standing for at least ten minutes watching the road where the van disappeared. Real ten minutes just standing is a long time. The house is quiet now. Occasional slams of doors but nothing much else. You're waiting. Daddy will stick to his word. He'll be digging the grave. How long does it take to dig a grave? How deep do you need to go to stop her smell leaking out when her juices start to seep? How many years before Jessie is earth? Must you look at her to say goodbye? Will Your People think you didn't love her enough if you don't look at her? You want her blanket to be gone too. Could that go into the grave? Or does it have man-made fibres? Will the blanket be dug up by a tractor in fifty years' time, washed and put on somebody's sofa? You're going inside. Star's curled on the sofa with Great Uncle Elizabeth and a heap of comics.

"Where did you get those?" You.

"Wolfie. Don't mess them up when you read them. They're on loan." Star. Words.

"Has he done it yet?" You.

"They're still digging." Star. Going back to the comic.

Summon every single bit of bravery you have and go to the back door. Not looking towards the freezer as you're opening the back door, walking to the hilly bit of garden that drops to the field and going down. You're stopping beside the hen hut. There they are at the tippety top of the field. Just the men. But it is all the men. Daddy, Eric, Rod, Pretty Justin and even the Hairy Dolly. Didn't know there were that many spades. They're all at it. Looks as if they're drinking home brew. They've got the big blue bucket that brew's made in. They dig then stop, dip a mug, drink then dig a bit more. Eric's jumping into the hole. Daddy's passing him a spade.

"Do you want to say some words?" Mummy. Softly. Suddenly beside you.

"Argh!" You. Six foot in the air.

"So sorry, darling, I didn't mean to startle. Sorry. Do you?" Mummy.

"It isn't a baby blackbird we've found dropped from its nest and are doing a pretend funeral for, with stupid droopy garlands, singing and fucking ashes. No. Thanks." You. Landing.

"Please don't be nasty. I know what 'it' is. It is our precious dog and it is very, very sad and you are allowed to cry and be sad but please don't be a bitch. It won't help you and it won't help me." Mummy. Crying. Will you ever be able to cry for your dear best most beloved dog? Or is Mummy using up all the tears?

They're burying Jessie without you. Take that pile of comics to your room and read them. All. Better start that *Golden Bough* too. Two pages. Bloody hell, really? Put that back. At least it's been dusted. The burying's taking a very long time. Go to the landing window Again. Try and watch but it's round the corner and you can't see. Might that be singing? Back to bed. Quite like *The Dandy*. Re-read the opening chapter of *Mallory Towers*. Enid at her best. Searching your book pile, under your bed, for *The Lark In The Morn* by Elfrida Vipont.

"Knock, knock, knock." Bedroom door.

The Lark In The Morn is by far and away the best book ever written. Guaranteed to induce an aching need to have been born to an Ancient Quaker Family. Not a family of old people. A family of people who have been Quakers for ever.

"Knock." Bedroom door. Who is it?

"Who is it?" You.

"Yeah. Me." Pretty Justin. He's taking advantage of the house position on locks by pushing the door open.

"I think, yeah, like, really, do think, yeah you should come." Pretty Justin. In the door.

"No." You.

"It's like too heavy, yeah? Way too heavy and if you, like, you know? I think it'll. Yeah?" Pretty Justin. Come to think of it you haven't spoken to Pretty Justin for so long now. When was the last time you cuddled?

"No." You.

"Come." Pretty Justin.

"No." You. He's checking behind him and coming into your room. Going to have to cash-in those post office stamps and get a fucking big bolt.

"I, yeah, I, Just. I wanted to, like, say something, yeah?' Pretty Justin. Something like – might it be possible to enter your private room. Please?

"Um. The other night, yeah?" Pretty Justin. Ah.

"Yes?" You. Unhelpful.

"He doesn't remember, yeah? Like totally doesn't like... you know, yeah?" Pretty Justin.

"What?" You. Very unhelpful.

"It was so, I mean, so, yeah? Obscene. It was like, oppression. I wouldn't, I want you to, yeah? To know, yeah? I wouldn't be, like, ever, sleeping, yeah? Bryan and me, yeah? We are, like so, a couple. I mean, yeah? He won't admit, you know? He won't... but I would never, couldn't, you know? I wouldn't be with him, yeah? If he wanted that? You know? From you? Yeah? What he said? He, like, totally can't remember, yeah? He thinks, you are like, you are, yeah? He says 'sweet kiddo', you know? Just like teasing? Yeah?" Might as well attempt discussion of pacifist politics with Prune.

The Hairy Dolly doesn't remember? Was it very drunk? Is it lying? Does Pretty Justin believe what he's saying? Yes. And Pretty Justin and the Hairy Dolly are sleeping together. Is the Hairy Dolly a queer? You'd be interested in being a lesbian so you could say – I'm a queer. Sounds excellent. But only homosexuals can actually say it. Or it's offensive. Like when those kids from the village were chanting about Clarissa being a 'Nig Nog Black Bastard'. You saw white light all round the biggest boy's head. Real white light. You were so angry it didn't even feel like anger. Something more and something simpler to deal with. You flew at that boy's eyes screaming 'She's not black she's brown!' You made him bleed copiously. Calling people black, who were born in Africa and are also more English than a strawberry, is offensive. Black is for horrid little imps that live under bridges in fairy tales. Clarissa always says the strawberry thing. Although she won't eat them. Too watery. Clarissa likes meat dishes best.

"What's it like sleeping with Bryan?" You. Been meaning to get a grown-up to tell you a few solid details and now you can because Pretty Justin wants you to do things. Like come downstairs and believe the Hairy Dolly. Look at him, he's aching to tell. And you did ask.

"Perfect. His skin. Yeah? You know his nose? When his eyes look in, yeah? When he is..." Pretty Justin. Working out exactly what to tell and sitting on your bed. "He does have the, yeah, problem, yeah but you know? He says, yeah? He says, yeah? It was the same with your mom so it's not about, you know? Not about, yeah? Men. It's always been. He gets so. I mean he is so. He gets so excited he can't like help it, yeah?" Help what?

"Is he furry all over?" You. Meaning The Penis.

"Yeah." Must like it. Or not have understood. Can it really be hairy?

"And I know it's yeah? It's you know? It's small. But I mean, I like so love that. You see how all of him, yeah? He's small all over. Yeah?" You'll just have to ask someone else about sex. Bloody Star would be more help.

"Knock, knock, knock." Door.

Who the bloody hell's that? Pretty Justin's bumped his head falling off the bed. You look very relaxed and comfy. That some other bloody bastard's just opening your door. Surprise. It's the Hairy Dolly. And its hairy willy.

"Where's my girlfriend? I've been delegated to fetch you. What're you doing here?" Hairy Dolly. To you then Pretty Justin.

"I'm like fetching yeah?" Pretty Justin. Off his own back? Pretty Justin's beside the Hairy Dolly. Close beside.

"You're becoming a master of initiative." Hairy Dolly. Putting its arm round Pretty Justin's waist.

"Come on Nearly Thirteen. It's just one of those things you need to learn to do. Pay your respects at the grave. Stop moping. It makes your pretty plump mouth all droopy." Hairy Dolly. "What? What? It is pretty." To Pretty Justin.

"Is all the earth back up top?" You. To either of them.

"Fuck yes. Hours ago. That was the easy bit. You should have helped with the hole. It's possible that everyone should dig the hole for their loved one's grave. It's fucking hard work and you're sick of them by the time it's dug. And you've got blisters. Come on down and drink some beer. Take your meds, Kiddo." Hairy Dolly. It's kissing Pretty Justin and leaving.

BEER TO DRINK AT THE WAKE OF A DOG

Big bowl
Big bag hops. The only one you can buy.
3lbs gran sugar. Beer has a lot of sugar. Far more than cake.
2lbs malt extract. Another kind of sugar.
Dried yeast. Not brewer's yeast. This is better.

Hops into massive pan, fill with water, simmer ¾ hour. Strain into bucket. Into saucepan with sugar, malt, fill pan with water, heat to dissolve. Pour into bucket. Sprinkle teaspoon yeast up top. Put near Aga with tray over for two days. Then skim off yucky froth. Stinks. You can smell fizz in the froth's smell. Not in a tasty way. Leave another five days. Might need to scrape again during. Sieve into couple Corona bottles with screw lids. Don't fill to brim. Like Ginger beer. Might turn into a beer-bomb. 1 teaspoon sugar into each bottle.

More sugar. Screw down lid, drink about a week later. Absolutely disgusting but useful for sadness.

Just give up. You're getting off your bed putting the comics back on Star's pillow. Following. Pretty Justin's trying to take your hand as you pass. You're pretending not to have felt and are off downstairs. No more droopy mouth for you. Into the Big Room. Laura's writing sat at the table. She's glancing up, smiling but in a normal way not a 'Oh it's so sad' way. Thank you, Laura.

"Good. About time. Thank you for the food. We saved you some soup." Mummy. Soup? What about the home-made jelly?

The adults have been infected by Star and Wolfie and have caught Joni Mitchel. They're playing 'Both Sides Now'. This is actually too much. You're nipping straight over to the blue box of the record player, got that off and you're searching the record stack. Star's beside you. She's got earth under her finger nails. Hairy Dolly's getting the jugs, going to the money drawer, filling its pockets and going out of the front door. Star's flashing you The Bay City Rollers, 'Bye Bye Baby'. She's got it on. You're doing checking this will do, listening with each other. Bit of a nod and Star goes back to her comics. Nobody's really doing anything. Why have they all made such a fuss about getting you down here? The beer's all gone. Someone will be drunk. Hard to tell who. That's the back door opening. Must be Daddy. Go out to meet him, he's coming into the kitchen, his hands are crusted in grave mud. He's got Jessie's food bowl and his beer mug standing inside it. Jessie's bowl's still covered in food scraps. Daddy's taking it to the sink, scrubbing and scrubbing. Using his long nails to pick the dried-hard food off. The water's suddenly steaming hot, Daddy's leaning his arms on the sink, the grave mud and scraps water is pouring down the plug and Daddy is crying. Oh. You've never seen your daddy cry. You're turning off the tap, taking the bowl. He's still crying. You're finishing washing it looking back into the Big Room. Laura and Mummy are watching. Eric and Tammie are watching but pretending not to. Rod's starting to cry. Rod's such a cry baby. Pretty Justin's reading one of Star's comics and Star's reading hers. Star's a big fan of the comic. Hairy Dolly's coming in the front door. It has three jugs of beer. It has whizzed to the pub.

"Hullllooooo Hullllooooo Hulloooo I am the Beer Man." Hairy Dolly. Stating the obvious. Filling up the empty and eager mugs.

"That fucking bald arsehole. I can't get him out of my head. How dare he patronize us? All that shit about undermining craft. Fuck him." Rod. To no one in particular. Is it Rod that's the really drunk one? The Bay City Rollers have finished. Daddy has too. Hairy Dolly's found a mug and is pouring for you.

"Anthony? Is this cool?" Hairy Dolly. About your beer.

"It's fine. Only one cup. She had her first wine when she was ten. Watered Barsac. At Christmas. Like the French. It's important for children to develop a palate." Mummy. Answering for Daddy. Surely she's told them this before? And was it ten? Star's been having the watered Barsac for years.

"Takes a craft mangler to know a craft mangler. Poet know thy self." Daddy. Normal again reaching across the table to get a letter for him that hasn't been opened. "Cheers Man." To the Hairy Dolly as it's pouring beer for him.

You're sipping your beer. Just get it drunk. Don't want to waste the opportunity of alcohol. Not because it's tasty but it's important to be allowed it. Good job they aren't giving Star any, it's almost impossible not to burp each sip you take.

"Okaaay." Daddy. Quietly but so fully that everyone's pausing in their doing not much and glancing up at him. And his letter. Another letter?

"Whadda they wanna screw us over for this time?" Hairy Dolly.

"The Oracle want to publish 'The Plough'." Daddy. Re-reading the letter. Not looking at anyone.

"The poem, yes?" Rod. Looks like he's been poured from concrete.

"Apparently not. Apparently they want the full collection. All twenty-six poems." Daddy. Still not looking up.

"The Oracle? New York The Oracle?" Rod.

"Darling, how marvellous." Mummy.

"Anthony man, you will rock NY. Hey, hey, hey. The fucking Oracle has spoken, man. Twenty fucking six poems." Hairy Dolly. Really, really happy for Daddy, up and banging Daddy on his back and pouring so much beer.

"Congratulations. That's grand." Eric. Tammie's nodding, Star has her arms wrapped round Daddy's waist, he's tapping her shoulders, smiling and he still hasn't looked up from the letter. You're going to hug him too. You are.

"Oh wonderful, wonderful day." Mummy. Well not completely. You're going to have a report filed and your dog is up the field under the earth but the poems are very good news.

"Thank you. All." Daddy. Looking up.

"But that's a book." Rod. Still looks like concrete. Bemused concrete.

"I think it is. Finally. A book." Daddy. Oh. Daddy will live.

"Do they say why they want your poems?" Rod. Why aren't you hugging your Daddy?

"Because he's the best writer, Rodders. Anthony is the friggin' winner." Hairy Dolly. Brimming over with glee. And beer.

So. Your daddy is a serious writer. Better send Orion a letter.

CHAPTER EIGHT

Dear Orion,
I hope you enjoyed the pies. We ate ours at the wake for my dog. You may remember my telling you my dog has died...

Dear Orion,
If someone gives you a bag full of pies you really should send them a thank you letter. And you did say you were going to send me a book list. I know our Dads...

Dear Ryan,
Hi! I hope you are very well. Did you like the pies? Would you like the recipe? So what has been happening to you these last few weeks? Things have been pretty normal here apart from my dad getting his book...

Hello Ryan,
Do you still want to be called Ryan or has your dad made you swap back again? My dad is getting some poems published. Are you...

Dear Orion,
I know you want to be called Ryan but I am not sure if that is correct when corresponding via post so please forgive my use of

your old name. Please can you send me the titles of some good star books? I find myself more and more fascinated by stars, these days. My dad is getting his book published in the States. Are you lot going to the Winter Solstice Medieval Fayre in Suffolk? Did I tell you...

Orion,
You are quite rude not sending a thank you letter for those pies I made for you. Are you going to the solstice thing? My dad says that your dad is typically...

Dear Ryan,
Star and Wolfie seem to be getting on very well. She's always sloping off to the phone box by Ma Burts with stolen 2ps. I suppose they are very close in age. When are you going to send me that book list? Or are you too busy building your own spaceship so you can see them for yourself? Ha, Ha. I think we will all be...

ORION?
PIES????

Before you can send any of them one arrives for you.

My sincere apologies for the delay. Please find enclosed a list of books to commence your studies. Ensure you read them in the order indicated.

And that is it. Apart from the bloody list. You bin his bloody stupid list. You couldn't be less interested in bloody stars. Apart from Astrology. Which is obviously a remarkably accurate system that's been in place for millennia. Unlike Astronomy which is just modern science. Anyway, you and Star have costumes to make. When you can get her out of the phone box that is. It's December, it's cold, but not cold enough for snow. You spend a great deal of most winters longing for snow. It's so cleansing. Unless you tread in buried dog poos. But that won't happen so much anymore as most of Jessie's are disintegrated now. The only real negative with snow is Mummy's allergy to it. 'Where the hell are my bloody fucking sunglasses? I. Can. Not. Step. Out. Of. The. Fucking. House. Without. Them. I will go blind.' Strawberries and crab have a similar effect on her. Clarissa's the same. Not the blindness but she hates snow too. Not that keen on the strawbs either obviously but that's just an opinion. It's better if it snows when Clarissa's visiting because then her and Mummy can go back to bed for the day and read *Vogue*. 'I'm a major snow freak. These kids need to learn to ski. Where can we take them? It's a friggin' life skill.' Laura. Two winters ago. When there was enough snow to use the Aga trays to sledge down the hill on the road to Aylsham. You wrecked the Aga trays. It was utterly marvellous. Laura and The Hairy Dolly stood in the road at the top and stopped any cars that came along and made them wait whilst you and Star, and then them, hurtled down the ice path you'd made by pouring water onto the road. Cars got pretty irritated and there was a lot of hooting. Star almost broke her legs smashing into the gate at the bottom but she ignored it. Gargantuan bruise. Aga tray buckled and all pies baked in it since have a hill in the middle where the buckle pushes the tray up.

There's been a suggestion that it might well snow at Christmas. It'd be even better if it snowed at the Solstice Fayre. Everyone's hopeful. Apart from Mummy. Not that she's wanting the snow to stop the Fayre. The Fayre's something Mummy manages every year. Daddy and her stay together holding hands, she sometimes does have a few spitting in hankies times but only really if the 'My Pots' aren't selling too well. 'I adore the Fayre more than my life. It's so blissfully timeless.' Mummy. At the House Meeting to plan this year's trip. 'Good job it's timeless since it's a celebration of an event first recognized by our brothers the cave men set in a quasi Medieval land but actually taking place in the late December of 1974.' Daddy. 'And our sisters.' Mummy. Daddy's pretty anti the dressing up in Medieval costumes, says he's just going to wear his mole. He always wears his mole. Every winter, all winter long, inside the house and out. The mole's exactly what it sounds like. A big ladies coat made out of hundreds of mole skins. 'The rest of you can freeze your arses off titting around in anything you can find with absurdly long sleeves. Just make sure the kids don't go near any camp fires if they insist on those hats with the veils trailing down the back. Again.' Daddy. You've worn one of those for the last four years and although they're beautiful and make you feel beautiful, this year it's time for a change. Hand-made, full, court jester costume. Even with the little doll on a stick to wag at people when they don't like your jokes. Or are just annoying. Been dying heavy weight T-shirting in batches of red and yellow for two days. Cut into strips, sewn into sideways stripes.

The Work Room. You're lying on the stripes and Star's drawing round you with chalk. Twice. Once for the front once for the back. Done. Time to cut yourself out. Twice. Done. Time to thread the dilapidated treadle sewing machine. Sewing your self-bits together. Hey Presto. A sleeping bag with legs. And stripes. You're staring at yourself inside it trying to work out why it isn't perfect.

"Hot air balloon." Star.

"Yes. Very funny. I know. It's just the start." You.

"No. You can't wear it. You can't." Star. Choking on her own laughter snot bubbles. Oh just mute-up why don't you. There're acres of red and yellow stripes all over the Work Room.

"How fat do you think you are? Snort, snort, snot." Star.

"It's a template." You. What is wrong with it?

"For a hot air balloon." Star. Ignore her, she's so childish.

"You need to cut the bottoms off. Needs to be just the balloon jacket, then wear tights and make a three pointy hat out of the balloon too. Have we got any bells?" Star.

"And sew some balloon onto some shoes." You. She's absolutely right. It's going to be brilliant. Although risk of shoe stripes un-curling in potential snow?

"Budge up. I'm doing my hat." Star. And she is. The only Medieval thing she's going to wear is the hat. The rest's going to be warm. Daddy's old sheep. Much like the mole. Two old sheepskins sewn together at their legs worn draped over the shoulders. Needs a belt to work as a coat waistcoat thing. Last year Star got lost for a day and a half and got very cold indeed. The Fayre's in a five-acre field with un-countable acres of woods. She couldn't find her way back to either of the kid's teepees, had to sleep under someone's van. It was very lucky indeed she didn't actually die. Mummy sobbed and sobbed when she turned up at the pottery stall for breakfast. Although no one had realized she was missing until about an hour before The Return. Everyone blamed everyone else and thought she was with the others. You still blame yourself. So does Star. Rightly. And Mummy. 'Christ almighty she's your sister. What were you thinking letting her go off like that?' Mummy. You were watching a magic show and refused to go begging with Star, that's when she stropped off and you didn't bother finding her. Then you assumed she was sleeping in the other teepee. Which was bloody stupid of you as she'd never not sleep with you. You missed her all night but there's no point in telling her that. You'll never ever lose anyone ever again. On purpose.

Few days later. Fayre time. Your people will find spaces in someone else's teepees to sleep in and you and Star will be in the North Field kid's teepee. Like you were supposed to be last year. The White Saab's rammed with old fruit boxes full of Mummy's 'My Pots' pots. 'There'll be Artists and Makers everywhere. There's absolutely no point in taking Domestic Wear. No one with Serious Taste will be interested in bloody stew pots.' Mummy. About why her stall will be the wibbly wobbly hand-built stuff with the holes cut out. Daddy and Mummy are travelling with the pots, you and Star are in the van with Your People.

"Make sure you come to the stall when you first arrive. To orientate. Then you can do what you want. Apart from abandon your sister again." Mummy. As she's sliding into the White Saab. Look at Mummy. She's head to toe in purple velvet robes. Not robes like Tammie's I'm-A-Christian-Now robes but more like a dress that flows. It's tied up on her little boy's hips with a rope that she plaited out of silver wool. She's got her hair down 'Oh god, it's just to keep me warm.' Mummy. To the Hairy Dolly when it gave her a tug. She's got a same purple velvet pointy hat to wear up top. She can't wear the hat in the White Saab, it's very tall indeed. She's made a silver river to drip down from the peak of the hat out of the silver wool.

"Shame there isn't a Miss Medieval Fayre beauty pageant. You'd take the crown." Daddy.

"Not sure you'd get a crown on over the giant's ice cream cone." Hairy Dolly. Hopping into the driving seat of the van.

"Don't stand too close to that hat, Bryan, it's taller than you." Rod. Mummy's snapping a look his way. "Magnificently tall. Great lady of the greatest Isle, whose lights

Like phoebus lampe, throughout the world doth shine,

Shed they faire beams into my feeble eyene. Puff."

Mummy's blessing him with her finger tips trailed over his shoulders, then tucking herself in the White Saab. Having a think about winning a pageant. Wish there was one. Although there's no way you could enter dressed as a fool and this jester costume is most pleasing apart from, can you feel the wind on your legs, dressed only in tights, as you're waiting for your turn to clamber into the back of the van? It's cold. Properly. Your bum's poking out from under the jacket and that's especially frozz. You will have to be careful of the shoes. Had to glue the red and yellow stripes onto a pair of old, slightly too small, wellies, cut off at the ankle. The glue – Copydex – is already coming unstuck. Snow? Imperative to do at least the first day with full stripes so as many people as achievable can appreciate the extent of this creation.

"Right. Swallow's Farmhouse, we'll see you in three days. Hens? Don't gorge on your corn supplies. Uncle Elizabeth, keep an eye on Prune. Ta-Ra." Daddy. Calling out the White Saab window as they reverse back out of the drive. Jessie always used to come too. Hens are designed to be a bit wild. A cat can fend for itself because winter's especially rich in mice and Prune's ok inside her shed, with loads of hay, for just three days. She's just stopped lactating so she won't be in pain. She'll be toastie. You're straining for your last glimpse of Mummy. Mummy's turning and doing her little wave. She's done it. It's going to happen. Cinderella will go to the ball. Hurry up rats, get that fucking pumpkin on the road.

"Let's get outta here before she gets him to turn back cos she simply cannot leave without one more friggin' bath." Hairy Dolly. In a lady voice. Silence. People piling into van.

Everyone's crouched on their rolls of bedding holding on to the sides of the van. There aren't any windows in the back so the grown-ups will swap halfway through the journey to make sure everyone gets a go up front. Eric and Rod are in the front with the Hairy Dolly, to start off. Pretty Justin looks annoyed that he's with the kids in the back. You heard him telling Hairy Dolly to sit next to him for the whole drive. The Hairy Dolly looked as if it hadn't heard him. It's very relaxing since the Hairy Dolly and Pretty Justin have become lovers. They don't do much talking to anyone else, quite like Eric and Tammie come to think of it, but they don't do much talking to each other either. Unlike Eric and Tammie who're always talking to each other. In whispers. Making big, constantly surprised faces. Pretty Justin and Hairy Dolly are quite grumpy when they do talk. Pretty Justin always goes to bed really early then Hairy Dolly doesn't notice then it looks towards the upstairs door, for about an hour, does yawning, then it slopes off to bed early too. You and Star are always up later than those two these days. Hairy Dolly's lost all interest in your mouth. Great. You do see it having some looks at you when you aren't expecting it but these aren't serious looks. Is it in love with Pretty Justin? 'Who'd be a queer? Looks especially grim work being someone's bum boy.' Daddy. To Rod one night as the Hairy Dolly sulked off to bed. 'Not to mention the bumming.' Rod. Snickering like a little pony. 'Oh, I'm sure that bit has its charms.' Daddy. Rod looked amazed. Laura and Mummy were watching Eric and Tammie who were pretending not to listen. Again. But about the bumming Tammie and Eric did do some head shaking then Mummy and Laura did some smiling. You and Star just carried on doing Poker Face. You were playing Poker. For the house stash of half p's. What's bumming?

"Please can you bang on the driver's wall. I need to be sick." You. To Tammie who's nearest the driver's end of the van. And as the van takes a particularly swervy bend.

Van humping up onto a verge, Eric opening the back, you're clambering over legs to the air beside the van and whoops. More sick. This is your third time.

"Eric? For god's sake let her swap with you. She needs to see where the road turns before it does." Laura. Good idea. Eric looks reluctant. "You can support Tammie's bump. It's pretty bouncy back here." Laura. Persuasive.

"Rod. Get out and let her in." Eric. About you. "Tammie, Doll, you take ma place. Someone should've told me about this. It's dangerous for you in here." Eric. Swooping Tammie out of the back.

"Star can sit on my lap. In case she gets sick too." You. Star's right on this, jumping up and onto you.

Off you go again. Much comfier. Apart from the stink. Damp old sheep. Star.

"Put your foot down then." You. To the Hairy Dolly. See it wink at you? Woah, feel that jerky lurch?

"I think that's enough pass the parcel for one journey. Let's just get there shall we?" Hairy Dolly. Foot down.

It's the long, straight, last bit of road, the Hairy Dolly's winding down its window to see if you can hear the Fayre. The van's hurtling along.

"These fields have been truly fucked. Norfolk's the weanus twin of Texas. Guess that's why we yanks love it so." Hairy Dolly. Scanning the giant patchwork ghost fields. Weanus is a Norfolk word. All Your People adore it. Means runt of the litter. You learnt it from Bad Dog Farm. 'You wanna keep your weanus away from our dogs. They'll have her.' Bad Dog Farmer. To Daddy and gesturing at Star. It was too funny not to laugh. Unless you were Star. But you're not. So. Ha, ha. Weanus.

Good thing about all this hedge-less decimation is that sound carries. Here that? That is it. There must be at least four or five different music happenings going on. Trumpets are the sound that sing out over the top of the rest. Great. Trumpets mean the People's Collective Of Brass and Beastuary are playing again this year. They're a band, they do hits from musicals and dance hall numbers, dressed as beasts. It's yours and Pretty Justin's best thing, it's why Pretty Justin taught you to dance. So you could clear the dance floor. Not that it's a floor just The Beasts' bit of field. Here it comes. The Winter Solstice Medieval Fayre Happenings And Creative Expression 1974. Acres and acres of teepees and flags. The haze-umbrella is covering all those fields. It's coming from the bonfires, of all sizes, dotted everywhere. There's the patchwork, of green tarp roofs of the stalls, up on the West Hill. The Commercial sector. That's where Mummy will have her stall. You and Star have to do a two-hour stint working the stall each day. Two hours each. So it isn't all work for Mummy and she gets her chance to experience the Fayre fully. Working the stall's fine, you have a system, you double up, doing the four hours together as a selling team. The Entertainment sector's over the other side, in front of the trees. Experimental Happenings will be inside the trees. You and Star aren't forbidden from going into the trees but you do have to go together. 'Grown-ups can get into some seriously weird shit up there. It isn't just Awaken Your Inner Wild Man and the likes.' Daddy. He says this every year in some form or other. Daddy always does one Inner Wild Man Happening. 'I need all the support to my masculine side I can get living in this house.' Daddy. Rod spends most of his time doing everything Inner Wild Man. Pretty Justin tried it once but said it was a little bit silly and he preferred dancing. Daddy did agree about it being silly but said that was ok too. And actually they do dancing because you must never give a sword to a man who can't dance. The Inner Wild Men strap antlers to their heads and canter about.

Hairy Dolly's dropping you and Star off at the entrance gate, going to park the van with the others still inside. Smell that. Pig, pig and more pig. Roast not rooting. And sugar. The air at the Fayre swirls with that improbable combination. All day and all night long. You and Star are gently manoeuvring your way to your rightful positions at the front of the queue. You've your bedding rolls and your grubby, twisted-tickets clutched. There isn't too much queue to piss off by jumping it; most serious people will already be inside. You're late.

"Excuse us, please? We're really sorry but we've lost our mummy and daddy and we need to get inside, please. So sorry. Please can we go first? We've lost our mummy." You. To queue. Who could refuse?

"Hey Guys, nice hat Star, get to the back of the queue, both of you." Ticket checking man. Might be called Big Leftie. Why?

Mummy took quite a long time packing. Then she needed a bath before the off. This is entirely normal. Mummy nearly always has a last-minute surprise bath before leaving the house. It's imperative that Mummy feels as beautiful as possible. You're both scouting the queue from your degrading positions at the back of it. Everyone's done a costume. Daddy's going to stick out in the green velvet trews and mole. Star's nudging you and pointing. Good looking gang, they look quite young, maybe fourteenish? There're five of them, they come from a commune, you can tell from the fringes. Must be a new one or they'd know this is too late to be arriving. They've come as a team. They're a team of beggars. Why the hell didn't you think of this? It'd be so warm and the look could only improve as the weekend goes along and you get dirtier and dirtier. Look that brown one's smiling. Do not smile back at the competition. Begging's how you and Star spend most of the time you aren't working the stall, dancing, eating or sleeping. You're the Fayre's most seasoned real beggars. People recognize you each year. It's very good money indeed, especially at night when people are out of it. So, no random smiling at new people. Now is not the time to make friends. Not that you need any. The other way to make good money's to get up early and go to the site where last night's main gig was and search the ground for cash that's fallen from the stoned audiences floppy pockets. You once found twenty pounds. Which was amazing luck as Mummy and Daddy can only spare two pounds a day for food. There's a proper variety of food here that really does need to be tasted. Sometimes more than once a day.

FAYRE FOOD YOU CANNOT IGNORE. Smell or taste.

Home-made sausages with heaps of fried onions on white bread rolls with tomato ketchup. Yes. It's true.
Waffles with cream and maple syrup and bananas.

HOME-MADE SAUSAGES. Roast pig smell.

Absolutely no idea how sausages are made. 'You don't ever want to know, Darling.' Mummy. When you asked. This blows her executioner theory but when Mummy contradicts herself it's not worth pursuing. There'll be heaps of reasons. Sausages do, however, involve pig or indeed even quite unpleasant sections of pig. Could it be the pig's willy? Its eyeballs? Pretty much certainly its brain. Lots of people find they enjoy a bit of brain. Never been tempted so far. Sausage will be crammed with weanus, no doubt about that. You and Star did have pet pigs. Once. Apple and Pear. Because they lived in a borrowed derelict orchard. They lived there for a year. Then they were delicious, very orchardy in taste, interestingly. Idea was you'd become realistic about slaughter from petting your food. It'd desentimentalize said food, to be so actively involved in its production. More evolved version of executioner theory. What actually happened was the adults were a bit shocked by how interested you both were in all the blood. You had to do some pretend crying about dear dead piggies on the way home from the slaughter house, whilst cradling said piggies all jointed and laid out in cardboard boxes, to make them feel less anxious. Adults not dead pigs. The Fayre Sausage stall has a massive fire and an even massive-er frying pan which is always full of huge and exceptional sausages. They've another pan for the onions. The onions need to be almost burnt. You've to insist on it, wait if there's a queue and they're tempted to rip you off rushing things by chucking the onions on half done. They're a Butchery Collective. Red faces. Must be all that blood. They told Daddy they make enough money from one Fayre to live, frugally, for six months. Butchery's to be considered. But the most important thing here is the Tom Ketch. Which you've never had anywhere else. The Butchers didn't cook or invent this they just bought it and sold it on so maybe it's a kind of cheat but who cares? Managed seven of these rolls of sausage last Fayre. Not bad over only three full days.

WAFFLES WITH CREAM, MAPLE SYRUP AND BANANAS.
Almost burnt sugar smell.

Eggs
Milk
Self-raising flour
Vanilla essence
Butter
Cream

Bananas
Maple syrup

Know how to make these because this is an American recipe and Tammie told you. She also told you she'd send you a waffle iron when she went 'home'. You have to have the iron or they're just fluffy pancakes. As you have no iron, presently, you've never actually made these but having watched and watched the waffle stall could entirely whip up the first batch in your bloody sleep.

Separate eggs, whip white until just before meringue stiffness. Beat egg yolks add vanilla, melted butter. Add flour, add milk. Beat. Add fluffy whites. Fold in. Must grease both sides of iron, heat until smoking. Iron does four in a go. The stall has four irons. If the Red Faces are anything to go by this lot (of very white faces come to think of it. Could it be the egg whites?) must turn over enough to live on for about eight months. People can eat sugar without licence when they're feeling festive. Especially when stoned too. The waffles fly off this stall from about nine at night. The High Waffle Priestess is busy baking and staking them, in readiness for their flight, from about six. Dollop the mix into the iron put the lid down, as they cook they're so swollen they push the lid back up. Steam escapes in a happy squirt. Each little light brown square's covered in its own little square dents. These get filled with a drip of melted butter, a flash of syrup, a huge heap of banana slices then a big enough mound of softly whipped cream. When you've searched and searched and found that you can't get maple syrup then you can swap it for a big sprinkle of dark brown sugar that you've mixed up with a good shake of cinnamon. Tricky to squash it all in your mouth in one go but it can be done. Practice. The maple syrup's from The States too. Maybe the High Waffle Priestess is? You've never actually heard her speak. She has no time for idle chit-chat. Unlike you.

"Hi, I'm here. Best ever waffles this year." You.

"Guess who? So glad you haven't changed the recipe. What is the recipe? By the way." You.

"The second one I had yesterday was a tiny bit burnt. I didn't mind. Was just wondering how hot you think the iron needs to be?" You.

"Hi. Please can I have a waffle? You must be exhausted. Are you exhausted? Would you like me to help? I'm always looking for jobs. I could make the mix. If you tell me the recipe." You.

"Thank you. Thank you for the extra cream. Please will you just tell me the recipe? I promise I won't tell anyone else. Promise." You. Fingers crossed behind back.

You try every year to break her silence but it's not possible. She's in a trance. You managed eight of these beauties last Fayre. These are all Star ever eats. All Fayre long. Don't tell Mummy.

Look. You and Star clambering up the West Hill. See your hands? You've a sausage pocket and Star has her usual. You're stopping by the Ancient Oak. The oak's hung all over with millions of letters all dripping from the tree just like falling blossom. The letters are tied on with coloured wools, they're twisting and flapping in the cold breeze. Feel your bum, which may as well be nude, prickling in that breeze? Please don't let it fucking snow. You and Star are huddled behind the tree polishing off today's (supposedly) rations, before you meet Mummy and Daddy. You're both silent, chewing hard. You've your jester's doll on a stick tucked between your legs. He's going to get annoying. Star and you are both looking up into the oak. The letters are people's wishes. They hang on the tree until the actual moment of the Solstice when they're gathered and thrown on the Great Fire. In the entertainment sector. You're casually reading a few as you munch. 'Bread. We need hard dough this year.' Wants to watch out they don't just end up with a load of stale bread. 'To witness the rosy finger of dawn from an Aegean shore.' Sounds like Rod. 'A Hamster. Please.' In absolutely beautiful brown ink handwriting. Can't be a kid. You're turning to Star holding out your one but last mouthful of saus to her. She's shaking her head.

"What? No? Why? Since when?" You. Outraged and appalled. You've been swapping your last but one mouthful of your completely different choices for years. It's part of what makes having to choose bearable.

"No thanks. I'm feeling veggie." Star. Pretending to be interested in the Oak.

"Balls. You are not. You will never be a bloody veggie. Swap." You. Pushing the bite at her.

"No. Ta." Eating both her last mouthfuls in one go. "I only really like this."

"Food can never truly satisfy your body if it isn't satisfying your soul. Sharing's vital for the soul." So much easier to work with Star when she was mute. This new talking again Star is fraying at her seams.

Why are you shaking? Look at Star. She's raising an eyebrow and walking away from you. And your last two mouthfuls of cooling sausage. Shame you ate all the onions with the first three bites. You're eating the sausage. Of course. Why wouldn't you? Great. You get an extra mouthful. The sausages are better than ever. Definitely must have a waffle next. When did Star learn to raise an eyebrow?

You're trailing Star. Undignified. The stall's up this next bit of hill. Sauntering past the woman who sells the dried flower head-dress-garlands. She's only been here for three years. The first year she came she must've made herself a millionaire over night. Everyone wanted one. Men too. Even the High Waffle Priestess found time to purchase. Then waffled away in it for the next three days. It was too easy to work out how Garland Woman had wound the silver fuse wire round the stems of the Everlasting Dried Flowers laying them flat, tucking them in. You and Star got a packet of everlasting flower seeds next spring and made a heap. Did one of your top-of-the-drive roadside stalls. Sold a fair few but not enough to properly break even. Brought the rest to the Fayre and did some Black Market. Undercut her by half. Quite good money. Give her a jaunty wave of your stick doll. She's waving back. With a purple pinky garland.

Next bit of hill, past the wooden puppet man then the Hobbit's stools made from gnarled branches couple, Indian bed-spreads man, hand-tooled leather placemats. Who uses them? There you are... Mummy's stall. But no. Where is it? It's been on the top, where two lines of stalls meet, for years. 'The only pitch worth having in the whole of the Western Sector.' Mummy. Rightly proud as she always comes away with her order book stuffed. Then the phone calls start.

Oh, god, where is Mummy? There are too many bloody new people. How much Indian jewellery do people need? There's a Tarot reading woman. Someone doing home-made sweets. Bugger them. And a man with some kind of machine where Mummy should be. Oh phew there she is. Five stalls down on the other bank. A really tipped up, because it's trying to balance on a hill, stall. Daddy and her have wedged up the down the hill end of the stall with heaps of boxes but it still looks tragically unhappy. Stall's mostly unpacked and it's been covered in the usual Hessian. 'Hessian's such an honest weave. The texture compliments clay to perfection.'

Mummy. On why Hessian every year. Hessian also covers more boxes piled up. It's on top of these box towers that the 'My Pots' are displayed. But look now. Never mind the drunken stall, they're selling stuff. Mummy's under the stall rummaging for old *Observer*s to do the wrapping and Daddy's being funny and smiley and piling up really quite a substantial heap of pots. Wow. See those three people doing the buying? Two little men, one very tall, white-haired woman. They're in no way doing Medieval. The men have matching leather jackets. Very shiny and black. And matching hair styles. Very shiny and black. The woman's wearing the best boots you have ever seen. They look leather too, they come all the way up her legs to the middle of her thighs, they're the colour of toasted oats, they've very flat and nearly splayed heels and at their eventual top there's a chunk of black woolly tights. Warm. Then more leather. Patchwork. A little flarey skirt. She's got a sheepskin jacket. It's short too, wrapped around and tied with a big man's leather belt. A big man's leather belt must surely be the only extra thing that a person really needs. Tooled placemats should diverge. Star's behind Mummy grinning at White Hair Long Boots. She looks very childish and has a cream blob on her mouth corner. Ha.

"It's the process. Everything's hand-built. All the glazes are wood ash. We gather from hedgerows, burn it and use the ash as my starting point. These are fruit. I think it's the acid from the wild raspberries that gives this sheen. And of course they're burnished before I fire. I violently disapprove of chemical glazes." Mummy. Emerging from under the stall and knocking her whopper hat sideways as she does.

"Although obviously we recognize that what we're doing is creating a chemical reaction. Just from a less processed starting point." Daddy. Looking a bit shy at Mummy.

"No, Anthony, I mean exactly what I say. Commercial glaze is chemical. This is organic." Mummy. Not smiling and starting to wrap. Daddy is smiling but at Long Hair White Boots and not Mummy, now.

"Yes, Love, I know, but glazing, by its very nature, is a chemical reaction." Daddy. Still doing most of the smiling at White Hair Long Boots.

"Either way, I think they're tremendous. We're finishing our place in Tuscany. These will give exactly the hand-built finish we adore. Right?" White Hair Long Boots. To her two shiny men.

"See. See. See." Both the Shiny Ones. See what? You're risking a quick glance round to try and work it out. Nothing. Back to White Hair Long Boots and shuffling forwards, edging in on the experience. She's turning to you, she must sense your arrival. And look. It's Prawnie! That white hair's really just truly blonde.

"Oh, hello." The Prawn. To you. She completely recognizes you. Why are you shaking your sticky little man at her?

"Ha, ha. You look immaculate. I hope you know that you've a genius for fancy dress." The Prawn. Immaculate, eh? Yes, she may well be right. As usual. Maybe that's where the real money lies? The Prawn's turning to Star.

"I am so sorry I didn't recognize you without your straw. Look at you in that marvellous hat." To Star then reaching across the precipitous stall taking Mummy's hand. Mummy's going to have to pause her wrapping up. This'll be tough for Mummy because the one golden rule of the stall is – chat away all through their choosing, encourage them to un-choose as much as they like but the minute they've committed, wrap like a fucking manic so they can't walk away. The Prawn's pointing a long leather-gloved finger at Star.

"Is she your daughter?" The Prawn. To Mummy.

"Yes." Why's she looking so bloody fondly at Star? Star's looking particularly fairy. Even with the cream.

"My god she's beautiful." The Prawn. Is she? Mummy and Daddy are having a look to decide. Hard to tell what they're deciding. Good job Star's got her hat. Covers the scabby patches.

"Bella. Bella." The Shiny Ones.

"No. Star." You. Helping them out with the name thing. Where the hell did they get hold of Bella? Grown-up laughing. What? The Prawn's turning back to you.

"So, what's the scheme this weekend?" The Prawn. She really is very quick witted and glad she asked.

"We always work the stall but essentially we'll be begging." You.

"Of course. And you're a dab hand at that, I'll bet." The Prawn. Is she going to just give you money? The group's having the tiniest of waits. No. You'll have to earn it and she's buying right now so that would be bad business. Nip in and take over that speed wrap from Mummy.

"I'm sorry did I miss something? Have you met my eldest?" Mummy. To The Prawn and a bit to the Shiny Ones too.

"Both of them. Guying. And of course I know Anthony too. Just a very little." The Prawn. All to Mummy. Look at Mummy. She's looking sideways at Daddy. Why's Daddy still doing his selling stuff big smiling? You're wrappety-wrapping and motioning Star into holding the biggest orange box for packing.

"How?" Mummy. Little bit too stern. Be better if she smiled too. The cheque hasn't actually been written.

"Very briefest of hellos on bonfire night. We saw your fireworks from our lawn. They were so tempting we tried to crash your party."

The Prawn. Is she going to tell that you invited her? "We were so sad to hear about your pet." To you. One Shiny One has laid his head on the shoulder of the other Shiny One. They are looking very sad. Clown mouths all turned down. At you. Then same clown sadness to Star.

"When did you meet Anthony?" Mummy. In before you can tell The Prawn a bit about Jessie. In case she needs to know.

"At the door. We coincided with your friend, the American guy? He had the body. We helped him down the drive. And waited with him until Anthony arrived. We had a very quick drink. Your friend seemed to need it." The Prawn. The Prawn has touched your dead dog?

"What did you all drink? Was there time?" Mummy. Taking off her whopping wonky hat shaking her hair around herself. Still stern.

"Love? We all knocked back a Mouse Cupboard Sherry and I came straight back out to all of you. Dahlia was immensely kind. To Bryan." Daddy. Finally.

"Eel car sarh eh moll toe bella." The Shiny Ones. Really truly together. They're speaking in a different language. That's what it is. Isn't French. Easy to recognize French. Mummy and Daddy have conversations about secrets like birthdays (when they remember them) in French. How come Mummy can speak Shiny? She understands it all.

"Bless you. Both. And you too, Dahlia. I do wish you'd introduced me, Anthony. Sometimes you can be horribly Croydon." Mummy. Croydon's where Daddy grew up. When your grandpa had his heart attack, before he died, he woke up a bit mad and told everyone he had been Mayor of Croydon. He hadn't been. He'd worked in a little office for the Council. 'Unutterably dreary. Can you blame him with the self aggrandisement? I'd have promoted myself far higher than Mayor.' Mummy. When they got home from burying Grandpa. "Bethan. Please call me Beth." Mummy. Sounds very un-Croydon. The sun's shot out behind Mummy's head, she has a little halo and her hair's sparkling.

"It's easy to see where your children get their exquisite looks, Beth. I'm so pleased to finally meet you and we really are thrilled with your work. How much do we owe?" The Prawn. The sun's shining its egalitarian rays on Prawnie too. Exquisite looks? So, what about this jester garb? Honestly? Is it exquisite? Back to the pointy hat next year.

"One hundred and sixteen pounds." Mummy. She's breathing in.

"With the friends and family discount that's ninety pounds, please Dahlia. And I am so sorry but I don't recall having been introduced to..." Daddy. He's nodding towards the Shiny Ones executing the second golden rule. Very smoothly. The second golden rule is when you mention the price then ask a question in the same breath. This distracts the buyer from money anxieties. Everyone suffers money anxieties, especially the rich. That's how they got rich. It seems highly likely Dahlia and the Shiny Ones might very well be real live true rich people. Oh dear, Mummy's bobbed down behind the stall where she's hitting Daddy's legs. Hard. No one on the other side of the stall will see this. Blimey. Daddy's taking a step sideways and actually kicking Mummy. You and Star are clearing out to the front of the stall. Mummy's straight back up with more *Observer* to pretend to tuck round the top of the pots. She'll have a problem getting that in. Those pots have been packed by a professional. Mummy knows this, she's fake scrunching the paper rubbing the kicked leg against the un-kicked leg.

"Anthony you're a lovely man but no. Thank you. We always pay crafts people properly. This is Bethan's art." The Prawn. She's leaning on the stall writing the cheque. In a very large looking cheque book.

Hope she doesn't lean too hard, that stall absolutely isn't finished. Listen. Silence. Look at the four of you. You're all, and especially Mummy, delighted with The Prawn. "Riccardo e Corrado." The Prawn. Teaching which Shiny One is which, with the tip of her lovely navy blue real ink pen. The Shiny Ones are doing a little bow. Together. Another mini routine. See Star? She's interested in those two. Will you tell Mummy and Daddy that it was you who actually discovered The Prawn?

The box's being handed over with kissing goodbye and waving at you and Star. They're off. But no, The Prawn's half turning back, ducking down to your ear.

"You do deserve to make your fortune." Gone. Back down the Oak side of the hill.

"What? What was that?" Mummy. About the whispered blessing.

"Just bye." You. Busy yourself with helpfully clearing that shredded *Observer*.

"Right. Girls? Your shift. Get your hat, Bethan. Let's go." Daddy. And he is. Just like that. Striding off after The Prawn and her team. Look at Mummy. Wishing she didn't have to. But she does and she is. But no hat.

"I am so sorry you felt the need to resort to the Croydon dig. Great boots didn't you think?" Daddy. To Mummy. Voice fading out over his shoulder to her. That will definitely go on for a while. Although the hundred and sixteen pounds might make it swifter than usual.

Star's reorganized the stall to fill the empty patches and is ditching her pointy hat. It's all hats off over here on the West Hill. She's got the bloody bobble hat out of her jeans pocket and has that on. Instead.

"You can do the first two and I'll come back for mine. Me and..." Star. Pausing in this second unwritten-contract-breaking speech of the day to nod towards... Look. Towards Wolfie. Wolfie's lurking a couple of stalls away in his matted old bobble hat. How long has he been waiting?

"Great. Have fun." You. Do not give her the satisfaction. Why the hell's she looking sad for you? Well she can pack that in for a start.

"Hiya, Wolfie. Head warm?" You. Waving stick man in his general direction. Turning your attention to an interesting article in the scrunched *Observer*. No need to inform Star of the cream beside mouth smear. Oh. You didn't need to. Wolfie's taking the corner of his massive old army jacket and wiping it off. Star doesn't seem to have noticed him doing this. They're off. Towards the entertainment sector holding hands. Neither of them in a scrap of Medieval. What is going on? People really must learn to make more of an effort. You on the other hand look immaculate. If bloody freezing.

Over the course of your two hours you receive visitors.

Visitor One

"Hello you, need any company?" Laura. Looking very good. Laura has a genius for dressing up too. Look at that hat-cap with a perfect pheasant's feather trailing behind it. Where did she get the massive bow and arrow from? Completes her, all over green, King's Archer costume to perfection.

"Hello. Where did you get those from? Can you use them?" You. Expecting nothing less than a yes.

"Yes. Not brilliantly but I have been known to hit my mark." Laura. Those antlered Inner Wild Men had better watch their backs.

"Will you teach me?"

"Sure. Sold anything?"

"Nope."

"Need me?"

"Nope."

"Ok, Honey Bunch. Catch you later." Striding off. Turning a lot of heads. Don't her legs look long and all over muscle in all that green tight?

Visitor Two

"Why's the stall hidden away over here?" Rod.

"Hello, Rod. I don't know." You.

"Where's Anthony? Is he already in the woods?" Rod.

"I don't know." You.

Visitor Three

"How much is this?" Customer. About the smallest pot. Tiny hand-pinched bowl with three little trees cut out of the rim. Just a glaze sample. Not a 'My Pot'. Mummy only put it on the stall as a joke. 'That little piece of commercial tat will be the first thing to go. Mark my words.' Mummy. About this pot.

"Five pounds." You. Over charging like a mental patient. Just to thoroughly test Mummy's theory.

"Why is it the only one?" Customer. Handing over the five.

"Because the Ceramic Artist who makes this work has a complete process. This is a very new direction for her. You'll have the prototype." You. He's looking a bit hard at you. Possibly you've gone a little far. But no. He's off. Five pounds poorer.

Visitor Four

"Are your parents around?" Man Who Takes The Fee For The Stall.

"No." You.

"When will they be back?" Man Who Takes The Fee For The Stall.

"Three hours-ish. Why haven't we got the usual pitch?" You.

"Not you as well. I've told your mother. You can't just tip up and demand the best pitch in the West Sector. It's not an inherited privilege. She needs to learn to pick up the phone and book." Very sneery. But he might have a point about Mummy and phones. Although you'd think he'd be glad when people make money but he doesn't seem to like it.

"Who has got it?" You.

"Terry's Tats." Man Who Takes The Fee For The Stall. Leaving.

Visitor Five

"Did you read them in the correct order." Orion. Look at you. Alert but un-moving.

You've been lolling on the stall with your arms hanging down by your sides and your chin pressed into the stall top, so your head looks like one of the pots. You've stick man's stick in your mouth and are trying to bang his head against the stall top using only the power of your jaw. You are now, very slowly, extracting the stick. Don't move fast or it'll look as if you feel silly. Placing Sticky down and smiling at Orion. But not raising your head from its resting place. Arms back down to dangling by your sides so it's just the head on display again.

"I haven't read them at all, Orion. I discovered I was less interested in stars, and the like, than I had previously suspected." You. Head maintaining dignity in resting place.

"How did you make that discovery if you didn't apply yourself to the literature? How is that possible?" Orion. Clearly fuming.

"By looking at the real Stars, Orion. They seemed so much more impressive than anything a book could teach me." Using his name excessively helps with the dignity aspect of this meeting, you are finding.

"I think my dad's right. You don't want to help yourself."

"Does your dad know about my dad's book?" Remembering your absolute trump card.

"Why do you have to keep your head on the stall like that? You look as though you've been be-headed."

"I am practising, Orion, practising." Hope he doesn't ask what for.

"What book?" And oh yes you are in charge and now is the moment to very slowly raise your head. So you are. Whilst also bringing your arms out from their hiding place, balancing your elbows on the stall, cupping your chin in as fetching a pose as possible. Done.

"Have you heard of The Oracle?"

"In classical antiquity an oracle was a person or agency considered to provide prophetic predictions, or precognition of the future, inspired by the gods. As such it was a form of divination. Pythia the priestess to Apollo at Delphia is commonly considered to have been the most important Oracle." Right.

"Oh yes, yes, yes, Mr Clever Clogs, not that oracle. The Oracle."

"No." Damn.

"Oh well, they're the most important publishing house in New York. They're publishing Daddy's complete works."

"People only publish complete works when they've had some books published in the first place." Damn. Damn. Damn him.

"Yes of course I know that, it's what they said. They want a book full of just his poems." Scampering. Slightly. "What is your costume?" Let's move things along.

"I am The Court Magician." That would explain what can only be one of his mother's nighties dyed navy and finished with a couple of large, badly cut out, yellow felt stars. Same old jeans and sneakers sticking out of the bottom. And a cardboard cone hat that he's scribbled all over to try and make blue too.

"Where's your magic wand?"

"I felt it might get in the way rather." Surprisingly he's right. Really quite seriously considering a divorce from Sticky. Even so early on in the partnership.

"Always pays to finish a costume." Standing, waving Sticky at him.

"Fool."

"Yes." Sitting again. Long silent bit. Orion's doing his toe in the earth thing. You're watching him. "Want a bit of bale?" Well he clearly isn't trotting off anywhere. He's squeezing around the back of the stall, you're budging up on the straw bale, he's sitting down too. Another long silent bit of watching all the rag-tail Medievals passing by. Nobody, apart from Prawnie and Co. seems that interested in hand-built ceramics. This year.

"Come and buy. Don't be shy." You. To passing trade. No takers. Bit more silent watching.

"Have you got any food with you?" Orion.

"Like what?" You.

"Some of those biscuits? Or even those pies?" Orion.

"Why 'even'? What was wrong with the bloody pies?" Touchy but he really should have said thank you, you did give him six.

"No. No. No. Sorry. No really sorry. That was exceptionally rude. The pies were the nicest pies I have ever eaten. They sort of crumbled and then disappeared in the mouth but then you were also chewing the inside bit for a while too so the flavour maintained. The cheese was so cheese like. I ate them all. All six. I didn't give any to Wolfie or anyone. I just sat and ate them all and I was really, really grateful and it's just that they reminded me of how good the biscuits were and I tried to make some myself but they were... not at all the same. I've done a bit of reading and I understand that there's a science element to baking but I can't seem to master it. It's worrying me." Oh how lovely. This could be your chance to practise having a row. Rows work best when one of the rowers is disadvantaged. Like now. They can escalate pretty swiftly. Have a go.

"Is that all I am to you? A kitchen maid?" Is it too soon to try crying?

"God. No, no, no. I am so sorry. I lo, lo, lo, lo, lo, lo, lo, lo. I lo, lo, lo, lo. Oh. I mean I love you being good at pies and everything. I love your baking. Not you. Not at all. I mean. I can't say it. I mean I love your biscuits. Really that's just it. I love your biscuits. And your pies." What did he just say? Both scanning wildly. No takers for hand-built ceramics as far as the eye can see. Luckily. Now is really not the moment to have to demean oneself with sales. Will you or won't you pursue the row idea? Why's your heart thumping a bit fast? Nothing like the knocking on a distant door thing that happened with The Hairy Dolly, this is just a tiny clock-bell hammer. Tonk. Tonk. Tonk. Big quiet breath in.

"The thing about baking, Orion, is that it is a science. A very serious one. An ounce here or there can over balance everything but, and this is the bit that you clearly need to learn, it's also an art. Art's about intuition isn't it? Do you have access to your intuitive side, Orion? Or are you just a bit too clever?" No need to pursue rowing for the minute. Or rather not shouty rowing. You're clearly a born rower so why bother with practice? It'll come naturally. It'll flow. That irritating tonking's calming itself nicely.

"Oh for god's sake. It isn't possible to be too clever." He must be enjoying the shouty row bit.

"I think you'll find it is." Look at you doing a mystical face. Captivating.

"I phoned Giles. When I got home. He gave me his direct line." Bit muttery. Haven't heard that for a while.

"What? Why?" What has Inspector Giles got to do with baking and intelligence or love for that matter? Golly you're having a serious conversation. When Orion can spit his words out.

"I asked him to do a proper inspection. I told him he needed to examine my dad. See if he was up to the job. In all the sciences. Dad failed the mock papers Giles gave him. Even Eng. lit. I asked Giles to get me into a proper school. He did. I got into St Marks. I'm starting in their sixth form in January. Full scholarship. My dad isn't speaking to me. He says he'll drive me to the bus into Norwich and pick me up but he won't speak to me on the journey. I'm having to earn the money for the uniform. Wolfie has to go to the village school. Wolfie isn't speaking to me either. My mum has left too. Nothing to do with schools. She's decided that to make a full contribution she must live in a separatist feminist community. She thinks women have to abandon the oppression of motherhood." Just wait 'til you tell your, fully functioning, Mother about the failed mocks. Ha.

"Do you want to go dancing? When my shift's over?" Taking off your jester's hat, popping Sticky up top of it. Farewell foolish garb. All you've got left are the weeny wellies and little jacket. What does that little jacket remind you of? What is it? Oh yes. It's Prawnie's little jacket. The only difference is you don't have a leather mini skirt. Or the big man's belt. Just your green snake belt. And you've all your legs and all your bottom in wooly tights. You're standing up and walking around to the front of the stall. Let Orion have a look at what's left of your fool's silhouette. And he is. A hard look. Why not lean over, a touch?

"Dancing?" You. Twisting back round and up. Giving him a flavour of your dancey moves.

"Um. I don't have a memory of ever having danced." Orion.

“Well, Ryan, It will be my pleasure to teach you.” Will it? What the hell have you got yourself into? “Go away now. I need to sell something. I’ll see you at The Beasts whenever they next get going.” He’s off. Not even glancing back. Right, get the ‘Pots Sold’ book, enter the tree pot. Marking it down as three, no, two pounds. Mummy will still be pleased and that leaves you with enough for your waffle. To get your energy up for the task of dancing with Orion.

Orion hasn’t turned up. Jolly good, no broken toes for you. The Beasts are the best they’ve ever been and this year they’ve three new members in the Brass section. All women. Trumpet, a bear. Cornet, a made up thing with a hairy back, extra long green ears and a shaved head. Sax, some kind of cat. How does she keep the whiskers on? You really must ask someone to teach you to play an instrument. Any instrument will do. Probably ask Laura, she’s laden with useful hidden skills and she can sing. The Beasts are surrounded by twirling Medievals. It’s still early, about fiveish but it’s pitch dark. Light is from wobbly arc lights, strings of fairy lights and bonfires. The Beasts always play next to their own fire. They’ve a huge metal arch that they sort of stake over the top of their fire. One of them must be a welder. It’s got Beasts, real ones, dancing and having painful metal sex along the top of it. When their fire gets going the metal heats and glows red. It’s red now. When you first arrived half an hour ago you asked The Bear if they would be doing ‘Beyond The Sea’ this year. ‘This year and every year for the rest of my life. Isn’t it the best piece of music ever written?’ The Bear. This is when you started wishing for musical talents. ‘It’s my favourite.’ You. To The Bear. Bit feeble. But not to worry, you’ve got your excessively good dancing skills up your red and yellow foolish sleeves to redeem yourself in the eyes of all and any Beasts.

Look at you now. Hugging your knees. Sat on the slope bit of field opposite them. Hugging to try and warm yourself. Listening. Completely. You gave up on Orion ages ago. Here it comes. Trumpets.

"Somewhere, beyond the sea, somewhere waiting for me, my lover stands on golden sands and watches the ships that go sailing." Trumpet. Trumpet. The Beast that sings is a very tall, very thin, but with an odd pokey out pregnant belly, nearly bald male beast. He fixes extra long points to his front teeth. Which you'd think might make it tricky to sing but it doesn't stop him. Is that the deepest voice you've ever heard? That actual growling's remarkable too. Look at you aching to get up and at it. But there's no Pretty Justin and nearly everyone else's dancing with someone. It's that kind of music. It has a system. But here comes the middle eight and you can resist no longer. Go. Up and twirling into the mash of Medievals. Medievals scattering like sweet wrappers in a gale. The drums are going mad. The trumpets are going mad. You are going mad. It's the swoopy lace curtain blowing in a breeze section and you are that swoopy curtain. BANG, BANG, BANG, here come the trumpets again. Have the drums ever been louder? Don't think so. It's a storm of perfect sound. Feeling it inside every bone and muscle? Knowing, with all your little body, exactly what will come next? Dancing the perfect thing for that next bit right on top of its beat. Not because you know this tune but because you are this tune. You are a beast. Caring not a fig what anyone thinks. Just for this perfect dancing time. Right inside yourself. Flinging yourself at this music. It's reaching its perfect end. "Happy we'll feel beyond the sea and never again. I'll go sailing." Trumpets. "No more sailing, so long sailing." Trumpets. "Bye, bye sailing." Trumpets. "Bye, bye." Done. Breathe. Breathe. Breathe the icy night air. Listen. The Beasts are all applauding you. Random Medievals are too. Oh. That feeling will be exceptionally hard to forget. You're full, stuffed to the gills, but really truly modest about it too. The modest bit is the most surprising element of all. The glorious clapping's finished. Trot on. Back to your bit of slope. Nobody's bothering with you now. Thud. Thud. Thud.

Almost back at the stall. Mummy and Daddy are clearly just arriving. Star and her gentleman assistant Wolfie are perched on that bale looking jolly pleased. The stall on the other hand looks windswept. Where are all the pots?

"Where are all the pots?" Mummy. From a few strides away.

"Gone." Star.

"I can see that. Where?" Mummy. Arriving. With Daddy. Holding hands. Good. Mummy's wearing a very long, right to her little ankles, sheepskin coat. That's beautiful. It's been sort of Henna painted all over its skin in swirly pale purple swoops. So warm. So un-Medieval.

"Good work, Star, really good work. You too, Wolfie. Wow." Daddy.

"Where?" Mummy. Clearly onto something.

"Um. Well." Star.

"Oh Christ all mighty. Where? That's a year's worth of work." Mummy. White knuckles. Already.

"It's good. It's ok." Star. Instinctively looking to you to speak. She got herself into this, she can get herself out of it. Little Miss Rule-Bender. Or maybe her Hero will.

"Where are my pots? For fuck's sake Star, now is not the time to go all droopy and hush fucking hush." Mummy. Star's trying Wolfie for intervention. Feel that? That's a tidal-wave rushing, need to take charge. Moving sharply forward. Mummy's hand's slamming into your chest. Holding you back.

"For fuck's sake let her speak." Mummy. This is completely the wrong way to be with Star. Wouldn't be surprised if Star muted up for another year now and frankly that'd serve Mummy right.

"A bloke from a shop in London came. Said you owed them two hundred pounds worth of stock. He said he'd waited a year. He was quite friendly. He took pots." Wolfie.

"I'll bet he bloody was. I cannot believe you let him steal my best work to date. Star, you fucking idiot. Why the hell didn't you come and find me? Which fucking shop?" Mummy. Too livid for tears.

"Can I speak to your mother please? Oh I see. Can I speak to any responsible adult then? That shop." Star. You're wrong about the next year's silence. Little disappointed? Given the recent shifts. Yes. "He only took a hundred and fifty pounds worth. He said these were different to the stuff he'd ordered and he was glad he'd waited. He liked these better. Said he could put more mark-up on them." Star. In-ter-est-ing. See your family, and it's newest recruit, Wolfie, all deciding this is actually a good thing?

"Then another shop came and wanted to put in an order and I suggested they buy what they want and invent their own mark-up. For their gallery." Wolfie. This could go badly wrong all over again. Third golden rule. Never part with stock if you can get an order. Stock is money in the bank. An order is also money in the bank. And you've still got the stock. Win, win.

"Did you get a name for the gallery?" Daddy.

"South Creek Ceramics. Yorkshire." Wolfie. Mummy's been wishing and wishing they might take her work for years. Look at Mummy working out if she's livid or thrilled.

"They paid in cash." Star. Mummy is thrilled. Star's handing over the wodge of cash. You're all goggle eyed, staring at the glittering pile.

"Someone find an axe and chop down the beanstalk before the giant comes thundering down and snatches back his fucking heap of gold." Daddy.

"Quick, quick, quick all hands on deck let's get this shitty little stall packed up and into the car before that miserable bald weasel comes sniffing round demanding his pitch fee. We can get out of here without paying." Mummy. "Darling Starlight I am very pleased with you." Mummy. Talking at the same time as Daddy.

"It was Star who suggested South Creek buy their stock as well. Not me." Wolfie. He really is a Hero.

"Well whoever it was, bloody good work. You kids take a box each and get it into the van, it's closer than the Saab. We'll bring the rest. Then we'll stay until after the Solstice Happening tomorrow but we won't stay tomorrow night. If you see The Weasel pretend you haven't and clear out. Got it?" Daddy. Of course you have. Simple plan. Oddly you'll be glad to go tomorrow. You are made of ice. And you've already had the best food.

Bonfire. You, Star, Wolfie and now Orion – who was nowhere to be seen all last night and all today but floated up, still in his nightie, about half an hour ago – got to the Solstice fire pitch two hours ago. You've been helping to ferry the wishes from the Ancient Oak to beside the fire.

"Handle those with extreme care. You carry dreams." Druid Boss. Very bossy, and wrong. Wishes are not dreams.

The Druid Boss needs to be charmed cos he'll light the fire. Not correcting his lazy thinking, trudging back and forth for hours, means you've earnt the right to be up front when it all happens.

People are starting to push, bunching, trying to get as close to the front as possible. Hey you, Medieval queue jumpers, get back. You have to earn your place at the front. It's all self-self-self with you lot, isn't it? Can't just float up and stick out your fucking elbows. Some people have been working for their privileged positioning. The Druid Boss's sloshing petrol all over the fire. Getting ready. Totally unnecessary. As you had to tell him. Just needs to be stacked better. You did offer. But.

"I don't think I'm going to attend next year." Orion. To no one in particular although there're so many Medievals crammed round, anyone might answer. They don't. So you may as well.

"What not even to learn how to dance? It's a life-skill, you know." Don't turn to look at him. Keep an eye on that lunatic Druid Boss, he's gone petrol crazy.

"You didn't look as if you needed anyone to dance with." That's got you. You're snapping round to him. Why's he not looking at you?

"You spied on me dancing? Are you a Peeping Tom, Orion?" Give him a very hard look. Plus a swift elbow back to the pushiest Medieval.

"It was a public place. Dancing is a public pastime. I was wandering past, I caught a glimpse of you." Panicky. Means he's guilty. He is a Peeping Tom.

Lunatic Druid Boss has got another can of petrol. Only a blatant idiot would apply a second can. Some of the Medievals think that too. Space's opening up behind you. People are trying to wriggle back again. Too many people. Where are Your People? Haven't seen Tammie and Eric at all. Keep bumping into Laura, nearly always with the shaved headed Beast, they always ask 'Ok Sweetheart?' When you say 'Ok' they go off. To do Beast stuff. Or Archer's stuff. Who knows. You've seen Pretty Justin and The Hairy Dolly. They were at the man with the machine who stole Mummy's best pitch, who must be Terry's Tats. Turns out Terry's machine does tattoos. You watched as Pretty Justin and The Dolly had one each. Absolutely disgusting and so sore looking. Pretty Justin was very annoyed because he did his first and it was something to do with The Hairy Dolly although hard to tell under all that blood. Then it changed its mind and just had the Ying and Yang sign. It was supposed to have had something to do with Pretty Justin. Pretty Justin cried. Not just the pain. You've seen a fair bit of Rod too, eating, then whizzing back into the woods. Mummy and Daddy came and found you and Star and Wolfie, of course, in the kid's teepee to say night-night, last night. They also gave you three pounds each from the giant's gold, including Wolfie, to celebrate. You sent Wolfie out for seven waffles (with your regular's discount) then split the leftover Waffle between you. None of Your People are anywhere to be seen now. When you might need them. Star's taken hold of your hand. Where the hell are the grown-ups? All this petrol's serious. This might be going to be dangerous. And that'll be exceptionally interesting and excellent experiential learning but enough is enough.

"We need to go. That's going to explode. We're too close. Star, now! Come!" You. See the four of you holding hands? All four pushing through the Medievals. Look out, you've started an historical stampede. Wolfie's got Star on his back, she's shoving Medievals. Orion's in front of them pushing a path, You're yelling;

"Medical emergency! Medical emergency! Wounded kids. Medical emergency! Let us through. Please!" You.

It is sort of working. There're a lot of pissed and pissed off Medievals but you're getting out. Star's off Wolfie's back and you've returned to holding hands, in a long line, and running. Clambering up the Ancient Oak hill, shouting and running, hands gripped tight, tripping, hauling each other up, running, sucking in chest-squeezing gulps of ice night air. All turning back watching the masses herding themselves into new formations. This is actually a much better view than before. You can see everything. All that slogging around for the lunatic Druid Boss for nothing. Those masses are still swirling. The Medievals are getting themselves safely away from the lunatic Druid Boss. You've saved lives. Orion's letting go. You're letting go of Star.

"Medical emergency?" Orion.

"Yup." You.

"Quite good actually." Orion.

"Thank you, Wise Wizard." You.

"It's hard to run in a dress." Orion.

"Only when it isn't a dress. It's a nightie. They're tighter. To help keep them in place. When one is having one's wild dreams." Look at Orion. He's wriggling and tugging and trying to get it off but his shoulders are stuck. He is trapped in his wizard's robes.

"Can you help me. Please." Bit strangled sounding. Thinking about leaving him inside and just walking off?

"Don't you have a magic spell for this kind of crisis?" Tugging it off and ripping it in the process. "Do you want this again or can we use it to sit on? My bum's frozen." Orion is unable to stop himself checking for icicles.

What was that? What was it? That very far away and monstrously loud crump. A sound that should burst ear drums but to your team on the hill, sounds as if it's coming from under the ground. Can you feel that sound too? Boom. Thud. Like the door knocking feeling. But just once and under your feet, not inside you. All four of you are turning slowly to observe the lunatic Druid Boss's petrol bomb going up. A ball of fire, quite round like the sun, gently puffing up to the stars. It's gone and it's leaving, in its wake, what under normal circs might be described as a bonfire but this is unlike any bonfire you've ever seen and you and Star are experts at dangerous bonfires. This really is dangerous. Hear the screaming? There's Medieval panic erupting down the hill. Is it possible that Mummy and Daddy are blown up? Star and Wolfie are leaning into each other a bit away from you and Orion. You and Orion are crouched on his nightie, backs to the Ancient Oak. Long silent watching bit. Now Star and Wolfie are getting up and heading off back down the hill. The swirling Medievals are calming. No more screaming anyway. Drums starting up. Maybe no one was killed. Would they be drumming if their lunatic boss had perished? Probably.

There must be thousands of people here but none of them are up this hill. It is dark night under the Ancient Oak. No people. No fires. No nothing. Just abandoned stalls. Bit like derelict buildings. Row upon row of abandoned factories. The kind of buildings that only pigeons live in. Stalls draped in tarpaulins to stop people stealing the tempting stock nestled underneath. Although all a serious thief would have to do is lift the tarps and do a bit of rummaging. But people don't seem to. At night. They're too busy getting marmalized by Druids. Or possibly they already have all the hand-tooled leather and branchy Hobbit furniture they need. Turning to consider Orion. He has his head back and is staring at the stars. Surprise. His too-long hair's in a plait. It looks better like that. That really is one hell of a beaky nose. Does he know it's moist and cerise at its tip? Why's he swallowing and swallowing? What's he eaten?

"Do you think he managed to set it off at exactly five thirty-five?" You.

"What are you talking about?" It really is most vexing how Orion persists in assuming you are an imbecile.

“Five thirty-five is the moment of ‘the turning of the sun’. This year. Might be that his ball of flame was a symbolic representation of the sun.” Generously sharing your extensive knowledge of Solstice celebrations.

“As we now have the vantage point of space we know that solstice is an astronomical event caused by the earth’s tilt on its axis, and its motion in orbit around the sun. It has nothing to do with fairies removing their affection from humanity and punishing us by making us chilly for a few months. It’s because earth doesn’t orbit upright, it’s tilted on its axis by twenty-three point five degrees. Earth’s northern and southern hemispheres trade places in receiving the sun’s light and warmth most directly. It is the tilt of the earth and not our distance from the sun that causes winter and summer.”

“And, this year it does its tilting at five thirty-five.” Hazarding a guess that the numbers add up with Orion’s bit.

“The tilt is continuous. Which you would know if you’d applied yourself to the reading list.” Bored sounding. Silence. You’re having another look at Orion. Swallow. Swallow.

“Are you imagining my delicious baked goods?” About the swallow.

“Not presently. No. I, I, I, I, would like to ah, ah, ah, ah, ah, ah, ah, ask you something.” Goody. What?

“What?”

“When you got your boyfriend did he ask you out or did you do it?” What boyfriend?

“Oh. Um. Well. It was. Actually that’s a private moment. I don’t feel comfortable sharing it with you.” This could be a very risky line to take because of course the last thing you want is him to stop talking like this. What boyfriend?

"Yes. I thought it might be. I have no practical experience in social situations. People don't seem to consider educating young men in these areas important. I have searched for books but I can only find *The Joy of Sex* and they wouldn't let me take it out of the traveling library." *The Joy of Sex*? Wouldn't mind a swift gander at that one.

"Yes. It's very like baking. You can't really learn the art bit out of a book." Meaning the fine art of asking out. But maybe you can. Maybe *The Joy of Sex* is rammed with asking out chapters.

"No. I thought it'd be useless. It was all clitoral stimulation and oral sex and everybody knows about all of that. I'll simply master that in a practical setting. It was more how one approaches someone one is in lo, lo, lo, lo, lo, lo, lo, lo, lo, love with. Formally." Clitoral stimulation? Oral sex?

"As I said, I feel unsure about sharing any actual details with you." This is a first. Stalling? You want, immensely, to share as many actual details as possible, you just need to find out what those details are supposed to be. You have an urgent need to find out everything Orion seems to know. But you must not reveal your massive ignorance. Or woeful lack of boyfriend. Why oh why didn't you just ask someone, like Laura, for solid actual sex details bloody years ago?

"Dad said you read a poem that was 'terrifyingly explicit' and 'appallingly knowing'. I thought that sounded hopeful." Looks decidedly unhopeful.

"Who are you in love with?"

"I can't tell you. Don't make me. Please tell me how to do it." Begging. There's nothing for it, his obstinate silence will have to be solved with some body work. You're sitting up very straight and tall, putting your head back against the tree and sort of arching your back then stretching your arms to the stars. Doing a great big Mummy-yawn letting your knees flop open and down to the earth. Something of a natural at those stretches that slow down the chat, aren't you? Yes. It's working, he can't resist turning to watch. Reluctantly? Oh my goodness. Is it you he is in lo, lo, lo, lo, love with? Pastry and crotches. It might be. It might be. It might not be too. Test him. Oh please let it be you.

"You should have come dancing with me, Ryan." Testing out some slow smiling too.

"I know that. I was embarrassed. Ok?" Are you falling in love with him?

"This is all so intense. I can't believe this is happening. My boyfriend and I do share everything but I don't think I should share this with him. Should I?" This is what it means to be alive.

"No. No. Please don't tell him. Promise you won't." Crikey, don't flinch, he's put one moist palm over the one of yours that's next to him. Yours isn't moist. It's ice.

"I promise." You're gazing at each other. Could this be it? Falling, nay, tumbling in love with each other? Hear that? He's done one of Rod's grunts. Only his is a bit higher pitched. You're doing a big breath in and pushing your breasts up. As far as they will go. Which obviously isn't far enough. Breathe out. Slowly. Both still gazing. Oh. Oh. The pretending's stopped. Just like that. Why?

"I don't want to take advantage of you." Orion. See yourself working quite hard not to shout pies?

"Ok. Good." You. Really no idea how it might be possible that Orion, of all people, could take advantage.

"Then I would like to attempt a French kiss." Kiss? Kiss? Kiss? What is the French bit? Do you want a kiss from Orion? In any language.

"*Oui.*"

"Please be serious." You are trying. Look. Eyes closed. Deep breath.

Orion has leant over and put his mouth onto yours and he is pushing very hard at you. Right. Look out, he's opened his mouth, making you do it too. Eyes open. He seems to be moving his head around so you'd better too. Waggle, waggle go your heads. Joined at the lips. Mouths open like drowning fish, he is poking his tongue into your mouth. Like a long, thin strip of hard, raw bacon. But wet. He is poking it at your tongue. Retreat. Retreat. Snail into shell. It isn't possible to actually swallow your own tongue. You're pulling away. Damn. You shouldn't have pulled away. Orion is too. Both sitting back.

"That was absolutely disgusting." Orion. How dare he? What a horrible thing to say.

"That is a horrible thing to say. You just stole my first ever grown-up kiss and that is just really hurtful and aggressive and I hated it too but I would never say such a mean thing." You. You're crying and shaking. Not just with the fucking cold. Oh please no. Real crying. You haven't cried since Grandpa died and then you only cried because it was the first time you'd considered being locked in a coffin under the earth but discovering you were alive. You cried in case Grandpa was slowly dying all over again. In his coffin. You didn't even really like Grandpa. Apart from the piles of real sweets like Mars and Twix he left on the pillow for you and Star that time you stayed the two days. And that was probably Grandma.

"What do you mean? You have a boyfriend? You are enlightening me. I said about advantage. I am not an oppressor." Orion. And he isn't. And he is right about the boyfriend lie. You fool. Crying fool.

"Sorry." You. Crying. "Sorry." You. More crying. "Sorry." You. Bloody hell. Stop bloody crying. You aren't Rod for fuck's sake. Crying stopping.

"Was it your first ever kiss?" Orion.

"Yes." You. Still at bit cryee.

"Why did Bryan say that about your boyfriend?" Orion. Ah.

"That's what he says he is. He isn't. He's busy doing bumming with Justin." You. Wiping eyes, nose. Sorting self out. Sorted.

"He's an adult. You are... well I suppose now you are nearly thirteen. But still." Orion.

"It's a joke." You.

"Why?" Orion. But as you still haven't heard Orion laugh, at anything, how can you possibly try and explain that? You're deciding not to. Maybe there's no point in explaining at all? How would you explain your leaking eyes?

You and Orion are looking at each other again. This looking's making you both slide towards each other. Kissing again. How did that happen? Just a kiss. A night-night variety of kiss. There are Orion's pale brown eyes. Then another kiss. Eyes. Then another. Eyes. Nose bump. Wet nose bump. Kiss. Having a shuffle towards each other rucking up the nightie and kissing again. This time you've opened your mouths. How did that happen? Pulling away at the same time having another look. A smile from you. Orion's making his mouth go up a bit at the corners. Maybe he just can't smile. Back to the little quick kisses. Oh go on try the open mouth again. Go on, put your tongue inside his mouth. Done. Thought so, his is there. Of course it's there. He isn't doing a snail. You're sort of wiping them around each others. Pulling apart and listen. Orion is snuffling. Might that be laughter? Kiss, kiss, kiss and another French kiss. It isn't horrible. You're pulling away, looking again. Ok. Now to try something very different. Just try it. You're kissing his eyes. Do you hear that? Orion's Rod grunt. Good. Kiss his cheeks, now down to his neck. Lots of grunting. Lots of neck. Try a bit of sucking of the neck. Lots of grunts. More sucking. Tastes filthy. Orion's pushing right against you. Orion's getting up onto all fours and he's gently pushing you down flat on the cold, hard earth.

"I'm not an oppressor. I'm not." Orion. Why is he bringing that up again? Look, you've left red suction marks on him. Yikes. You are a squid.

Orion's lying down on top of you. He's surprisingly heavy. But he is warm. Now you're really having a lot of the French kissing. In between kissing Orion's grunting away. Why's he stopped? He's levering himself up to leaning on one elbow.

"I watched you eating. I saw you eating a sausage sandwich and I thought about this and I never ever thought it might really happen. That you would let me." Orion. He is a Peeping Tom. But it is you he is in love with. Wish he hadn't seen you eating. Can he taste the pig? Listen to the drums? Not Hairy Dolly Drums. Not at all. These are real drums. Solstice drums. Bang, bang, bang, up floats the wailing chanting. "I definitely won't attend next year." Orion.

"Have you ever eaten that sausage?" You. Wriggling a bit out from under him. Ow. Feel him clamping your right thigh with both his broom-stick legs? Feel him pushing his, well frankly, his penis against your thigh? Penises must be more woody than they look. Oh what the heck, ignore it. In the pursuit of knowledge. Christ, think yourself lucky. Imagine having to drag one of those bouncy poles around with you all day. No wonder he didn't fancy dancing. No harm in being friendly to the poor thing. You're letting your thigh give it a welcoming rub. Hear that? Might as well be Rod up top there. What a kerfuffle.

"Massive swallowed puff. No. I was observing you opening and closing your mouth and I decided that, if I could possibly arrange it,

I would attempt to French kiss it." He has gone the same deep red that angry Gandalf can. Suction marks and all. And, oh. Inside. Inside. That must be what the Hairy Dolly wanted too. A French Kiss. Ok. Good. Now you know. Scary but good. Maybe your mouth will be your best feature. Mummy's is her raven hair. But also, actually, her gamine body. And her chocolate eyes. And her enormous mouth. And her walk is supposed to be 'Impossible to walk behind without tripping over your own tongue'. Rod. Weirdly and to The Hairy Dolly. No use tripping over your own tongue, Rod, you might be needing that for French kissing. Although Who would French kiss Rod? A needy weedy poetess possibly? Laura's sadly got to deal with the fat issue but it's a fact that no one can stop themselves looking at her, a lot, and you understand she's supposed to be big but she's mainly just very, very strong so possibly her best feature is her strongness? 'Tammie has absolutely nothing to recommend her physically. Great thing for her she found God. Who it turns out is a bloke after all.' Mummy. To Laura. Laura didn't say anything. Anyway, to develop fully as a woman one must evolve a best feature. So. Mouth it is. You're now opening yours slightly and running your tongue over your teeth. You've noticed that Mummy sometimes does that to Daddy when there's a boring bit in a House Meeting, or something. He seems quite pleased by it. Yes. Orion is too. Rub. Rub. Rub. Puff.

"Ryan?" You. Whispering.

"Puff." Orion. Rub.

"Please will you tell me who you're in love with?" Whispering and smiling. How can he resist? He can't.

"Valerie Singleton." That is a bitter blow. Never let him know this. And who the hell is she? How does Orion even know any other girls? Is there a girl living at his? His mother was one of the only women at his commune and now she's buggered off. Might be she's gone leaving just Valerie's mum in charge?

"How do you know her?" Shifting your thigh helpfully and to make sure he has absolutely no idea how silly and. Um. Yes. How lumpy you now feel. Why did you cry?

"Don't you know *Blue Peter*?"

"Not personally." Why is this Peter blue?

"I'm going to build a relatively powerful telescope, using only domestic materials, and earn myself a badge. That's why I need to have some appropriate dialogue ready. And some basic experience. Before you say anything I am aware she's at least twelve years older than me but my father's twelve years my mother's senior and they had a successful relationship." Rubbing away.

"Until she became a separatist feminist." Bit mean but fair enough. So Valerie must be a mum. Yuck. You're shifting the thigh again but this time because it's going a bit dead. This isn't clear to Orion, he's still doing as many rub-attacks as possible.

"I think it was more that she became a lesbian." The lesbians are everywhere these days. What's happening now? He's clambering to stand and is sort of bent over. "I am very sorry. I do really mean it about oppression and I do not wish to insinuate that you might be a prick tease but I think I'm about to develop what I understand are commonly known as blue balls. Please will you not look?" Does he know you so little? And what's with all this blueness?

"Of course not." Turning your back on him. And instantly peeking back over your shoulder. Look at that. Orion has his jeans undone and pulled a bit down, so you can see the top of his weeny bum. He's hunched over, his right arm's flying up and down like that little metal toy soldier Star was given to sort out the gender balance in your play things. You wind it up, it salutes over and over at a frantic pace. Orion's soldier arm has stopped. Just like the soldier's does. Clunk. Orion's weeny bum's flicking back and forth a couple of times. Stopped. He's breathing out very loudly. He's shaking something off his right hand. It won't come off. Whatever it is. He's scraping his hand on the bark of the Ancient Oak. He's pulling his trews back up. Stop peeking you horrible Peeping Tom. You have.

"Can I turn round yet?"

"Yes." You are doing. He's sitting back down. Both watching the Medieval Druids who're now skipping around the fire. More distant wailing. Quiet thinking between you and your first French kisser.

"Does Blue Peter have blue balls too? Is that why he got that name?"

"What is the point of your sense of humour? I don't understand what you are saying. That's one of the reasons I could never be in love with someone like you. I am searching for a helpmeet. Like Dad is. It's a shame. Your baking is really very good."

Can't think of a thing to say, or a thing to do, to make right out of this. Look at you standing. Jester's jacket coming apart at its rushed seams. Tights bagging down uncomfortably around your bum. You're having a great big pull up of your tights. May as well be comfy. How about finding that Hairiest of Dolls? How about seeing if it still wants to French kiss with you? Setting off down the hill at a little run.

"Thank you very much. And if you wanted to do it ag, ag, ag, ag, ag, ag, ag, ag." Orion. Fading into the distance.

Hairy Dolly, Hairy Dolly where is it? See as you slip slide down the hill and veer off away from the Medievals? It's unlikely The Hairy Dolly will be skipping. And Pretty Justin certainly won't be. So. Woods or a Music Happening? Very little apart from skipping going on. Lots of dark areas all over the fields. Woods. The woods are perfect for a Medieval Fayre. 'Oh, blessed Oak of Olde England.' Rod. He'd done a thing where they had to find their talisman tree-spirit lurking in a tree. 'No way of knowing how long I held that trunk in my arms, the gentle breeze of morning lifting my fringe eventually roused me from our embrace, guiding me back from our travels on the psychic plane. Unlocking my arms, from that deep connection, was the hardest of goodbyes.' That'll mean crying. You're stopping at the edge of those Oaks. No Inner Wild Men being awakened by cuddling trees tonight. Bloody hell, they are big trees. See those few bonfires dotted about? All quite far apart. Smell the stinky hash haze? Why are you here? Just because. And it's fate now because there's Pretty Justin. He's about fifteen trees away moving fast out of the woods. Looks like he's in a bad mood. Septic tattoo? You're ducking behind your tree. No spirit in sight. Pretty Justin's gone. You're trotting into the darkness. Follow the hash whiff. That Dolly won't be far from it. Ha. There it sits. It's got its own little fire. Good. Warmth. It's playing its guitar. It's all on its own. It can teach you how to play guitar. The guitar can be your instrument.

"Will you teach me how to play the guitar?" You. The Hairy Dolly has leapt to its feet and sent the guitar spinning dangerously close to its little fire.

"Fucking-fucking-fuck. You fucking terrified me. What the fuck are you doing creeping around? There are no kids allowed here. Jesus, my fucking heart." Hairy Dolly. Bit surprised by you.

"But will you? I am not a kid. I am nearly thirteen. Juliet was twelve." Seating yourself as close to its fire as possible. That feels very good indeed.

"So they say." It's getting its big, black, thick, long coat and putting it over your shoulders. It's kneeling in front of you and it's buttoning it around you. Wrapping your arms, and tucked-up knees, in the coat-parcel. It's moving round to your back rubbing and rubbing. You're rolling around and pushing back against its hands. Oh how heavenly, it's warming you up properly. Like when you and Star were tiny babies and came toddling out of the rough and icy Norfolk sea and Daddy or Mummy would be crouched with a massive towel all open for you and they would sausage roll you into it and rub-a-dub-dub until there was a layer of tingle all over your salt encrusted skin. You can roast things like whole fish in a crust of thick salt. May this normal kind of rubbing never end. Oh. It is. The Hairy Dolly's sitting down behind you pulling you to it. It has its whole front against your back and its little legs round yours and it's putting its stumpy arms round you and cuddling you. Giving you a hot potato on each shoulder and now in the middle of your back. Feel yourself slump? Sleep. That's the thing. Like when you were tiny and sleep just was suddenly there. Close your eyes. Sleep. When you're grown up, and when you have kids, you will not stop giving them cuddles when they get their first period. Especially if that period is a false start.

"Better?" Hairy Dolly. Chin on your shoulder.

"Yeah. Bit." You.

"You've looked bluer and bluer each time I've bumped into you. Apart from the traffic light jacket." Hairy Dolly. Traffic light? There's no green.

"What's blue balls?" Sliding softly towards sleep. Feel it shift?

"Right. Ok." It's moving away and round to beside you. Rescuing its roast guitar on the way. Your back feels huge and cold and lonely. No more sleepiness.

"Please just tell me." You look like a lump of coal sat huddled there.

You're working your fingers up, undoing a few top buttons and giving yourself a bit of movement.

"Stop wriggling and stay where I put you or I'll be able to show you what they are. Fuck. Mother Fucker." Hairy Dolly. In a sighing voice.

"What?" Looking at it looking at you. Thud. Just a little thud. One of the many tricky things about this Dolly are its eyes. Too dark to read. Even in the daylight it's impossible to get a reading off them. Blue eyes are the thing for silent communication.

"I'm leaving Swallow's Farmhouse. Don't tell your parents. Yeah? I have to like go. I am drowning." Hairy Dolly. Head in hairy hands.

"How?" You.

"This fucking nonsense with Justin. Fuck. Why am I telling you? What is the fucking point? You're a child." Looking up at you again. "Ok. You're not a child. Obviously you aren't. Look at you." Not much to see huddled in the coal-sack coat. Are the children all in bed for now it's eight o'clock?

"What's bumming?" May as well try and get some solid facts. The Hairy Dolly's doing its high tinkley laughing. Must be stoned.

"I've missed you, Nearly Thirteen. Where have you been? Why did you abandon me to that Faggy Nag?" It has a thing about nagging.

"When are you going?" Will it be good if it goes? Or is The Hairy Dolly your one true friend?

"Pronto. Pronto. Pronto."

Sitting and looking at the fire. Smell the singe from tights' proximity to fire. Here we go. Druid wailing's packed up and real music's starting all over the site. Why do trumpets carry so much clearer than say, the sax? Maybe that's why people always draw fat baby angels with them. Extra clear tooting to get all the devils to shut the fuck up and listen. It's amazing that there could be not a single other person in these woods. Haven't seen a soul.

"Where are all the Inner Wild Men?" You.

"Covering themselves in earth somewhere." Hairy Dolly.

"It's quiet." You. The Hairy Dolly's turning to you so you do to it. Smiles. Thud. It's coming towards you with its face. Just like that. Here it comes again. French kissing. My, my you'll be able to sit exams in this by tomorrow. Oh. Different. It's got your fat bottom lip in its teeth and is sucking. Nearly pulling it and hurting but not. It's sucking then letting go, sucking then letting go. Why isn't that getting boring? Now it's the top lips turn. This is French kissing. Why aren't you scared of this?

Knock, knock. Who's there?

Hey, you were right with what you did for Orion, the Hairy Dolly's kissing your neck and sucking a tiny bit there too. No wonder Orion went loony. Eat that neck. Eat it all. You're pushing against your Dolly. Like Jessie used to for more scratches. It's blowing warm gentle air into your ears, nibbling, chewing. Your dirty neck is stretched and backwards. Head's lolling down almost at the ground. The Hairy Dolly's got an arm under the curved up bit of your back, kind of holding you, draped over it. It's licking cold wetness on all neck and ear bits. Shivery. See your eyes? Rolling around in your head. Focus eyes.

Look. Behind that tree. Your neck's gone rigid. What is that? Pushing the Hairy Dolly away. It's not stopping its licking. No. You do not want to see what you are seeing. Pushing the Hairy Dolly to stop.

"Bryan? Excuse me but... look." You. Too quiet, it won't hear that.

"What?" Hairy Dolly. It has. Both of you have gone to statue. One of those marble ones of gods caught up in tumultuous activity.

Stopped for all time in wild embrace. You with your head hanging down. Seeing the wrong way up.

"Him." You.

"Who? Whadda ya? Who?" Hairy Dolly. You're staying as close as you can to its hairiness but twisting too. To show it.

"Him. There." You. Crouched underneath and pointing. A man. But only the outline of one. He's grey. Like he's made of cloud. "There. Him." You. How can it not see him too?

"Please, Bryan. There." You. Stab pointing.

"Nada. Not a thang." Hairy Dolly. Craning everywhere. Holding you tight.

"Go away." You. Pathetic squeaking. But, he is. Moving too fast backwards. Eye-shaped bits on you.

"That's the way, Thirteen. Claim your space." Hairy Dolly. Twisting you back to its tummy.

The man is leaving a trail of his cloud-ness. He's disintegrating. Far inside the trees.

"He's evaporated." You. He seems to have. That grey is only mist. "He was watching." You. Twisting your little face back to its doll.

"Lucky guy, hey?" Hairy Dolly. Hoicking you up to sort of sitting on its hips. Like it did on the windowsill. When it first started wanting French kissing.

"Hey, Mister? You wanna join in? You wanna share?!" Hairy Dolly. Bit of a stumble carrying you into a tree trunk. Yelling, laughing at the mist. Silence. Apart from your heart. Thrashing inside you like a hooked fish. Long quiet staring at each other. Then. The Hairy Dolly is strong. It's got you pushed to the tree by your hips. It's pulling you up and slowly back down. Rubbing your fanny pretty toughly against its willy. Staring. Both your escaped air is twirling, like the gone-man's cloud, between your faces. You could tell it to stop.

"Just us, hey?" Hairy Dolly.

"Are you sure?" You. You've got hold of it on top of its shoulders. Holding on. When the slow bit in front of your fanny comes it's easiest to push down. To keep held.

"Fuck that feels good." Hairy Dolly. Does it? It feels buzzing. Your fanny is a hive. Push down.

"Yeah. Do that." Hairy Dolly. You are. But a smaller push than before.

"Do you think he was an Inner Wild Man who maybe got a bit lost?" You. You look like Star on her beam, trying to do a handstand, pushing up, but not back down now, on that Hairy Dolly's shoulders.

"Come on, Thirteen. Don't be a tease. Push." Hairy Dolly. Tease?

"I don't think he was a ghost. Or anything, um, corporal." You. Elbows fully locked, holding you high.

"Tee hee hee. Corporal? You mean, jesus, Thirteen, the opposite, that's the body, what you saw was a friggin' spook, a friggin', come on, kiddo, get it right, a friggin' phantom, a wraith an appa- friggin' – rition. Tee hee. Come here to put me off my stroke." Hairy Dolly. There's no such thing as ghosts.

The Hairy Dolly's shoving you down its tree.

"I don't find that funny. I know it means, um, OW! No. I meant. OW! No. I meant he looked..." You. Your head is not working like it's supposed to.

Everything's gone away from you. It's all whizzing. Whizzing away.

Bryan's got your face in his hands, he's undoing his trousers and he's pushing you and your head against the tree. Firmly. He's got his willy in his hand. It isn't hairy. It's bouncing on its own. He's doing the soldier pump.

"Please, Bryan. Juliet wasn't real. Please." You.

"Eurngh. Yeah. Beg me." Bryan.

He's pushing the end of his willy against your mouth. Clenched jaw. Your mouth is sore, bruised from his bites. Bleeding. His hands are hurting very badly. Escape. You're twisting, twisting. He's too little to be able to hold you with one hand on your head but he is. Kick. Get him with your legs. He's sitting on your legs and soldier pumping. Escape. Your head's thrashing, trying to get away, he's back up and banging your head to make it still against the tree. Oh. No. No. How did he get his fingers inside your mouth? He's got your mouth jammed open. He's pushing his willy right inside your mouth. There's no air. You can't breathe, he's going to choke you, he's pushing it in and out. Crashing it right against, into your tonsils. Gag. Must, must, must breathe.

Bite it. Can't move your jaw he's holding too tight. Argh, your throat is full of liquid. Breathe. Gag. Breathe. He's getting out of you. You're spitting, spitting yeast-froth-slime. Be quiet. He still has your head, he's back in his trousers, his face is the closest you've ever seen anyone. Can you read his eyes now?

"What? Not fancy a gobble on my seed? I am so far gone. Oh man. This is done. It's fucking over. I'm taking up my place at Harvard. Yes I fucking am. I'm majoring in law. Yes I fucking will. If you tell anyone I will know and I will creep up on you and sue you so hard. You know what that means? That means you and your pouty little mouth will end up in jail. Oh yes. Giving a man blue balls for months on end is a sueable offence. Goodbye, Nearly Thirteen. You asked for it." Bryan. Picking you up by your head walking you away from the tree knocking your feet out so you plop down on your knees giving you a friendly tap on the back sending you over, like a dog, onto all fours. Then going. He is going. Hear that? Crashing and smashing of dead wood. He's walking fast. Gone from the woods.

Seed? By far and away the best thing to taste involving seeds is this:

SUMMER PUDDING

What is it that goes in summer pudding? You're spitting. Crouched. The ground is covered in teeny, tiny needles. Where are the oak leaves? A needle has pierced you. It's sticking right up inside the underneath of your middle fingernail. See that? It's going purplish beyond your fingernails dirt. You're watching an actual bruise as it really forms. Stop spitting.

You've been left quite close to the last of Bryan's fire. He's forgotten his guitar. Too much juddering. Crouched. You need to start breathing.

Summer Pudding has raspberries and, it, it has those other berries that are? Well, oh for goodness sake come on, they are, red. And they hang off a string. Mummy wears them as earrings when... Red currants! That's it.

SUMMER PUDDING

½ pound raspberries
½ pound red currants

Breathe then you need to get that needle thing out of your finger. Your nail is plumping up with blood that's queuing, waiting to burst past its pine needle cork. Pine needles. That's what's up top this bit of earth. Stop staring at the earth. Get up. Stop spitting. And? And summer pudding has bread in it. And, sugar. It has sugar. And seeds.

Breathe. You're raising your needled finger more slowly than a clock moves. Up. To. Your. Teeth. You've stopped spitting. You're taking that pine needle under your right front tooth. How funny, your tooth is soft, it can't bite down. Your teeth are turned to fudge. You need to find your mummy.

Go. Go now. Get up and get out of those woods they are very, very dangerous.

Look at you move. Pulling the needle with your other hand and hurtling it out. Blood. You have to put weights on summer pudding to squash it and make the juice. Where's the path gone? Pushing through brambles, skin flaying, smashing those little wellies down, crushing your way through. There's no such thing as ghosts. You are not being followed. Out. Now – Run!

Where are Mummy and Daddy? Where is Star? Passing the kid's teepee, nearly at the adult teepee. Argh. No. See over there? That's the gang of rival beggars. Why is there no one else anywhere around? Swerve. Get away. No. The brown one's running after you.

"Hey. Hey. Come here. We want to talk. We want to ask you... come here. Why are you... ?" Brown One. He's stopped chasing. You haven't stopped running. Breathing is burning up your throat. Chest squeezing too hard. Smaller and smaller air gulps getting through. Smash into...

"Hello, Sweetheart." Laura. Catching you, sending you back onto your feet. She's holding hands with The Bear. You're squeezing her other hand. Panting. Staring at them. Why can't you say anything?

"Sweetie? Ok?" Laura. Her and her Bear are so smiley. Still no response?

"Sweetheart?" Laura. Crouching down but holding on to her Bear Anchor. You're doing your staring at The Bear. The Bear's crouching too. Tell them.

"Have you seen my parents?" You. Can they see the cracks on your mouth? Your mouth's blood? The scratch by your eye? Why can't they hear your breathing? Stop wheezing. Get some air in past your throat. You're going to fucking faint if you don't let the air get inside you.

"Um. Yes, Sweetie, we have. They've gone out to dinner with that woman from the village that imports the gross sheepskin. A hotel somewhere." Laura. She's let go of her Bear. She's putting both hands on your shoulders. You're doing a hot-hop backwards and pushing hard on the soft bit between your ribs. Secretly punching self, shocking your lungs into opening. Shuddering breath. In. Finally.

"I'm ok. I'm off to bed. Night." You. Going. Doubling back to the kids' teepee. Walking nearly backwards to keep seeing them. Taking each other's hands. Laura's raising The Bear's paw to her lips and kissing, neither of them stopping watching you until you're inside the kids' teepee and blinking into the blackness. Adjusting. Take in more air. Fetid air. Get yourself inside. Eyes coming to, like morning starting. The tent is filled with molehill humped bodies. A children's graveyard from *Oliver Twist*. Who do all these bodies belong to? Who is going to come in and kiss these bodies good night? Oh. Corporal? Like Corpse. That's why you got it confused. Scanning, crawling through the dank, dark, fire-smoke-thick air to the little heap of Star. Her heap's curled into the bigger heap of Wolfie. No Orion. Good. Good. You're huddling as close to your sister as you dare. Don't wake them. Please just try to lie down. Stop juddering. You're still wearing Bryan's coat. Scratched hands jumping like the nerves in a freshly beheaded chicken, getting out of his stink. Pushing his coat away with just your feet. Stop juddering. So cold.

Next morning.

The van's turning into the drive back home. Daddy's flying into the house to find Bryan and hit him. Everyone's crowding in after him. To experience the hitting. Pretty Justin's lying on the dark green velvet buttony sofa with all its straw hanging out underneath.

"Where is he? Where is that shitty little doe-eyed fucker?" Daddy. To Pretty Justin. About Bryan. And needing to hit him.

"Gone. Home." Pretty Justin. Hot, huge tears drip, drip, dripping off his face. Laura's going to him, sort of picking him up and leading him upstairs. Bryan has gone.

Hear that scream going on and on and on? Everyone, including Pretty Justin and Laura, who are falling back down the stairs, are rushing out of the back door. Star's holding open the door to Prune's hut, she's emitting the highest most throat-raw screaming you'll ever hear. Running to the hut. Looking in. Pulling Star away. You and Star being pulled away.

"Justin, you fucking idiot. Jesus Jesus Jesus. Beth get them inside. Everyone stay back. Fuck. Didn't you check in here? Didn't you check when you got home? What did Bryan do? Did he check on the fucking goat?" Daddy. Nearly as loud as Star's scream.

"What has happened, Anthony? Please. I can't bear to look." Mummy. She has Star's face into her and Laura has your hand.

"Sorry, like, oh, like, so sorry, so sorry. I am going to Japan. I am like so going. So sorry. I didn't think I didn't." Pretty Justin.

"Some thing has got in. Cornered her. What could do that? What would do that? It's very messy." Daddy. Sort of pushing everyone back inside the house.

CHAPTER NINE

The Big Room. It's only the next morning. You're on the limping stool wrapped around the house hot water bottle – Poseidon – every muscle working to hold the stool still. The stool's limping. Independently. Poseidon's only working on your tummy. All of your legs, all of your arms, all of your back and all of your head are numb. Cold has taken up residence. It's blown down doors, pushed through walls, creating an ice vacuum inside you. You're now echoing with cold and this fucking stool needs to grow up its stupid wonky leg and stop it's fucking free-style juddering.

Pretty Justin's bags are lumped against the white wicker chipped chair. Everyone, apart from Tammie and Eric, is here. Everyone's sitting at the table watching Daddy. Daddy was the last to come down. He went to the bottom oven of the Aga, he took out the French porridge and he chucked it in the bin. He made two pots of coffee and he served you and Star first with the coffee. He made it extra top of the milk milky and loads of sugar. Look at him now. He's smudged he's cooking so fast. Mixing, dolloping, greasing.

Food to nurture The Group after a nasty shock.

DROP SCONES

Not as perfect a breakfast as Frozen Chocolate Cake but a very, very close second.
1oz butter, melted
10 oz self-raising flour. Really are nicest with wholemeal.
1 oz sugar
couple eggs
Bit less than half pint milk. Slosh in until thick pouring mix.

Whip eggs, add to milk mix. When butter's coolish add, then add dry stuff. Remarkably like waffles. Grease hot plate of Aga, dollop little puddles of this all over. Rise then flip. Drip of butter on each then drip of wonderful, forbidden golden syrup. These quants make enough for about five people to have ten each. Which you all need. No matter how many waffles you had before. This is now.

No. No. The syrup is trickling to inside your mouth cracks. It's hurting too much. Don't cry. It's only sugar.

"You don't have a flight booked, baby. Is there even a flight to Japan this week?" Laura. To Pretty Justin. His face is still slidey with tears. Has Bryan left because he's in love with you? What is sue? Open your mouth a tiny bit. Do some pussy cat licks to the sweet, and a bit bloody, crack to get the syrup out. Jaw's very achey. Your head has lumps and one cut at the back of it but you've washed your hair so people won't look. There was no hot water left. Will your seaweed hair ever dry?

"And what the fuck does Japan have that we don't?" Daddy. Trying to make up for blaming Pretty Justin for Prune's slaughter. Although he might be to blame. Why didn't they remember her? Too busy sitting about bumming.

"Stay, darling. Let us organize this properly." Mummy.

"I can't stay. I like so can't yeah? I can't be near. I can't like." Pretty Justin. Why does he keep looking at you like that? Tell him not to leave. Try a smile at him. How long will it be before you can smile without it burning? Eric and Tammie are coming into the Big Room.

"What the fuck is this? The family Von Trapp scarper into the mountains? Where are you two tripping off to?" Daddy. Flipping and using his fish slice to point at their rucksacks. Why is nobody noticing Eric has no beard? Easy to see why he used to have one. Lips like wet balloons.

"Eric and I need to find a home. Somewhere substantial. Somewhere in The States. We will always value the time we spent here but that time is now over. We're mindful that someone will be driving Justin to the train and we thought it would be kind if we shared that lift." Tammie. Oh. But these are Your People. Whether you want them or not. You need to open your mouth wide enough to get the half-chewed drop scone out. It's too much. Spit-plopping it into your hand. It's got flecks of blood on it. Scrunch it up.

"That is disgusting. Put that into the bin immediately and for christ's sake share Poseidon with your sister. It was her pet, we're all feeling the same thing." Mummy. Are they? Hurling Poseidon at Star. Electric shock speed. Star has Great Uncle Elizabeth under an arm. Fumbled catch.

"Sorry. No sorry." You. Mouth seriously failing. Drop scone sludge in bin. Scrambling back on useless stool. Tummy instantly ice-numb again.

"Great. Sure. I'll take you after I've finished feeding everyone. The petrol will be two quid a piece. I have no change so exact money only. Please." Daddy.

"I don't like have oh I don't have yeah? Two. Yeah? I don't have it." Pretty Justin. He is wailing.

"Not you, Sweet Boy. You ride free." Daddy. More wailing. Is Rod going too?

"How will you pay for your flight? Where will you live? Justin, please be sensible." Mummy. Why is Mummy wearing lipstick? Star is coming over to you. With her free arm she's pushing Poseidon up against your back. That is the nicest feeling ever. Tears are coming out of your eyes. In waves. They are scouring your mouth cracks. It is agony. Salt is an antiseptic.

"I have a. Yeah? Bryan found me a, like a, like a cooperative. Like Raku cooperative. He said we would, you know? Together. I have like yeah? I need to make some like pots? I will get like I will do some waiting tables in London. I will like, find the like money." Pretty Justin. Pretty Justin loves Bryan more than he loves you. Why? Pretty Justin is your nearly brother. He is yours. He said he would be yours forever, that he'd dance at your wedding. Then he laughed and said you'd be too clever for weddings but he would be there, no matter what, whatever it was, to bay at the moon with you. It was a long time ago, early one morning, with your underneath of finger nails full of his back grease, as you tickled away, but he did say it. It was a promise. And now it's broken. Your waves of tears are the tide coming in. Look at Mummy. Her red mouth's wonky.

"Hang on, let me get this straight. Bryan has organized a sabbatical placement for you in a pottery in Japan specializing in Raku? And you are just going? Just abandoning all the work we have together?" Mummy. It's Mummy's dream to work in Raku and to learn it in Japan, where they're the masters and where Mummy will never, ever be able to go. This will be too much. Norwich would be too much.

"You know what? I think that is just cool, Justin. It's a friendly thing Bryan has done for you. You can hold that thought. I can advance the cash for your flight. Come on, let's get your bags sorted. You're done here." Laura. Heading towards his bags. There is snot mixing with your tears. Star's pushing harder. Your right arm's curled backwards pulling her in. Poseidon's crushed between you, eking out his last.

"Hey, Lady, that's my assistant you're marching out of the door. He has an unwritten contract with me to fulfil." Mummy. Standing.

"No. No. He doesn't. Please be careful now. Everyone in this room, and I include your husband and your kids, is witness to the fact that Justin hasn't made a single pot in his time with you. This is not a positive learning environment." Laura.

"Puff." Rod. Look at him glowing. Not a tear in sight, now. Rod would like to do French kissing with Laura. Not the inside kind of French kissing. The proper kind.

"Right that is it. Anthony, I give up. Justin you have my fucking blessing with your fucking Raku fantasy. It will fail. It will fail because you're a good assistant. And that is all. I was doing you a favour by not teaching you the reality. You need a profound and resonating sense of self to be an artist. Who are you, Justin? I'll tell you. You are a dream thief. Tammie and Eric? Really I have very little to say to you apart from Eric, you were a reasonable fuck and Tammie, I would be amazed if you can make him shake when he comes quite as effectively as I do. My blow jobs will haunt your marriage. Rod? You're a good man. A little dull but good. Maybe you should think about applying to the Police Force. Please pack a bag and leave. Laura, you too. This house is mine. I demand it back. My family demand their own space back. Good fucking bye. Oh, and Laura? You are fat. Sorry but it's true. And it needed saying. Girls? Come upstairs now.

We are going to read a story whilst these people clear out." Mummy. Star has stepped backwards and sideways to your flank. Two sets of greenish sludge eyes wide. Yours are pure liquid because your tears have broken through the sea-wall, they're flooding the fields. This is not a House Meeting. This is real. Mummy is wrong. This is very, very wrong. Laura's laughing at Mummy. Her mouth's wide open, full of snow-white teeth.

"You're a piece of work, beautiful Beth. And you're right, we are done here. But thank you, thank you for all the good and strange times. Thank you especially for the privilege of knowing your girls. I'm going to pack but then I'd like to take a couple of minutes to say a proper farewell to them and I'm sure these guys feel the same." Laura. No more Laura? If you tell about the seeds will they stay? Oh god. Are the seeds growing? Like mustard and cress on damp cotton wool sprouting down the walls of your throat?

"No. Please. I don't want. No." You. Can they understand you? The Big Room's looking at you and Star. Star has hair in her hands. "Please? Mummy? Please?" Laura is wrong. It isn't always about the fucking words. Or at least not from a child.

"Let's slow things down. Beth, please stay. Just a moment. There's something I have to say. Can you get her under some kind of control, please?" Daddy. Head nod towards your sad, wet face. Mummy is staying. "We now know who she takes after with the water works. And, please, stop that, it's irritating." Interrupting himself to prevent your limping-stool. Can't he see its uncontrollable shaking? Tears done. It'll be thirty-four years before you cry like that again. "Ok. So. Firstly, does everyone have the breakfast they need? I am loath to suggest it but there's a big bowl of yoghurt that needs eating. Who needs a yog whizz?"

YOG WHIZZ

Yoghurt. Must be goat. There's a particular, almost stinky, taste to goat's yog that gives an acid flavour that stops the sweetness from being wrong. Yog is the easiest thing in the whole wide world. A dollop of last yog batch into warm milk then onto back of Aga over night. Yoghurt. Prune's yog could well live on. For years to come.

Honey.

Going off bananas. Might be fine with fresh but never tried that. They're always a bit brown. At Swallow's Farmhouse.

Handful of oatmeal. 'Something to balance all the cursed dairy.' Mummy. When she first started chucking it in. Doesn't wreck the taste too much.

Whizz all up. This is a drink. 'It's profoundly nutritious. Did you know honey's so potent it can kill spunk?' Mummy. To Tammie. When Tammie first joined in and Mummy was 'attempting to fathom her'. What is spunk?

"Ok." Daddy. Pouring. Look at Star clutching Great Uncle Elizabeth. Star hasn't let go of him since you got home. Surprised she hasn't got a couple of hens up her jumper too. There are two bleeding bits on her head. "Ok." Done pouring. Everyone in the Big Room's waiting for Daddy. Even Mummy. "So. I have been asked to go to The States. The Oracle folk need me there. Just for nine days. Signing stuff, meeting people and then there's a festival. It's important. I need to go." Mummy has gone grey. Face not mane. Silence.

There is an opening out of the gaps between people and things happening. Air feels to be rushing in. Like the roof came off and there was the sky. Pouring down, pulling you up, so much bigger than the little toys stacked inside the Swallow's Farmhouse doll's house. The toys cannot imagine what to do next. They only know that the Mummy toy will disintegrate if the Daddy toy leaves the house. Who will brush her hair each morning, squeeze her orange juice, kiss her eyes awake? Who will keep the sky from falling into the doll's house? Why does the Daddy toy need to go? Does the Daddy toy love his poems more than you?

"To Prune. A fine and crazy beast." Rod. Raising yog whizz to his dry lips and gulping. Go on. Try it. Just a sip. The others are glugging it back. Eric's holding the cup so his bairn gets its share. Star's absolutely not drinking, she's doing another big yank. You're sticking your tongue into the whizz. No. Too much deadness.

"Everyone, mewl, fed? Anthony, love, it's simple, let's just have a little holiday in New York. The girls will adore the adventure." Mummy. The Big Room's contents are slack jawed, staring at Mummy. Brave Mummy's looking at them too. Silence. Um. Oh. Mummy's dropped her face down. She's looking at the table. She's putting both her hands on the table and pushing herself up.

"It seems I might be getting a migraine. I am so sorry. This is clearly turning into an important House Meeting. Much to be sorted. Love, thank you for such a delicious breakfast. I think I need to take my silly old head off to bed. So sorry, Lovely People." Mummy. Going. Everyone watching her go. She's rubbing her eyes, hear those little squeaks? Star's turning. Head shake from you. Star's choosing Mummy. Leaving too. You're running in front of them. Got the door. Holding it open. Pushing Poseidon into Mummy's hands.

"Bless you." Mummy. They've gone. Soft double clunk of upstairs door shutting.

"She means I walk like a Police Man. She's remarked upon it before." Rod.

"Rod? You and I need to stay until Anthony's home. Anthony? How many days do you really need to make this work?" Laura. Daddy's reaching his hand across the table, putting his up top of hers. He's shaking their hands together softly, letting go, now he's looking at the table.

"I can't yeah. I just can't. Please don't make me. I'm like gonna hitch to Norwich yeah. I have to." Pretty Justin.

"I will drive you. As I said. The three of you. Do you want to go now?" Daddy. Stopping looking at the table.

"Now." Pretty Justin. Getting up. Getting his bag. Hoicking it onto his baby frail shoulders. Going straight out of the door. Not even a glance to you.

"Eric, final blow job? Or off?" Daddy.

"Thank you, Anthony. Off." Eric. The mountain's standing. The mountain's stretching and yawning and offering its little love its hand. "Come away, Hen. Home."

"Please know that we meant it when we said there would always be a place for you with us. God bless you and Star." Tammie. Straight out of the door they go. Will Tammie remember her promise to you? Daddy's following then stopping in the door and turning back.

"Thank you. Both. I need two weeks. They want me there in four weeks time. I will understand if you want to leave and come back, just for these two weeks, but you're welcome to stay until then. My guess is Beth will now be completely cool with you staying until well after I'm home. I have to go. Regardless. So. Thank you." Daddy.

"I can't promise I'll be effective but Rod? You may be. If you've got the stomach for it. I ain't sure Beth will put up with me. It's a lethal ingredient in her sorry mix, that scrabbling need to be adored. Her belief that it's worship, not kindness, that keeps us all here, propping her up. She doesn't believe it from me, anymore. And she ain't stupid. She's right not to. I will not buy into it." Laura. Stern and tall and sure. Daddy looks absolutely amazed.

"Is that how you read it too?" Daddy. To Rod. Of course Rod doesn't read it. Rod only reads books.

"This house is an important venture. It's important what we've embarked upon here. Together. We're a family of creative impulses. The energy we create, communally, could power a factory. A factory of ideas." Rod. That is not what Daddy asked. Daddy's pushing his thin fringe away from his eyes.

"Why are you offering to stay? Considering." Daddy. To Laura.

"Old times' sake. And y'know, them." Laura. Head tilt to you.

"Ok. If you need a break when I'm gone then Dahlia, sheepskin Dahlia, knows all of this and has offered to step in for a few hours." Daddy. He's about to leave but has changed his mind and is running up stairs to Mummy. Two weeks without Daddy.

"It'll be fine. Really, really good actually and Rod, you can go, or whatever you want because I can do everything. Daddy will be back, so soon, and I can do everything. Laura you can stay too and it'll be fun." You. Words are dripping out of your mouth like nonsense-jam. Laura's tulip-green eyes are full, not of tears but of something unreadable and complete. She's smiling at you. The stack of un-touched drop scones has butter solidifying round its golden syrup. The smell of golden syrup now means goodbye. Get away. Get outside. You are.

Eric and Tammie are jammed into the front of the van. Tammie's kneeling up on her bit of seat so Eric's legs can have her share of the floor. Eric's giving you a final, under the red eyebrows, look. The day's coming when that look will haunt health food shops the world over. Turns out Eric was up to his muddy elbows in ideas. Mostly regarding hedges. Useful if you're going to invent organic farming. God's Good Earth (Inc.) will produce plenty of other stuff besides pressed corn. And every single packet will have Farmer Eric, plus reinstated organic beard, staring out from it. With Vicar Tammie, just recognizable under her layers and layers of rosy cheeked plumpness, snuggled against his shoulder. Must have stood on a box. Probably a golden one as they're clearly absolutely soaked in real money.

Pretty Justin's at the back doors trying to shove his rucksack in beside all the Fayre stuff, that's not had a chance to be unpacked, and Eric and Tammie's massive rucksacks. He's pushing with his back. Has he seen you coming? Yes. He's stopping pushing. Bracing himself against the doors. Saying goodbye to the Norfolk sky, with his eyes.

"Thank you very much for teaching me to dance properly. Please will you send me lots of letters and don't forget to give me your address as soon as you have one. I really don't think Mummy meant any of that. I know she thinks you're very pretty and very sweet. And I will write to you every week. I promise. Oh, I know, we can be pen pals. And then you can come home for holidays. Anytime. Really anytime, you won't even need to phone or anything. So. Um. Bye, Justin. Bye, bye." You. There's fresh blood in one small crack. From all your smiling.

"I will never, like, I will never contact you. Yeah? If you ever, yeah? Fall in love, you will know, Yeah? What you have done. I am going to practise, yeah? Pity for you. That you begged him, yeah? To do that. Yeah? That is like sickness. You have like taken from me. Yeah? I know you are like so a child and so everything but I don't think you are. I think, yeah? You know." Pretty Justin. Pushing and squashing his bag into the van. Slamming the door. Hear it make that tiny little click closed? That'll be popping back open before they get to the trains.

Pretty Justin will never contact you again. Laura will pay his air fare to Japan. He will live in Japan for six years. Laura will pay his return fare to The States. Where he will die of AIDS. You will never find out if his practice paid off.

One week later.

Mummy has had a couple more migraines. A letter arrives for you.

Dear Boudicca,

I find I am compelled to communicate with you. I no longer have those feelings for Valerie Singleton. I don't understand how a feeling so certain can change. I have decided I do not believe in love. Love must be a chemical reaction. Possibly created by the shift in blood from the head to the penis when aroused. I am searching for some reading matter to support this new theory.

What I wanted to discuss with you is the interesting fact that the feelings I once had, or rather it would be fairer to say, the chemical reaction that Valerie Singleton once effected in me seems to have shifted its effect to you. I am not in love with you. I am certain of that. There is no such thing as love. I am, however, keen to test out my ideas. I think that will only be possible if we meet again.

Please write to me at the address above and let me know how I can arrange this meeting.

Best wishes,

Ryan.

You pen a reply.

Orion,
Chocolate idiot biscuits.
4 oz butter
2 oz sugar
4 oz plain flour
1 tablespoon cocoa
Vanilla essence. I'll leave you to work out how much.

Cream fat, sugar and essence. Stir in other ingredients. Roll into large marble-sized balls. Place on baking tray. Push them flat, slightly, with the back of a fork. Bake for a minimum of six minutes, a maximum of ten.

Boude x

Two weeks after that.

Mummy has had five more migraines.

More letters about how interesting chemical reactions can be and do you want to take part in what might be a first scientific experiment on this subject and really, really wanting to know how much vanilla essence, as he has wasted quite lot of house money on ingredients, have arrived. You haven't replied. The letters chase you on and off for the next two years.

One week, two and a half days later.

Daddy's been gone for nine days. Laura's broken her promise and left before Daddy's return. Laura left before but came back when Daddy went to New York. She whispered to you that it was just to get herself used to being without you and Star. Rod stayed the whole time. But. Now. Laura's gone. Forever. To New York.

Amazing thing. Laura's a millionaire. She has a granny who's swimming in cash. Old money. Does old money die? When the old granny does? 'That is the question that keeps Dodie's wily accountants awake all night.' Laura. About Dodie – her granny – and her old money. Daddy's staying in one of Laura's granny Dodie's apartments. High up towards the sky. On the Upper East Side. It has glass walls. What's it like sleeping in a greenhouse? If the weather wasn't so sodding January you'd try it. But mainly, how unfair that Laura has this granny. Bet Laura's granny doesn't put a saucer of milk out for the fairies every night. In her sky greenhouse. How would the hedgehogs get up there to steal the milk and trick the granny it was actually the fairies that drank it? Your grandma must have wasted hundreds of pints on the bloody hedgehogs. No wonder she hasn't got any spare old money hanging around.

So, Laura left. She did say goodbye. She took you and Star up the field. Not the Jessie's grave-end but the end near Star's subsiding den. She sat you down, said Rod was ok and it'd be ok, and she sang a song to you. It was quite a long song.

"If the sky above you should grow dark and full of cloud and that old north wind should begin to blow." Laura. Singing for a fair while. Bit too quiet to catch it properly and the old north wind really was blowing a gale. You and Star were trying to sit still, it was so blowy, but Laura had clearly rehearsed so you let her finish. "Keep your head together and call my name out loud. Soon I'll be knocking on your door. You just call out my name and you know where ever I am I'll come running. To see you again." Then a bit more about being a friend. Then Laura hugged you both. Too hard. And walked out of the house with just one small bag slung across her bone and elastic body.

"Goody, goody, good. I have been looking forward to watching that enormous bottom making its way back the way it came pretty much since its arrival." Mummy. To Rod.

"Aye. Enormous bottom gruuuunt. Puffff." But all whispered. They both watched Laura's bottom until it disappeared over the horizon. Then Mummy had another migraine.

One year after Laura's return to New York she publishes an international best seller. *The Major Arcana.* About life in a commune in north Norfolk, England. Laura's as good as her word. She returns from The States, the hour she's called, when you suspect Star's having a second breakdown. She takes Star to live with her and her girlfriend and their son. By this point Laura's a film producer living in LA. In another five years she'll be one of *the* film producers living in LA. Laura will always understand, fully, the meaning of friendship and that it's different from family.

One week, three days later.

Who'd have thought it'd be Tammie who kept her promises? Your waffle iron arrives. With a whopping jar of maple syrup strapped to its side. There's a pink box with real pink pointe ballet shoes for Star. They even have satin ribbons.

One week, three days and the middle of that night later.

You wake up with such a jump you're standing up out of bed when your eyes open. Takes a few seconds to realize what it is that's done it. There's so much noise. Then you get it. It's that noise. It's the grain lorry reversing sound. But far louder. Is Mummy having a migraine? No. There's a creature loose in the house. The only adults in the house are Mummy and Rod.

Two weeks later, afternoon.

Daddy is home. Daddy had a bag of New York sweets for you and

Star. The best thing was sugar in crystallized lumps stuck together and hung on strings looking just like real uneven lumps of jewels. You wore them until the lure to suck was too much. Forty-six minutes.

Just before bedtime.

"Girls? Mummy, Rod and I want to share something with you. We all love you very much." Daddy. Rod loves you? "We know you're both old souls and we know you both have a very grown-up understanding of what a mess adults often make and we want to try very hard and make sure this is not a mess. We also want very much to treat you with the respect you deserve. So. The thing is. Mummy and I will always love each other but Mummy isn't in love with me anymore. She is in love with Rod and they want to get married. We think, maybe, we just loved too much, too young. Anyway. Nothing's going to change. I will still live here. I'll just sleep in a different bed. Possibly Dahlia, that nice woman who you met when she bought all Mummy's pots, might share my bed sometimes but that'll be the only change. I promise I'm not going anywhere." Daddy. Smile, smile, smiling.

Rod has promised Mummy he'll cure her agoraphobia. Apparently you can cure sickness by naming it. Keith? But most importantly by being the kind of masculine energy that can match Mummy's powerful feminine energy. Once Rod gets going on names he has another surprise for The House. Your People have been mispronouncing your name. Since birth. It isn't Bo-di-see-er. Like, in fact, the whole world thinks. It's Bo-dicker. Dicker is not a name you fancy much. You stick with Boude. Rhymes with woad.

When Rod cures the agoraphobia Mummy and he leave Norfolk. Liberated, Mummy branches out into Feng Shui. She travels. It's the migraines that get to be the problem next. Mummy doesn't have the actual agoraphobia but if there's something happening that she's desperate to attend, her head trips her up. She's forced to stay home. The migraines go on for ten years. Then her tummy joins in. Then it's fainting, then legs. Mummy gradually shifts her loyalty from Biba to a clothes catalogue called Lands End. 'Darling, do you know them? They do everything in wonderful rich colours, in this amazing cloth. It's called fleece. Have you heard of it? So toasty.' It gets cold sat on the sofa. All day. Surrounded by half-eaten pots of honey. But, Rod is always there. Caring for Mummy. Giving her troubles their Latin names. And his novels win awards, despite how much more he would have written had he not chosen her. Until the wretched day when Beth's beloved head packs up for real. Alzheimer's.

Middle of the night.

The noise. You lie in bed for as long as you can bear but Mummy and Rod have Mummy and Daddy's bed in the attic and that's above your head. You go to Daddy's room. Bryan's old room. You wait outside the door. You don't want to wake him up. You don't want Daddy to hear the creature. You wait as long as you can bear. You knock on Daddy's door.

"Come in." Daddy. Sitting up in bed.

"I don't like it. It's too loud. Can you make them stop." You.

"I don't like it either. No. I can't. It's all a bit of a surprise. Sorry. I stayed away too long. I needed to work. For myself. It will stop. Do you need to sleep with me?" Daddy. Yes.

"No. I'll be alright." You.

"Rod's a good man. He has a good mind." Daddy.

Two weeks and one day later.

Middle of the night.

Same wake up. Same journey to Daddy. Same return to bed.

Two weeks and four days later.

Morning.

Daddy's standing in the Big Room. He has two plastic bags full of clothes. He has two single roses from a real flower shop. Each rose is wrapped in its own twist of paper. Star's is pure yellow, yours is yellow streaked with red.

"I am very sorry. We do love you. Sometimes adults have to do what is best for them in the hopes that it'll be best for the kids. I'll only be at the other side of the village." Daddy.

Daddy stays at the other side of the village for four weeks. During those weeks Clarissa visits, she and Dahlia have so much in common that Clarissa abandons her loyalty to French Sun. Tuscany becomes the only place really worth one's time. Daddy lives in a series of squats in Norwich for the next nine years. If you and Star need to see him you have to ask for the bus fare, which causes a bit of an argument, or hitch. Daddy will live with a couple of other women, raising their children beautifully. He will always be the best poet. He never does get to hit Bryan. For stealing the White Saab.

Bryan does graduate from Harvard. He does become a lawyer. He does have his own law firm. It specialises in family law. Laura keeps you informed of his family's progress in her Christmas round-up cards.

CHAPTER TEN

April 1975

It's dawn in Swallow's Farmhouse. You haven't slept. You've been powering your way through *The Lark In The Morn*. Now it's the actual real morn. Not a lark in the endless bloody sky. Just a couple of blackbirds. 'Christ, those fucking birds. They sound like nothing so much as polystyrene being dragged down glass.' Mummy. In early March, when the blackbirds got busy on the nest. The only other sounds are the echoes made by nobody, trudging round your empty home. Turning your head to get a good old stare at Sleeping Baby Star, before she grumbles awake. Ah. She is awake. Staring at you. Be appropriate to think of something epic, or funny, or tender to say. So this morn will be printed on her, for all time.

"Mornin'." You. Oh, well done, most excellent word-smithing.

"Yup." Star. Quarter of a second more staring then, up. Both of you flying into clothes.

But hang on. Slow down. There's your careful pile of completely new clothes. Even the knicks and bra. 'Too, too divine. Of course you can have it. Your choice what we spend this on but really darling, it is gargantuan. Looks like you're part-way through being mummified by a particularly inept spastic. Ha, ha, ha.' Mummy. Last week. Helping with shopping. In Norwich. Rod sitting on the floor outside the changing room, writing odes to Mummy and looking about four times fatter due to being so puffed up with all his masculine healing energy. 'Do I get one?' Star. That swung it. Into the yes pile with the masseevo bra.

The Big Room. Mummy and Rod are both up, both perched behind the table, both fully dressed, both with a mug of coffee, fantastically wide eyes and horse-shoe shaped smiles. Looks painful. Great Uncle Elizabeth's been brushed. The table's empty. Take a proper deep sniff. Damp earth and all its components. Fill your lungs. Don't let them see you doing this. Sly glance round and wham. There, by the door, is your trunk. Closed. Has Mummy filled a secret tuck box for you and snuck it into the middle?

"Right. Who wants what for breakfast?" Mummy. Rising. Like a mermaid from a lake. She's dressed in a pair of silver trousers that never end. They go on from her legs into a shirt and then a hood. Where were they when you did your choosing? Are you hungry?

"I'm not hungry. Lets just go. Shall we? Will I be too early?" You.

"Oh darling, please have something. You're making me sad. You're never nervous. You're going to adore it. What about some flum flum?" Mummy. Flum fucking flum? Who's ill?

"Yuck. No thanks. I'm excited. That's all." You. You could have waffles. Swimming in syrup. Three, easily. You could have cornflakes. You could make Mummy, make Rod, gallop to Ma Burt's for said flakes. You could even see what's lurking in the deep freeze.

"Can I have some?" Star.

"Are you ill?" Mummy.

"I feel a bit sick." Star.

"Then no. Come on. Lets get this lovely old thing in the car." Mummy. Up and stroking your trunk. It used to be hers. Giles was most efficient. He got you and Star expelled from The Rainbow School, too. Orion isn't the only kid of scholarship eligibility. Yours is to a child-self-governing, co-educational, vegetarian Boarding School. Hundreds of miles from Swallow's Farmhouse.

The driveway to school. It's long and straight. At the end there's a huge car park full of the shiniest most navy blue cars you've ever witnessed. Some have blacked out windows and people in uniforms standing beside them. And there's the bread van. With the bonnet up, and look, there's Daddy's arse sticking out from under it. Rod's doing a perky honk on the White Saab horn. Daddy's jolting out of the engine, thwacking his head on the bonnet of the bread van.

"Fuck off. That fucking hurt." Daddy. Rubbing oil into his hair. Daddy's dressed in a suit. Looks like a clown at a rival clown's funeral.

"Hey, Anthony Man, so sorry. Just a cheery greeting on this auspicious day. Merely attempting to keep things light and easy for our girl." Rod. Out of the open White Saab window, swinging into land beside the bread van. Whose girl?

"Does she have bags that need carrying?" Daddy. Ignoring Rod, going round to Mummy's side. Star and you are pressed into the back seats. If you press hard enough maybe a door to Narnia will melt open. You can both float through for a natter with Aslan. Let this lot get on with The Arrival. Christ. Look at the other cars. Many, many expensive people are watching the tatty remains of Your People as they negotiate the removal of the trunk from the boot of the White Saab. Out you get. Why didn't you think to wash the fucking White Saab? It's practically navy itself, it's so filthy. Or better still, why didn't you shut the fuck up about that rural inbred flagging down your bike to say he'd found the sodding White Saab loitering in a ditch at the edge of one of his fields? Halfway to Norwich.

Big Four. This is the name on the room that's your dorm. It's at the top of the bit of the school with Dorms for Girls. Everywhere is white, with black wood. The windows have criss-crosses of grey, soft looking, metal over them. This is the noisiest place on earth. There are constant screams ricocheting off the whiteness. Could that be joy? The screams of joy are ringing out over about seven hundred different musics. It's an infernal fairground racket. Very few people hanging round available for meeting. The joy's all leaking from behind closed doors. Here's yours. Open. Called, Big Four. Looks like you'll be sharing with three others. And the little one said, roll over, roll over. Heave, heave, thunk. Trunk arrived. Your Tatty People have no more purpose.

"Hear that?" Mummy. Perching on your trunk, teetering on the end of your school bed.

"How could we fail to?" Daddy. Hands in pockets. Is he about to pull out a clown's honky horn?

"That, my darlings, is the sound of pure oestrogen. Heaven. Let's swap. I'll even wear those horrid scratchy trews you insisted on." Mummy. Happy.

Daddy, Rod and Star are lurking beside your bed. Rod's sweating. Daddy got him to carry the back end of the trunk, up all the stairs, without stopping. Your bed's nearest the door. The two beds beside the window have posters of exhibitions of French, real, paintings pinned up round them. Look, two girls, dressed in the simplest white T-shirts, jeans and sneakers, hanging out the window. Smoking. This is not Malory Towers. Should you saunter over and get the ball rolling? They're not giving The Tatty Gang a glance. Maybe hold off on the idle chit-chat, for now. These girls are identical to the shiny navy car lot. They're giraffes, with hair like Mummy's and the tightest, cleanest, skin. Real money, no doubt about it. Old or new? Who cares. These two are talking French, only drawing breath to do Frenchie screams of joy out the open window, alongside their puffed out smokes.

"Rod? Rod? Home time. For fuck's sake they're twelve. Thirteen, tops. Come, on." Mummy. Sliding down the trunk and swooping door-wards. "Do you want a hug? Or shall we just hit the road? Right. Road." Mummy. Blowing you a kiss, skipping off down the corridor. Rod in tow. Where are you? Follow them. Then you'll be able to map your way back here. You are. Fast.

Base of stairs beside the school front door.

"Oh come here. Don't be wet. Buck up. Keep bucked up, especially at night, then, before you know it, you'll never be able to un-buck again." Mummy. Pulling you tight to her chest. Kissing the top of your head, swooshing her silver hood into place, taking Rod's hand, swinging it and going. "Star? Pick up the pace. It's easier." Mummy. Halfway to the White Saab.

"Farewell." Rod. Doing a little semi-hop to get back in time with Mummy's exit.

Star's glued to a herd of giraffes who've just swept past. Males. Not as tall as the females. Stocky zebras? For some un-fathomable (at present) reason, they're pissing themselves laughing and all making the same sound. Loudly. Surprised? It seems to go something like – Wah-erh-ahhh. With an upward inflection on the final syllable. War cry?

"Star? Your mother." Daddy. Pointing at Mummy flapping a hand from the White Saab. You're about to say goodbye to your little sister. You do not want to say goodbye to your little sister. Ever. 'How come Star doesn't get this scholarship? Why am just I going?' You. When

Mummy announced her plans. 'Are you mad? Ten's far too young. She'd be destroyed by it. It'll suit you. You're unsinkable.' Mummy. Star's bobble hat has risen right up, like a gnome's. You could pull it back into shape for her. Screams are receding. Why's it gone all quiet? Why's your chest tight? Say something. Star's tip-toe leaning up to your ear.

"Trot on." Star. Whispered.

"Trot on." You. Whispered back. She's gone. The White Saab is gone.

"So. Boude. School and all that jazz, hey?" Daddy. Hands in pockets. Still not located his clown's honky horn.

"Why?" Why's your voice gone scratchy?

"Ha. Yeah. Very good question. To which, I'm afraid, I honestly do not have the answer. I think you're a pretty remarkable person. By the way." Not remarkable enough to take back.

Another flock of leggy beasts is gusting past. Screams swelling back. There's a tray of inedible looking hunks of what can only be described as slightly burnt wholemeal rusks balanced on a radiator beside the front door. One of those Serengeti Plains dwellers is going to send them flying. Daddy's moving towards you. It'd be better if he didn't hug you. You're turning back up the endless stairs.

"See ya, Anthony." Over your shoulder. He'll have to sort the bread van engine for himself.

Little jumping Joan. When no one's with her, she's all alone.

And so it starts. The week of silence. Not one single person says a thing to you for the first day. No one. Not even the female grown-up who lives behind a door that says 'private' and only comes gliding out dressed in a man's dressing gown and enormous slippers she can't lift off the ground with her four strands of greasy grey hair draped over her shoulders to do Lights Out. She's your House Mother. In all your time at Boarding School you exchange not one word with her.

Big Four. Made it. The French giraffes have gone. Good. Are you allowed to close the door? Shut out the joy? Best not. But do need to plan. On bed. One thing's frighteningly clear, you have to get your fucking clothes sorted. What were you thinking with the grey wool trousers that have pleats at the waist, bag out like a compact beach ball round tummy and bum, and are itchy as fuck? And actually, never mind them, what was the plan with the electric blue jumper? It's more of a tube and goes down over the endless pleats of the blanket-based trews, ending, at your knees, to create a swiss roll effect round what might, once, have been your waist. Why, why, why did you force Mummy to cut your hair like Liza Minnelli? You just look like Ma fucking Burt. Is there time, before more giraffes descend, to fashion a simple-something from a sheet? You've got a sewing kit. You're a quick fucking worker. Can't think straight. Noise. Look, the bed opposite you has been claimed, in your absence. Cripes. How come it took so long to notice that? Above bed three is a poster, as big as the wall. A man waving a red cape at a massively cheesed-off bull. Both man and bull have the same bottoms. Has Daddy gone?

Base of the stairs beside the high oak front door. Really only open it a tiny crack. Done. Weeny peek. Still there. Two of the men in uniforms are leaning on the bread van smoking with Daddy. Laughing. Bonnet down. You could saunter up. Tell him to take you home. Obviously he doesn't actually have a home, currently, but you can sleep anywhere. Bread van would be fine. Why did Jessie die? If Jessie was alive they'd have needed you at home. Daddy's stubbing out his ciggie. Shaking hands happening. Run. Now. Now's the moment. Run to your Daddy. What if Daddy says no? The bread van's leaving.

Braking at the bottom of the drive. Indicating right. Both its brake lights are broken.

Big Four. Still empty. Unpack. No secret tuck box. Nothing, apart from books, two pilfered Lil-lets (in case periods pluck up courage) and shampoo. All the rest of this crap must never see the light of the Big Four day. Look, oh blessed delight, the red jeans. Quick. On. By the window's a full-length mirror. The only one you've ever lived with. This'll be your first look in a mirror since. Hello, face. Surely to buggery you must have a plain T-shirt somewhere? Plain is the thing. Or rather plain with one interesting bit. Not everything interesting. Rummaging like crazy beans in the trunk of shame. Colour and interesting-bloody-texture as far as wild eyes can see.

Creeping back to full-length mirror. What else are you supposed to be doing? No one has come to say hello, tell you where to go or what to do. You look like a particularly drab sweet shop. Stop gawping. Listen. Screams are subsiding and shifting location. Downstairs? Must be an event taking place. Should you be attending? Don't be a fool, of course you bloody should.

Dining room. Explosive levels of sound. Smells of farts, frying and apple shampoo. Hovering in its archway entrance. About twenty tables. Every place taken. Extra giraffes perched on zebra's knees. Can't see a single grown-up. There's a long food table, piled with raw, terminally ill veg. Plus two bowls with peanuts and grated cheese. Didn't know cheese could change colour with sweat-effort. Thought the bloody veggies were keen on keeping stuff alive. Only one thing anyone could possibly eat. Peanut for supper anyone? Round the corner there's a huge hatch, open, with a miniature Chinese man, running up and down ladling food from metal churns.

"Mr Chow's Chinese Chow. You want? You want? You want?" Mr

Chow. No, you do not want. Nowhere to sit. No one to ask about sitting and eating. Or anything. You're on your own here, kiddo. Can only just see in the churns but it looks like clumped bean-sprouts floating in greasy hot water. This time next week, when it's Mr Chow's Chinese Chow again, you try some. It is exactly that.

"Wah-erh-ahhh." Table Of Zebras At The Far End. Is that about you? Not remotely hungry. Giving the blue jumper-tube a subtle and yet massive stretch outwards from pretend waist area.

"Screams of joy." Table Of Giraffes Right Beside You. All staring at, at. Yes, at you.

"Hello." You. Is that shyness?

"Venetia. Scream. Scream. Venetia. Scream. Venetia. Come here. Scream. I thought I was going to die, the holiday was so long. Scream." Table Of Giraffes Right Beside You. You're flicking round. It's Venetia. Who else could it possibly be? Another endless beauty.

Return trip to Big Four. No desiccated rusks in sight now. Worst luck. Oh peanut, peanut, most fragrant of nuts, where art thou now? What time is it? You have two ten p's for phoning Swallow's Farmhouse in emergencies. Is this one? If it is can you hitch over two hundred miles? You have no money. Of any kind. Might be best to get into your nightie. No doubt it's the ugliest thing anyone has ever slept in so may as well get it hidden under still intact sheets. This bed's too narrow. Will you fall out of bed when sleeping? Do you need cot bars?

Right, time to buck up hard, sweat it out until French girls return.

"Ahhhh weee, hee hee hee, weee, weee. Ahhh, non, hee hee hee, non. Ahhh hee hee hee, non." One French Girl. Entering.

"Saaavah." Other French Girl. Also.

"Olar." Bed Opposite Yours Girl. Jumping up with a hand on each French girl's shoulders, swinging herself into room. Close your eyes.

So, what the fuck-sticks is bed-opposite-girl? Ah yes, bull and bottom. Spanish. That is really all you need. The foreigners are now hanging out the window. Delicious looking men's PJs. Smoking night-night ciggies. Whispering. Why're they bothering? Must be able to tell you only speak English. Maybe being kind? Don't want you to know what a Mon-fucking-Dure they think you are.

Bit more smoking. Bit of whispered Frenchie-Spanishie joy. All out window. Clambering back in. Endless kissing on cheeks. Bed.

This is the first time, in your twelve and three quarter years, you've eaten and drunk not one single thing for a whole day. You'll starve at Boarding School.

Now you know what the Ginger Bread Peoples feel like, layered up top of each other, sliding about in their tins, with their burnt-currant eyes getting knocked out. Waiting. Who's going to get it in the neck first? Or the leg? Or the head? Rattle, rattle goes the lid. Look out fellow Gingery Ones. Here comes The Hand. Run, run as fast as you can, you can't catch me I'm the Ginger Bread Olympic Athlete. Sleep. Finally.

6.30 a.m. Next morning. What the bloody buggering hell is that? There's a bell knocking your brains out right beside your lug-holes. Shattering you awake.

"Bun jaw cherries." Frenchie. Drifting past, patting the other two's toes. Still in excellent PJs, carrying what you now know, having been forced to waste money on one by Mummy, is a sponge bag. It's for fanny-flannels and the like. Follow that Frenchie. You are.

The girl's bathroom. Three basins. Three cubicles. A pretend wall with two showers behind it. Ten thousand giraffes brushing hair. Each other's. Cleaning teeth. Own. Rubbing soap all over, in full showers, each other. Truly.

"Joy, joy. Morning joy." Ten Thousand Giraffes. Crammed into corner beside the door. Your nightie's fine. Apparently night-time doesn't adhere to the same rules. Men's PJs or snuggly-I've had this since I was an infant-nighties. Back right against wall. How many more giraffes can ram in here? There's a constant flow, in. None going out. Gallop-a-trot here comes another herd. All in nude, bar towels. The whole room's pausing and re-directing its joy. All flocking around one golden, extra tall, giraffe.

"Ahhh. You found us. Oh, we're so jealous you're in Big Six. We want you. Don't we want her? We do. We want you in Big Four." One Of Your Frenchies. Speaking English like someone pretending to be royal. English royal.

"Yes yes yes. What is your name? What's her name?" Your Other Frenchie. Also bloody doing perfect English. Completely stripped off and tip-toe running into shower. "Do me, someone. Veet veet. I'm totally dying of cold." Someone is doing her. Soap flowing so fast it's flooding the whole room.

"Oh, it's so shaming. I can't say. My parents are imbeciles. I reject them from this moment forth. Lets just make up a name for me. We can all call me it for ever." Clearly New Girl. Flinging towel to floor and prancing into shower. Blinking heck. This girl is not a girl. She's a woman. Her breasts are orbs. "Do me. Quick. Oh, you are so right. It's disgustingly cold. How dare they do this to us. Let's just insist, at the next school meeting. Let's just say we demand heat." Clearly New Woman. Hurling herself out of shower, before the heap of giraffes all desperate to be the ones to do her get a chance.

"Oh god, yes yes, scream, yes let's. We'll demand it." Most Assembled Giraffes.

Stand back. Giraffes are stampeding out of the bathroom. Who gave the order?

You're now alone in the apple-scented, soapy flood-plains of the bathroom. Empty sponge bag. Forgot to pack your flannel. Or toothbrush. Toothpaste never even occurred to you. Look, over there, someone's left their toothpaste. Opening sponge-bag. Squirting in a big worm. Supplies. Taking a finger-full and doing own teeth.

Breakfast. Funereal veg table now replete with bowls of flakes and jugs of milk. That's more like it. At the first school meeting of term (disappointingly indistinguishable from a House Meeting. Complete with crying from giraffes who've had their feelings hurt by mean zebras) you're accidentally voted onto the breakfast-duty Rota. Dozy idiot. But, bobble hats off to your fellow boarders for spying out what a natural you are for a Rota.

Breakfast–duty means up, alone, at 5.45. Creeping downstairs, willing self not to think about dead past pupils, and letting self into the cavernous empty kitchen. You're trusted with the key. Beautiful ovens. Three of them. First morning in there you open one, take out the shelves and fold yourself inside. You don't close the door. You aren't demented. Think to self – could defo roast a whole pig in here. Small one. Weanus – clamber out and commence first ever kitchen job. Rolling person-sized milk churns, prizing off huge lids and dipping jug after jug into creamy depths. Delivering jugs to dining room, sorting breakfast.

Right now doing a swift bit of necking at Mr Chow's hatch. Open. Only one urn. Tea. And, piles of thick wholemeal bread plus an ocean liner of a toaster. Breakfast at Boarding School is worthy of gods and, infinitely more important, goddesses.

Sitting down in public. Couple of grazing zebras looking up. Considering a sleepy war cry? Stare 'em out. Cowed. Searching round. Tables half empty. Random pairings of, mostly, zebras. Do giraffes not eat breakfast? You appear to be the only person who's considered it polite to dress for the occasion. PJs as far as worried eyes can see. Stripy ones. Table nearest the funereal one. Empty. You've done it. You're sat.

Sliding your bowl, with as mountainous a pile of flakes as is seemly in one so young, onto table. And slice of toast. Only a loony bin escapee would let self be noticed snaffling two slices. Raising spoon. Milk dripping off spoon back into bowl. Slow motion drops. Spoon in. Whole mouth contracting, like with lemon. That's actual jets of saliva squirting in there. Christ knows why cos these bloody flakes are stale. But. They are flakes and they are inside you.

Big Four. Did they evaporate whilst you were breaking your fast? Where is everyone, fucking France? The echoey, white and wooden room is deserted. There are now flags draped from the high black beams. Spanish. Nobody's made their beds. Apart from you. Not very well, it's the first time you've attempted such extreme reaches of domesticity but thought it might be best. Wrong. Sat on bed. Knees hugged to chest. Tummy ache. Why? You've eaten. Flipping over, getting into fart-position. Kneeling with bottom high in air, chest on bed, arms stretched along in front.

"Hilarious laughter. Screams. Horror not joy." Two Pairs Of Feet Rattling Past Open Door. Do you care? No. Simply wish you'd been blessed with a Jessie sized rasper, to blow them on their childish way. Ow. Not wind then. Flipping back over. Heart attack? Um. No. So. Well. Here you are. This is school. There will be lessons somewhere. Final check in full-length mirror. Yup. Clothes still a shocking bore.

Courtyard. Rather lovely. There's music everywhere. High, proper bricks, building, you've just stepped out of, now on your right. Then, rest of buildings, clustered, which are low, crumbly and wooden. Your Boarding School is made of garden huts. Look inside open doors of Wendy-house size huts. Beds. Stables for zebras. This school costs a fortune. Where does all the money go? Bribes to butchers, stopping them setting up camp in one of the crappy huts? The Delicious Hammy Baked Goods Hut. None of these huts has a label. You'll have to employ wits to work out which is what. Takes a week.

English Hut – Kicked out, due to lack of grasp of verbs.

French Hut – Kicked out, due to lack of grasp of verbs.

Woodwork Hut – Welcomed, due to hut being full of wildlife who think you spell verb, berv.

Science Huts – Kicked out, due to lack of grasp of verbs.

Sex Huts – Welcomed, not for sex but as a go-between, for one virginity-losing giraffe (loser) and her history teacher (taker).

Drama Hut – Decide to stick at Boarding School, for another couple of weeks, on discovery of this almost self-consciously decrepit hovel. Drama Hut is, essentially, a more prolonged version of 'We're these two girls.' You. To Star. Starting every game of pretend you ever played. There's going to be a production, *A Midsummer Night's Dream*. They do it every year. Whilst perfecting your escape plan you get cast as Puck. Causes a bit of a who-ha. Who do you think you are sauntering into their Drama Hut and taking one of the only parts that involves body paint and a Lycra body suit? You give your Puck as a two-hundred-year-old man. On first entrance, you spook the hell out of everyone by emerging from a heap of leaves. Real. Sporting a bald-head swim cap, dead leaves attached. A granddad shirt (mossy bank on left shoulder) and old bloke's trews. One Lycra-free costume. Only concession to trad. fairy look is bare feet. Blue. The mistress stroke insight, of your interpretation, is that Puck is a fucking sarcastic, miserable old bastard. Instant Drama Hut stardom. Being a Drama Hut star's much the same as being a star in the real Land of Drama. Only the other Drama Hut wildlife have the faintest idea of your importance and all they're after is making sure you don't nab all the Lycra-based casting. Never fear. It's only when you end up at a real Drama School, aged nineteen, that Lycra rears her ugly, stretchy, head again. And by then you weigh six stone. So it fits a treat.

Big Four. Sat on bed rubbing tum. Three rusks beside you. Please get rid of this pain. What to do with your endless time? Full-length mirror? May as well have another gander at all of you.

Right. Go on. It's what you're standing here for. Look at it.

Mouth.

Not fat. Top lip pleasantly cushiony and bottom a tad fuller. Soft. A mouth. Normal.

Noise starting up. Must be lunch. Thank Christ. Get some. Most people will've registered the clothes. Just keep your badly coiffured head – down.

Lunch. Bowls of funereal veg fading into distance. Boarding School is a farm. This is goat food. Scraping yours into the leftovers urn. Bloody good job it's an urn and not a bowl. You aren't alone in your disdain.

"Do not despair. We'll take you to the CPO straight after school. You can fill up then. And we'll get you an exeat, on Saturday we can all go down town and absolutely stuff ourselves with sausage rolls. We're binning your vile grub, Mr Chow. So sorry but it's wretched." Frenchie. To Orby, then Mr Chow. Blithe and bonny and gay. You're doing the same, whilst also stuffing pockets with peanuts. For later.

Later. Here they come. Both Frenchies, Orby, six other giraffes. They're linked, like one of those lines that ice skaters make where they twirl faster and faster round the rink with more and more skaters joining the ends of the line until the whole ice rink is full of the turning line-up.

"But you gave away the things you loved and one of them was me,

I had some dreams, they were clouds in my coffee, clouds in my coffee and...

You're so vain, you probably think this song is about you." Giraffes. Singing.

Way up ahead of you now. That's truly lovely. Quite loud, naturally, but so full of tenderness and togetherness. You ache to be a girl. Have to follow them. Need to know what the CPO is and what'll be there that's better than goat's grub. Across school field you all go. Through a hole in a hedge they go. You're scramble-wedging inside the hedge and spying. Look. It's Hansel and Gretel's witch's cottage. In they're all trooping. Waiting. Here they come. They have brown paper bags. Giggling back through the hedge hole. Keep very still. Gone.

Inside cottage. It's a shop.

"Hello. What's this place called?" You.

"We're the Corner Post Office. Do you want stamps?" Smiley Witch.

"What did they have?" You. Head flick towards door.

"Usual. One of these and a packet of these." Smiley Witch.

"How much is that?" You.

"Twelve pence. Have you got a slate?" Smiley Witch. Picking up navy ledger. A slate? Bliss. But. How will you pay off beloved slate?

"I'm new. Please can I have one?" You. Sort the finer details later.

Food To Sustain When All Else Fails. Badly.

STUFFED WHITE ROLL

1 Bread roll. White. Never give bowels another thought. Rusks will be your constant companions from hence forth.
1 Packet salt and vinegar crisps. Can have plain but these are best. The exquisite rasp is ameliorated by softness and sweetness of roll.

Take roll from bag immediately through hedge hole. Rip open with both hands, lodge crisps under arm. When roll open pull out soggy dough centre. Eat. Stock-still in field. Try not to eat too quickly. Savour this goodness. When last squodged-crumb swallowed take packet of crisps, crush slightly, open and tip into empty white roll cavity. Push roll firmly closed over crisp filling. Allow teeth to dig confidently through slight toughness of roll then crunch through thick layers of crisp. What a texture. There are no words to describe the perfection of this subtle, nourishing meal.

Big Four. Alone. Again. Sat on bed. Picking white thing that keeps re-growing on middle fingernail. Listen. That's the sound of Boarding School at night. Such a quantity of private sound. If you step gently, from one door to another, hut to hut, you'll hear sighs and crying. Music loud and fast, quiet and slow. Talking. One voice on and on. Stabs of laughter. Cricket on the radio. Pens gouging paper. Hair being untangled. Crack of teeth on rusks. Tea being made. Wine being poured. Smoking. Kissing. This, all behind doors. Children making their little harbours safe for the night. Fall asleep this second night before anyone returns to haunt you whilst you're still alive.

You pass a week like this.

A week.

Same routine re-trailing giraffes on Saturday. Now know what an exeat is and having no money to name, plus no one interested in whereabouts, there seems no point in booking one. Yet. Simply hang about for ice dancers, then follow. Straight down drive. Get lie of the Market Place, in town. Where you lose them. On purpose. Sausage rolls will have to wait. Bet there's no slate at the blessed butchers. What cannot wait, a single other moment, are clothes. And thank fuckity-fuck-wind you've been taught to shoplift by an expert. 'Four lovely oranges. Four lovely oranges. Four lovely oranges.' You. Forty-five mins later and you're availed of the basics.

Big Four. Mistakes gone. Had to shove them up white T-shirt, get to bins at back of kitchen, scrabble hole in muddy carrot peelings and bury the vile things. Almost correct jeans and, white with green stripes, sneakers upon your dainty toes. You're happily engaged in wall papering. Also nicked six rolls of crepe paper. Each roll a colour of the rainbow. Balanced on bed, drawing-pinning whole rolls up, in order, along the wall at the head of your bed. Got to green.

"Oh, hey. That's lovely. Great idea. I like that idea." Frenchie. Bloody hell. Had entirely given up on chat for ever more. Had decided to see what life was like as a Star kind of person.

"Right. Thanks." You. Do not turn round. Do not stop pinning.

"Are you ready for the blue? Shall I pass it or have you got a system?" Frenchie. Shoving blue roll into your arm pit. Quite helpful actually.

"Ta." You.

"Good jeans." Frenchie. Ha. Pin, pin, pinning away.

"Yeah. My other clothes are dirty. So I changed. Those other clothes were a present from my little sister. I promised I'd wear them for the first week. So she could still feel, um, connected to me. She'll be so lonely without me. We really only have each other. I really believe in keeping my promises. It doesn't really matter what people think about the outside of you. It's really the soul that counts." You. Bollocks it is. Wonder if this is really making Frenchie weep with sorry-ness? Do not turn round to check. "She also insisted on cutting my hair. Like hers. She's recently had a brain operation thing. Purple, please." You. Purple being handed up. Feel that bed-lilt? That is a Frenchie bum-cheek descending on your bed. Sorry Star.

"Horrors. What is your name?" Frenchie. Right. Here you go. With all the bloody time you've had lounging around, clasping your aching sides, and you haven't thought to prepare for this question? Moron. Is your name shaming? Are your parents imbeciles? Do you reject them from this day forth? Yes. Mouth attempting to shape name. It will not say Boudicca. In either pronunciation. And, nope, it won't even get itself round Boude, which, it now occurs, can lead to only one thing – 'that doesn't bode well' – jokes. Shame. Bye, bye name.

"Bo. As in Bo Peep." You. Can't cross fingers as doing last purple stripe's drawing pin.

"Or Bo Diddley. Don't you love his guitar jumping thing?" Frenchie. Getting up and going over for her baccie tin. Coming back and starting rolling. You're sitting down too. Side by side.

"Yeah." You. Not even a whisper of an idea what the hell she's on about.

"Wild riffs, right?" Frenchie.

"Wild." You. It's quiet in Big Four.

"Wah-er-ahhh." Ever so far away.

"What is that?" You.

"No idea." Frenchie. Going to window and leaning out with ciggie. "What kind of music do you like?"

"Elgar. Paul Tortellier playing his concerto in D minor. So much grief in waiting." You. Couldn't say the Bay City Fucking Rollers.

"Really? Do you play?" Frenchie. Bloody idiot. Why don't you play?

"What kind of music do you like?" You. Will she notice you didn't answer?

"Everything. Even rubbish like the Bay City Rollers. I wish I could eat music. I'm seriously into reggae. I think I'd have had to exterminate myself, when I had to come here, without Marley and Delroy Wilson." Frenchie. It's tempting to touch her barley sugar twisted hair where the sun's licking it.

"Better must come, better must come, yeah

Better must come one day

Better must come, yeah, yeah, yeah, yeah, yeah." Frenchie. Singing. Coming back to you. Sitting. Tucking her brown toes under her bum, knees touching yours. This Frenchie sounds like she's coming out of an LP.

"I had a look at your books the other day. What's the Chinese one?" Frenchie. Joy. Silent, joy.

"That? Oh, just the *I-Ching*." You. Thank you, oh thank you dearest Rod.

It takes so little. In half an hour you go from being nobody to being...

"Everybody? This is Bo. We picked the wrong one. We should have picked Bo, she's like us. She can read fortunes. She can do them in Chinese and Tarot cards. She knows about dreams. She's wise." Frenchie. To all giraffes gathered in a secret kitchen meant only for the upper sixth but where your year are tolerated. Until grey-hair-slidey-slippers has her termly alcy fit. Turfs out all toast addicts, locks the door. For two days.

Your wisdom's universally admired. People, especially giraffes, like nothing better than talking about themselves, under the impression you're talking about yourself too. You're needed. If a little disappointed when every term it turns out you've been given Big One, the Dorm for giraffes that's a single. You're so mature for your tiny years they say you're the only one who can cope with sleeping alone. How to turn down the honour?

In the secret kitchen your Frenchie cooks for you.

TOAST WITH BUTTER AND JAM

Just as it sounds. Main thing is quants. Toast's thick, white plastic bag bread, butter's a molten lava flow, jam's strawb and must have been placed up top by a tractor, the heap's so copious.

You'll know this Frenchie for many years. It's for her birthday that you abuse your insider's kitchen key knowledge. Your Frenchie misses her mum. Very badly. Her mum isn't allowed to see her. By her dad. Because her mum fell in love with someone. Frenchie's mum used to cook meringues for Frenchie's every birthday. How hard could that be? And the toast debt was big. You snuck into the real kitchen straight after lights out. Got those beautiful ovens going. On low. Packed them with meringues. Got up before the poor breakfast Rota sod. Took 'em out. Skimmed off the milk-churn creamy bit. Whipped it. Filled meringues. Binned stale flakes. Piled funereal table with meringues and cream. Breakfast. For everyone. On your Frenchie's birthday morning. Didn't say it was you. Let her pretend it was her mum.

"Tuck in. You're not on a diet are you?" Frenchie. About toast.

"Diet?" You. Isn't that just a list of the food stuff one eats?

"You know. Weight." Frenchie. Turns out diet's what you do not eat.

Your hungry tummy ache will take another thirty-three years to subside. Never eat breakfast. Doesn't stop it. Always eat breakfast. Doesn't stop it. Live off powdered food substitute. Doesn't stop it. Live off pineapples. Doesn't stop it. Stick fingers down sore throat. Doesn't stop it. Eat handfuls of laxatives a day. Doesn't stop it. Eat sixty calories per meal. Eat six thousand calories per meal. Only carbs. Only protein. Like a cave woman. In restaurants every night. Eat only at home, at midnight. Eat only in public, when travelling. Have gallstones removed. Eat chips, marge by the tub, six buns in a row. You're hypnotized, irrigated and analysed. Carnivorous, omnivorous, a veggie. A vegan, a fruit and nut-arian. Massaged, medicated and melted. Book a stomach staple. You, aged forty-six, become a mother. Re-acquainted with your old pal fear, your hunger ebbs. Cancel appointment.

You don't commit to Boarding School until after your first real exeat. Used one emergency ten pence. Phoned Swallow's Farmhouse. Told Mummy you'd be coming home for half term. 'Darling, it'd be divine to clap eyes on you but we're so broke. Really not sure how we'll scrape together the train fare.' Mummy. 'It's ok. There are slates everywhere now. I just have to apply for an exeat then they buy the ticket for me. I got some apple shampoo from the school supplies-shop too.' You. 'Fucking hell darling. Who do you think will end up having to pay your massive slates off?' Mummy. 'Your parents? Aren't they doing my "scholarship" too?' You. 'Weeell. Yes. But you being so lively and entertaining in that phone chat you had with school helped, you know.' Mummy. You got off the train in Norwich. Didn't bother finding a 178 to the village. Walked and asked likely looking people until you found Daddy's squat. He wasn't home. Some bloke sitting in the front garden in a rotten armchair, skinning up, said Star's band, The Lemmings On Smack, were playing that night in the Three Magpies. You find that too.

Doorway of The Three Magpies pub. Dense ciggie smoke, pub half full, sound of two electric guitars and a drum kit being crashed over and over the same two keys. The band are on stage. Dressed in black with black eyes and hair that looks as if it's been electrocuted. Star's perched on the edge of the stage. Same black clothes, same punched eyes, same frazzled hair. She's knitting, with insanely large knitting needles, an endless mohair cobweb. Star is ten. Ten-year-olds are not allowed in pubs. But look at Star. Angry, sad, wicked, fairy Star. Who could possibly tell how old she is, or isn't? This band, and Star being so tiny and defiant, are frightening. You leave without saying hello.

Star doesn't do much talking to anyone, apart from Wolfie, for the next three years. During which she lives with Mummy and Rod, goes to the village school and gets chased home by boys with dogs, most days. When Great Uncle Elizabeth dies (natural causes), and Rod hits Star for teasing him about giving up smoking, Star and Wolfie move into a house in Norwich that Daddy has a room in. There's a room in this house for kids in Norwich that aren't sure where they live. There's a cushion in that room which used to live in Swallow's Farmhouse too.

You'll never have a home with your parents again.

There's a morning coming where you and your sister will pause. It's twenty-six years away but it is coming. You're arriving. Star's in the garden of her basement flat in London, dancing with her daughters. Propping your bike against their warm wall. Star's tilting her head, running a hand through short brown hair. Seeing you. Star's girls are turning. Blue and brown eyes, wide. Here they come, toddling into you. Your heart's flipping and twisting. Crouching. Holding them, for a wriggling second.

You can love a child. You will love your own child. When you meet him.

Boarding School. It's a late, wet, Friday night. Returning from the exeat with a whole weekend in front of you. The walk up that drive is hard. School's twinkling in the distance. The different musics are a dull thud away. It's Friday night. Go on. Friday night supper is the zenith of Mr Chow's talents. It's always egg and chips. Pushing open the heavy oak door. In you come. Letting it do its endless drag closing behind you. Lolling head gentle against it. Breathing in the four-week-old egg and chip oil smell. Reaching hand out to right. Not even turning head. Taking rusks. Biting down. Dropping damp carrier bag, with spare pants and George Eliot in, on floor, for collection later. Slouching towards the dining hall. In doorway.

"Screams." Giraffes. All for you. Raising a tired paw. Leaning against the white wall. These children are your people now. This is it. This is your place. You're back.

ACKNOWLEDGEMENTS

I owe a debt of profound gratitude to my first readers for their rigorous notes, encouragement and not laughing at my spelling.

Deena Gornick, Kate Reich, Sue Baynton, Jason Morell and Rebecca Lyon. Thank you dear pals.

Thank you Amelia Bullmore for passing *Devoured* on. To St John Donald for seizing the day and Anna Webber, the agent of agents, for her relentless graft and unshakeable belief.

Henry Layte, thank you for your excellent taste, certainty and drive. You have massive balls and I salute you.

Lindsay Clarke, thank you for first suggesting I might be capable of this.

Phoebe Clare Clarke, thank you for your undying faith in me. It lives on.

Thank you Michael Mackmin for your blessings and pride.

Scarlett Mackmin, here's to all our yesterdays, thank you. My love to your girls for their tomorrows.

And, Stephen Russell, this book owes everything to you. Thank you. Thank you too for still bringing me laughter, bringing me sunshine and bringing me love. And our son. The beginning.